ARCLIGHT

ARCLIGHT

JOSIN L. MCQUEIN

GREENWILLOW BOOKS
An Imprint of HarperCollins*Publishers*

Epigraph excerpted from "Darkness," by Lord Byron

Arclight

Copyright © 2013 by Josin L. McQuein

www.epicreads.com

The text of this book is set in 11-point Hoefler Text.

Book design by Paul Zakris

Library of Congress Cataloging-in-Publication Data

McQuein, Josin L.

Arclight / Josin L. McQuein.

pages cm

"Greenwillow Books."

Summary: The first person to cross the barrier that protects Arclight from the Fade, teenaged Marina has no memory when she is rescued but when one of the Fade infiltrates Arclight, she recognizes it and begins to unlock secrets she never knew she had.

ISBN 978-0-06-213014-3 (hardback)

[1. Amnesia—Fiction. 2. Identity—Fiction. 3. Science fiction.] I. Title.

PZ7.M478829Arc 2013

[Fic]—dc23   2013002929

13 14 15 16 17 LP/RRDH 10 9 8 7 6 5 4 3 2 1

First Edition

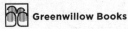
Greenwillow Books

Dedicated to Ms. Rob and Mrs. Soriano: teachers who took a kid who liked to write and taught her how to be an author, and who knew that dreaming isn't a waste of time. Consider this a promise kept.

A fearful hope was all the world contain'd;

Forests were set on fire—but hour by hour

They fell and faded—and the crackling trunks

Extinguish'd with a crash—and all was black.

CHAPTER 1

SOMEONE'S attention shouldn't have physical weight, but it does. Hate's a heavy burden; hope is worse. It's a mix of the two that beats against my skin as my classmates condemn me, and I do what I always do—pretend not to notice the burn gathering at the base of my neck that says I'm being watched.

I focus on the front of the room, where Dr. Wolff's wrapping up his presentation. Like the nine who spoke before him, he extols the virtues of his occupation in hope that someone listening will choose to follow his path.

"There's no rush," he says. "But please consider how few take up the caduceus. I fear that one day we'll see a generation without healers, and regardless of what else comes, that will be our true end."

I know he's speaking to me, but I don't want to hear him,

or indulge his belief that I show promise. I don't want to be a doctor.

By my less-than-scientific calculations, sixty percent of my memory is framed by white hospital walls and backed by an antiseptic sting so strong it lingers for days. Pain and injury are my past; they can't be my future, too.

Besides, it's hard to heal someone when everyone who comes near you cringes if you touch them.

Dr. Wolff steps aside to allow Mr. Pace his spot at the front, and an uncomfortable shift ripples through the room. Instead of his regular clothes, Mr. Pace wears fatigues and a dark green field vest with stitched stars on the pocket marking him as our acting security chief. Tonight, he's speaking not as our teacher but as one of the Arclight's protectors, standing in the place of the man I killed. This presentation should belong to Tobin's father.

Somewhere behind me, I know Tobin's there, being forced to bear another reminder of what he's lost, but I don't turn. This time, I leave him the peace of not having to see my face, and give myself respite from the rancor I've come to expect on his.

I keep staring straight ahead, past Mr. Pace to the patched crack in the writing board bolted to the front wall. Mr. Pace speaks of guard details and patrols, honor and responsibility, but none of those are for me either. Even if I wanted to join our security team, no one would allow it, so I let his words break around me and continue on to those more suited for them.

When he's finished, the other presenters go back to their assignments, leaving me with a quandary. No offered trade or task feels right. Is it my destiny to always be the burden I became when Mr. Pace and the others dragged me, bleeding and unconscious, through the front gate? When I became proof that the Arclight isn't the only human enclave left in the world?

Or at least that it hadn't been.

Mr. Pace picks up his stylus and fills the board with a series of problems, as though this is any other night and he isn't dressed for armed combat. His voice settles into its familiar drone, tempting me to close my eyes for a nap and claim a rare few minutes without pain. Five or four or even three without having to adjust my leg to stop its throbbing, or patting my inhaler on the end of its chain to make sure it's there. I'd be grateful for anything.

But then the green light on the wall starts blinking blue.

I *hate* the color blue.

Everyone sits straighter in their seats. The stylus's tip crushes against the board when Mr. Pace stops writing to check the alarm over the window. He takes a breath, erases his work, and starts over with something new as the glow from his bracelet lights up his skin.

This time everyone listens because his voice gives us something to think about other than the alarm reflecting off our desks a half-beat out of time with the pulse in my ears. It doesn't matter that his words are artificially slow, or that our lesson no longer involves numbers or equations but reminders of the escape routes we're supposed to know by heart.

"M-Mr. Pace?" Dante's one of the bigger guys in class, someone others turn to when they're scared, but there's nothing sure about his voice now. "Shouldn't you close the shutters?"

"If they need to close, they'll close," Mr. Pace says. He sketches a rough map of the halls, marks our room, and calls for a volunteer to join him at the board. "Dante?"

Dante shakes his head and presses himself deeper into his chair.

"Becca?"

But Becca, too, refuses to move.

Jove bites out a pointed "no way," and anchors his feet. The caution light's blinking; of course they're cautious.

"Marina?"

I push back from my desk, using the short walk to shake the stiffness from my leg. I grasp at my inhaler to make sure it's there, even though I never take it off. I could die without it.

I could die anyway.

"Primary route," Mr. Pace says, and I draw a line representing our fastest way to safety.

He sets his stylus to another color and strikes through one of the halls, creating a blockade in the path I made.

"Alter the route," he instructs.

I draw a new line, and count it a personal victory that I can remember where I'm supposed to go. *Anything* I can remember is a personal victory.

"Again," he says, making another change.

Then the blue light turns violet and shatters the room's strained calm.

I also hate the color purple.

Chairs scrape across the floor as people scoot toward their neighbors so they don't have to face the moment alone. Someone tries to cover a whimper with a cough.

I turn to see my best, and only, friend, Anne-Marie, sitting at attention with her knuckles clenched around the edges of her desk. Sweat and tears roll down her nose, to where her bobbed curls stop on either side, while the personal alarm on her wrist blips in rhythm to her knee bouncing off the underside of her desk with a tiny *thwack*.

The sirens come a minute later, followed by the rattle of security shutters dropping into place. A hiss of air expels from the room as the door seals shut, and the ventilation system kicks over to a self-contained unit.

I jam my hands over my ears, ducking to the floor beside Mr. Pace and counting the seconds until the seal's set. It's an awful sound, too much like being shoved into a cage and having the door slam shut. Sure, the Fade can't get in, but we can't get out, either. The line between protected and entombed is much too thin.

In the far corner of the room, Tobin sits alone, choosing fury over fear. Hard, brown eyes narrow toward the door, as his hands bend his stylus nearly in half. His rage is no less terrifying when it isn't directed at me.

The alarm changes one last time, reaching its peak color. The blinking bulbs above our door and window stop, and instead each side of the room begins to glow. Backlit panels pulse red, painting us all the color of fear. And when the others run for the safety point on the back wall, Tobin still doesn't move.

We're at Red-Wall; hiding under a table isn't going to help anything.

In the weeks since I've been here, I've *never* seen an alarm go Red-Wall. It always stops on blue caution when the Fade are at the outer perimeter, or purple warning when they come close enough to test our defenses. Before now, the light's always driven them back. Tonight something's changed.

They're inside.

CHAPTER 2

LIGHT is safety; light is life.

Blink.

Flash.

Blink.

Flash.

The room doesn't look the same glowing red as it does in the pause between lights, and the surging bursts of color set me off balance.

"Everyone under, now!" Mr. Pace shouts.

Anne-Marie crawls over from her desk, tugging my hands away from my ears where I've covered them.

"Marina, come on," she begs, as we scramble into the huddle at the back of the room.

We become a massive khaki tangle, with a single heartbeat

..d breath we all try to hold, like everyone but me holds hands. The Fade want me bad enough to risk death under the high beams, so tonight, my peers shrink from me more than usual.

And still Tobin sits, waiting. The stylus in his hand finally snaps, staining his hands and uniform. He catches me staring and looks away.

Mr. Pace uses the bracelet on his wrist to unlock a cabinet we aren't allowed to touch and reaches for the high-powered rifle kept there. He checks the scope, palming a couple of clips to stash in the long pocket of his camo pants. He snaps one into the gun with a loud click before shouldering it with the sight trained on the door—our human fail-safe, in case the locks don't hold. Not that a flesh-and-blood man will be much of a barricade if concrete and steel crumble, but if he's willing to stand between us and death, we're willing to pretend it'll make a difference.

"Where are they?" someone on the other end of the tangle whispers.

"What's going on?"

There are plenty of questions, but no answers. This can't be all I get.

My time's been spent adjusting to my wounded leg and figuring out how much medicine it takes to kill the pain without killing me. Weeks and weeks of fielding questions about my life before the Arclight, shrugging my shoulders when I get tired of saying "I don't know what happened."

I just got my life back; it's too soon to lose it.

I know I'm *supposed* to be dead, and I know the others would be better off without me, but allowing the Fade to kill me won't bring back the ones who died for me.

"Tobin, get under," Mr. Pace orders, checking to see if we're in position.

Tobin doesn't say a word, but his posture screams defiance while the rest of us cower beneath our useless shelter.

No one survives the Fade.

I hear those words every night, but my survival tells me there's a chance. Why should we accept defeat? Why not fight back? Why not live?

I rise to a crouch, with my weight on my good toe, ready to spring when the time comes, and try to fill in the blanks of my memory. All I need is a jolt to start me in the right direction.

Gunfire ignites in the hall outside our door, though I'm not sure anyone else recognizes the clustered pops for what they are. Practice hasn't prepared my classmates for the terror of live ammo flying overhead; they don't know the hot sting of a bullet ripping flesh and muscle, nearly breaking bone. To them, it's a lesson—one I hope they've learned.

I tip forward until the weight of my body burns my fingertips, tilting my head to catch the sounds beyond our room and breathing deep to center my nerves. Gunfire's a good thing,

I tell myself—only humans use weapons, so there are still humans left.

"Tobin!" Mr. Pace tries again, but he doesn't abandon his post. "We're running out of—"

Everything goes pitch-black.

Time. We're running out of time.

There's a scream, just one, but it comes from everyone and everywhere at the same time. This is the worst part, even in practice. Humans can't see in the dark, but the Fade can.

At least I can still hear. Our elders tell us the Dark is dead silent, and that my time there made my senses sharper. When I first came here, my eyes weren't much better than a Fade's for taking light, but they've adjusted. So far my hearing hasn't, and I don't want it to.

"Shades!"

Mr. Pace shouts over our panic, and the training sequences take over. We reach into our pockets for the tinted glasses kept there, so we'll be prepared when the lights turn back on.

If the lights . . .

"Gloves!"

Mr. Pace turns this into a drill. Compliance is automatic.

"Hands!"

Everyone stands and we sort ourselves out in the dark. Jonah emerges from the jumble first, pulling himself hand to hand along the crowd until he's at the door and calling out his name to say he's in place. We've done this so often, I know how he fidgets, and the way he hunches to look smaller.

Another hand grabs mine as the next of us moves into place.

"Anne-Marie," she yells back. If she's keeping up, she'll be sliding her right hand onto Jonah's shoulder so she can follow him blind, and the routine continues. The only pause comes when Tobin doesn't take his place.

"Marina!" I shout in turn, claiming my spot at the end of the line.

Silver's tall enough that I have to stretch my arm up to grasp the loop on her uniform. There's an expected twitch of her shoulders rolling under my hand as she ties her hair up so it won't hit me in the face when we run.

"Tobin!"

The feel of his hand on my shoulder makes me jump, but I force a scream down. No one's supposed to go behind me. And yet his hands are on my shoulders and his fingers are tugging at my jacket.

"Step," Mr. Pace orders.

Everyone takes one measured step forward, closing the gaps between us.

"Can you march?"

Tobin's voice comes as a breath beside my ear, his face pulled low and close. We're not supposed to talk in step, so I don't answer.

Those who speak become prey.

"Can you?" Another warm puff tickles the inside of my ear. "With your leg?"

I nod; we're close enough that he should feel it.

There's comfort in having warmth behind me, an illusion of protection I've never had with my back exposed. My skin pimples up as an odd electric shock races down my arms, and I can almost convince myself he's concerned about me rather than the likelihood I'll trip and bring the whole line down.

"I'll be f—"

Something huge and solid slams the window from outside, shaking the room. Another scream goes up as a horrible truth sets in—they didn't come in from the front. The Fade always come in from the front during our drills, but this one came straight to me.

Mr. Pace spins, the toe of his boot sliding against the tile so he's facing the window before the echo has a chance to die. Claws scrabble against a surface with no traction, trying to dig through, but the shutters hold behind a half-foot of bullet-proof glass set into concrete.

This is really happening.

"I've got you," Tobin says against my hair. His hand drops around my waist. He pulls me tight until I feel his chest at my back, shuffling forward so I won't lose my grip on Silver. The surprise of unexpected contact sends my heart beating through my back so hard I'm sure he can count my pulse.

Pressure's building at the back of my skull, creating sparks behind my eyes. This is too much like my snatches of before, all screams and terror and confusion. I grab for the disk on the chain around my neck and suck in, counting down the pattern for a dose, and welcoming the familiar queasiness that settles in my stomach from the medication.

"Hold!" Mr. Pace must have heard us move, and I think surely the thing outside did, too.

Any hope that the Fade believes our room is empty dies when the creature slams against the window again, and again, until I realize it isn't just one of them out there. There are at least a dozen, each with its own tone and pitch when it strikes.

The room goes still, folded into another held breath until a new nightmare emerges with the sound of cracking glass that says they're breaking through.

The Arclight's falling.

"Stay with me, guys," Mr. Pace pleads over a surge of muffled whimpers. "Just a little longer."

As we wait for the signal that will release our door, I feel suddenly lighter, and this time it isn't the inhaler putting a fog in my brain. Half my weight rises off my feet, so I barely feel the muscles burning in my leg.

"Just step with me," Tobin says. "I've got you."

And I have no idea what to say to that. Normally, when Tobin speaks, it's a grunted one-syllable yes or no. But he hardly ever speaks, and never to me. For me, it's a glare like ice dropped down my back. *His* father led the rescue party into the Grey. *His* father made the choice to save me over the others. *His* father didn't return. Why should Tobin be kind?

There's a knock from the hall, a set of very human knuckles rapping out a prearranged rhythm before Mr. Pace unlatches the door with his bracelet.

"Go," he orders, touching each shoulder to count us as we pass.

"If we have to run, go limp," Tobin says. "I can carry you faster than you can move on your own."

Before I can protest that I don't need to be carried, Tobin gasps, lurching forward as though someone's shoved him. The force cascades through our chain of hands. Elbows and knees hit hard on the ground, and the yelps that come after are followed by frantic shushing.

"They're through!" Mr. Pace shouts behind us.

At first I think he's saying everyone's out of the room, but when he empties a cartridge into thin air, I realize he isn't speaking to us at all. The Fade have broken in.

We're dead.

"Move! Move! Move!" Lt. Sykes's high and nasal voice shouts somewhere in the blackout.

Everything goes to pieces. We've only ever marched in silence with no real sense of urgency or danger. Now we're a hive mind with a massive case of brain freeze. All our drills mean nothing, especially for the youngest children who spill out of the rooms on either side of ours, calling for their parents

ARCLIGHT

and crying "Fade!" when they run into us because they can't
see to know we aren't the enemy.

Their voices are swallowed up by louder sounds as the corridor erupts with gunfire and something that is in no way
human. I ball up on the floor with my hands over my ears.

"That's not what I meant by limp, Marina!"

Tobin pulls me up by one arm, and then he's racing toward
the shelter beyond the maze of hallways, dragging me along
the glowing line that's been painted on the floor to guide us
there. I try to keep up, but my leg can't take it.

Good to his promise, Tobin lifts me off my feet, and over
his shoulder I watch Mr. Pace and Lt. Sykes appear and disappear with every ammunition flash. Three others I can't name
shoot at shadows in the dark, their bodies twisting from the
impact of the rifles against their shoulders.

"Don't hold so tight, you'll pull us down," Tobin gasps. At
some point I clenched my arms around his neck and didn't
even notice.

"Sorry."

"I won't drop you," he promises, tightening his grip as I
loosen mine.

Pairs of our elders line the hallway, guarding our retreat as
they spur us forward. A flare illuminates the face of Honoria
Whit with the odd bald V scarred into her hairline.

Easily the oldest surviving citizen of the Arclight, Honoria
grew up defending her home, and she's not going to stop now.

15

While the rest of us scatter, she stands sentry, repelling the enemy with the force of her determination, shouting orders I can't hear over the gunfire.

Behind Honoria, through the door of our classroom, I finally match an image to the idea of the monsters from my past as the Fade appear. They're ghosts made of shadows, with their faces covered in decaying grey cloth. Silvered eyes glitter under monochrome hoods, visible only in the barrel flashes from our elders' weapons. A haze of dark robes flies in all directions, making it impossible to see where one ends and his brother begins. Bullets cut through cloth and air, emerging on the other side to embed in our own walls.

This is pointless—bullets won't stop the Fade. How do you kill pure evil?

"Bring it down," Honoria orders, closer now, as she and the others join our retreat. "Collapse the corridor!"

Chunks of ceiling break loose and crash to the ground, creating a new obstacle for the Fade to cross.

"Get away from the walls!"

"It's coming," I say, and straighten Tobin's shades, unsure if he's paying as much attention to Honoria as he is to the destruction. He pushes off the wall, prepared for another sprint.

The passageway begins to vibrate, growing hotter as the redirected power collecting behind the walls reaches capacity. Generators snap on with a hum, flooding the complex with lights as intense as a second sun. In their wake come the screams and howls missing from the battle, and I know we've finally hurt them.

Panels that blinked red only minutes earlier burn hot enough to turn my alarm into a branding iron when it knocks against the wall as we flee.

Our shades protect us, but the Fade recoil, burned by light their pale eyes can't handle. Some crumple like they've hit a solid barrier, but Honoria stays put, ready for the next wave.

The people who are close enough pick up the smallest children and run with them. I focus on the sound of boots and voices because it's easier to make out than the obscure outlines my shades provide, but the noise leaves me dizzy, disoriented by fractured memories dredged up with the sounds of screaming Fade. I tuck my head into Tobin's shoulder as he sprints to the only refuge we have left. I don't even realize we've reached the bunker until the door slams behind us. My feet find their way back to the floor as I slip my shades back into their pocket.

I turn to say thank you, but Tobin wanders off to a corner by himself.

He's the ghost again, and it's with a pang I'm reminded he has more reason to hate me than most. So why is he the one who saved me?

CHAPTER 3

I'VE lived a short life, most of which I can't remember, and it doesn't take long for the rest to flash through my mind while I wonder if it's already over.

The wait reminds me of stories we've read in class. Our teachers claim things like art and literature are as important to survival as food and water, and they've preserved all they could of things written in the world before the Fade, including those of a place called Purgatory. There's no sense of time, and no beginning or end, only the torment of an uncertain outcome over which you have no control. I didn't believe it was real, but now I know we're there.

I try counting off seconds in my head, but lose track around six thousand, at the point people thaw out enough to risk talking. Everyone's in motion; nerves make settling down impossible.

"We should just give her to them."

Hearing Jove make the suggestion isn't as surprising as having him wait nearly two hours to do it.

"Shh!" Anne-Marie, feeling guilty for choosing a seat with the crowd, no doubt. She shouldn't. Safety in numbers is the first rule of self-defense. "You're scaring the babies."

Jove has the sense to look ashamed when he realizes that several pairs of very small ears are listening, but it only lasts until his attention strays back to me.

"We were doing fine until she got here."

His argument's always the same. It was my scent the Fade caught when I ran through the Dark, and it was me they followed through the Grey to the Arclight's boundary, so the attacks are my fault. I can't even say he's wrong. There hadn't been a Red-Wall for years before I came.

"Shove it, Jove," Anne-Marie snaps. The last time he went off on this tangent, she dunked him in the ice bin from the Common Hall. *Twice.*

She reaches for a terrified bundle of curls and tears, and totes the girl to a quieter part of the room. A small troop of others follows her.

"Sorry," she mouths when they pass me.

Anne-Marie busies herself with soothing the babies by having them sing lesson songs from class. Other, older voices drift in, thankful for the distraction, and soon the danger of the night is set to verses about numbers and silly sounds.

Tobin finds a seat under a table full of supply boxes. He draws his knees up to his chest and buries his face against them, rocking to the tempo of the children's voices, while matching their cadence with a bump against the wall.

"Hey, Fade-bait." Jove's boot toes the side of my bad leg.

I tell myself I will not answer.

Anne-Marie's voice notches louder, attempting to drown out Jove's with the days of the week.

"If we toss you out a window, would the Fade really choke on your blood?"

I will not answer . . . I will not. . . .

"That's what happens, right? You're poison to them?"

I will not . . . I will not. . . .

He drops to his haunches directly in front of me. Have his eyes always been this cold? Was he a different person before I came?

"What's the matter, freak?" he asks. "Forget how to talk?"

I cut my eyes sideways, not seeking permission so much as encouragement. Anne-Marie nods; I snatch Jove's hand, and lick the back of his wrist.

"You're still breathing, so I can't be that toxic," I say when he sputters backward, tripping over his own feet and landing hard.

A round of snickers runs through the room. Jove spits on his hand to wash it off, and climbs back to his feet.

"How's it feel to know so many of *us* died because of *you*?"

He shoves my shoulders, knocking me back when I try to stand and face him. "You *do* know it's your fault, right? If you're Fade-proof, they died for nothing."

No, they died for the hope that a human coming through the Dark alive meant . . . *something.* I just wish I knew what. Then they'd stop asking me.

Jove grabs my inhaler, using the cord to hoist me off the ground.

"Do they really eat the bodies they can't use? Keep them as pets? What? What'd they do with your bunch?"

I'd bite him if I wasn't sure he'd leave a sour taste in my mouth.

"Jove, let her go." Anne-Marie's on her feet now, too.

"Did you watch it happen?" Our faces are barely an inch apart. "Did you hear them scream? Did they beg for mercy?"

I pull back, but so does he, digging the cord into my skin.

He's not worth it, I tell myself.

"Jove! Knock it off."

"Shut up, Annie." Every emotion from anguish to hate to terror shows on his face. But his eyes are pure misery, locked on mine, as though staring will somehow transfer his pain to me so he can be rid of it. "How many of those things out there used to be our people? You think William Bryce is out there? Or Elaine Crowder? Colonel Lutrell?"

Jove's mouth just outran his brain.

He could have antagonized me all night, and no one but

Anne-Marie would have said a word, but he should have left Tobin's father out of it. Jove slams sideways, hit full force by someone a lot bigger.

"Get off me," Jove yells. Tobin pins him to the floor, sitting on his legs. "I didn't mean it. Get off!"

I assume the broken nose means his apology isn't accepted.

One punch comes, then another, until they blur so fast the impact sounds like perverse applause. Jove gets out one good scream before his mouth floods with blood, sending flecks of crimson to pepper the front of Tobin's face and clothes.

"Stop it!" Anne-Marie cries, but her feet are still stuck to the ground. Dante and Silver hurry the babies away from the fight.

This is something else the drills never prepared us for. We've never been locked in long enough for friends to become enemies.

"Toby, don't!" Anne-Marie tries again, but he doesn't hear her.

I don't think Tobin even sees Jove anymore. He's hitting his own agony, exorcising his own mourning.

He's crying.

"Tobin, stop."

I grab his arm on a backswing and go along for the ride when he pushes forward.

"Tobin!" I splay both of my hands on his shoulders as I duck my head into the space between his arms so we're face-to-face.

"He said he didn't mean it," I say, knowing Jove meant every hateful word. "Enough, he gets the point."

Because of me, Jove lost his mother the same way Tobin lost his father, and he's just as much an orphan. He doesn't need a beating to understand that hurt.

So many here only have one parent; they're not forgotten so much as never mentioned. Anne-Marie won't discuss her father even when I ask. She says it's not the sort of thing people talk about, but she can't tell me why. If I had a family, I wouldn't keep quiet about it.

Jove moans, unable to get away. Tobin's still on his legs; I'm bent over his head, keeping myself in the line of fire.

"Get out of my way, Marina," Tobin snarls, fist frozen at midswing.

"Look at him, Tobin. You'll kill him. You cannot murder someone in the Safe Room, okay?"

It's weird what arguments your brain comes up with at the worst possible moments.

"Move, or I'll move you." Tobin shifts his position for better leverage.

Desperation and lack of ideas make me stupid. I grab Tobin's face with both hands, close my eyes, and kiss him on the mouth.

Anne-Marie says guys don't think straight if you kiss them out of the blue; I guess she knows what she's talking about. Tobin drops his fist. His body goes rigid; he even stops breathing. When I open my eyes, his are wide and bewildered.

That's a good word for the whole room, because there's nothing but silence until the babies start to sniffle and someone drags Jove out from under us.

In total, the kiss buys about ten seconds before Tobin snaps back to reality and pushes me away; we sit there for another five on our knees. He stands, wipes his mouth, and goes back to his corner without even glancing in Jove's direction.

But he looks at me.

His eyes are clear and focused, without anger now, only loss and confusion. He collapses in on himself, so we're back where we started. Me on my side, Tobin on his, both isolated in a crowd. This isn't Purgatory. It's Hell.

CHAPTER 4

IT'S too hot in here, too close.

Anne-Marie sits with Jove's unconscious body, trying to clean him off as best she can with her bare hands and shirt-tail. I unbutton my jacket and bunch it up under his head to help him breathe while she strokes his hand.

"Someone's going to have to set his nose," she says. "I don't know how."

"Doctor Wolff will fix it," I answer. Besides the nose, Jove's lost a couple of teeth. The rest of his face is swollen; he winces when I touch his side.

"But what if they lose Doctor Wolff?"

"They won't."

"I think I should get help," she says. "Don't you think I should get help? Someone needs to know what happened—or is happening—or could happen. I don't think Toby meant it. Oh . . . how did this happen?"

She ends up gasping. Anne-Marie always seems to forget that she needs air.

"And how do you plan on getting out of here? The door's locked."

It's the wrong question to ask.

She starts in on the horror of being locked in a small space—which she never thought was small until now—straying from one extreme to the other until she comes to the conclusion that we're all going to run out of oxygen and collapse.

She's abandoned her gloves, and the only two of her fingernails that managed to survive the run brush over Jove's swollen eyes. She pats his hair down over his forehead, but all that does is leave it tacky against the drying blood.

"I should have made him stop," she says. "Jove's really not this bad . . . at least he didn't used to be, but he lost his dad three years ago, and now his mom. . . . I didn't know he'd gotten so—I'm sorry."

"It's the Fade's fault, not yours," I say quietly, but her attention's still on Jove.

"He's bleeding on the floor."

Untold years have left the cement surface cracked, and each spidered line acts as a thin channel for Jove's blood to travel. Anne-Marie shakes her shoe to clear what's pooled by her toe.

"I never thought he'd do something like this—Toby, I mean. He only ever hits walls, and I thought he'd stop that when the last one wrecked his knuckles." She worries the edge of her sleeve with her teeth, leaving it with tiny holes along the cuff. "I should have stepped between them, not you. But I—"

"Anne-Marie, stop!" I cup my hand over her mouth. "Help me get Jove's jacket off. He's too big for me to maneuver on my own."

Keeping her busy is the only way to stop her from talking, or at least change the subject.

"Are you sure?" she asks nervously. "We could make him worse. Marina, I don't want to kill anybody. Please don't make me." Her hands are ice-cold and sweating over mine, trying to keep me from working his buttons.

"I want to make sure the blood's only coming from his face. Otherwise, we need to stop it."

"Yeah . . . okay. That makes sense." Anne-Marie bites her cheeks to cut off whatever automatic protest she wants to make. I'd laugh at the effect if we were anywhere else.

"I can do this," she chants as we roll Jove to one side and free his arm from his jacket. "I can— I can— I *can't*— I can't do this."

Anne-Marie rocks back on her heels as soon as we lay him back down. It's not fair that Jove caused the problem, Tobin did the damage, and we're the ones with blood on our hands.

"Is he all right?" she asks, chewing on her sleeve again.

"We got lucky. Jove doesn't know how to do laundry."

It's a black shirt day, but Jove's wearing his khaki one. If he was hurt, the whole thing would be caked as red as his face. How can a person bleed so much from just his face?

"We should keep him still until Doctor Wolff can take him in the morning."

Anne-Marie nods, shrugging her jacket off to drape over Jove's body.

"We need to wash him off, and he needs water. See how much the dispenser will let you have."

Anne-Marie hugs her arms around herself, grumbling about the lack of plumbing as she picks her way over to a tall black box in the corner. She holds her bracelet out to the sensor on the front, prompting a single canister to roll into her hand. No matter how many times she shakes her bracelet, that's all the box gives her, and kicking it doesn't change its mind.

Our bunkers aren't meant to be lived in. They were storerooms initially, then converted to short-term shelters when the need arose. They're nothing but a dash-away hole where we can hide until the Fade retreat into the Dark at dawn.

Cinder block and steel dampen our scents and voices, but if pipes ran through here, or power lines, the Fade could follow the sound of flowing water and humming cables. We have to make do with a night's rations and a twelve-hour generator.

"It's all I could get." Anne-Marie returns with the one

slim can of water, huffing from her assault on the dispenser. "Maybe we can use the babies' bracelets for more."

"Did you ask it for bandages?" I ask.

"I want a shower," she sniffles. "And my own room. And my mom. And I really, really, really want Jove to not have so much gunk on his face I can't see his skin. I can't believe my stupid brother hasn't even offered to help! I'm telling Mom exactly what he—" Her voice hitches as she scans the room. "Marina, have you seen Trey?"

"Maybe he fell behind and had to go in with the adults. Did you see him in the hall?"

"I don't know," she cries, searching for anyone the right shape or size to be Trey.

"He doubled back."

I peer up at Tobin, smoothing away the white hair that falls in my eyes when I turn my head. I'm not sure if I should be angry with him for what he's put us through or grateful for his help during the run.

"I saw him as we were coming in. Trey turned around as soon as you were inside, Annie."

"Why didn't you stop him?" Anne-Marie's voice barely makes it out of her throat.

The only reason Trey would have gone back is to help on the line. That means he's out there—with *them*. Anne-Marie heaves on the floor, but there's nothing in her stomach to come up.

29

"Drink this," Tobin says. "The adrenaline's wiped out your blood sugar."

He holds out two bottles of pale amber liquid, but she refuses them. She sets her jaw and glares like she wants to replay the fight with him in Jove's place and her in Tobin's.

"It's apple juice," he says, showing off three more in his other hand. "It'll dry sticky, but you can wash your hands and face with it. The acid should help loosen the blood. Save the water for if Jove wakes up."

"You'd better not be lying about this, Tobin Lutrell." Anne-Marie snatches one of the bottles out of his hand.

"It's just juice, Annie. I gave half of it to the ankle-biters."

In their corner, the youngest children sit in a circle slurping drinks and wiping their noses with their sleeves. Somehow, in the last ten minutes, Dante's been elected jungle gym and a couple try to climb on his back, bottles and all.

"Where'd you get it?" I ask. Glass bottles are used for the younger kids because they're easy to sanitize and the tops screw on and off without needing a can opener, but they're stored in the kitchen coolers, not down here.

"This place has a lot of secrets, you just have to know where to look." Tobin sets the last bottles on the floor, taking a seat on Jove's other side. "It's the same kind of dispenser they use for snack time in the lower-year classes. Juice is provided in bulk, in response to whatever number of students the teacher puts in, but water's rationed to one bottle per person. They switch out the machines for maintenance, but always over-look the juice bottles and cookies."

He pulls off his jacket, biting a hole in it so he can rip the material. Within minutes, he's got a pile of long khaki strips.

"Bandages," he says. "You okay, Annie?"

"No. And I do *not* want to talk to you right now." After downing the first bottle in one long gulp, she takes a handful of strips, pours some juice on one, and starts cleaning the dried blood away from Jove's mouth.

He's a mess. His bumps and bruises have gained definition, changing the lines of his face and darkening his skin in places. He barely looks human.

"At least he's not awake to feel it," I say as I wash off his knuckles.

"Careful," Tobin warns. "Only clean his skin, not the wounds. The sugar could give him an infection."

"Don't you tell her to be careful, Toby," Anne-Marie snaps, but she listens well enough to skirt the split on Jove's eyebrow. "You should thank her for stopping you."

She takes a long swipe down Jove's cheek, accidentally snag-ging one of the cuts. Tobin presses a clean bandage against it to stop the bleeding.

"You know you didn't have to hit him, or you could have just hit him once, but you didn't. If Marina hadn't made you stop, you could have killed him."

Apple juice sloshes out of the bottle as she shakes it at

2

another bandage to clean off Jove's cracked lips.

"He's burning hot, Toby. Feel his face." Anne-Marie grabs Tobin's hand, not giving him a choice. "When he wakes up you're going to apologize or . . . well, I don't know what I'll do, but you're not going to like it!"

Her voice dies down to half-mumbled threats. If Jove weren't already unconscious, she'd talk him into a coma.

Tobin and I ease away once most of Jove's injuries are checked, leaving Anne-Marie to take care of him.

"We need a clock in here," Tobin says.

Or windows. Or a radio. Anything to tell us how close it is to dawn, and what might be happening outside.

I check my personal alarm, hoping I can figure out a way to coax information from it, but the face is still flooded with blinking red light. It's a shock to see the burn from where I'd hit the wall during the run. I hadn't really registered the pain until now.

That claustrophobic feeling that had Anne-Marie so keyed up settles in. It really *is* a small room once it's packed full, and yet I somehow end up picking a spot close to Tobin rather than one where I'm alone. He doesn't flinch away from me like the others would.

"You know what it is, don't you?" Tobin's voice is distant.

"What?"

"Why they're afraid of you?" He nods to the room. Every once in a while, someone will glance my way, but they divert their attention as soon as they realize I can see them.

"They blame me," I say.

He shakes his head. "It's your ears."

"My ears?" I grasp at them, confused. They feel normal.

"I don't know what the stories are like where you came from, but here people who can hear the Fade and those who can see in the Dark are bad omens. They're the ones we lost first. You know, before."

"But I can't see in the Dark anymore."

"You can still hear," he says. "You try to hide it, but I've seen you with your head cocked to the side, like you're counting off a rhythm that doesn't exist. Honoria tells us stories, and . . . never mind. It's not a time for stories."

"No. I want to know. Her stories are about people who could hear?"

"Some of them." He nods again without looking at me. "They walked into the Dark on their own. They said they heard voices calling them out . . . people they knew. . . . The next time they were seen, *if* they were ever seen, they were Fade. It hasn't happened in years, but Honoria's brother was one of the last. They grabbed him on a forage run or something. He was just a kid."

"But I don't hear voices," I argue. "I hear real sounds."

"It still scares them. My dad trained himself to do the same thing, but he doesn't tell people. You have to hide it better."

I don't mean to stare at Tobin, and really I'm not, but he's been so many different people in such a short time. He's gone from the boy slinking into rooms after everyone else was in place, to my protector, to the hurt son defending his father's memory with feral determination, to . . . whatever he is now. His posture changes, followed by his expression, but not quickly enough to spare me the expectation there, as though I hold all his answers.

"How much longer do you think we have to wait?" I ask, because I can't figure out how to ask him anything else. "Will they turn the alert back to normal so we know it's over?"

"Maybe." He scratches at the bloodstains on his fingers. The bandages he'd worn earlier are gone, lost either in the run or the fight, exposing purplish-black bruises on his knuckles. "Or maybe we died and nobody bothered to tell us."

"That's not funny," I say.

"I didn't mean it to be," he says. "We have no idea what dead feels like. Maybe we're there. Death would be simpler. No more mourning, no more waiting."

"You don't really think that, do you?"

"I guess not." He shrugs. "If we were dead, someone would have let us out by now."

"You think that's how it works?" I ask. "Easy as opening the door?"

"That's what Dad told me when my mom died." Another

shrug, like his brain's linked the motion to ending a sentence.

"I don't even know how my mom died . . . if she's dead . . . nothing."

We've become not friends, exactly, but tolerable allies through the bond of common loss and lack of options.

Tobin shifts again, fixating on Anne-Marie and Jove in the middle of the room.

"I didn't mean to hurt him." He slides to the floor, resting his hands on his knees.

"I know." I slide down beside him, using the wall as an anchor for more than my posture.

"Do you ever wonder why Honoria and the others separate us like this?" he asks. "Why they stick us in a hole while they stand guard?"

"To protect us." Obviously. The elders protect the young, like my parents did with me. I have to believe they drew off the Fade so I could reach the Light. They did *not* throw me away; I refuse to be an outcast to two worlds.

"They didn't think it through," Tobin says. "What happens if they fall?"

"The locks open at dawn and we do the best we can," I say.

"But if the Fade take them, we're next. They're gone, the defenses are shot, the ammo's spent, and we get twelve hours to tick off what's left of our lives before they come back to kill us. We're penned in."

He stops, like he hadn't realized he was speaking out loud.

"Sorry, I've been around Annie too long," he says. "I'm starting to babble."

Anne-Marie's oblivious to our staring, still sitting cross-legged with her mouth going ninety miles a minute, and using her teeth to even her fingernails in the pauses between words. She takes a marker from her pocket and starts coloring them in.

"Almost makes things feel normal, doesn't she?" Tobin asks.

Absurd and normal, a perfect description of Anne-Marie.

A group of toddlers has Dante subdued, while Silver tries to pull them off. She has one upside down by the leg, which the kid finds hilarious. A boy named Jerome, a mid-year according to his gold name tag and sleeve patch, stuffs another up under his arm while threatening similar treatment for the next one who doesn't behave.

"I guess we could sic the babies on them, if it came to a fight," I offer.

It's weird to realize this is the first time I've laughed, but it's true. There's not a lot of call for humor when you're sandwiched between the probable massacre of one people and the possible extermination of another.

"Outfit them with flashlights and we might have a shot," Tobin says. It's the first time I've heard him laugh, too, but it doesn't last long.

A rolling tumbler and the click of a lock stops everyone short.

We all stand, braced for whatever waits on the other side of our door. Anne-Marie leans over Jove's body; the upper-years form a defensive line to guard the babies. Tobin angles himself in front of me, one arm out to hold me back and away from the unknown.

The door opens slowly, allowing a foreign scent to flood the room with a metallic bite that brings cool, fresh air behind it.

"Cordite," Tobin says. "From fresh rounds. Stay back, we don't know—"

"It's not the Fade," I say, tapping my ear. The Fade don't wear boots like the ones marching through the hall outside.

Our personal alarms switch from blinking red back to blue—not safe, but not danger, either—and Tobin drops his arm.

"Looks like you were right. We're not dead after all," Tobin says with a tired smile.

No one survives the Fade, but I've done it twice.

CHAPTER 5

"GET a head count," Lt. Sykes orders one of the men who entered with him. He looks terrible, with his hair plastered to his face like sandy mud. "Make sure they're all here."

That's not as easy as it sounds. Parents rush the room, searching for their children; children run to their parents. No one stays still long enough to be counted. Those like me and Tobin hang back; we don't have anyone to check on.

Mr. Pace shuffles through, kicking spent shells down the ramp. His face is drawn. The butt end of his rifle hits the ground with a hollow thunk when he spots Jove, and his whole frame slumps.

"Do I want to know what happened?" Mr. Pace asks, looking straight at me.

He kneels beside Jove, presses a hand to his throat, then

passes it over Jove's mouth and nose to make sure he's still breathing. He snaps his fingers, and a man and woman in rumpled fatigues come to carry Jove to the hospital.

"It's not as bad as you think," Anne-Marie says. "We tried to clean him up—Marina, Toby, and me." She makes a circular motion with her finger in our general direction. "But we didn't have enough water and the dispenser wouldn't give us bandages."

What's left of Tobin's shredded jacket litters the floor beyond the rust-colored spatter left behind when Jove's taken up.

"Don't be mad, please." Anne-Marie goes quiet, which tells him more than if she'd kept yammering. "He and Toby . . . it was an accident. *Sort of.*"

Sure. Jove accidentally painted a bull's-eye on his face.

Everyone still inside the bunker listens to hear if she'll recount the whole story. No one has to tell me they'll gladly let me take the blame if Anne-Marie turns on me.

"Tell me the truth, Annie."

"He said something about Toby's dad," Anne-Marie says, gnawing on the fingernails she just fixed.

Tobin slips out from beside me, coming forward to answer for what he's done, but doesn't get the chance.

"Annie!"

Her mother runs toward her, with Trey right behind. She starts tugging at Anne-Marie's uniform where it's stained with Jove's blood.

"Mom, stop it." Anne-Marie swats at her hands.

Trey rescues her with a bear hug that has her off the ground and out of their mother's reach.

"You look awful," he says. "What's all this blood?"

"It's not mine." Anne-Marie dissolves into tears, hugging him. "I thought I lost you."

"Not a chance."

Trey looks the perfect imitation of Mr. Pace, standing next to him with a rifle hung over his shoulder. The same posture and resolve in the set of his jaw; he's even shaved his hair down the same way. A week ago, Trey was a kid like the rest of us; now he's one of those determined to make sure we live long enough to call ourselves adults.

"You should have told me." Anne-Marie punches him in the arm as she lets go of him.

"Are you okay?" her mother asks.

"Can we use the showers?" Anne-Marie asks in return.

"Honoria told us to switch over to our individual generators until noon, but the water should be warm in twenty minutes."

"Then I'll be fine in twenty minutes."

The whole family heads off in a clump, while I'm left behind without anyone to take me home or worry if the blood on my face and hands is mine or not.

Halfway to the door, Anne-Marie shrieks "Mom!" as her mother resumes her attempt to strip her in public.

"Do you need any help?" Tobin asks Mr. Pace once they're gone.

"I think you've done enough."

"I didn't mean—"

"You never mean it, Tobin. But that doesn't make the damage any less, and it doesn't deal with what you refuse to. *Deal with it!* I'm tired of cleaning up what happens because you won't."

"Jove attacked her, and no one made a move to stop it, so I did." Tobin meets our teacher's accusation without flinching. This time he wins over the rage; his hands never quite make the transition into fists. He stomps up the ramp and out of sight.

"You, too," Mr. Pace says to me. "Get out of here." He twitches his head toward the exit.

"He wasn't lying," I say. "Jove snapped. He was about to choke me."

Mr. Pace takes a quick look at my throat, drawing in a hiss when he touches the cord marks left from my inhaler. He inspects my arm where the burn's spread from under my alarm band.

"Get yourself checked out before you turn in for the day."

"It's not bad," I protest. "Doctor Wolff has his hands full without me taking up space."

Mr. Pace straightens into his "lecture" posture. Then he sighs, and lets it go. He's not in the mood for another argument, and he knows there'll be one if he tries to force me into the hospital. I'd hate that place even if Jove wasn't there to remind me of what happened last night.

"Go straight to your room, and *don't* tell Honoria I did this." He overrides the code on my wristband, unlocking it, before pulling a small tube out of one of the pockets on his vest and squeezing cold, blue gel onto my skin.

"It tingles."

"Good. That means the burn didn't damage your nerves." He caps the tube and hands it to me. "Keep the alarm in reach, on the other wrist or in your pocket, but not over the burn. If it bleeds or goes numb, promise me you'll get it looked at."

"I promise."

"Good. Now get out of here. I don't want to see you again until twenty-one hundred, got it?"

"Yes, sir."

When we entered the bunker, all I wanted was a way out and fresh air. But now my leg's heavy and uncoordinated; it drags with an ache I thought I'd healed past having to feel again. One side of me wants to run, the other can hardly walk.

By the time I'm back to the domicile halls, following the green line on the floor toward my room, I'm pulling myself along the rails. I pass people at intervals, but most pretend they can't see me. They certainly don't offer to help.

I pause to rest against the sign listing the procedure for finding a broken light, and spare a quick glance to the station at the middle of the hall to make sure the emergency call's still in one piece. It's weird not to have my alarm on my wrist. The band isn't heavy, but it's always there. The steady bump of the bracelet in my pocket with each step becomes a talisman to keep me focused until I reach my door and lock myself inside.

I dispose of my blood-soaked clothes and wash off before digging out the blue pajama shirt and pants assigned to kids in my year. I fall into bed and close my eyes, but the individual generators are louder than the main power supply, causing slight vibrations through the wall.

My brain refuses to calm, jumping from one frantic thought to another. If the Fade can make it through the Arc at high power, what's to stop them from coming in during the day while we're all asleep? In the place I came from, did we live our lives at night the way we do here? Was I odd there, too? Did I have friends?

I lie awake counting holes in ceiling tiles, and wonder how old I am. Fifteen to seventeen is Dr. Wolff's best guess. Two years isn't a wide spread, but it seems wrong to not know.

Everything seems wrong.

I pull my blankets over my head and try to shut the world out, but it blocks the thrum of machinery within the walls, and I can't stand the silence, so I kick the covers loose and climb out of bed in the dark.

The Arclight trains its children to fear the dark, but I can't fear the familiar. Darkness is all I know, and the passing weeks don't change that. I don't remember a world before the fluke of my survival was deemed a miracle.

I don't *feel* like a miracle. I feel like a scared and lost little girl who doesn't remember how to find her way home.

It has to be a mistake—the Fade are too powerful. They rip down walls with their bare hands. I can't be stronger than that. No one can.

I stare at myself in the mirror and don't know what I'm looking at. A face, of course. Eyes for seeing, a mouth for talking, and nose and ears for all the rest. The parts I get, but not the whole. I'm a puzzle with the pieces still jumbled.

Everyone looks like someone here. Anne-Marie has dark skin like her mother and brother, with the same eyes and mouth. My yearmates share features common among themselves, but no one looks like me. Silver's hair is blonde, but not the white of sun-bleached stone. Dante's eyes are blue, but his are dark and wide; mine aren't. Honoria and Lt. Sykes are fair, but at least they have freckles. A paleness clings to my skin, no matter how long I stay in the sun.

How far did I run to be so different?

I don't know, and that's terrifying.

My first memory is throwing up. Retching over the bed rail in what they later told me was the hospital. I sat up and looked around a room I didn't know, saw the backs of people I couldn't name. I couldn't even name myself.

"Where was she found?" Honoria's voice was the first sound I heard other than my own sickness.

"Klick and a half into the Grey, on the short side. She was hiding in the water."

Honoria talked with others in a huddle off to the side. A fog around my brain made it impossible to think straight or understand what they were saying. It was only later that I was able to sort the words into real sentences.

Putrid water and black bile hemorrhaged out of my mouth, clearing the Dark from my body, and by the time the spasms calmed, I barely had the strength to wipe my face, so someone else did it for me. That was my introduction to Dr. Wolff.

"Easy there." He peeled me off the bed rail, laying me back against a pillow, but I was convulsing too hard to lie still. "It's the medicine, but it'll get better. I promise."

All I could see clearly was white clothes and a man with brown skin and no hair. Everything else was a blur of flat walls and the intrusion of shapes in front of them.

Where am I?

The words sounded right in my head, but when I tried to speak, it didn't work. I knew what I wanted to say, but my tongue was too heavy to twist around the syllables.

Why am I here?

"Don't try to talk, yet," Dr. Wolff said. "Your vocal cords are raw."

I didn't know what that meant, and couldn't ask, but I still tried.

Where are the others?

There had to be others. I couldn't be the only one left.

A glass came close to my mouth, resting on my lips to give me a drink. Fresh water was a foreign thing after what I'd thrown up. I couldn't get the bitter taste of the Dark out of my mouth, or the smell out of my nose.

Why am I alone?

My questions came with tears that did nothing to cool my cheeks. My leg burned where it was bandaged, my throat was seared from screaming questions, and my skin flared every time someone touched me. I was on fire.

"Calm down, sweetheart, no one wants to hurt you."

Please . . . let me go. . . .

"Do you remember me?" another voice asked. Now I know it was Mr. Pace, but then it was just more noise.

Someone took the glass away, and I was back on the pillow.

"You had us worried, kid. But you're home now." Lt. Sykes's voice wasn't as comforting as Dr. Wolff's, and he lied. I wasn't home. Home wasn't that bed and that pain. Home didn't hurt. There were no strangers who hid their faces or their voices from me. Home held no secrets.

I tried to scream what I wanted, but there was only volume and no words. I cried, stretching toward my wound as well as I could manage.

"I'll give you something for the pain. It'll help you sleep," Dr. Wolff said.

Something jabbed into my arm before I could make them

understand I wanted to stay awake and aware.

"You're safe here, Marina. There's nothing to be afraid of."

My whole body stopped, and my last thought before I lost consciousness was: *Who's Marina?*

I'm still trying to answer that question.

The face in my mirror feels smooth and cold, without the contours my fingers find on my flesh. Stray thoughts and half-pictures fill my head, memories maybe, and I smack the glass, as if it's my reflection's fault for keeping secrets.

And then I scream.

It isn't intentional, but I can't stop it once the pain starts. I dig the fingers of one hand into my scalp, as I puff another breath from my inhaler to kill the sudden head-ache. Something hot stings my leg, and my calf snaps like an overstretched rubber band. Sharp, shooting fiery pains rage through the muscle even after I'm on the ground.

I reach for my inhaler again and resign myself to needing the hospital after all. I just don't know how I'll get there.

One . . . two . . . three . . . I count off the dosage as I breathe the medication in.

During a pause, low and softer than the machine hum in the walls, comes a *click-clack*—a sound that doesn't belong in my room, or anywhere else within the Arclight. I turn my head from side to side, but I don't see anything.

Click-clack. Click-clack.

When I stop, it stops.

Three . . . no, I already did that one . . . *four* . . .

Click-clack. Click-clack.

It's a real sound, slithering its way through the echo of the security system, and filling the gaps between generator hums. I open my mouth to call for help, but all that comes out is a cloud of white vapor that leaves me hacking.

I slam my hand down to hit the alarm on my wrist, only to remember too late that I'm not wearing it; it's still by my bed. Slapping raw skin is almost as painful as the original burn, but I swallow the scream.

"Thanks, Mr. Pace. Thanks a lot," I whisper.

Sanity breaks through and tells me I'm imagining things. I'm exhausted and overloaded with adrenaline, like what Tobin told Anne-Marie. My blood sugar's crashed, that's all. . . .

Then my wall begins to move.

I see it first from the corner of my eye, just a hint of motion like a flickering candle. The wall's surface melts to form an outline of something hanging between the wall and ceiling, clutching at it with clawed hands that clack against the surface when it moves.

There's a Fade in my room.

It drops to the floor in a whoosh of flared robes, still wearing the wall's texture. Boiling smoke churns around its legs as it advances through my space. The pattern on its skin and clothes transitions to match whatever it passes, and unless I catch it just right, the creature's as invisible as our lessons say.

My lamp takes a step, then turns into my bed; back into the wall as it reaches the middle of the room.

The only sounds are my skipping heart and hitching breath. Fear and life . . . I'm still alive, and it's still moving.

Its hands, wrapped in tight cloth, turn dark. Its face is the same, covered so only a pair of burning eyes peek out—silver rimmed in red.

I want to shout that this can't be real and drive the monster back to the shadows, but the dull ache in the back of my head says I'm wrong. My shaking hand raises my inhaler from habit, but the Fade takes hold of my wrist before I can reach my mouth.

"Do you understand?" There's no volume or voice to the question, but I hear it in my head.

"L-l-let go."

An odd, pervasive chill coats my arms everywhere but the one patch of skin on my wrist that sears like it's being burned again.

"You're hurting me," I say, as though a monster can be moved by words.

"Do you understand?"

Each time it speaks, my wrist burns hotter. Much more and I'll black out.

"Do you—"

"No, I don't understand! What do you want from me?"

Stupid question. Stupid, stupid, stupid question.

Instinct takes over, and I'm wheeling, jerking, punching—anything to loosen the creature's grip. I kick through it, hitting air where there should be a solid body. I scream, and don't stop, raising my pitch until my voice threatens to mangle the inside of my throat, hoping to drive the monster away.

The red rims of its eyes bleed toward a silver center while what I assume are its eyebrows pull closer together. I throw all my weight behind one, hard kick, setting my aim for the very solid arm holding mine. But it lifts me off the ground by my wrist before I make contact.

"Let go," I order through clenched teeth. My life won't end like this. I didn't survive the Dark to die in the Light. "What do you want?"

"Help," the Fade says finally, releasing me so I fall to the ground, where the world shatters into a thousand shards of light as I sit up in bed and pull my blankets from my face.

There's no Fade. The room's as bright as ever, with sunlight streaming through the sheer curtains, and my alarm's right there on the side table. Under the covers, my leg's fine, if a little sore from last night's escape; my wrist is the only thing that really hurts.

I let my body crash back against the pillows, wondering when the nightmares will finally end.

CHAPTER 6

THE world consists of three things: the Arclight, the Grey, and the Dark.

The Arclight is human territory, existing under the protection of perpetual day. A solid wall would create shade and shadows, so we have a barrier of light. Massive lamps embedded in the ground and mounted on posts and buildings shine through the night to keep us safe. We're packed inside with buildings and gardens, a few pens for dwindling animal stock, and stories of the world that was. They say it takes more than a day to walk the perimeter, but I've never tested the theory.

The Grey is a wide expanse where our lights blend with the darkness beyond, a buffer zone created when those who came before set a ring of fire to clear the brush and flatten anything that could be used for cover. That was before we knew the

Fade could fade, and we thought we'd see them coming.

The Dark is lost to us, filling the gaps on the map between areas of light. To get from one to another, you must first believe there's somewhere to go. And should you be so stupid as to believe that, you still have to cross the Dark and pray the Fade can't see you any better than you can see them. That was the mistake my people made, and now there's nowhere left to run. Only the Arclight remains, and I'm its only immigrant.

A dozen men and women risked the Grey the night I ran out of the Dark. Nine of them never made it back, including Tobin's father and Jove's mother. They were all volunteers who had no way of knowing if the anomaly on the perimeter sensors was human or not. All they had was hope, and all they found was me. One stupid teenager who didn't know where she was going, or why she was alone. I just saw light and ran toward it.

Light is safety; light is life.

The first rule of the Arclight.

The second rule is that things taken into the Dark don't return. It's not an official rule, and our elders have tried to make me an exception, but it's not easy overriding programming that's been in force for generations. Maybe if I knew what happened out there, I could make them understand that I'm no different than they are.

Mr. Pace said once that I should count my amnesia as a blessing, like the truth could be worse than what I imagine piecing together the fragments, but any past is better than the void, no matter how horrible the details.

After hours of attempting to force myself back to sleep, I give up. Inside doesn't feel safe anymore, so I break the third rule and go outside alone.

Outside is beautiful. It's alive and green in a way that doesn't mean mold or mildew like it does inside. It's warmer, without the taint of recycled chemicals in the air to make me choke, and sunlight replaces the stark fluorescent glare from the halls, giving my skin a healthier glow.

I toe my shoes off and toss my socks with them, not wanting anything between me and the ground.

Trees, kept manicured in narrow shapes and planted far enough apart that they can't make true shade, make up the Arclight's orchard. It's definitely meant for necessity rather than beauty, but here and there, something breaks ranks: a stray branch cuts out at a sharp angle or drags low enough that I can pull myself up for a better view.

Beyond the narrow orchard lies our garden, where rows of green stalks frame one side of the Common Hall and vines snake up its windowless face. Against the shed that houses our tools, there's a pile of crates filled with liquid vitamins for the soil. No matter what Dr. Wolff thinks, out here's where I belong. It's my favorite place in what's left of the world, and it conceals the evidence of another rule I've broken.

I drop out of the tree to make sure my secret's still safe.

Camouflaged by an empty crate, a vibrant pink and white flower bush grows where it has no right to exist—like me. I don't know where the seed came from, if it was dropped by a bird or if it already existed in the soil, but it thrives despite the measures required to keep it a secret. I'm relieved to see it's still here, welcoming me back. If it's found, it'll be destroyed for fear that it came from beyond the light, but for now, it's mine. Something about it has always struck me as familiar; I can't help but think that in whatever place I came from, these flowers exist. Maybe I grew them there, too.

I sit with my back against the shed, turning the fragrant dirt in my bare hands, without the gloves we're supposed to wear outside, and simply watch my flower bush exist. No secret scowls or eyes at my back to make me cringe. It's a rare moment of freedom, so it's a surprise to find that I have company.

Small, feathered company.

Stuck between a climbing cage and the tangle of berry vines threading through it, a bird the color of a thundercloud struggles to free itself. It shakes the cage and pulls up hard but can't disentangle its feet and captured wing.

"Hello," I say, as though the bird can understand me. "How'd you get in there?"

The bird cocks its head and flaps again—bird speak for "Would you help me?"

I wind my hand inside the cage and pull. Sensing freedom,

the bird pecks at the last of the vines with its beak until it spills out of its tiny prison. Delicate and light, it perches in my hand, testing one wing and then the other, shaking itself with an explosion of down feathers.

"Tough little thing, aren't you?"

It's not a native bird, like our ducks and chickens or the bright things kept inside with their wings clipped so they can't pass beyond our border, and the protocol is clear—I should kill it and hand its body over to one of my elders. But I can't.

What sense is there in ending another life when we're trying to keep the world from dying? I have to let it go, and that means breaking another rule by sneaking out to the Arc.

On this side of the compound, our boundary is a stone path where everything green and good ends at the mouth of the Grey. In the first days, there were bonfires here, lit and tended around the clock, but they were too easy to put out, and every rainstorm meant calamity. Over the years, the stones were laid so electric lights could be permanently set into the ground, and the fires drifted into memory. The Arc of Light became the Arclight.

Here, lampposts replace brown tree trunks. The bulbs are on standby, in these last moments before night falls, charging for another marathon burn, and leaving the Arc cold, but a faultless guardian to keep the gloom of the Grey from encroaching.

"Get somewhere safe," I say, opening my hands.

The bird looks at me with intelligent, sharp eyes. Its feathers, sleek now, bear a pattern of steel and white with swirls of black along its head and tail. It lifts off with a smooth beat of its wings and slips above the Arc, but it doesn't turn the way I expect. It shoots across the Grey, making straight for the Dark.

"Not that way!"

The bird's gone, and far too high, but trying to stop it comes automatically. My hand slices the space between the lights to disturb the churning, waist-high fog beyond. I stumble back, landing hard in the rocky soil, and stare at the horizon past the Grey.

The Dark doesn't look like much, out there on the edge of the world, just a smudge in the distance where light goes to die. Shadows shift with the movement of the sun, growing longer and racing away as though they want no more to do with this place than the Arclight wants with them. Hopefully my little bird has the sense not to go so far.

I don't want to be here anymore, or think that something I saved threw itself into the abyss for no reason. So I stand and turn away, surprised by the sudden appearance of a red glow hovering beyond the compound's main building. Something's burning.

Embers float along, dying as they fall, until I have to push through them to find their source. They settle solid on my arms and face, the warmer air becoming thick with smoke the nearer I come to a tramped-down hedgerow that's ablaze, tended by Honoria and a group wearing security uniforms. This is why no one was patrolling the halls to stop me when I left alone; they're all out here, guarding the breach until it can be reinforced.

Something beyond the boundary catches her attention, and Honoria's hand goes to the silver pistol she keeps tucked against her back. Whatever it is, it passes quickly or isn't worth her attention. Her hand goes slack on the gun's handle, and she throws another bundle of cut brush into the fire.

Thankfully, no one sees me.

The air turns dry and brittle, filled with ash that stings my lungs. I hold my breath to stop the smell from entering my nose and the grit from sticking on my tongue, but that makes it worse. Each time I run out of air, I end up swallowing heat, until I'm forced to flee back the way I came.

I think of Tobin and his stories of the world before. People who walked out into the night because they heard the voices no one else could hear, calling them to a home that never existed. If someone sees me out here, skirting the Grey, they'll think the same of me.

I follow the curve of the Arc away from the fire, and again, I find I'm not alone. Tobin approaches the boundary cautiously, pausing to scan the area every few feet, and I duck behind the switch box for the external alarm. It's barely wide enough to hide me, but I doubt he sees me. It's not people he's looking for. Not out here so close to night.

Fear flits across his face, followed by an uncertainty he doesn't know anyone can see as he rubs the back of his neck. He shakes his head and talks to himself, though his words die in the din of the fire and the churlish wind beyond the Arc.

The closer he comes to the boundary, the more frequent his glances to the side, toward the fire. There's no way he can get to the breach point unnoticed. And there's no explanation for being caught at the Arc, other than a desire to cross it. No one's going to admit to that—not even Tobin. Not even for his father.

He starts pacing, venting his frustration through his feet.

Maybe, like me, he wants to watch the world change hands, and see the sun set, if only to prove life doesn't end at moonrise. More likely, he's hoping for a glimpse of something familiar. A figure in the distance, headed home. Walking, staggering, or carried by others, it won't matter, so long as it's recognizable as James Lutrell. If I knew what my parents looked like, I'd be searching, too.

Tobin's hands run up his arms and through his hair. He bends to inspect a large rock wedged between two lamps at the divide between Light and Grey. It looks the same on both sides, which seems strange to me. What good is a barrier if nothing changes once you cross it?

He kicks at the rock until he works it loose, then picks it up, testing its heft in his hand. I hold my breath as he draws back for a throw, but he loses his nerve. It isn't wise to disturb the silence beyond. This rule he's not willing to break.

The rock drops with a heavy thud.

A sudden chill curls around the lamps, drawing fog into the perimeter. Tobin waves the misty trails away, frantically; I try blowing on them, hoping my breath will scatter them back to nothing.

The shadows shift again, stretching out, and when they reach their farthest point and join the Dark at the horizon, the Arc's lamps come on in succession, early enough to change the bulbs or do repairs if one stops working. The lamps below our feet send columns of light into the sky, threading their beams into the horizontal lines cast by lamps on the poles. The ones atop our buildings create a canopy to cover the rest. Together they create a perfect weave, tight enough to beat back even the smallest creatures that might try to drag the Dark across our boundary on their feet and fur.

Anne-Marie says once a raccoon had the misfortune of crossing the Arc as it ignited. There was only a singe line left, and the scent of burnt hair. It's absurd, but she swears her brother told the story when she was little.

Everything snaps back into view: grass and trees and animals like owls and Anne-Marie's raccoon who've forgotten what it's like to be nocturnal. A soft white glow bounces back from the building's walls to match the polished shine of poured walkways set with crushed glass and reflective minerals. Somewhere, the night is black, but not here. Bugs from both sides hit the bulbs and incinerate, sparking and popping as they fall.

This is the time the world is divided, with no Grey in between. This is when it's dangerous. The lines no longer blur and everything I lost is still out there, almost in sight, but beyond my reach. I rest my hand against the smooth metal of the nearest pole as Tobin leans his head against another. Power hums beneath my fingers and feet. The invisible wall between us falls away, and Tobin finally acknowledges that he's not alone. His eyes, when they meet mine, have that distant look again, as though they're not focused on the here or now. They grow stormy, then he turns toward the main building without a word.

A persistent plea of "Go" rattles around my brain, but there's no answer when I ask it where I'm supposed to go to. Nothing lives beyond the Arc but death. There's no way back to wherever I came from.

"I thought we had a deal."

I cringe, knowing exactly who that voice belongs to. I'm an idiot. I'm not the one Tobin ran from.

Mr. Pace stands behind me, arms crossed. Trailing him, Honoria approaches with half of her patrolmen from the fire, ready to pick up the slack of our weakened perimeter. They're going back to their assigned places for the night, still wearing the exhaustion that comes from working through the day.

"You were supposed to stay in your room until first meal," Mr. Pace says. "Not wander out to the boundary and set off the proximity alarms."

I'm going to kill Tobin for picking up that stone; he must have tripped a sensor.

"I promised I'd stay out of sight, not in my room," I say weakly.

"What's she doing out here?" Honoria asks, ignoring me, as though I can't answer for myself.

Hateful and hard, she snaps her fingers toward Mr. Pace and draws him away, pointing to me and then to the switch-box I'd used to hide from Tobin.

She thinks I was going to run; I can see it in her face.

She'll turn me out to die in the Dark, or lock me up so the others can forget I ever disturbed their routine. If she's decided that those lost to the Fade really *did* die in vain because of me . . .

I bob from one foot to the other, giving the Arc a long glance and struggling not to give in to the voice telling me to leave and never look back. If I run, no one would follow.

No! Such thoughts are madness. Whatever Honoria decides, it's not worth venturing into certain death to escape.

Finally, it ends. She jabs the air with an insistent finger, sending Mr. Pace back toward me.

"Sorry," I whisper to my teacher. "I wasn't running. I don't hear voices like the people before."

Honoria hasn't taken her eyes off me, so I shift my attention to my feet.

"Is she going to make me leave?"

Mr. Pace steps sideways, turning his body into a blockade. "Marina, even if you did hear voices, that wouldn't happen. Those who left in the first days weren't tossed aside; the people here tried to keep them. Why were you at the switchbox?"

"I wanted to see what was burning, but then the sun started to go down and . . . I got scared, so I hid." It sounds better than the truth.

"The fire's nothing to worry about," he says, and tries to smile.

"People only say that when they mean the opposite."

"Not me."

"It's where they broke through, isn't it?"

Mr. Pace hesitates, checking over his shoulder to see what Honoria's doing. Once he's sure she's occupied with inspecting the switchbox, he answers.

"Yes."

"How'd they get so close?" If Tobin and I were enough to trigger a sensor, they should have, too.

"Most people think of the Arclight and Dark as rings, with the Grey between them." He drops to the ground and draws three concentric circles in the dirt. "But there are places where the Dark comes so close that the Grey's almost gone."

He nods in the direction my little bird disappeared and

wipes the drawing away to make another. A tiny circle in the center, with an amorphous blob surrounding it. The band that separates the two grows wide on one side, and nonexistent on the other.

"Our territory is shrinking, while the Dark is always growing wider, consuming the terrain around it. Another decade, and we may not have the luxury of going outside at all."

With his finger, he drags the blob's line closer until it touches the rim of the Arclight's circle.

"That's why the boundaries are forbidden for you and the others who are too young to appreciate the danger."

Danger isn't something to be appreciated; it's something to be avoided. And if he thinks I don't understand that, then he's not half as smart as I give him credit for.

"So long as the lights are on, the Fade can get close, but not cross over," he says.

"But last night—"

"We pulled too much power too fast," he says. "They hit the barrier from three sides, overloading the system by tripping all the main sensors simultaneously. Most of the lights dimmed, but the ones at the fire point shut off completely."

"You mean they just walked through?"

He nods.

"It was a worst-case scenario. Circuits for the Arc are supposed to be isolated, but if things happen in a certain order, the base grid defaults to its original programming, glitches included. The system couldn't tell the security lights from the room lights."

"Do you think—"

I can't bring myself to ask him if it was someone taken during my rescue who told the Fade how to get past our security.

"I think they got lucky," he says. Mr. Pace puts a hand on my shoulder, but removes it when I flinch. "They've always tested us. It was only a matter of time before they found a way in."

"That's the difference between us, Pace." Honoria invites herself into our conversation. "I don't *expect* the Fade to find weakness. What I *expect* is that the people who live here will stick to their assigned places." She turns her temper on me. "Keep away from the power boxes, they can kill you."

"I didn't touch the box," I say. "I was only hiding behind it."

"From what?" she demands. "Did you see something?"

"The lights startled me. It was the closest thing to hide behind."

"Well, at least you kept your head . . ." She never finishes the halfway compliment. Instead, she snatches my burnt wrist up to eye level. "Where's your bracelet?"

"She got burned in the run," Mr. Pace says. "I told her to put it on her other arm until she healed."

I hold up my left arm so Honoria can see the alarm's really there. Thankfully, she doesn't test the latch.

"You should have gone to the hospital."

"I gave her some salve, and told her to keep an eye on it," Mr. Pace says. "Doc had his hands full. He'd have done the same thing."

"Why are you out here?" Honoria's fingers are rough on my ragged skin as she prods the burn and new scrapes.

"It started to bother me, so I put some cold water on it. Then I couldn't go back to sleep. I smelled the fire, and—"

"From inside?"

I stare back, hoping my expression is as blank as everyone claims. I don't know what to say, and thinking quickly usually ends with me tripping over my own tongue.

"Her room's on that side of the building, Honoria," Mr. Pace says.

"Get that wrist treated before it gets infected," she says. "And have her window resealed. I won't tolerate another weak point on this facility, especially not on a priority target."

Priority target . . . no way is that a good thing.

"And next time you take a stroll outside, wear your gloves. You'll have a harder time scraping your hands."

I dig my bare toes into the dirt, thankful she doesn't look at my feet.

Honoria stalks past us. Mr. Pace gives a heavy sigh.

"You didn't smell the smoke inside, did you?"

"I could have," I offer lamely.

"The burn's been going for hours. If it had bothered you inside . . . please tell me you haven't been out here for hours."

Yes, I'm definitely going to kill Tobin. This should be his lecture, too.

"Marina, I know it's technically safe inside the Arc, and the sun's only just set, but after last night—"

"Nowhere's safe."

"That's not what I meant." His hand falls heavy on my shoulder, but this time he doesn't move it. "The Arclight *is* safe. Last night was an aberration, but it still happened."

"Will it happen again?"

"We're doing what we can to make sure it doesn't, but we've stagnated on drills so long that we forgot the Fade aren't simply monsters in some children's story, easily overcome because they're on the wrong side. They don't move in the ways most convenient to us. They're intelligent, and they can plan. Last night, their plans proved superior to ours. Next time we'll have to be better. And that will be easier if you stay where you're supposed to be."

This wasn't what I had in mind when I left my room. All I wanted was air and open space, not to cause more trouble for people who've already given too much to protect me.

"Where'd I come from?" I ask, nudging the edge of his dirt diagram with my toe. "Which side?"

"The short side," he says. "We found you hiding in the Grey."

"In the water?"

"Yeah," he says. "There's an old boat platform out there.

You'd gotten into the water behind the pier supports. We almost missed you."

"Sorry."

"Don't apologize. We weren't the only ones who couldn't find you."

He heads toward the main building, stopping when I pause to collect my shoes and socks. It's a harder decision to follow him than it should be. There shouldn't be anything out here daring me to stay, but there is. An itch I can't quite reach kicks in every time I turn away from the horizon.

I wonder if this is what it was like for those who came before, if that itch is the first hint of hearing the call to join the Dark.

But I won't. Not ever.

CHAPTER 7

"**I**'LL have to scrape it before I can bandage it," Dr. Wolff says after examining my arm.

Mr. Pace abandoned me promptly upon delivering me to the hospital. I suspect his quick exit had something to do with Dr. Wolff's dirty looks and muttered promises of unspecified pain for those who thought they were better equipped to treat his patients.

"Hold still" is the only warning he gives, and when he's done, tiny dots of blood glisten on my skin where he scraped away more than one layer of flesh. But unlike Honoria, Dr. Wolff tries for gentle. "That wasn't too bad, I hope."

I grit my teeth, determined not to let the tears show.

"How's your inhaler?"

"Why won't it work on anything but my headaches?"

"What else would you need it for?"

"My leg," I say, kicking it for emphasis.

"You pushed it too hard last night, didn't you?" he asks.

I shrug. Dr. Wolff isn't intimidating in the least when he's not armed with medical instruments, but my throat threatens to close up every time I come here.

"Does it hurt now?" he asks.

"It's a little sore," I lie. The echo of pain from my nightmare has plagued me since I woke up.

"You didn't break the wound open?"

"No," I say quickly, afraid he'll decide he needs to examine it again, which will only lead to more questions and a longer stay.

"You're sure?"

"Yes, sir."

Dr. Wolff eyes me suspiciously for the too-polite answer, but I imagine he's seen plenty of people acting strange since last night.

"How's Jove?" I ask, redirecting him.

Several beds are curtained off, so I assume he's behind one of the partitions, but I'd sort of like to know that what Anne-Marie and I did last night made a difference. It would be nice to be the answer to a problem for once, rather than the cause.

"He'll be all right," Dr. Wolff says. "I understand he has you to thank for that."

"I didn't do much."

"Not many people would have made the choice you did." My face must show my confusion because he explains. "You and Annie kept him from going into shock. It takes a great deal of compassion to offer aid after someone's hurt you."

Somehow I don't think he'd appreciate my saying I was more concerned with keeping Anne-Marie from losing it than keeping Jove comfortable.

"Jove was scared," I say. "He thought . . . you know . . . that his mom was one of *them*. He thought she'd come with the Fade to take him back to the Dark."

"And he blamed you?"

"He always has."

"Do you think his opinions have changed?"

"I doubt he can tell me. I'm pretty sure his jaw was broken."

"Dislocated and fractured," Dr. Wolff corrects. "But it should heal good as new."

He picks up an empty syringe. I'd hoped we could skip the blood sample this visit, but the man is nothing if not consistent. I roll up my sleeve and give him my arm, watching the tube in his hand as it fills.

"Have you given any consideration to where you'd like to focus your studies once you age up?" he asks.

"It sort of slipped my mind."

Along with everything else that wasn't "run for your life or die trying."

"Well, should it happen to slip back in, I hope you'll

consider what I've said. There are some things a person's born to, whether they want to believe it or not," he says. He removes the needle and taps me on the head with my hospital file while I bend my elbow to stop the bleeding.

"You might as well let me refill your inhaler while you're here. If you've been using it for your leg, you've probably depleted it. I'm surprised you haven't overdosed."

I pull the cord over my head and hand it to him without mentioning that most of my inhaler usage was in a dream.

"It'll be a minute or two; the new batch isn't mixed."

Dr. Wolff disappears into the back room where he keeps his supplies locked up, leaving me to wait alone. He wasn't exaggerating the need for healers when he spoke in class. In all the time I've spent in this room, I've seen maybe a dozen people wearing patches that denote medical service, and none are here consistently. They only come when called to assist.

I close my eyes again, straining for sounds to give the moment depth. Pinging machines, or the whoosh of air from the overhead vent, even my own heartbeat. Often, finding that faint layer beneath the usual clamor or quiet is the only way I can function. Absolute silence terrifies me.

I'm counting the ticks of a wall clock when I hear footsteps approach from the door on the opposite side of the hospital, stopping behind the curtain next to my bed.

"I'm sorry, man." It's Tobin, talking to Jove. "I know you can't hear me, but I'm sorry."

I should tell him I'm here, but I already know I won't. I can be very still when I want, and right now, I'm grateful for it. He'd never talk like this if he knew I could hear him.

"And don't think I'm only apologizing because Annie threatened unspecified yet terrifying retribution if I didn't."

He pauses every few words, but no matter how hard I listen, there's never a response. He must be filling in Jove's half of the conversation with his own imagined answers.

I do that—imagine conversations with Tobin. I apologize for his father's death and he accepts, or I apologize and he curses me; it depends on my mood. I don't have to pretend with Jove or the others, because I know where I stand with them, but Tobin won't even acknowledge that his dad's dead. Somehow my offense seems greater with him, like it's worse because his father was the one who made the call to save me over the rest.

"And Mr. Pace didn't make me come, either. I just wanted to apologize. I'll do it again when you're awake, okay?"

Tobin's words may be friendly and familiar, but his voice comes thin and hurried, punctuated by bouts of swallowing.

"I'm probably rambling you into a deeper coma, but I haven't slept, so it's not my fault. I doubt anyone slept after last night. Well, maybe Annie."

He laughs; I put my hand over my mouth so I can't. Anne-Marie can sleep anywhere. I've even seen her do it standing up when we were in formation too long. She dropped her forehead onto Jonah's back and started snoring.

"And, when you wake up, we're going to talk about Marina. You have to step off. You can't keep—"

The door on the other side of the room slides open again. This time someone enters with the sound of heavy boots rather than student shoes.

Can't keep what? I want to shout.

"I'll go," Tobin says. "I just wanted to check on him."

"Why were you at the perimeter?" Mr. Pace's voice comes through the curtain. "How'd you get out there?"

"Doors are usually the easiest way."

"And I've got yours monitored."

"You can't do that. You're not my father."

"I keep tabs on all my kids, Tobin. And I'm trying to help you."

Adults' alarms can be set to track their children, so they know if anyone goes across the Arc. I didn't know teachers could do the same for their students.

"I don't need help," Tobin snaps.

"Tell that to Jove."

"I've already told him everything I came to say."

My stomach flips again. I search for something to hide behind in case Tobin comes my way rather than passing Mr. Pace, but everything large enough is bolted to the floor and walls.

"You cannot keep walking away from your problems like

that's the solution to them, Tobin," Mr. Pace says. "If you keep running away, I'll just keep following until you talk to me."

"I don't want to talk about my dad."

"Fine, then you can tell me what's happening with you and Marina."

I lean forward to make sure Dr. Wolff isn't on his way back yet. The way my luck runs, he'll show up before Tobin can answer.

"Marina?" Tobin asks.

"Normally you two won't even look at each other. I saw you pick her up during the run."

"She couldn't make it on her own, so I helped. End of story."

"Middle of story," Mr. Pace corrects with the infernal, maddening calm that always marks his temper. "Jove's got two broken ribs, a busted nose, and bruises that say it's nowhere near the end. I've got Annie telling me you plastered him because he insulted your father, and I've got Marina's version telling me you did it to protect her. Which is it?"

"What difference does it make?"

"I want to know why she's covering for you," Mr. Pace says. "The truth. No threats of punishment. No teacher. No student. Just the guy who's known you since you were born and needs to know why you were outside with Marina, at sunset, by the Arc."

"I didn't know she was there," Tobin says.

"Fair enough," Mr. Pace says. "But she knew you were, and

she didn't tell anyone, not even when Honoria cornered her."

"You can't expect me to understand what goes on inside her head."

"Do you even understand what's going on inside yours?"

Silent defiance is his only answer.

"You're not your father, Tobin. You don't have to be, and you don't have to bear his burdens." He pauses. "I know you're not going to want to hear this, but are you sure you want to stay in the apartment by yourself? Dominique's offered—"

"You're not taking my house away from me!"

"It's not good for you to be wandering around a space that big with nothing to do but sit and wallow."

"When my dad gets back—"

"Tobin . . ."

"Mr. Pace, please—"

"What's all this noise?" Dr. Wolff rushes past me.

My luck's worse than I thought. It's when Tobin is at his lowest, begging, that Dr. Wolff returns and yanks the curtain open. On the other side, Tobin stands with his back to Mr. Pace, which means he was facing the curtain. With it gone, he's facing me.

A rush of heat floods my cheeks. Tobin's face goes the other way, losing his tan to bleached-out ash.

"Sorry, Doc," Mr. Pace says.

"This is a hospital, Elias. You can't bang around like you're on maneuvers."

"Let's go, Tobin. We'll finish this later."

But Tobin doesn't move. Neither he nor I have blinked since the curtain was pulled away. He stands; I sit. We stare without a word—one accusing, one apologizing—until that same, stubborn piece of hair falls forward. I tuck it behind my ear, but with the connection between us severed, he wastes no time leaving.

"Tobin, wait," I call after him. "I'm—"

He pushes past Dr. Wolff, close enough to my bed to bump it sideways.

"—sorry," I finish, too late.

"That could have gone better," Mr. Pace says.

I nod, scooting off the hospital bed as Dr. Wolff hands me my inhaler. The ring feels heavy and cold against my skin when I tuck it in, not comforting at all.

"If I'd known you were still here, I would have waited," Mr. Pace says.

"S'okay," I mumble. It's not like he ruined a friendship; he only pushed the wedge a little wider. "Can I leave?" I ask.

"Go on," Dr. Wolff says. "Honoria's arranged something special for you kids at first meal. You don't want to miss the surprise."

Yes I do.

Unexpected variables rarely prove to be good for me. They lead to running and screaming and things that can kill me, so talk of something mysterious waiting in the Common Hall isn't an incentive to get there any faster.

I hesitate near the door, balanced between two bad decisions. At least with the hospital, I know what kind of misery to expect. I've pretty much lost my appetite anyway.

"Doctor Wolff," I begin. It isn't easy convincing my mouth to explain my nightmares and endure whatever reactions he has to them. I anticipate a lot of needles.

"Yes?" He inclines his head, not looking at me while he sterilizes the scraper with an open flame.

My hesitation costs me the chance to answer.

The door on the far side of the room slams open. Lt. Sykes and another guard hurry in, shuffling to manage a third person between them—Anne-Marie's brother, Trey.

Burned and bloodied.

CHAPTER 8

TREY holds his arm against his chest. His jacket and shirt are burned through, the skin beneath them melted, as though someone roasted it over an open flame. It's going to take more than a dab of cold blue gel to fix that.

"What happened?" Dr. Wolff asks.

"Briar bush at the burn site," the man I don't know says.

"It had gone black," Lt. Sykes adds.

Lt. Sykes is young, barely older than Trey, and strangely pretty for a guy. There's something off about him, like he's always marching a half-step out of time with everyone else. And he certainly doesn't act like someone who's only recently aged out. He isn't treated like it either.

"She burned me." Trey gags on his own words, shaking as the others hold him up. Dr. Wolff extends Trey's arm farther, and Trey vomits onto the floor.

I step toward him automatically, but Mr. Pace seizes my injured wrist, only loosening his grip when I yelp. He doesn't even apologize.

"Don't touch him."

"But . . ."

This is Anne-Marie's brother. How can I not help?

"Get to the Common Hall." Mr. Pace tows me toward the exit, still by the wrist.

"Was he attacked?" I ask.

It's barely dark. If Trey was attacked, that means the Fade have moved faster than they did last night, or that they were closer. Either way, we're in trouble. We should be at Red-Wall.

"Is he okay?" I try to get a clear view of Trey, but Mr. Pace keeps his body in the way.

"Go!" He dismisses me, then doubles back.

I position myself in the hall outside the door where I can watch from the side. If I tell Anne-Marie I saw Trey delivered to the hospital, she'll drive everyone crazy until she gets details. Staying to eavesdrop is a mission of mercy, really. It's not just to satisfy my own curiosity, at all. . . .

"What were you thinking, taking him out there?" Mr. Pace snarls at Lt. Sykes—actually snarls. His face twists into something grotesque. "He hasn't even aged out."

"He showed up on his own, same as last night."

"What happened to his gloves?"

"He said they made it too hard to work."

"You let him take them off?"

"He's about as reasonable as his old man."

I've never heard Lt. Sykes speak back at Mr. Pace before.

"Stop!" Dr. Wolff splits them apart when it seems Mr. Pace is going to do more than yell. "Elias, you can exact your pound of flesh once I'm sure I won't have to do the same with our young patient. I need details. Are you sure the bush was infested?"

"The kid tore it up before we could warn him not to," the man I don't know says. "Confirmed punctures. His skin started to halo around the wounds."

"How long?"

Lt. Sykes checks his alarm for the time. "Less than three minutes."

"What'd she use, a blowtorch?" Mr. Pace touches Trey's abused arm with the tips of his fingers, and Trey winces.

"There was no time for neat," Lt. Sykes says. "Honoria held his arm over the flame until it flaked."

Honoria?

She couldn't have. She wouldn't harm one of the Arclight's own—not on purpose.

"Get him downstairs," Dr. Wolff orders. "We need him contained so I can do a proper assessment."

But Trey goes berserk before they can go anywhere.

"Make them stop," he cries, trying to raise his hands to

cover his ears. "They won't shut up. Make them stop."

Trey claws at his wounded arm, jerking against the men holding him.

"Get them off! They're everywhere! I can feel them!"

"We're losing him," Lt. Sykes says. He wraps his arms completely around Trey in an attempt to steady him. He and Mr. Pace pull Trey to the floor to brace his body.

"I need morphine," Dr. Wolff says, kneeling down to press Trey's head against the floor. He swipes his free hand toward the cabinets, and the guard I don't know starts opening drawers. "Third, left. Orange lettering on the package."

"Got it."

The guard tosses a plastic wrapper. Mr. Pace catches it and holds a syringe out to Dr. Wolff, who slides the needle into Trey's upper arm.

"Relax, son," he says softly. "I know that's easier for me to say than it is for you to do, but the medicine should kick in soon."

"He won't make the trip downstairs," Mr. Pace says in a rough voice. "Honoria sees him like this and—"

"Get him into a bed," Dr. Wolff says, nodding. "I'll do what I can. Hopefully he'll be in the clear before Honoria ever sees him."

Mr. Pace closes the curtain between Jove's bed and the one I had used, and once Jove's sequestered, they deposit Trey on my bed. The short drop when they lower him down is too much for his stomach. He throws up again.

"She overdid it," Mr. Pace says.

Trey's out of it, thrashing with the sheets tangled around his feet. Sweat explodes from his skin as he tries to speak, but no real words come out.

"She saved his life, Elias." Dr. Wolff becomes the voice of reason in the room. "There's a chance to stop them before they trench in. If we're lucky, he'll keep his arm."

"Don't lecture me on that sort of luck, Doc. I'm more than familiar with the concept."

Another few seconds pass with Mr. Pace trying to get a response from Trey, but Trey's gone—hopefully to the morphine rather than his injuries. His eyes roll up into his head and close. Even after he's out, he shakes so much that Lt. Sykes and the other guard have to hold him down.

Dr. Wolff cuts the sleeve away from Trey's mangled skin before reaching for the same scraper he'd used on me. I have a feeling that the next emptied stomach will be mine if I watch, so I hide my face against the wall, grateful for Trey's sake that he isn't conscious.

I keep my eyes closed until I hear the scraper hit a metal bowl. Trey's arm now sports a shallow trench in the muscle where Dr. Wolff cut deep. Flecks of black ash fall to the floor, and both of the men who carried him in back away from it. Mr. Pace sweeps it into a bin, adding Trey's ruined shirt and the bloody bandages to the pile. Torn pieces of the green patch declaring his status as a final-year student land on top.

"Clothes," Mr. Pace orders.

Both men shuck their jackets and remove their gloves.

"You need these, Doc?"

"They're active." Dr. Wolff bites the words, bitter like a sour lemon. "Use the incinerator downstairs."

Down? The only stairs I've ever seen take workmen to the roof so they can replace lightbulbs. All that's under the Arclight is dirt.

Mr. Pace sprints toward the medicine room with the bin held at arm's length.

Dr. Wolff turns the light over Trey's bed on so high it bounces back off his skin with a pale violet glow, then snaps a breathing mask over his nose and mouth and turns on the pump beside his bed so it fills with medical smoke.

"Portman, your hand," Lt. Sykes says. Surprise makes the nasal whine to his voice worse. "You're cut."

The other man, Portman, glances down at the hand he was using to steady Trey's arm, raising it toward the light. A scrape stretches across his palm, below the thumb. The skin's red and irritated in the center, but nothing serious. Around the scrape, a sooty black halo traces the shape.

"You must've ripped a glove," Lt. Sykes says.

"Secondary transfer," Portman argues, trying to wipe the halo away, but the stain sticks fast. "Doc . . ."

"They're not in the tissue, yet." Dr. Wolff rounds Trey's bed.

"Do something!" Portman screams, grating his skin with his fingernails.

"Don't!" Dr. Wolff grabs his hand and holds on tight. "Speed your heart and you'll spread them faster. I need a tourniquet."

Lt. Sykes rips off his belt, one-handed.

"Keep your other hand clear, or we'll end up with cross-contamination," Dr. Wolff warns as he ties off Portman's hand at the wrist.

They've completely forgotten about Trey. None of them are watching when foam starts forming under his breather and the convulsions start again.

I'm out of my hiding place and beside the bed, and I don't even remember moving.

"Doctor Wolff!" I don't decide to shout either, but that's how it happens. "Trey . . . calm down." I try patting his shoulder, but he seizes up off the bed with the slightest touch. "Trey!"

"Elias, we need you!" Dr. Wolff leaves Portman to Lt. Sykes and returns to Trey's bedside. Mr. Pace finally reappears from the back room—he's not happy to see me.

"You can yell at me later, Mr. Pace. Trey's dying!"

All I can think about is how Anne-Marie will look when she finds out her brother's dead because of me, too. She'll hate me; I won't have anyone left.

"He's not dying," Dr. Wolff argues. "The Fade carry a contagion. It was on the bush that cut him. His body's fighting it."

He slides his hand beneath the mattress of Trey's bed, retrieving a cuff he uses to strap Trey's leg down. Mr. Pace does the same on the other side. They bind Trey's hands, careful of his forearm.

Trey's burn begins to weep a slow-moving ooze. Dr. Wolff reaches for a metal bowl off the counter, positioning Trey's arm over it to catch the runoff. By the time it's done, there's about an inch-deep puddle of murky glop mixed with blood in the tray. Dr. Wolff lights a wooden dowel on fire and tosses it into the . . . whatever it is that came out of Trey's body. It burns quicker than paper, igniting in a brilliant emerald flash that leaves only fine black powder and the scent of decay.

"He'll be fine," Dr. Wolff says. "Once it's burned out, it becomes inert."

I turn my head back to where Lt. Sykes is still holding on to Portman's translucent, bloodless hand. If feelings have colors, I've just turned chartreuse.

"Stay clear," Dr. Wolff says to me.

While I watch, he heats a long, flat blade. When it's glowing, Lt. Sykes and Mr. Pace hold Portman tightly by his shoulders, forcing him down into a chair. Portman wraps his feet around the chair's legs. He bites down on the towel they put in his mouth, so when he screams, it comes out muffled. All the fingers on the hand with no tourniquet flex, bending back against their joints from the agony of being branded. His feet pound in place along the slick tile, gaining just enough traction to tip his chair. The tendons in his neck pull taut; his eyes pop. And he keeps on screaming.

Dr. Wolff watches the clock with one hand in the air, counting down, and drops it when he says, "That's enough, let him go."

Portman slumps, shaking, in the chair. Dr. Wolff pulls the blade away, takes the towel from Portman's mouth, and uses it to brush new black ash from his hand into another tray.

"Only skin contact," he says. "It didn't go deep."

They all relax like they didn't just sear a man's palm with a knife. Lt. Sykes helps Portman to a bed, fitting him with his own mask and light, while Dr. Wolff carts both bins of black ash to the back room. Mr. Pace comes for me.

"I'm sorry," I say automatically. "I was worried about Trey. Anne-Marie—"

"Does not need to know about this."

"But—"

"Marina, we don't tell you not to do things and not to go places because we're horrible. We're trying to keep you safe, so what you saw doesn't become a necessity for more people. If you constantly do the opposite of what you're told, it's harder for us to do that. Go to first meal and let us handle this. There's no need to mention the Fade at all. It would just worry people."

"But what about Anne-Marie and her mom?"

"I'm going to tell Dominique myself. Annie can wait, but I promise she'll be told."

"Thanks, Mr. Pace," I say. "And I really *am* sorry."

"Stop apologizing and start paying attention." He taps my forehead with his finger. "Now get out of here before I decide to tell Honoria you were prowling around where you weren't supposed to be, again."

That's all the motivation I need. One run in with Honoria's enough for the day. I leave Trey to our teacher, and start the walk down the brown line to the Common Hall. Halfway there, I remember that Trey's catastrophe wasn't the only one I'd witnessed in the hospital. Not only do I have to get through first meal with Anne-Marie, but I have to face Tobin, too.

CHAPTER 9

I lay my head against the table, hoping the cool metal will numb my senses, but the twitch at the base of my skull says it's no use. The voices are too loud, the lights too bright, and it'll only get worse if I raise my face.

Normally, this would be the time we prepare for our first classes, but we can't actually reach any of the rooms beneath the rubble. Our elders are understandably preoccupied, and the few adults available for handling night-to-night tasks have their hands full with the babies. The rest of us were told the rec rooms are open and we should stay inside the building. So my choices for the next several hours are either to participate in rec room games I don't enjoy, or cling to the pain and go back to my room to stew.

"Can I sit down?"

I crack one eye open to get my bearings and have to fight the urge to use my tray as a shield. Anne-Marie stands on the other side of the table, waiting for my answer just like she did the first time we met. No act of kindness, that, just a dare to see if anyone would approach the only outsider any of them had ever known. Anne-Marie was the only one willing—and now I'm supposed to lie to her about her brother.

Memories of Trey mix with those of my first days, when it was me stuck in a bed with my arms and legs tied down so I couldn't hurt myself. I don't have any scars to tell me someone had to boil Fade poison out of my blood, but close enough is bad enough. For once I'm happy I can't remember.

Anne-Marie hooks her leg over the bench and sits with her tray on the seat in front of her. She's broken dress code and worn a hooded sweatshirt over her uniform. From the size, it has to be Trey's. The brown's so close to her skin color, the only real difference is in her fingernails. She's scribbled them in green, like the flames that burned her brother's blood.

"Headache?" she asks.

I nod against the table. This way I can't look her in the eye.

"That bad, huh?"

"Worse." I can't get the smell of scorched skin out of my nose.

"Well, suck down some magic air and get it over with. You can't be sick today."

Like the inhaler smoke can fix everything. It didn't do Trey any good.

"Don't wanna." The medicine dulls my mind as well as the pain, replacing my brain with something sluggish. I don't want my perceptions diluted; people who lie to their friends deserve to be in pain.

"Come on, Marina. I want to go back for seconds before the guys inhale everything that's not oatmeal. Either the freezer's down, or they feel bad for all the duck and cover yesterday. Someone broke out the *real* sweets today."

Anne-Marie picks up a plate of baked goo in a flaky crust and shakes it at me so a blob of amber jelly falls out. I grimace at a similar one on my own plate; it doesn't look appetizing in the least, and it smells like the vomit on the hospital floor.

"Last time we got real sugar, Jove and Toby chomped through half their body weight. They were sick for two days, but it was worth it. There was this thing called coconut cake— it was amazing. You couldn't even taste the vitamin syrup hidden in it. I'm going back to see if someone made one this time."

"Coconut? You mean like cocoa?" I ask. They gave me that in the hospital; it's one of my first good memories.

"You are so weird." Anne Marie smiles through a mouthful of goo.

Her whole tray's filled with dessert. Mr. Pace was right, telling her about Trey would spoil this for her, and if she can't even see him yet, there's no reason.

"And look . . . coffee! It's been a year since there was a crop big enough to make coffee, and they said we were too young then. I got three cups just in case someone decides we still are." She frowns at the taste before dunking a chocolate cookie and shoving the whole thing in her mouth. "Much better."

Anne-Marie's enthusiasm crosses the table, chipping through my misery, and I end up picking at the crust of my flaky thing.

"Try it," she says. "I'd never steer the new girl wrong."

Food vanishes into the shadows created by her hood as she talks, and only the lightest parts of her eyes and the edges of her hair are visible where her curls reflect the fluorescent lights.

"I've been here for almost two months. I'm not that new," I say. I'll play along if she wants to pretend nothing's wrong. If she's controlling the conversation, there's no chance for me to mention Trey.

"You're the first survivor who's ever reached the Arclight," Anne-Marie says through another bite. "Trust me, you're new." She wipes her mouth with the back of her hand and picks the stray crumbs off her fingers. "You'll probably die the new girl." She realizes what she said too late to stop the words. "I don't mean you're going to die. I mean . . ."

A spray of sticky debris flies out of her mouth as she splutters over her mistake, and the next thing I know, I've been attacked by a lemonade-soaked napkin as she tries to wipe my face.

I reach for the only thing I know she'll respond to and pull my inhaler up to my mouth. She jumps back, while I breathe through the ring longer than I should.

"Sorry." Her natural energy takes a nosedive.

"What are you apologizing for?" Dante's voice comes from behind us, with no indication of how long he's been there. I take another breath from my inhaler to give myself a reason not to answer him. "You're right. She'll die the new girl, and we'll all go with her. Right, Fade-bait?"

Dante acts like he might sit, but a loud clang at the far end of our table makes him change his mind. Tobin drops into his seat, with a silent warning to move along written in the way he glares.

"I'd hate to waste a dessert day where the smell turns my stomach anyway," Dante says, backing down. "Coming with us, Annie?"

"Of course I'm coming. That's why I sat *here* instead of *there*. Moron."

"Catch you later, Fade-bait. *Without* the guard dog."

He turns and heads to a table across the room where his friends are waiting. One scans our table and makes a motion with his hand like he's clearing the air from something that stinks. The others laugh.

"Idiots," Anne-Marie says.

"A lot of idiots," I grumble.

"That's what happens when too many people share one brain. Dante used to be a nice guy, before—"

She lets the word hang. Apparently a lot of things were different before. *Nice* before. *Good* before. *Still living* before. And every one of those sentences ends with me.

"I didn't mean it, Marina," Anne-Marie says. Her lip trembles as she totters on the edge of another meltdown.

"I know."

"Really . . ."

The only diversion I can find is the odd mass on my plate, so I stab it like I hate it.

"You don't like cobbler?" she asks, taking the nudge.

"I'll tell you once I figure out what it is."

Tobin snorts from his end of the table. He certainly knows what cobbler is; he's already taken bites off three different pieces.

I poke at the mass of jellied fruit in front of me, peeling back the layers with my fork. Red liquid catches a crack in the plate, tracing it to the edge.

"You want the apple instead? I'll trade if you don't like cherry," she offers.

I shake my head no. Cherry's interesting. It's warm and sticky, like running blood without the horror of death attached.

A shrill whine and flickering lights cut my musing short.

The alarm on my wrist flashes straight from green to violet, and all the noise I found so confusing stops.

People scan the room to its edges, searching the shadows for darker things.

Only three or four blips pass before it's over. Silver's voice carries through the empty air, telling a joke that isn't funny. Nerves make everyone laugh, but we credit the joke, and everything starts over. The chatter, the tink, tink, tink of fast-moving forks and spoons, the slurping and swallowing just to have something to occupy our time.

At the end of our table, Tobin's lost interest in his desserts. He's carving swirls into his tray with a pocketknife.

"They're just resetting the grid, to make sure it wasn't damaged yesterday," Anne-Marie says.

I don't think anyone believes her.

Fingers drum. Toes tap. Legs shake. The room's attention keeps drifting back to me—one here, two there, never at the same time. Some glare, like Dante, while others foster a foreign hope in their expression that disappears as quickly as it forms. A few haven't come out from under their tables. No one told us to get under, but a dozen or so did it anyway.

The lights flicker again, and this time they cut out completely. I clap my hands over my ears, anticipating the scream I know is coming.

"Get down." Anne-Marie pulls my pant leg from under the table. Now I'm the only one *not* hiding.

Everywhere I turn, people are huddled together in the pale glow of mounted track lights around the edges of each table. They're lost without orders from an elder, and all looking at me.

What do you expect me to do? I want to scream.

"Stay in the light," Anne-Marie pleads.

Light is safety; light is life.

Tobin's less civil; he grabs my arm and yanks hard. I tumble down, so close to striking my head on the table that it skims my hair as I fall into his lap. My bad leg takes the brunt of my weight, making me bite my cheek to not cry out.

"Stay down, and stay close," he orders.

"I'm sorry," I say. "About the hospital."

Not the best time to apologize, but it's what I've got.

"And stay quiet," he says.

"I'm trying to apologize."

"The rest of us are trying not to die."

"If I annoy you that much, I'll go cower elsewhere."

I lean up to crawl away, but Tobin drags me back down.

"Ow!"

"Sorry," he says, loosening his fingers. "But it's not safe."

He's right. A violet light isn't a good thing, or a calm thing. I shouldn't be in such a hurry to get away from him, not when he's the one who watched my back last night.

"Why do you even care?" I ask.

"I don't know." Barely a whisper.

Tobin scoots back, making a small gap between us. He

crosses his arms over his chest, turning sideways to watch the door. That's how we stay until the alarm stands down to blue, the lights return, and we all take our seats.

Tobin retakes his station at the far end of the table; I slink back into the spot across from Anne-Marie. We chew through our cobbler-things mechanically. Anne-Marie doesn't say a word.

This is our aboveground evac point if we can't reach the bunkers, and being here feels like we're closer to Red-Wall than anyone wants to admit.

"I'm going for a walk . . . maybe to the rec rooms," Silver says, breaking the stifling silence. It's an idea the others take up quickly—the rec rooms are closer to the security hub.

She and Dante start the exodus. They clear their trays, scrape the gunk into the trash, stack them on the counter. Always slow, calculated movements that don't quite succeed at looking normal. They reach the door, and another group stands. Whole tables vacate, but no one walks alone.

"Annie," one of Trey's friends calls back just before she escapes. "Come with us." She checks over her shoulder to make sure the others haven't left without her.

"Marina, I don't want to get left behind," Anne-Marie says, tray in hand.

"Go on." This is my chance to actually talk to Tobin without all of the extra eyes and ears. I have a hunch he won't leave the room until I do.

"But—"

"Annie, move it!"

Anne-Marie gives me one last, pleading look, tosses her tray, and runs for the exit.

I switch seats, taking one directly in front of Tobin.

"I'm sorry," I say again. The annoying throb in my skull returns as my nerves get the best of me, so I suck in a quick breath through my inhaler to stop it before it gets worse. Tobin glances up, watching, but doesn't say anything. "I'm sorry about the Arc. I didn't want to interrupt you, or have you think I was following you, so I hid."

"You didn't turn me in," he says.

"Whatever took you out there was personal. It wasn't Honoria's business." We both know I'm talking about his father. "What you said to Jove was personal, too . . . I shouldn't have listened in. I still don't know what to say or do most of the time, and I keep choosing the wrong thing."

He continues staring at his tray, tracing the same lines over and over with his knife. This feels like all those times in class, when there was so much fury in him that it spread across the room, slashing at me without his having to move at all.

"I don't understand you, Tobin. One minute you act like you hate me, and the next you're going out of your way to make sure I'm safe. Why?" Normally, I'd have accepted his silence by now and backed down, but I press on, my brain buzzing from my inhaler meds. I really shouldn't have taken so many hits off of it so fast. "Is it what Mr. Pace said? You think this is what your dad would want?"

"You don't know anything about my father or what I'd do for him." He hunches down, tracing faster.

I guess I hit a nerve.

"If you think you can just sit there and ignore me, you should know I've been around Anne-Marie long enough to know how to talk someone into submission."

The knife in Tobin's hand stops midstroke. He shoves the tray hard enough to send it skidding off the far edge of the table, and he's gone before it stops bouncing side to side off the floor.

The steady blue blink lights up the tables. The soft vibration of my alarm itches my wrist until I have to pick at it. And I'm suddenly very aware of being alone in a big, empty space where every sound echoes back to the center.

I sail my tray through the air toward the others before going back for the one Tobin abandoned. Red sludge mixed with amber coats the main compartment. Beneath it, four words are etched into the plastic, scratched over and over with his knife.

"*I promise*" is cut the deepest, as though that was his first thought. Then below it, in a shallower groove, "*For you.*"

CHAPTER 10

CATCHING up with Tobin isn't hard.

There are only two ways you can go from the Common Hall. Turn left and you'll end up in the rec rooms; turn right and you'll be in the domiciles. And I'm sure he isn't in the mood to play games with the rest of the refugees.

"Tobin!"

As soon as he sees me, he disappears around the corner.

It would easy to spin on my heel and leave Tobin to whatever quest he's outlined for himself, to say he can choose to find me if that's what he wants, but making him follow me would bare an open wound as much as if I'd betrayed him at the Arc.

Stupid conscience.

"I blame you for this," I tell my inhaler, but it's not the

chemicals causing me trouble—it's me and my newly discovered talent for being in the right place at the wrong time, and listening in on things I'm not supposed to hear.

This is worse than eavesdropping in the hospital. This is mind-dropping or mind-snooping or whatever the word is for me knowing what he's thinking when I have no right to. If I hadn't heard his argument with Mr. Pace, I wouldn't know what those four words on his tray meant.

I don't want to be Tobin's burden, or compulsion in his father's name, and I *don't* need another martyr, so I follow him, wishing the hallway were longer. At the junction, he's still not moving fast enough to make me believe he's trying to outpace me, not knowing how fast he ran during the Red-Wall.

"Tobin!" He's stopped at his door, hand raised toward the scanner that will let him inside. "Please, we both know you were waiting anyway."

The struggle's there in the way his shoulders tense, then droop. He tightens his grip on the door handle, leaning into it.

"Leave me alone," he says.

"I can't."

"Yes you can. You can walk past here, go to your room, and get inside where it's safe."

"I can't let you do this," I correct him. "You don't have to be your father."

"You don't know what you're talking about."

"I know that if it wasn't for me, he'd be here. I wish—I wish

I was as brave or selfless or good as the people you lost for my sake, but I'm not—I'm scared."

The words come out in a rush, without a pause for him to break in.

"And I don't want you to think you have to throw yourself into the fire for me because it's what your father did, but I'm also too big of a coward to tell you not to. You were the only one in that room last night who was worried *about* me instead of what would happen *because of* me."

How does Anne-Marie do this without passing out? I'm so light-headed, I have to rest my shoulder against the wall before gravity can take me to the floor.

"Marina?" Tobin asks, concerned.

"I think I took too much off my inhaler."

"Do you need Doctor Wolff?"

"No." Shaking my head's a mistake. The entire hall wobbles; Tobin splits in half, so there are two of him with four eyes fixed on me. "I'm finishing what I came to say. If I pass out when I'm done, then one of you can go. I know you blame me for your dad not coming home, and I know—"

Whatever I knew is gone. Thoughts don't matter anymore. Neither do headaches, double vision, or the light show going off inside my brain.

The wall beside Tobin's head shimmers, moving with a grace and precision only possible for a living thing. It's crawling toward the floor with an all-too-familiar *click-clack*

I wish I could blame on my meds.

I take one shaky step, and like before, my movement makes the Fade move. A fraction of a turn, the smallest shift in the way it distributes its weight, and it's out of sight.

Click-clack. Click-clack.

It's happening again, only I'm not asleep this time, and I'm not alone.

"Look, I'm not in the mood for . . . whatever this is." Tobin presses the door handle, disengaging the lock.

"Can't you hear it?" I ask, though it barely comes out as a squeak.

Click-clack. Click-clack.

I risk my fingers, wrapping my hand around the side of the door, and hold tight with strength enough to surprise us both.

"We have to stay still."

The Fade shredded our outer walls; a door will hold one back about as well as tin foil on a hinge. Our only option is to let it pass, then we can alert someone.

"That's it, I'm getting Doctor Wolff," Tobin says.

"No!"

The vents kick on overhead, and the sudden burst catches the Fade's robe, pulling the edge into sight. It's closer. Close enough that it could reach out with one of its poison hands and slice through Tobin. Another burst, and the robes billow out as extensions of the wall itself. The Fade's backing away from us, toward the ceiling.

"You can't feel it?" I ask.

"Feel what?"

The oppressive choke of being watched. Death waiting for the perfect moment to drop out of the sky.

"It's—"

A very human squeal stops my warning. Loud and just around the corner, it's followed by laughter and chatter, announcing that we're no longer the only ones I have to worry about. Silver didn't go to the rec rooms after all. Her walk has brought her all this way, and Anne-Marie and Dante are with her.

"Hey!" Anne-Marie chirps. The lights in the dormitories are bright and strong; our bracelets have turned green. She thinks the danger's passed. "Is this why you didn't want to come with me? If it is, I'll back us right out of here and leave you—"

"Annie, what's on the wall?" Tobin asks. He's finally caught on that I'm staring behind him, not at him.

"Paint?" she guesses, coming closer.

"Someone hit the alarm," I say, forcing the words through my teeth. "It's watching me. If I move, it will, too." I can't make the word *Fade* come out of my mouth.

Tobin cuts his eyes sideways, toward the wall.

"Farther up," I whisper. "Near the signs."

I see the exact second he realizes he's close enough to death to touch it. His body takes on that same surreal calm he had during the Red-Wall.

"You see it?" I ask.

He nods.

Anne-Marie crosses her arms. "Would somebody please—"

Tobin grabs her arm and wrenches her sideways, putting the light at the right angle to show what can't be seen head-on. She gasps, covering her mouth with her hands.

"What?" Silver demands.

"I don't get it either." Dante frowns. "What's the joke?"

Anne-Marie slaps the alarm on her wrist at the same time Tobin activates his own, and she launches herself at the emergency station down the hall hard enough that I hear it when she hits.

In the instant the corridor goes Red-Wall, Silver and Dante shift into reverse, running backward until they're on the wall with Anne-Marie, who still hasn't taken her weight off the emergency call. Tobin twists, grabbing the now-visible Fade by its robes. Dislodged and confused, it crumples, leaving it as a Fade-shaped piece of wall on the floor. It howls through the blue-and-white DOMICILE 27 sign where its mouth should be as Tobin pins it down.

Tobin's eyes go feral with his first strike, but never unfocused like they were when it was Jove on the other end of his fist. This time, he knows exactly who and what he's hitting, and that makes him all the more vicious.

The Fade flails its arms and legs, thrashes its entire body with enough force to bring them both off the floor, but Tobin locks his knees and never falls off.

No two noises from its mouth are the same. One comes out birdlike, the next as the hiss of some great cat, then odd guttural sounds with a rhythm like spoken words. The planes of the Fade's face shift beneath its wrappings as though its bone structure is in flux. A brutal jab connects to an angular cheekbone that crumbles away and re-forms in a new configuration, so no matter how many times Tobin actually succeeds, he never hits the same target twice. Its limbs lengthen and shorten, and its girth flexes from wide to wiry and back again.

Eventually, the Fade finds its center, settling into one form. The pebbled off-white appearance it stole from our wall dissolves into wrapped hands and a face under some kind of long shroud or robe that covers everything but a pair of furious silver eyes ringed dark blue around the irises. Instead of using the leverage of its superior strength, the Fade stops struggling. Those horrible eyes close under lids that are bone white.

Something's coming. I can feel it, smell it, even taste it. The air crackles.

"Tobin, stop." My voice croaks, dry and harsh. "Something's not right."

The Fade takes each blow without a flinch. Not a whimper, no more strange sounds, but it's not as still as it appears. Between the blows, where a person would take a breath, there's a rustle.

"Get back!" I shout.

Tobin has no time to heed my warning. The Fade comes alive, shrieking, and the invisible force that's been holding me still breaks. I drop to the floor, wondering if my ears have ruptured from the sound. To the side, I catch a glimpse of Anne-Marie and her friends with their hands over their ears, cringing together against the wall.

The Fade wedges a foot between itself and Tobin's chest and sends him flying into the far wall; he lands in a heap, at least dazed, most likely unconscious.

The Fade collects itself, pouring up against gravity, until it's balanced on whatever it has for feet. The wrappings that protected it from the light now hang limp from the struggle, an odd sort of decay—second skin falling off a body.

Staring up, I realize that the Fade is on its feet and I'm not. Anne-Marie and Silver are on the floor. Dante's down. Even Tobin, with all that unstoppable rage—useless. It knocked us all out of the fight with barely an effort.

It turns its attention down, meeting my eyes with its silver ones. A connection sparks, raising bile in my throat.

This is familiar.

I've felt this . . . thought this . . . before.

Somewhere.

The headache I've been trying to suppress pokes at the back of my brain. The air charges again, and the Fade drops to a squat in front of me, with its hands rested on its knees, weight forward on its toes.

Blue into silver, then back into blue, the Fade's eyes cycle as they sweep my face. I want to run, but there's nowhere to go, and I can't leave the others. I pray the moan from down the hall means Tobin is conscious again.

"Stay away," I warn, hoping I sound braver than I am as I inch backward, into the opening of Tobin's apartment, and reach for the only weapon I have. I cup my hand around the bottom corner of the door, swinging hard, and hitting the Fade square in the face.

Surprising tears flood those inhuman eyes as it howls again. The Fade's chest heaves, struggling to find the air I knocked out of it. Fade aren't supposed to breathe—there's one of our assumptions blown.

This time, when it finds its feet, the filthy thing lunges. Wicked claws pop through shredded bandages to rip my shield out of my hands. The door hinges groan, but keep their settings.

"Get away from her!" Tobin, back on his feet, leaps at the creature, using his momentum to bring it down.

The others are standing now, made bolder by the knowledge that the Fade can feel pain. Dante tries to help, but Tobin and the Fade move too fast. The Fade's whirling robes make it impossible to keep track of who's where until one or the other of them lands a solid strike, knocking the other one clear.

And suddenly, Anne-Marie's the hero of the night.

Out of nowhere, a shower of freezing water pours into

the middle of the hall. She's climbed up on Silver's shoulders, banging away at a metal sprinkler with her shoe. Sprayers pop on in sequence down the full length of the corridor. Enraged, the Fade tries to find the source of the water as its coverings soak down heavy against its body, impeding its movements.

Tobin and Dante are waiting when their chance comes and knock the Fade off its feet. Anne-Marie grabs an arm; Silver takes one of its legs; I plant myself on its chest, pressing against its shoulders.

There are five of us holding on to this thing and it's still moving. One of them, stronger than five of us—that's one assumption proven.

I dig a knee harder into its side, and the Fade jerks. Our eyes connect again, causing a sensation like static. Not quite tickling, not quite pain. The Fade's eyes widen, forcing the blue to recede to the far edges of its silver irises. Shock, if I had to guess.

Recognition.

It appears as a word, an impression, and a picture all at once in my thoughts. The cool weight of still water washes over my arms and legs, so real I have to glance down to make sure I'm still here. If I close my eyes, I'm outside the Arclight, floating in water that has nothing to do with the sprinklers.

Whispers speak with voices I don't recognize. Flashes of shrouded trees, covered in black vines and moss. *I'm in the Dark.*

Figures appear from nowhere, ghostly white against the ground and nonexistent sky. Blank faces blur together, and all the voices become one.

"Do you know me?" I ask.

Then I'm running. I'm still holding the Fade to the Arclight's floor, but I can feel my legs pumping. Trees and bushes fly by, trampled in my frantic need to get somewhere.

A pinpoint of light appears beyond the darkness. Light means escape. It means safety. It means the monsters can't follow. My leg aches, but I keep running, and the light gets brighter. I'm almost there, and then . . .

Nothing.

White light explodes as though my eyes have burst, and the images retreat to make room for the pain. I can't use my inhaler and hold the Fade at the same time, so I make it suffer for my misery. Legs clenched tighter into its sides, fingers digging as deep as I dare on its throat. Let it feel the torture it's caused for once.

Remorse.

The word echoes softly, like the first moment after waking. It chases the ache with a cooling breeze, and phantom fingers brush the pain away.

Do not injure.

"Wh-what was that?"

The Fade shuts down, and the static dies to silence.

"What did you do?" A minute ago I was sure this creature

wanted to kill me, and could without much effort. Now I'm screaming in its face.

"Don't make it mad," Silver begs.

"It recognized me," I say. "It knows me from before."

"Answer her!" Tobin torques its arm higher over its head. "What happened to the people you took in the Grey?"

Do not injure. I hear again. *No pain.*

The Fade's eyes close. Its fists uncurl, and even the rise and fall of its chest goes to nothing as the sound of running boots flies around the corner and we're left at the center of a fast-forming circle of our elders.

The world's gone upside down.

This Fade knows me. It remembers me from when I was lost in the Dark, and because it remembers, it's surrendered and asked me not to hurt it.

It's afraid of me.

CHAPTER 11

"OH my God." Lt. Sykes stops cold at the sight of us on the floor. For once, his high whine of a voice is welcome.

"Get them out of there," Honoria shouts.

Silver lets go as soon as Mr. Pace touches her shoulder. Dante and Anne-Marie hold on until they're sure there's another pair of hands ready to replace their own, but it takes two men to pull Tobin off.

That just leaves me, shivering on the Fade's chest and unable to let go of its robes.

"It wouldn't tell me anything. I tried to make it tell me, but it wouldn't."

"She's in shock." Honoria starts prying my fingers open one at a time. "Take her."

Mr. Pace grasps me about the waist, lifting me backward.

"No. It knows me!" I refuse to unlock my knees.

"Ease up," he says. "This is one of those things you need to let us handle."

"But—"

Honoria takes my face in one hand. "Marina, I promise you that if there's a way to make it communicate, we will. You've done more than enough."

I nod, letting Mr. Pace pull me away.

He deposits me with the others at the far end of the hall, a mix of anger and panic clouding his face. I'm sure the last thing any of them expected to find when Anne-Marie tripped the alarm was a bunch of kids soaked through and sitting on a Fade in the middle of the Arclight.

I chance looking at the others, expecting the usual disdain and suspicion to have amplified in the wake of this disaster, but there's a spark there instead.

Hope.

Silver rests a hand against my shoulder, squeezes it quickly, then pulls back. Anne-Marie hauls me closer, and this time, no one flinches away. They move me to the middle, so I've got a guard on all sides. I'm not the enemy anymore.

"Is it . . . is it dead?" Silver asks.

"You killed it." Dante says, staring at me. "You really did."

"But I didn't do anything."

The Fade *chose* to shut itself down; all I did was try to retain my sanity while it made me see and feel things that weren't happening.

We all stand clinging to one another, our hair dripping as our elders take possession of the Fade. Though the careful way they handle it speaks to how little confidence they have in their ability to hold it should the Fade decide it doesn't want to be dead anymore. But it stays inert, even when Lt. Sykes nudges it with his boot.

Honoria stops him from removing the Fade's loosened facial covering. "Not here," she says. "Get that thing down to the White Room. And somebody get this water turned off!"

He nods, not at all happy that he's going to have to lift the Fade with his own hands. He takes a deep breath, and signals for help.

"Did you draw blood on it?" Honoria asks me harshly. She slips the silvered pistol she'd been using as a pointer back into her waistband.

"I hit it with the door," I blurt. "But it didn't bleed."

"Show me your hands."

I hold them out to her without hesitation, turning them so she can see both sides. Honoria examines them closely, checking my fingernails to make sure I didn't take any of the Fade's skin away beneath them. After another inspection of my branded wrist, she seems satisfied, and lets go.

She turns to the other woman, whose name tag reads M. OLIVET. "Where do we stand?"

"All the living areas locked down," M. Olivet says. "The kids headed back to the check point in the Common Hall."

"Take Tran and Miller and get a head count. If anyone's missing, find them."

"Should we move people to the bunkers as we clear them?"

"Not so long as there's a chance we'll be locking our kids in with another one of those things. Take them to their parents. Pair the singles off with upper-years."

"Got it."

"And I want to know how that thing got into my compound. It should have tripped ten sensors before getting this deep."

M. Olivet hurries out, giving her a curt nod.

"Get them back to their rooms," Honoria orders Mr. Pace. The furious red tint that had overtaken her face recedes. "Annie can go to the hospital. Dominique's already there with Trey."

"What's wrong with Trey?" Anne-Marie asks.

"He had an accident," Honoria says.

Anne-Marie darts forward, but the adults won't let her pass.

"You are not roaming these halls alone, Anne-Marie Johnston," Honoria says. Her voice never softens, and her posture never relaxes; I'm not sure she's capable of anything short of harsh.

"Trey's asleep," Mr. Pace says. "He won't know if you're there, yet."

Anne-Marie starts in on her fingernails, ripping them with her teeth.

"Is anyone hurt?" Mr. Pace asks "Cuts, scratches, anything?"

I shudder at the thought of Trey and Portman, and the only way to "treat" someone poisoned by contact with the Fade.

"We're okay," Dante says through chattering teeth. "Marina killed it."

"I didn't—"

Oh, never mind. No one's listening to me.

"Tobin, what happened to your head?" Mr. Pace reaches for the rising welt on Tobin's forehead; Tobin knocks his hand away.

"It threw me into the wall." He points to the slight dent where he hit.

"I don't think it made contact with anyone," Silver says. "It was all covered up so the light couldn't get to its skin . . . it has skin, right?" She turns a strange shade of sickly pale at the prospect of the robes and bindings holding together a loosely packed mass of organs and arteries.

"They're clear," Mr. Pace says to Honoria Whit.

"Everyone get to where you're supposed to be. We're on alert until we get this sorted."

She tromps off down the corridor, back the way she came.

"You'd think she'd be happy we won," Anne-Marie whispers.

"I don't think she's ever happy about anything," Silver says.

Personally, I think "won" is overstating things. We lived through the confrontation, and the Fade gave up. That's not the same as winning. If we'd won, we wouldn't be at Red-Wall.

Lt. Sykes glances at me as he and the other guards prepare to take the Fade away. "The girl shouldn't be by herself," he says to Mr. Pace. "If there's one, there could be more."

Not something I want to hear.

"Tobin," Mr. Pace says. "Keep her with you until I come back."

Also not something I want to hear.

"Why me?" Tobin asks.

"Because if you're doing this, you won't be doing anything else—including trying to get another crack at that thing."

"You don't have to—" I start to argue, but Tobin runs over me.

"Fine."

No, not fine. I am not fine with this.

"Mr. Pace—"

"You're both alone, and frankly, I don't trust either one of you with anyone else. Get inside, and stay inside. That was most likely a scout, so it was probably alone."

I'm not so sure.

The idea that another one could be lurking on a wall or over a random door makes me shiver.

"You should be back in your own space in a couple of hours," Mr. Pace says. "Do *not* kill each other before I get back. Silver, Dante, stay together and set the locks. Annie, let's go."

Silver and Dante go deeper into the domicile wing, while Mr. Pace leads a subdued Anne-Marie toward the hospital.

"Come on." Tobin takes my sleeve, guiding me back to the door I used to bash the Fade's face. He grimaces as he pulls it open, struggling to make it stay on its hinges. His eyes shift downward, scanning the bottom, where it hit the Fade's body, to make sure it's clean.

We force the door into place and slide the locking bolt to secure it, leaving me with whichever version of Tobin decides to keep me company, and the knowledge that somewhere there's a Fade inside the Arclight.

"This is where you live?" I ask.

Unlike most of the residential areas, Tobin's is more home than barracks. The floor's laid with mismatched and uneven pieces of carpet, the walls covered with wooden planks from floor to ceiling. This isn't the plastic-and-steel monotony I'm used to. It's real furniture, uniquely beautiful and arranged in a semicircle of chairs and a worn-out couch.

"My dad didn't like the industrial look the place had when it was assigned," Tobin says. "So he copied a page out of a picture book. It took him years."

No wonder Tobin doesn't want to give this place up.

"He even switched out the door so it's got hinges instead of a slider like the rest of them. He put it in backward, though.

It's supposed to open into the apartment, not the hall."

"Lucky us."

Without the door, I'd have been defenseless out there. Tobin's father saved us all. Again.

"Yeah . . . lucky," he mumbles.

Considering what's just happened, and everything that came before, we should have plenty to talk about, but words don't come. I fidget with my inhaler, grateful for the excuse to use my hands for something. Tobin favors his right leg as he drops into a cushioned chair.

I don't talk to him. He doesn't talk to me. Together, we don't speak, until he leans forward to pick at his bootlaces, and an all-too-convenient topic of conversation presents itself.

"You're bleeding."

CHAPTER 12

A patch of dark red spreads along the base of Tobin's neck, stemming from his shoulder; it wasn't there when Mr. Pace checked us over. The split in his jacket's so neat, I couldn't see it until he moved, bunching the material, but blood's soaking through the khaki green of his uniform.

"Get your jacket off," I say.

He's on his feet, snatching at it to get a better look, and ends up turning in a tight circle. A thin red line runs from under his sleeve before dripping off.

That's no simple scratch or scrape.

"It bit you." Those three words take my breath away.

"No it didn't," Tobin says. He's not giving me an opinion; he's begging. "Its mouth was covered."

"Then it slashed you."

"Maybe it's not mine." He tries to get the jacket over his head without unfastening it. All the awkwardness falls away as I pop the clasps one flick at a time.

"Toss it," I order.

The jacket lands several feet away, and for a moment all we do is watch it, as though it could hop up and run away on freshly sprouted legs, but we don't have time to waste.

I reach for his shirt, shaking. What bled through his uniform was only the tiniest indication of what lay beneath, where the material's clinging to his skin. His blood's warm and slick, slipping through my fingers while I use the torn shirt to clean his shoulder. All I can do is keep wiping and hope I live up to my Fade-proof reputation.

"It's bad, isn't it?" he asks, swallowing at the sight of the mess in my hands. He recoils from his own blood, caught by the conditioning that tells him what's been touched by the Fade is tainted. "Can you see anything?"

Yes. I see blue carpet stained with red blood. There should be more left of a person than a splotch on the floor, but if this goes bad, that may be all Tobin leaves behind.

"It's not a bite." I throw his ruined shirt into the pile with his jacket and prod the wound with my fingers, brushing aside the chain for a set of dog tags he had tucked inside his clothes. "No jagged edges. It actually looks pretty clean."

Except for that same halo Portman had on his hand. I glance at the bandage over my burn and find it soaked with black encroaching on it, too. I rip it off, relieved there's nothing but clear skin beneath.

"There's a callbox in my dad's room," Tobin says. "The yellow button's for the hospital."

"You can't go anywhere." Something horrible lies down that road; I'm certain of it. Mr. Pace wouldn't have been so panicked over Honoria seeing Trey if there wasn't. "You're still bleeding."

"Can you fix it?"

There's too much hope in Tobin's expression to believe he only means the cut.

"Do you have any matches?"

"What for?" The suspicion is back in his voice. That's the Tobin I know and lo—

Well, that's the Tobin I know, anyway.

He listens, numb, as I recount what happened with the brush fire, Trey and Portman, and what it takes to purge the Fade.

"You want to set me on fire? I don't like that plan, Marina."

"The Fade poison burns up and flakes off as black ash. Black like what's on your back."

"You're sure?"

"Would you rather wait until Mr. Pace comes back and ask him yourself?"

There's an edge in his eyes, a challenge on his tongue for the sharp tone he's not used to, but he snaps his mouth shut and heads into the kitchen. I hear him slamming cabinets and banging drawers. When he returns, it's with a large knife, an oil-fueled lantern, dishtowels, and a first-aid kit.

"Show me." Tobin taps his foot near where his blood's spotted the carpet. "If you're right, we have to torch it anyway."

The carpet's haloing; I get what that means now. The patches of blood on fabric are no longer red, they're dark as ink. And the stain . . . the poison . . . *the Fade* is spreading. It branches from each spot, creeping across the carpet like rings of charcoal frost on water.

I strike one of the matches and let it drop. A flash of green sparks on contact, and Tobin stumbles back, repulsed by his own blood.

"That came out of me?" he asks.

When the flame dies to a weaker yellow, I stomp it out under my shoe, leaving clumped ash behind. The stink of Fade rot hangs heavy in the air.

"Do it." Tobin covers his mouth and nose.

"You know this is going to hurt, right?" I ask as I light the lantern and prop the blade of the knife into the flame.

"And?"

"Right." What's pain compared to the danger of death—or worse?

I take a towel and do my best to clean his wound again while I collect myself. It'll take a clear head to do what I'm about to, and steady hands. Right now, I have neither.

Tobin lies facedown on the couch. It makes it easier for me to work, but I think he does it so I won't be able to hear him scream. We both know he's going to scream.

My hand trembles as I reach for the knife.

"Do you want a warning?" I ask. "I can count it down, or—"

"No, just get it—"

The rest is torn away by a sound even the couch can't completely muffle. Tobin's free hand digs into the cushion; his face burrows into the corner between the arm and back. His legs kick at the other end.

It occurs to me that I have no idea how long I'm supposed to hold the knife in place. Tobin's skin turns red almost immediately, but if I pull away too soon, I'll have to start over. Even if he could stand it, I couldn't.

Another shriek vibrates through his back.

"Almost there," I assure him, laying my hand between his shoulders. The skin under my hand quivers. A thin coat of sweat breaks out down his spine, like it's crying, too.

I glance at my alarm for the time, trying to guess at how many seconds Dr. Wolff counted off on the hospital clock, then back to Tobin's shoulder. Where the skin's bubbled up around the knife, the halo darkens. His blood grows thick until the crust crumbles into that hideous powder, and I chance moving the blade.

I pull it up slowly, trying to be careful, but it sticks, bringing Tobin's already ravaged skin with it—and one more whimper comes through his back. I take the knife the rest of the way in one quick tug, then poke the blade back into the lantern flame.

He blinks at me, a new fear of fire evident in his features.

"Just cleaning it off," I say.

Tobin pushes himself up on his hands, steadying his body against the pain so he can sit forward while I dress the burn. I don't mention his red, damp eyes, or how smushing his face into the sofa left lines crisscrossing his skin.

"Did you get it?" he asks.

"It looks just like Trey's arm." The black powder brushes away with a swipe of a wet cloth.

"Good." He breathes the word in and uses his voice to cover his pain. "What about you? Your hands?"

"I don't think the Fade like me very much," I say, and wiggle my fingers.

There. I said it. *I'm Fade-proof.*

Tobin pulls his dog tags over his head, brushing his thumb over an inscription I can't see well enough to read; he drapes the chain into the flame to clean it. While he watches his blood bake away, I search the first-aid kit for some of that blue gel Mr. Pace used on my wrist, and layer a coat over the outline of the knife branded on Tobin's shoulder.

At some point, Dr. Wolff's going to hear about this, and, once again, he'll be after me to take up medical training when I age up next year.

Suddenly I realize that I think . . . *I know* . . . I'll be here next year. I'll be in this place and with these people. Somehow I've accepted that this is as close to home as I can get.

"How's that?" I ask.

Tobin tries to shrug, but his face betrays the pain he won't voice. He rips off strips of tape and hangs them from his hand, staring off into the hallway at something I can't see.

His hair's gotten longer since the first time I saw him; it falls forward into his eyes so he has to brush it back with his hand. The burn must catch him off guard because he breathes in sharply. His closes his eyes until it passes, then he opens them, straight at me. The gesture makes me want to run, like he can see through me to one of those parts of myself I've lost.

"I hated you when they brought you in," he says. "That's the one thing I've wanted to say to you this whole time."

Even though I've always known it, his simple confession hurts worse than the imagined versions I came up with on my own.

"But it's not for the reasons you think. When the call came in, my dad was the first one to the Arc. He left so fast I didn't get to tell him good luck. All I got was a note on the counter telling me he'd gone and promising he'd be back soon."

I pull one of the strips of tape off his hand so I have an excuse to look away; he hands me another bandage square.

"Dad said we needed you, and you needed him, but the thing is, I needed him, too. I still do, but he left me. I hated you because one of these days you might wake up with a memory I'll never have, and realize you got to say good-bye to my father. You might have seen what happened to him."

He winces when I slip and have to pull the tape off his burned skin.

"Sorry."

I'm not sure what else I can say. I'm sorry for hurting him, and it kills me that I've done it over and over. Not just with wounds that disappear beneath the pile of bandages and tape, but worse.

"People were so excited when they brought you back. We'd had false alarms before, but you were the real deal."

"They sure didn't act like it."

"That was my fault, too."

This time I do stare. I stop, holding the last layer of bandage in place, with the tape bunched up and twisted because I didn't set it straight.

"Dr. Wolff put you straight into quarantine," he says. "It was days before they gave us details, and all that time, all I did was fester, wondering why my dad chose you instead of coming home like he'd promised."

"You have to know he tried."

"I know, but it didn't matter. They told us you were injured, and I thought . . . I know my dad, Marina. They couldn't have gotten to you without going through him."

No one survives the Fade.

"I still don't think he's dead, but the idea that he's out there, wounded—"

"I'm sorry."

I'm sorry. I'm sorry. I'm sorry. I'm sorry. I'm sorry. I'm sorry. I'm sorry.

"That's the worst part of it," he says. "*I* was the one who got Jove riled up in the beginning. *I* was the one who convinced everyone to treat you like poison. Annie's the only one who wouldn't listen."

He stops talking, as though he expects me to start, but what can I say? I can't say it's a surprise, and I can't say it's all right. This kind of thing doesn't heal with bandages and a little salve.

"Aren't you angry?" he asks.

"I should be." Everything's jumbled, with flashes of anger being enveloped by something still and cool, like trying to spark a fire on soggy wood. We're both broken, and I don't know how to fix it.

"I'm trying to make up for what I did, especially after what happened to that Fade in the hall, and this, and—if there's even a chance Dad was right. It's . . . *you're* . . . worth it."

"As far as I'm concerned, the hall's just another nightmare we shall never speak of again." And like a bad dream, it's best forgotten as soon as possible. I don't want any incentive to think about the Fade or its crawling skin and freezing metallic stare. I don't want the strange, dusty, moldy smell of its wrappings in my nose. I can exist happily without remembering the echo of that wailing screech that sent us all to the floor.

"You probably should have mentioned that to Annie. Once she's out of the hospital, she and Dante will make sure everyone knows you've lived up to your reputation."

"Yep. That's me. Fade-bait."

"Fade-*killer*," he corrects.

Hearing someone say it makes it worse. I'm not a killer. I'm the scared kid who forgets to hide when the lights go out.

"Do you really think your dad's still alive?" I pick the only subject I can think of to make him stop talking about my new status.

"I yell good-bye when I leave for class, and good morning when I go to bed. I keep expecting him to walk through the door. If he was dead, I'd feel it."

I think I understand. I haven't let go of the idea that my family still exists, either.

The itch I'd felt near the Arc returns, and I wonder if that's what's drawing me out—not the Dark or the Fade, but the buried knowledge that someone's waiting for me to find them.

"We have to burn everything," I say, stamping out the feeling.

"The sink in the kitchen is steel. We got lucky with the floor, but I don't want to risk a fire getting out of hand."

I gather the clothes and towels, assuming it's safer for me

to handle them, and pile them into the basin. Tobin throws the lantern in on top of it. Fire and light. With all our safety measures, and all our weapons, it's the primitive things that keep us safe.

Within the cracking pop of green flames, I hear the screams Portman couldn't muffle, the sound of Trey throwing up on the hospital floor, Tobin's agonized cries into the couch cushions. I think of that twisty V in Honoria's hairline, and wonder when she made her great mistake, who held the fire to her skin, and if saving her life cost her more than a little pain.

CHAPTER 13

THE room settles into a hush I can feel on my skin. It presses down, so heavy and uncomfortable I want to say something to end it, but I'm afraid to open my mouth. So I just watch until there's nothing left but ash we can wash down the sink.

"I'm . . . um . . ." Tobin fumbles over the room's new energy. "I'm going to go find a shirt that's a little less—"

"Cauterized?"

"Yeah."

I get a tiny smile before he takes off out of the kitchen.

I can't stay in the room we just used for a crematorium; it reeks of char and decay. I can't go back into the living room, where the echoes of what happened are waiting to get me alone. That only leaves me one option, which is to follow him.

A long passage, paneled like the main room, runs the

length of the apartment. The first door is a bathroom. I can smell the damp even before I see the pile of towels lumped against the wall. Next there's a smaller, closed door that can only be a closet.

Photographs line both sides of the hall—mostly Tobin, arranged in order from the time he was an infant. Collages of pictures show birthdays and achievements, ceremonies where new year-patches were awarded as he's aged up so he grows in a progression of official colors. His parents are here, too; now I know the face of the man who saved my life. Col. James Lutrell was . . . is . . . *was* tall with plain brown hair cut short like Mr. Pace's. His only defining features were prominent burn scars on the backs of his hands that say my rescue wasn't his first brush with the Fade.

The photographs of Tobin's mother stop when he's very small, but he has her black hair, her dark eyes.

Is this what family's like? Tobin in the middle, his mother's arms around him, his father's arms around her, the light around them all? I pick at the photos with my finger so I can see the ones below, but they all show combinations of the same three happy faces.

Tobin's so sad in the first pictures after his mother disappears, clinging to his father like he's afraid to let go. Suddenly it feels like I'm eavesdropping on another of his private moments, and knowing things to which I've no right. I smooth the pictures back in place and turn away.

"Tobin?"

"Down here."

My uninvited tour of Tobin's home takes me to a bedroom where I hear him from inside a closet that's spilled most of its contents onto the floor. There's stuff piled everywhere, even on the bed.

"Sorry, putting on a new shirt was more complicated than I expected. I gave up on buttons." Tobin's voice changes pitch as he tests the limits of his wounded shoulder, straining when the pain hits.

The next time we run, I'll be on my own. No way can he carry extra weight now.

"Are you okay?" I ask

"I want to show you something."

He maneuvers ahead of me into the last room on the hall. This one's neat. The bed's made, and the closest thing to clutter is a set of bags slung over the back of a chair.

"This is my dad's room," he says, disappearing into another closet. There's a crash, then a muffled avalanche, before a solid, repetitive thud announces his return.

He tries to drag a huge box through the room with one hand. After a few steps, he stops and kicks it, pushes it with his foot, but it doesn't move an inch farther.

"Let me," I say. "You fight the monsters; I'll handle the cardboard boxes."

"Kind of a one-sided deal, isn't it?"

"Yeah, but I'm willing to brave the spiders and closet crawlies."

Smiling's getting easier all the time—for both of us.

Tobin relinquishes his position, taking a seat on the floor while I flip the lid open for a better grip and haul the box over.

"I should've thought to open it." He scowls.

"Yes, well, you're a guy. . . ."

"I knew it was a mistake to let Annie talk to you," he grumbles.

"So . . . what's in the box?"

"Take a look."

I pick a glass ball out of a pile of tissue; it's filled with water and shimmering flecks that spin when I shake it. There's a dozen of them inside divided sections of the box.

"What is it?"

"A snow globe," he says. "Relics from before. They were my mother's, but Dad packed most of them up when she died. He only takes them out when he thinks I'm not looking."

"This is snow?"

It doesn't look right. It's browning in places, and clumps of it float in the water. In winter stories, snow's frozen and cold. It should melt in my hand.

"It's not real." Tobin takes the globe and sets it on the table. "But Mom kept dozens. They reminded her of outside."

"She lived outside?"

"Her fifth-greats-grandparents did. She had a book that

one of them had written in, but she read it so often it fell apart in her hands. Pages and pages about traveling the world to cities that don't exist anymore, huge ships that sailed across the water, night and day. They had machines that could fly anywhere you wanted to go."

I nod as though I believe him, but I'm only humoring him. Real flying machines are as unlikely as Anne-Marie's incinerated raccoon. If people could fly above the Dark, why would we still be trapped down here?

He pulls each snow globe out one at a time, making a semicircle on the floor around us, and telling me a story with each one.

"This is Paris," he says. "They called it the City of Lights." He winds up a key on the bottom, and a sad, tinkling song plays while a couple dances on a bridge in the snow inside the ball. "It was my mother's favorite, because all the stories about it were romantic. It's where her sixth-greats-grandparents got married."

"Is that them in the ball?"

"Maybe."

He names the others, Lisbon and London, Tokyo and Montreal. Five of them he says are all the same country, but different places: New York, Chicago, Los Angeles, Austin, and Miami. And the colors . . . there's so much color. The world outside wasn't painted white and grey and sallow yellow. It was bursting with color and music.

"Are we close to any of these?" I ask.

"New York's north of us. Miami's as far south as you can get before the continent ends. We're closer to the north, but there are hundreds of empty miles on every side."

"I like this one." It's not a glass ball on a pedestal; this one's a dome with no trees or houses covered in white. Instead, a green stick stands in the center. Silver glitter shaped like stars falls down around it.

"It's a desert," Tobin says, taking it out of my hands to shake it. "That green thing's a cactus; it's like a tree that doesn't need water."

"It's beautiful," I say.

"Don't you understand, Marina? *This* is what I wanted you to see—I think it's where you came from. If there are people still out there, then they have to be in a place like this where there's light and heat in every direction."

"Where is it?" I ask, peering deeper into the dome, searching for some clue or connection.

"On the other side of the Dark, maybe." He shrugs. "Close enough to reach at a run?"

I wish I could say his prompting spurs a memory, but it doesn't.

"Or maybe it's like the stories they tell children to help them sleep, and it never really existed," I say sadly. The green stick doesn't carry the same familiarity as my secret flower bush.

Tobin shakes the dome hard, setting it down so the stars fly and fall back to earth.

"And I think I'd remember seeing the stars swirl like that," I say.

"Watching the stars fall is definitely something you don't forget."

"Stars can't fall."

They light the night. If they fall, the darkness is absolute.

"Not like this, but . . . here, look."

He burrows through the box, lifting out a stack of old paper books. The pages are glossy and thin, with photographs and a lot of words blocked into columns. Right on the front, there's an image of giant cinders filling the night sky while people sit on a hill and watch.

"Falling stars," he says. "See?"

"What is this?"

"They're picture books from right before the evacuation to the Arclight," he says, passing me one. "These are all we have left."

The paper's so smooth and delicate, I'm afraid I'll tear it just by turning the pages, but Tobin handles his carelessly, flipping the sheets with his thumb.

"What happened to the others?"

"Some fell apart. I cut one up when I was little. I didn't know they were rare, I just liked the pictures."

Tobin reaches back into the box and retrieves another

bundle of pages, but these aren't bound. They're yellowed and crisp. Even with his cautious movements, bits flake off, coasting to the floor.

"The newspapers didn't last as well, but you can still read pieces if you're careful," he says.

Newspapers aren't as interesting as magazines. The pictures are smudged, and washed out in places. Some of the pages have holes where entire sections are missing. Large letters declare things like *Epidemic After Containment Failure* and *Military Maintains Silence. Affected Areas Devour Townships* and *Missing Persons Total Tops Four-Hundred-Thousand.* Tobin picks up a brittle page with a header of *Calvert County Quarantined: Symptoms to Watch,* but it goes to pieces in his hands.

"What's a nanite?" I ask, trying to decipher the diagram of a tiny machine that looks like a bug.

"I don't know what half of this means. They're old words no one uses anymore."

He sets what's left back in the box; I return to the magazine. "These are stars?"

Lighted streaks fall like rain with fire on their tails, as people on the hill point at the brightest and biggest. Children and adults, all with wonder on their faces, enjoying the night.

"They're fragments of rock that burn when they touch the sky," Tobin says. "People called them stars because of the glow."

"They're . . ." I don't know what to say. What's more than

beautiful? "I've never seen anything like them."

I lay my hand against the page, but it's false as a reflection. It's nothing but a memory someone else has forgotten.

"Come on." Tobin grabs my hand, abandoning the box of treasures in his dad's room, and drags me with him to that tiny door I passed in the hall. The few towels he hasn't gone through line the bottom shelf inside; sheets and blankets fill another. There's a pillow wedged between cardboard boxes on the highest one.

"It's a linen closet," I say.

"I told you, this place has a lot of secrets *if* you know where to look."

Tobin holds up one finger on his good hand, like he's going point to something, then reaches inside and flips a panel that's perfectly matched to the wall.

"Press there," he says, placing my fingers on a metal plate with tiny skids for traction.

The plate gives way under my hand, and the entire side-wall of the closet disappears into a pocket, revealing a narrow passage beyond.

CHAPTER 14

THE passage is long, empty, and more claustrophobic than the bunkers. Metal pipes run the length of the ceiling, snaking down the walls to disappear into the floor. Steam drifts back and forth at a lazy pace, blown around by the air from separate vents, never quite able to escape the middle ground between them, like the fog that fills the Grey.

"You want me to go in *there?*" I ask.

"You have to turn sideways and scoot through, but it gets wider inside."

Tobin shoulders past me and slips into the passage, turning a circle with his uninjured arm out wide.

"I'll pass," I say.

"I've used this tunnel since I was so small Dad had to carry me."

"But it's dark."

"Give me five minutes. If you're still scared after that, I'll bring you straight back." He reaches for a flashlight propped on the floor beside the opening, and turns it on. "Trust me."

A very real, very loud part of me wants to say no, turn around, and run screaming. It tells me I was too late treating his shoulder, and this is how the madness starts. A normal person, who looks and sounds like himself, who acts like himself, but gets the urge to walk into the darkness and never come back. Luring friends and family because the Fade have his mind.

However, that part of me disagrees with a tiny voice, growing stronger as I watch Tobin with his hopeful look, biting his lip, stretching his hand out for me to take. Slowly, I edge my hand toward his, closing my eyes as he wraps his fingers around it and tugs.

Once I've cleared the door, I look back and forth between the tunnel and Tobin's apartment. The flashlight's beam turns the passage an eerie brownish-green, casting shadows at sharp angles. But inside the apartment, the light's warm and sunny. It dims behind us as we walk, until all that remains is the thin streak from the flashlight and the dull blue glow from our alarm bracelets.

I try to get a look at Tobin's eyes, to see if they've taken on that metal shine like the Fade that attacked us in the hall, but his face is hidden in shadow. Just like his hands, and my hands, and our feet, and everything else that exists outside the beam.

"Almost there," Tobin says, as though he can feel my nerves choking me. "Step up."

At the other end of that command lies an open space with three more tunnels branching from it. An almost useless bulb hangs above us, dimmer than the flashlight. There could be a thousand Fade in here, and I'd never know.

"Hospital," he says, slashing the flashlight toward the tunnel on the left. "Common Hall," is the middle one. "The Well," he names the last.

He steers me right, and we start toward the Well, but he never tells me what it is.

The world behind us no longer exists. It's bleak and empty, and no matter how hard I try to keep my word, my legs are heavy, slowed by the twisted scenarios usurping my attention. Tobin could have turned Fade; he could be on his way to the Dark right now to join the others. Or, confident that I'm Fade-proof, he could have decided I'm a bargaining chip to trade for his father.

Neither possibility ends well for me.

At the point I'm ready to hit my alarm and alert security, something reflects the beam back at us. There's a metal panel set into the wall, identical to the one in his linen closet. Tobin hands me the flashlight, jogging ahead. I let the beam shine up and into his face, but the relief at seeing his eyes still brown is short-lived.

141

He presses the panel, and the door slides away. Fresh air floods the tunnel, warm and sweet, as the seal breaks.

It's a door to the outside. Out where *they* are.

How could I have been so stupid? *No one* is this at ease without light. Not after a Red-Wall. Not after a Fade slices into them. Not when there could be more of them anywhere.

"This way," he says, taking my hand to pull me out into the darkness.

I press my feet against the cement, but it's slick from the steam.

"Tobin, please don't give me to the Fade," I beg. "I know you think your dad's still alive, and after what happened back there, you think they can't hurt me, but it won't work."

"Give you to the Fade?"

I ignore the confusion on his face and pull against him, straining back the way we came.

"I won't survive out there . . . *please* . . . I don't want to die."

"Marina, snap out of it." Tobin shakes me by both shoulders, wincing when the motion pulls his wounded arm. That's when I see my escape.

I swing the flashlight, aiming for the tender spot where I held the knife against his skin, but he ducks, catching it when I try to swing it again.

"Stop it!" he orders.

Even with only one good arm, Tobin's strong enough to lift me off the ground. Either my flailing feet aren't connecting with his legs as often as it feels like, or he doesn't notice.

"Put me down! You are not giving me to the Fade!"

"No. I'm not," he says, and totes me out into the night.

There's no need for my eyes to adjust like when we entered the tunnels. When Tobin forces me through the door, it's from one dark place into another. He takes three steps, then drops me.

My first impulse is to run, but he's between me and the door. Behind me there's only open space, and beyond that lurks the Dark itself, in collusion with the night.

"Look up," he says, annoyed, plopping down on the grass with his legs crossed to do exactly that.

My curiosity wins out.

I crane my neck up, stiffly, as though my body's still fighting my better judgment.

The sky's ink-black, with barely a moon. Then the whole thing rips wide open as a cascade of burning streaks trail across in red and gold.

"Falling stars," he says. "Do you still want me to take you back?"

Two minutes ago, I'd have said yes, but now I'd rather have my two minutes back so I could make myself not act like an idiot. I'm furious with myself, and that's unacceptable, so I'll be mad at him instead. I give Tobin my best scowl.

He laughs at me.

"Marina, this is one of the Wells," he says, as though the answer explains everything, but it means no more now than it did inside the tunnel. "When the lights were first built, after the bonfires, they designed the Arc with pockets to see the night sky. They needed a window, so they made this."

"We're inside the boundaries?"

Tobin stands, taking a rock in his hand. He draws back, aims high, and lets it fly. The rock pings off something metal.

"We're inside the Arclight," he says. "The curve of the wall is designed to keep out ambient light."

It's a courtyard where the Arc's shine dulls to barely a glow around the upper edges, like we're surrounded by a giant halo. We must be near the center of the compound, between the rooftop lamps.

"It's screened, with no access from the outside. The Fade can't come here unless they breach the Arc again, and even if they did, no one knows this place exists anymore. It's been forgotten."

Tobin stretches his legs, leaning on his stronger arm. He looks peaceful, without the anger and frustration, or even fear I've seen on his face since the day I first came here.

"My dad loves the stars—so do I. People used to go up there, you know. That was the book I cut up when I was a kid—pictures of people standing on the moon, where the lights are brighter than you can imagine."

The Fade took that from us. They stole the moon, and robbed us of the stars.

Slowly, as my brain accepts that Tobin is telling the truth, I convince myself to scoot closer and sit beside him, mimicking his posture and staring up. You can't do this with the sun— it burns and blinds even those of us it protects. But at night, there's nothing to keep you from the size of the sky.

Tobin lies back, and so do I. He points out clusters of stars that were named by men who died long before the Fade were fears, and tells the stories he's heard from his father about how the shapes guided ships across oceans.

Every few minutes, another flare sparks to life from nothing. They sputter silently and disappear as though they'd never existed at all.

"Do they do this every night?" I ask.

"Every year, but not every night; Dad marks it on the calendar. I wasn't going to come this year. I didn't want to be alone."

He changes his position on the ground, and maybe not-so-accidentally moves closer. I lean in his direction and point up.

"That bunch there looks like Dante when the babies tried to climb him in the bunker," I say. "See the way it's bent from where one kneed him in the back?"

Tobin snorts.

"And that's Anne-Marie holding Jove's head in the ice bucket."

Over and over, we rename the stars to our liking. He points to one image, and I move into his space. I spy another, and he encroaches on mine. Maybe they'll lead us somewhere.

"What happened to you back there?" he asks without turning his head. "When we had the Fade on the ground, you kind of went somewhere else."

"It's hard to explain." I pull my inhaler up, fidgeting with the ring.

"Did it do something to you?"

"I don't know."

He tucks his arm behind his neck, covering the blinking light from his alarm.

"Well, something happened. That thing saw you and it just . . ."

"Gave up," I finish for him. I shiver as the sensation of cold water washes over my arms and legs again. "I saw things. I looked in its eyes, and I was in the Dark—running. I saw it, felt it, *everything*. It was like my mind split in half, or like the Fade had drilled into my head. It was searching for something."

That sinister chill that has nothing to do with temperature returns, and I cross my arms over myself. What little space remains between us, Tobin covers, so we're touching at the shoulder, and we both get the same idea at the same time. Our heads lean together, and the closeness kills the cold.

"Did it find what it wanted?" he asks.

"I don't think so. My headache cut the connection."

"Are headaches why you need this?"

He sits up and takes the inhaler out of my hand, holding it flat in his palm.

"Yeah."

"What's it like?"

My focus shifts again, as though my body is one place and my mind is another. "Everything buzzes. There's too much distraction to concentrate on anything except everything at once, because it's all too loud and too bright. My pulse crashes. There's no air in my lungs. Then it gets worse."

"That sucks."

"Like you couldn't imagine." He makes me laugh; I can't help it.

Tobin has many faces, but none are quite as endearing as the lopsided grin in front of me now. "At least the inhaler fixes it."

"Not really," I say.

He's like Anne-Marie, thinking that a puff or two of "magic air" makes me normal, but it's not like that. It's more . . . dying in reverse. Everything switches back on, but it doesn't pick up where I left off; I always lose something. All the color disappears beneath whitewash.

I pull the inhaler out of his hand and tuck it into my shirt, shaking the muffled feeling out of my head as I sit up completely and face him.

"Tobin, what's the White Room?"

The question comes out of nowhere, and I hadn't intended to ask it like that, but I need to know.

"A place that isn't supposed to exist anymore," he says, turning his attention to the ground.

"You mean like this one?"

"It's underground." He rips up a handful of grass and shreds the blades between his fingers.

Underground, like Dr. Wolff's incinerator.

"It was the original hospital, in the sections that were walled off when they sealed the tunnel system."

"But Honoria said that's where they took the Fade."

"I know."

A shadow passes over his face, blending him into the night. I reach to touch him, even though I know he hasn't moved.

"Tobin?"

"It's just a cloud," he says. "Hopefully they won't last long. Clouds mean we can't see the stars, and the real show hasn't even started yet."

"I want to see it," I say.

"We'll come back. By next week, they'll be falling like rain. Dad said this was going to be the best year in a decade."

"The Fade," I clarify. "I want to see it up close."

"We saw it close enough." His shirt rustles, testing the freshly dressed wound, and reminding me just how close we got to the Fade tonight.

"I want to know why it was here."

"You already do."

"And that makes it worse. I need to understand. I want to look it in the eyes."

No, really I don't want that at all. I want to see it, but I don't want it to see me.

"You think it's worth letting that thing dig around your skull again? It can't talk. How's it going to tell you anything?" Tobin demands.

"It gave me back a memory, Tobin. I remembered the water. I don't know what it means yet, but that thing knocked something loose, and if it can do it again—"

"No."

"What do you mean, 'no'?"

"No to what you're going to ask me. I'm not wandering the tunnels on the off chance we'll stumble across the White Room."

"Not even to know what happened to your father?" I feel guilty using his dad as leverage, especially since I accused him of using me for the same, but I'm desperate. This way we both get our questions answered. "If that Fade saw me, it could have seen him, too."

"How do you know it was even your memory?" Tobin asks. "It could have been a trick."

"I know what I saw."

It was too . . . *human* . . . to belong to a Fade.

"Some of the older tunnels opened into the Grey before they were sealed off. Others are so old they run under the Dark now. If the White Room still exists, it's in those older parts; I've never gone that deep."

"I want to try."

Tobin's scared. I can see it in the way he rubs the back of his neck with his good hand; I can nearly hear the argument in his thoughts. He's trying to do what he thinks his father would want, but that's at odds with what he wants himself.

"You were ready to claw me to pieces because you were afraid I was going to take you to the Fade, and now you want to go in search of one. Are you sure that thing didn't do something to your head?"

"Not really, no."

Tobin stands and starts to pace. Shadows cast across his face and arms. Dark circles fill the hollows of his cheeks and ring his eyes.

"The oldest tunnel I've ever used is the one that goes to the Common Hall. Dad only took me that way a couple of times, so I'd know how to find it if there was no other way out. It's a last resort passage, not one you'd use by choice, and I haven't been down there since I was ten. We'd have to start at the junction and mark the path as we go."

That sounds suspiciously like a "yes," despite his already having said "no."

"When?" I ask.

"Not tonight. Mr. Pace is going to come soon, and I'd rather not have him find my apartment empty."

The trip back feels shorter. I glance down the different shafts at the junction, repeating them to myself as he'd listed them off: Hospital . . . Common Hall . . . Well . . .

Common Hall . . .

Common Hall . . .

White Room . . .

"What's wrong?" Tobin asks. His earlier calm has passed to me, and he's absorbed my nerves in exchange.

"All my answers could be down that tunnel," I say. "Both our answers."

Tobin shifts, putting his body between me and the route to the Common Hall.

"Maybe, but Honoria will have people crawling all over that Fade tonight; she'll be there herself."

I'm struck with an almost unbearable desire to bolt around him and charge down that tunnel on my own.

"We can't risk getting caught down here, Marina. When I said no one knows about the Well, I meant it. It's supposed to be sealed. I'm not losing this, too."

He shuffles me along until we reach the point where that distant, muted hum becomes a constant once again. The tiny blip on my wrist that blinks in time to the wall alarms bounces off one wall. Tobin's bounces off the other, and the flashlight finds the door.

Light from inside his apartment floods the tunnel, no longer joyous or comforting but harsh. I hide my face against Tobin's side to block it. The scent of antiseptic and burnt skin from his shoulder mingles with the remnants of dirt and grass on his clothes from where he'd laid down in the Well.

The panel slides closed with a *thwack* and I let him lead me, blind, to the living room and the same couch where I'd burned him, to wait for Mr. Pace.

CHAPTER 15

MR. Pace is furious over Tobin's injury, not to mention the fact that we'd treated it ourselves. And I can live quite happily without ever seeing him return to the enraged caricature he became in Tobin's living room, just before he called reinforcements to sanitize the apartment.

"Do you have any idea what could have happened?" Mr. Pace keeps asking, stalking the floor. "Of course you don't. None of you know anything."

He looks so old, lines appearing around his eyes and mouth where none had been before.

Behind him, a team of three tears up the carpet swatches Tobin's father had installed and fire-washes the cement floors below.

They treat me and Tobin like we're contaminated, forcing

us into quarantine until Dr. Wolff arrives. He ensconces us in the makeshift hospital he sets up in the kitchen, so he can be sure I didn't miss anything when I burned Tobin's skin.

Tobin sits perched on his kitchen table, shirt off, watching his childhood disintegrate as the flames devour one more memory of his father.

"Dad's going to be mad," he says, still watching the sanitation team. "It took him forever to collect enough pieces to cover the whole floor."

"And what would he say about you, Tobin?" Mr. Pace asks. "How do you think he'd feel trying to put back the pieces of his son?"

"Leave them be, Elias." Dr. Wolff clucks his tongue when he peels the bandages away from Tobin's skin. "It was a near miss, but a miss nonetheless. His skin's clean, and the heat marks are well beyond the edges of the initial injury. Considering the conditions, and the skill level of the people involved, he was lucky."

Mr. Pace brushes his hands over his skull, five times, maybe ten, while Dr. Wolff selects the evil scraper from the instruments he brought with him. We may have been lucky, but he's not taking any chances. He double-checks everything, wearing multiple layers of gloves.

"Did Tobin's skin ever branch black or halo?" he asks me.

Mr. Pace stops and turns my way; Tobin's eyes plead silently for me to tell them no so this will end. Beyond them, blue flames lick at the cement floor, close enough to be convenient if they decide we're contaminated, so I choose the lie and hope I won't regret it later.

"No. I burned him because of what I'd seen with Trey and Portman."

"You still should have called for help," Mr. Pace says.

"We did the same thing you would have," Tobin charges. "You wouldn't have pulled anyone away from the bigger crisis."

"You shouldn't have been up here alone."

"I wasn't."

The exchange between them shifts from the timbre of a superior chastising someone under his command, or a teacher scolding a student, to something more informal. Here, there's no caste system enforced by the patches on our sleeves. Tobin and Mr. Pace become two people who care about each other, not because it's a regulation for the older to protect the younger, but because they're an extended family.

I *want* that feeling. I know I should have it, but I don't.

"There's a difference between a miss and a graze, Tobin," Mr. Pace continues.

"Elias, not now."

"Then when, Doc?" Mr. Pace demands. "Of all the unreasonable, bullheaded, senseless . . . *you* tell me when the right time is! Keeping these kids uninformed is only going to lead to more accidents—or worse. And you, of all people, should be agreeing with me. You're the one who has to clean up the ones who fall through the cracks we make, and I'm the one who has to do it when you're not fast enough."

"Be thankful Marina was with us today to see what she saw, or this would have been much worse."

Tobin's skin pales as he absorbs Dr. Wolff's words—*would*, not *could*. There are only absolutes with the Fade. Tobin came too close to needing more than a knife and a lantern to save his life.

"That's exactly my point!" Mr. Pace snaps, making me jump. "Sorry. I'm not angry with you—either of you, but I'm so tired of this. After Trey . . . Trey nearly lost his arm, and now, if this had happened to anyone else . . ."

He picks up the nearest instrument from the counter and hurls it the length of the room, shattering a glass pane in one of the cabinet doors.

"Wonderful lesson for the young ones, Elias. No wonder you're such a good teacher."

"Keep it up, Doc. Next time I'll aim for something else."

"Hold on to your right shoulder, Tobin," Dr. Wolff says, ignoring Mr. Pace. "You'll have to wear a sling for a few days so you don't do the muscle worse injury. I assume you know there'll be a scar."

Tobin nods, resting his hand against the top of his shoulder while Dr. Wolff ties his arm in place. When he's done, Tobin's arm lays anchored to his chest, beneath a cocoon of cotton bandages. It makes an ugly lump when Dr. Wolff helps him back into his shirt, leaving the empty sleeve to flop around limp.

"A few days with me and you'll be good as new."

"I don't do hospital stays. I had enough of that place when Mom was sick."

"Tobin, you can't even dress yourself," Mr. Pace says.

They think he's being difficult, the same way they believe he's deluding himself about his father, but I know better; he doesn't want to be separated from his apartment. Without the door in his closet, he loses the Well and the stars; we can't search out the White Room. Tobin isn't being difficult—he's clutching at hope.

"I can check on him," I offer.

Tobin relaxes, a change so small, it would be easy to assign it to the pain in his arm easing.

"I don't think that's such a good idea," Dr. Wolff says.

"Well, I do," Tobin argues.

"Marina's not capable of watching out for you, as well as herself, if another situation arises."

"She did pretty well from where I was sitting," Tobin snaps back.

"Honoria wants her somewhere safer than wandering the halls between her room and this one," Dr. Wolff says, then turns his attention to my hand. To my relief he reaches for a clean roll of bandages, rather than the scraper. "Back me up on this, Elias."

"Honoria's wants aren't too high on my priorities list right now." Something changes in Mr. Pace's posture. "Tobin, get up. You're coming with me," he says as he pulls Tobin from his perch on the table.

"That's going to take some getting used to," he says, familiarizing himself with the new balance of only having one mobile arm.

"Between my leg and your arm, we almost match," I add.

Dr. Wolff stands his ground, with the bandages hanging from his fingers and rolling across the floor, not ready to concede the argument, but Mr. Pace shoves past him, still towing Tobin along by his empty sleeve.

"You can come or not, Doc, but it's time Honoria was reminded that people have to deal with the consequences of her decisions. Marina, move it. You're coming, too."

I snap to attention at the command, too used to following his orders not to obey.

Mr. Pace ushers us into the deserted hall, past the torches with those colored flames that are so similar to the green blaze of Tobin's Fade-infested clothes. The reflection flickers in the eyes of those sanitizing the apartment, incinerating any human emotion that might be there.

"Are we in trouble?" I ask.

"You saved his life, Marina. I'm not going to punish you for that." Mr. Pace lets go of Tobin's sleeve, moving ahead of us.

"But when Honoria sees what happened—"

"Honoria means well. She's a good leader, but she keeps a certain distance from everyday life. Sometimes that distance is too great, and it gets hard to reconcile statistics with the people they represent. She might lose her temper, but she'll realize I'm right."

He sounds sure, but I still wish he'd picked someone else to be his visual aid.

"Trust me, I'm the only one she'll be angry with. *You*, she'll be proud of. There aren't a lot of people who could stomach what the two of you did."

We turn at the main hall, and then down another, with Mr. Pace walking so fast, I have to jog to keep up. The burn's returning to my leg, but I don't think trying to stop him is the best idea. Here the floor bears a red and gold line with RESTRICTED stenciled every three feet—we've passed into the security sector. Dr. Wolff catches up with us at a metal door that requires not only Mr. Pace's alarm bracelet to open, but a manual code as well.

"I thought you'd change your mind," Mr. Pace says.

"There's a very real chance that if I leave you and Honoria to your own devices, one or both of you will need medical attention before this is over. I think Marina's battlefield triage skills have been tested enough for one day."

The door slides on a hidden track like the one inside Tobin's apartment, but unlike there, the overhead lights still work, snapping on as we approach, and flooding the corridor with stark light that shows off brightly painted walls and pipes that are free of rust.

"We're going underground," I whisper to Tobin as the floor slopes downward.

"I know," he says gravely.

The decline extends at a gentle angle for more than three hundred meters. Raised letters show through the paint on the wall; I brush them with my fingers as we pass, tracing *USAF*, inscribed with three stars on each side.

At the end of the first passage, there's a turn and two steps down. We travel the next corridor in a tight group, taking another two steps at its end. Once we start a long, straight stretch, Tobin and I slow down to put some distance between us and our elders.

"Do you know where we're headed?" I ask.

"We're off the map, but if I had to guess, I'd say we're under the security hub. These are definitely the old tunnels, but they're supposed to be unstable."

Paneled walls and lights that activate as we pass don't exactly scream "Watch for falling objects." It's cleaner down here than the halls up top. More raised letters appear along the wall here and there, spelling out SUB-LEVEL, followed by a number sequence.

Thick glass windows show gardens and orchards that hang heavy with new fruit. They're overseen by Jonathan Shen, the gardening supervisor who teaches us to care for the pitiful growing rows outside. He's yet to speak to our class about following his trade, but even if he had, I don't think he would have mentioned this place.

Maeve Brecken didn't when she spoke to us about the necessity of maintaining our uniforms—she's here, too, bustling through a neat storage area that houses clothes on racks. There have to be enough here for twenty years.

Why hasn't anyone told us about this?

"What is this place?" I ask Tobin.

"I don't know," he says under his breath. People behind the glass begin to notice us, gaping as we pass. We're the youngest people here. "But we never would have made it if we'd wandered into this on our own."

Up top, in the Arclight aboveground, a red line leads you to the hospital, while a phosphoric green one takes you to the bunkers. There's blue for the Common Hall, and yellow, orange, purple, and brown for the different domicile wings. No matter where you go, so long as you follow the lines, you can get back to where you came from. Down here, it's blank.

"Stay close," Mr. Pace warns as the temperature drops and a stale draft blows the scent of dust and mold our way. "Keep to the right."

Ahead, the corridor splits into a T. To the right, the clean air and lights continue, but to the left, there are only echoes of distant wind, and the hint of a wrecked wall a few meters in.

"What's the other way?" I swing around for a glimpse. Cobwebs clump in dim corners, near pipes covered in cement. Rubble blocks the passage from floor to ceiling.

"The Grey. Those entrances are sealed."

Mr. Pace trudges onward, faster, so more lights ignite when he passes under them. He pauses to enter another code at a door that seems out of place for its plainness. I expected something more than steel on hinges.

There's a metal frame etched on the front, reading *Th. Whit: Micro-Mechanics + Biology* in heavy script. Inside is an office and more light, but muted yellow like true sun, and it's sweltering. Honoria sits rolling a small, dingy ball across the surface of her desk with one hand, while the other holds an inhaler ring to her mouth. I recognize the breathing pattern as she draws the medication in and out.

"What are you doing down here?" she demands, shooting to her feet. She stashes the inhaler in a drawer, along with the ball, and slaps a photograph of a boy wearing a blue cap and white shirt facedown against her desk. A slim orange cat leaps from her desk to a shelf, then sits there, flicking its tail.

Even with the grey streaks in her hair to hint at her age, Honoria's an imposing woman. She's tall, over six feet, and it's not easy to shoulder the full weight of her disapproval, but Tobin doesn't even flinch.

"Mr. Pace made us come," he says.

"This is no place for a pair of children who have the

unfortunate habit of attracting disaster—" Honoria's rant and her demeanor make a one-eighty shift as she zeros in on the empty sleeve hanging at Tobin's side. "What happened?"

"It seems the last bit of trouble they attracted hit closer to home than anyone realized," Dr. Wolff says.

"You were wounded?" She hooks a finger into the neck of Tobin's shirt and tugs it sideways sharp enough to unbalance him. "It broke skin?"

"The boy's fine. Thankfully, Marina is as suited to healing as I've tried to convince her she is."

He smiles, attempting to lighten the atmosphere; I suppress the urge to groan.

"What did you do?"

Honoria's question comes as an accusation.

"She branded my shoulder," Tobin answers for me. Unsure what to do or say, I mimic Tobin's confidence, hoping I can pull it off well enough to convince myself it's mine.

"Marina witnessed my treatment of young Mr. Johnston in the hospital earlier tonight," Dr. Wolff says, "and thought it a prudent precaution to take. He's clean."

"If you didn't bring him down here for quarantine, then—"

"I brought them because *you* could have prevented this," Mr. Pace says. "If they'd known the real danger of dealing with a Fade, they'd have been more careful. What if it had been someone else? Someone with no idea how to contain an infestation?"

"I thought it was poison," Tobin says.

"See? Ignorance will kill us faster than anything beyond the lights," Mr. Pace says. "Especially now."

Honoria's jaw pops so loud and hard I'm sure everyone in the room can hear it.

"I know Trey's accident has you on edge, Elias, and maybe, in light of recent events, we should reevaluate the idea of early instruction for our older children, but it's going to take time. I don't appreciate being cornered, and—"

"And I don't appreciate one of my students reaching the point where another has to hold a branding iron to his back because *you* don't think these kids can deal with the truth. I'd say these two proved you wrong."

They're toe-to-toe now. Nose-to-nose and eye-to-eye. Breathing the same breath.

"I'm trying not to lose my temper here." Honoria pinches the bridge of her nose, wincing behind her fingers. "But what little patience I have left is eroding fast. I'm not sure—"

"Please let us see it." To the surprise of everyone, myself included, the request that ends their argument comes from me. "I know it's down here. I . . . I *need* to see it."

"*We* need to," Tobin corrects. "Either I get answers from that thing, or find my own beyond the boundary."

Honoria and Dr. Wolff wear matching expressions of doubt and annoyance.

"Tell her I was the reason you were hiding behind the

switchbox," Tobin prompts me. "*I* was the one who set off the sensors, not you."

"It's true," I say. His fingers split the spaces between my own, turning our hands into a shared fist.

"Did you cross over?" Honoria asks.

"I will. When Dad first disappeared, I thought about it every night and day. I'd go to the Arc and look for any sign of movement." The fearless shell cracks; his voice softens to a plea. "He's still out there—I know it. I just need to know where to look. If you won't help me get my answers, I'll find them in the Grey. Marina survived out there, so can I."

"Confronting that thing's not going to give you what you want, Tobin," Honoria says. "Either of you."

"Seeing it's enough," I say. "Anything to tell me I'm not crazy or dreaming, because that's how it feels."

"You dream about the Fade?" she asks.

"Just nightmares." I shrug and buy myself another few seconds with my inhaler. "I tried to run away, but my leg gave out. It asked me for help, then I woke up. I can't trust that what I remember was any more real than the nightmare. I need to see it."

"I thought the inhaler was supposed to help," Mr. Pace says.

"It helps the pain, but doesn't stop the dreams," I say.

Honoria takes my inhaler, weighing it in her hand. She shakes it to make sure there's still medicine in it.

"You and Doctor Wolff go back to the hospital. Tell him

everything you can remember about these dreams. When you have them, what causes them, everything."

I feel Dr. Wolff's hand settle on my shoulder, as though he means to take me now.

"Can't we see it first?" I ask. "Please?"

"We caught it, we have a right," Tobin says. "Someone has to answer for what it did to my fath—our people. *Her* people."

We're coming to a deadlock. Tobin's weight shifts onto the balls of his feet; I hang on to his hand, not wanting him to challenge Honoria outright. But the impasse I'm expecting ends before it even starts.

"Fine. I suppose it won't hurt to let you take the tour," Honoria says.

We follow her out of the office and through a set of doors that lead into another long corridor. She stops at the end with her hand on another door.

"You want to go in, you follow the rules: One—no one finds out you were down here, or that the old base is still operational. Understood?"

We nod, and she continues.

"Two—whatever you think you're about to see, forget it."

Tobin goes cold and distant. Whatever's in the next room could destroy everything he's held on to; he could lose his father in a way worse than death.

"Even if it looks like him, it won't be him," I whisper.

"It's not James," Honoria says with surprising kindness.

166

She puts a hand on his shoulder. "Whatever notions you have, put them out of your mind. Your lessons didn't cover what's on the other side of that door, but try not to let your surprise show. Sudden movements are a bad idea."

Another nod.

"Rule three. When I say leave, you go, without argument or hesitation. And rule four—" She digs her fingers into Tobin's wound until he cringes down .

"Honoria!" Mr. Pace and Dr. Wolff shout together.

"Stop it!" I scream.

"Even think of challenging me again, and I'll have you in a cell before you can blink." She lets go so fast Tobin stumbles to the floor and I have to help him up.

Honoria flashes her wristband at the panel on the wall, and that same hiss I dread when we go on lockdown comes from the door in front of us. A rush of air fills the void as soon as the door's open, wrapping around us, and pulling us in.

"Keep your head down and walk straight," Mr. Pace says, pushing us along from behind. "It won't last long enough to use your shades."

I inch forward, still holding on to Tobin's hand, with my eyes less than half open beneath the glare of blinding panels on the ceiling and walls. Under our feet, the floor turns from cement to tile. And as the light tapers off to an intense glow, Tobin stops past the threshold of the very appropriately named White Room.

Almost identical to the hospital, the room is outfitted with reflective ceramic walls. There aren't any beds, but rather a glasslike partition that separates half the room into a containment cell. On our side, it's some kind of control room. Lt. Sykes stands behind a large console. M. Olivet patrols at an easy distance from the cell. They're both armed.

This is it.

We're going to have to face the Fade knowing that it could be the one that saw our loved ones die, or even be the one that killed them.

"I'll say it again," Dr. Wolff says. "I disagree with this decision. Adding another stimulus to the creature's environment could be—"

"A tipping point," Honoria says, ending the discussion. "Stay off the glass."

The containment area is small, without any remarkable features other than the large shadow taking up one corner. Tobin moves first, then me. Honoria's warnings fall forgotten in the instant we approach the containment wall.

"Are you going to tell Dante, or am I?" I ask.

"Tell him what?"

"I didn't kill it."

CHAPTER 16

THIS is it? The great fear? It looks so . . . *human*.

"Is it a kid?" I ask.

"A juvenile, yes, but mature enough to be a viable threat," Honoria answers.

It doesn't look like a threat. Barely taller than me, I doubt it weighs as much as Tobin. This Fade wearing an old pair of medical scrub pants bears no similarity to the creatures that tore down our wall.

Tobin steeples his fingers against the glass, smashing the pads into it. He cranes his neck, standing on his toes, but there's no way to get a better view. The Fade's got its back to us, hiding, trying to block the light from lamps on the ceiling and walls by putting its face in the corner and guarding it with its hands.

The cell's furniture lays in shattered pieces. Claw marks mar the glass where the Fade must have tried to dig its way free. Blackened patches on the vents overhead sit perfectly spaced for fingers where it must have tried to reach the lights but burned itself.

This cell was built to hold a Fade.

Someone expected to catch one.

I tap the glass, but the only response is a ripple of the muscles across the Fade's back. A strange sheer veil over its skin shimmers with the motion.

"Have you figured out how to kill it yet?" Tobin asks.

"We're learning a great deal, Tobin, too much to risk by destroying our only living specimen," Dr. Wolff says.

"You should kill it."

The Fade's muscles twitch beneath the veil again, and my skin warms. My heart races in time with my shallow breaths as I'm overcome with the sensation of wanting to strike out at something. It's anger without a trigger, and I'm not entirely sure it's mine.

"You're hurting it," I say.

"No." Dr. Wolff shakes his head. "The lights cause it to go dormant, but their wavelengths have been altered from that of true sun."

He's wrong; the Fade's too tense to be asleep, pulling its muscles close to control the pain. I'm familiar with the gesture, and I know just how well it doesn't work.

"You're torturing it," I say.

"Good," Tobin says. His fists clench at his sides. "Make it turn around. I want to see its face."

"If it gets agitated, monitoring its systems becomes more difficult," Dr. Wolff argues.

"Can't you turn a few of the lights off?" I ask.

"They're only at quarter power as it is."

"But it's in pain."

"What makes you so sure?" Honoria asks from right behind me.

"Just a feeling." Like the one that gives me chills from her proximity, and the clinical tone she tries to pass off as curiosity.

"Do it."

Dr. Wolff looks up at Honoria Whit's sharp command, but all she does is nod her head. He sighs, but crosses to the console and dims the lights; Tobin slaps his open palm against the glass.

"Hey!"

"Give it a minute," I say

"Hey, Fade! Look at me!"

If he'd calm down enough to pay attention, he'd realize something's happening in the cell. The unnatural lacelike shadows that screen the Fade recede, drawing into its body as they dissipate. Slowly, it relaxes and drops its hands. It twists, testing its arms and legs and neck before turning.

It's not the kind of face I expected. There's no damage. No rot. It's not the desiccated corpse form of some monster from a story. Monsters I can handle, but this . . .

It looks like a teenage boy.

Stripped of its robes and bindings, the Fade has skin as pale as the ghost moths that sneak in at night when the shutters stick open. Hair hangs loose around its face with the sheen of a bird's wing—jet-black, but reflecting other colors as it falls. It hardly looks like hair at all, more like a spray of fine crystals spun into strands. Eyes so light blue they're almost clear look straight at—and through—me. Well-formed muscles move under skin marked with the same blackened patterns I watched security burn out of Tobin's carpet when they turned his blood to ash. It's calm and quiet, and tracking me as I move. I can see intelligence behind its eyes.

"I'm talking to you!" Tobin hits the glass again.

The Fade takes a step toward us.

"Look at me, not her." Tobin slides in front of me.

The Fade startles, as though it hadn't noticed him before. Those sharp raptor's eyes change, turning darker around the rim so the color bleeds toward the centers. The Fade's eyes trace along Tobin's arm where it's stretched out like a security bar holding me back. It steps to the side and cocks its head, angling for a better look. The movement isn't human; it's too fluid.

The Fade studies Tobin's face, mirroring his stance and

putting its own arm out straight. It touches the glass, tapping out its own rhythm with one finger. It concentrates on Tobin, as though it recognizes him.

"What are you doing?" Tobin asks, confused, even panicked.

Its expression never changes, but its posture falls in apparent disappointment, and it moves on from Tobin to me. A vibration pricks the hairs along my arms, and warmth spreads through my whole body. Images invade my mind like a ribbon of negative light winding its way into my memory . . . looking for something.

Know.

I hear the word as an echo without a voice and grab my inhaler to stave off the headache drawn in its wake. I stumble backward, my head stuffed with cotton balls.

Aid. Assist.

Two more words, clear as speech from a voice I can't say I hear.

"What happened?"

Tobin is right beside me.

"I don't know."

But whatever it was, the pain's gone. I don't even need my inhaler.

Repentance.

The cool breeze soothing my mind becomes a nauseating sense of shame. The Fade's expression melts into downcast eyes and concern, its whole body on its fingertips against the glass in a pantomime of Tobin's earlier stance.

"You're sorry?" I ask.

Repentance.

The answer is solid, and accompanied by a nod so slight, its hair barely falls forward.

"Sorry for what?" Tobin asks.

"It apologized," I say. "I think it's talking. It tried to talk to you . . . you didn't answer."

Dr. Wolff steps out from behind the console. Honoria circles, mumbling under her breath. Mr. Pace and the others shift in place, worrying their rifles in their hands.

"I don't hear a voice," Tobin says defensively.

"Neither do I." I step closer to the glass and face the Fade. "You understand me, don't you?"

Affirmed.

A burst of hope and joy. Its answers aren't really words, more declarations through feeling and image, but they're enough to fix the idea that this Fade is definitely a *he* and not an *it*. I've never heard a monster ask for forgiveness.

"Do you have a name?" I ask.

He cocks his head again.

"Marina, stop. It doesn't know what you're saying," Tobin says.

Oh yes, he does. Maybe not exactly, but he gets the concept.

"Let her alone," Honoria says. "Something's happening on the monitors."

174

ARCLIGHT

"I'm Marina," I say, trying to send an impression of everything I remember about myself. "This is Tobin. Who are you?"

The next thing I hear is the sound of my own screams. Disjointed fragments of thoughts and ideas cut into my brain like razors. I see the Fade's face and others like it. More and more, until they're a horde.

The others disappear, leaving only two behind: the one in the cell, and beside him, a female with the same marked skin. She evaporates into steam, leaving him alone.

Understand. Aid.

It's a command, but I don't know how to follow it.

"What do you want me to do?"

His answer comes as pictures out of order, upside down and backward. A mass of whispers as chaotic as a hornet's nest.

Return . . . Taken. Lost . . . Find.

Dichotomous thoughts shred my brain, raking from one extreme to the other. I'm being pulled apart.

"Stop!"

I tumble, so disoriented that I'd swear the floor was rushing up to meet me halfway as a warm trickle of blood runs from my nose.

"Do something," Tobin begs. He pulls me into his lap so I can hide my face against his chest, but it doesn't help. What I see is projecting straight into my head.

"Shield your eyes," Honoria orders just before she notches the lights up to high power.

The images stop, and the Fade shrieks. He whirls and hits the back of the cell hard enough to dent the wall, shoulders heaving—furious beyond the pain. All those little lines and dots that make up his markings scatter into millions of individual points bursting off his body to become the veil again.

"It's a parrot fish ," Tobin says, and I wonder if that's something else from one of his picture books. I thought parrots were birds.

"Not a bad analogy," Dr. Wolff says. "The markings you saw are microorganisms that live off the host body. They're photosensitive themselves, but also exist in such a way that they prevent the production of melanin when bonded. Under normal levels of direct light, they'll darken the host's skin. Under extreme conditions, the nanites extend their shielding in a more dynamic way."

"Host? You mean they're parasites?" Tobin asks.

"They're the legacy of the world before," Honoria answers bitterly. "The nanites were designed for medical use—tiny, sentient machines that could save lives when human hands couldn't. But instead of that dream, we got this nightmare. They replicated and spread so fast, they couldn't be contained. Their creators lost control, and then we lost everything else."

I scramble off Tobin's lap for a closer look. What seems like a veil from a distance is made completely of those tiny black crystals. It's anchored to the Fade's body with wiry lines no thicker than a piece of hair. Without the patterns, his skin's milk white.

"Is its body alive?" Tobin asks hesitantly. "Is it human?"

"The host was, at one time. Now it's a shell."

"If Marina hadn't burned me . . ."

"The Fade would have overwhelmed your system until you became this," Honoria answers.

"Why not tell us this?" I ask.

"We would have—eventually. Children can't understand the nature of the Fade, so we allow the rumors and ghost stories to keep their curiosity in check. When you're older, we tell you tales that have been passed down for years—real ones about real people who were lost to the darkness. And when you cease to be children, we tell you the rest. You didn't need to know yet."

"You lied to us," Tobin says, angry again.

"Would you have preferred hearing that your father has most likely become a food source for a mobile colony of parasites?" Honoria asks. "That he was little more than a carrier of a sentient virus whose only goal is to replicate and spread until there's nothing left to consume?"

"If it's a virus, then cure it."

Suddenly the pieces of the puzzle I call a past start snapping into place. The only thing worth risking everything for is survival. Somehow, my people, the ones I was born to, found a way to combat the parasitic invasion that ravaged those lost to the Dark.

"That's why they sent me into the Dark, isn't it? My people found a way to undo it."

I wasn't thrown away; I was sent. And if I'm where I was meant to go, then I'm not lost. There could be others like me out there.

I'm not alone.

"That's what we hope," Honoria says. "It's what our people were willing to die for, and it's what *they're* willing to kill for."

She nods to the Fade, who's still trembling under the ultra-brights. I walk over and twist a dial on the wall to dim them back down.

"Marina, don't," Tobin warns.

"I want to ask him some—"

The words fall off my tongue as spectral shapes form inside my brain. A random burst of synapses drags voices and faces to the surface, but they move so fast I can't get a hold on any of them. The White Room disappears, taking Tobin, Honoria Whit, and everyone else with it.

I'm in the Dark again, and on my own.

CHAPTER 17

TEARING branches and biting thorns. Wind in my hair and the occasional strike of dim light against my hands casting strange patterns across them. It's cool, and the air smells different. My shoulder hurts, as though there's a thorn stuck in it. I have the barest impression of needing something.

I dip down in the water, hiding beneath a piece of weathered wood. Someone's looking for me, to take me home. All I have to do is hang on until they find me.

Heavy, running feet trample the ground nearby, and I choke on my own scream. If I scream, they'll know where I am.

The scene shifts. I'm running again, faster and harder, but it's not enough. An alien noise tears through the air and I topple toward the mud. Muscles groan around the searing, puckered wound in my leg; something hot and slippery pours through my fingers and soaks my skin, but it's too dark to see the blood.

My focus is shot.

The halting images turn to sounds and voices. Shouts of terror mix with reassurances that I'm safe. Behind it all, a whispered wall of static.

I snap back to myself and I'm in the White Room with Tobin on one side, and Dr. Wolff and Honoria on the other. My hand is still on the light dial.

"What was that?" Tobin demands.

"A memory . . . I think. Have I been here before?"

"In the beginning," Dr. Wolff says. "It was the only place we had set up for quarantine."

"You put her in there?" Tobin asks. "Like one of them?"

"We had no idea what her lengthy exposure to the Dark might lead to," Dr. Wolff says. "Once she was cleared, we moved her up to the hospital."

This has to be the place Dr. Wolff was going to put Trey.

"I remember," I say.

As quickly as it comes, the memory leaves my mind, ripped away as sure as if someone reached in and clawed it loose.

Pain races down my spine, along every nerve until even my feet are shrieking. The room swirls down a drain that shouldn't exist, coming to a point between my eyes. Everything flips from black and white to a sheet of red, then sickening green, before it's obliterated in a shower of sparks and spots that leaves me on the ground, seizing.

"Here." Tobin fishes the inhaler out from between my arms and holds it to my mouth. "Breathe."

Easier said than done. My first attempt fails miserably as though my lungs have collapsed and refuse to take in air. I try again and end up clawing at my throat.

In his cell, the Fade goes berserk. He launches himself at the glass partition, beating his body against it full force until a pool of dark blood forms under his palm. The impact rolls through the floor, knocking M. Olivet to the ground.

The room dims, growing smaller under my closing eyelids . . . this isn't so bad. It feels like falling asleep without the fear of nightmares coming to torment me. I see Honoria standing close, glancing back and forth between me and the Fade. Her face definitely isn't the last thing I want to see.

Then something warm blows into my mouth. A blurred Tobin has the inhaler in his hand, pulling the medicine into his own mouth and breathing it out into me.

Listen.

The command comes in the Fade's odd speech.

Calm.

Gentle rain falls against my skin. I can smell it even without the air passing through my nose. Slowly, the medicine sinks into my lungs.

Breathe.

I feel the air as though I'm part of it and as though it forms my body instead of flesh and blood and bone.

Breathe.

I exhale without a hitch and take the inhaler from Tobin, sucking down medication until it doesn't hurt anymore.

"Get her sleeve," Dr. Wolff's voice orders.

Someone strips my arm out of my shirt. A needle pricks my shoulder, followed by a flood of stinging nerves where he depresses the plunger, and the last of the weight lifts off my chest.

Tobin leaves me sitting there to face the Fade in the cage.

"What did you do to her?" He slams his fist against the glass.

"Stop." My valiant attempt at a shout falls flat as I struggle to stand.

I don't so much walk as pitch, but I make it to the wall, blocking Tobin as he reaches for the light dial.

"That thing almost killed you!"

"He helped me, Tobin," I say.

"That's crazy."

"Fine, I'm crazy. But I know what I felt."

"You're hallucinating."

"I am not!"

"Step away." Honoria drags me from the containment side, while the others in the room watch the Fade with their rifles at the ready.

"Let go," I demand. When I pull away, it's with marks from her fingernails where she tries to hold me still.

"It *was* you, wasn't it?" I ask the Fade.

He stands statue-still, eyes fixed on my face, his hand on the glass in a smear of his own blood; the broken skin behind it closes seamlessly into perfect flesh. On my side of the glass, spots form where Honoria's scratches bleed down my wrist.

Damaged.

"Just an accident," I say. "We take a little longer to heal."

But I've misunderstood; the Fade isn't talking about me. He falters and slips to the floor. The patterns on his skin come alive, branching out across his chest and down his limbs. They weave across his face into delicate lines more intricate than lace.

"Is he all right?" I look back, trusting my elders to have the answers I don't.

"I've never seen this behavior before," Dr. Wolff says, joining me by the glass.

"Then perhaps it's best we let the creature be and see what happens," Honoria suggests. "Between this incident and your nightmares, I think Doctor Wolff needs to reevaluate your medication. It's time to leave."

"But—"

"Rule three, no arguments," she says.

"Help . . ."

The Fade speaks. Hoarse and strained, but it's a real word.

"Tell me I hallucinated *that*."

"Did it just . . . talk?" Tobin asks.

The Fade slaps his open hand against the glass again. M. Olivet and Lt. Sykes back farther away from the cell.

"Everyone freeze," Honoria orders.

"Stolen," the Fade rasps, struggling over the words as though they cause him physical pain. "Removed . . . void . . ."

"What was stolen?" I ask. Honoria hooks the back of my belt with a finger, pulling me toward her when I try to get closer to the cell.

"Stay back."

"You want information, let me ask him for it," I say, then repeat my question to the Fade.

"Cherish," he says, after a pause where he seems to be deciding the best way to fit the word in his mouth.

"Cherish?"

"Mine . . . is blank."

I'm not in the White Room anymore; I'm on hill in a clearing between huge trees. Vines like the crystals that form the Fade's hair reach from the branches to the ground; black lines crisscross the terrain. The Fade from the cage is there, standing beside a female until she's ripped away—off the hill, out of his reach, and out of my sight.

"Stolen," he says.

"She's a friend?"

His brow knits together, frustrated, and his eyes make

that same constriction of the blue band into the iris. A gentle nudge in my brain picks out the words he needs to fill in the ones he doesn't know.

Cherish. Life.

Not aloud, but spoken to me with the dull thud of a heartbeat behind it, and the smell of open air.

Soul. Mine.

The heart beats faster, then dies into silence. Lost to the void.

Void.

He nods, assuming I understand things I'm not sure I can interpret.

"She's your mate?"

"Mine . . . Cherish . . . is blank. Is silent." He lays his hand against the glass, over my palm. "Return."

"What's your name?" I ask again.

The Fade sinks as the light leeches the last of his strength. A line of black blood streaks across the glass. "Return Cherish."

Help. Assist . . . Truth.

A last plea, for my ears only. His silvered eyes close and the veil draws tight around his face.

CHAPTER 18

MAYBE if I hadn't told Honoria about my dream, or maybe if the Fade had said anything other than *help* when it finally opened its mouth, things would have been different, but my fate was sealed as soon as he spoke. Honoria ordered me into the hospital; there was no sense arguing. Truth is, that one word made me want to beg Dr. Wolff for a bed.

Of course, I didn't expect that bed to come with a parade of people through the sliding doors to "check" on me.

The first day, I assumed they were visiting Jove. Without parents at home, Dr. Wolff kept him longer, and they all started off at *his* bedside; but without fail, they'd drift my way.

The second day, most of our classmates had used up their visitor privileges, so they manufactured excuses to wander through. Minor injuries, aches and pains, anything to provide a reason to poke their heads in the door and peek behind the curtains I kept closing.

Now into the fourth day, things haven't improved.

They keep coming with their robotic greetings and awkward words. I watch dozens of questions falter before they can be asked, and at least as many conversations stall before they start. Awe has replaced dread for my presence.

I blame the Fade. They haven't attacked once since we dog-piled the one outside Tobin's apartment. There've been no flashing lights, no alarms. The others think the Fade are scared, and count it as one more accomplishment on the list of things I haven't actually done.

But none of the irritation I feel around them compares to the stomach-sinking, skin-crawling uneasiness that hits every time I realize the eyes watching me belong to Honoria rather than someone my age. It would be easy to think she's keeping watch over all of the kids in the hospital, but she never says anything to Jove, and she doesn't approach the screened-off part of the room where Trey's been isolated. She haunts the space around my bed, the chill of her presence waking me every time, and then she leaves once she knows I've seen her.

It's weird.

Even Jove's being civil.

He actually wrote me an apology on a napkin. Dr. Wolff moved him across the room, but if I make the mistake of glancing his way, he'll catch my eye for some new attempt at reconciliation. I usually humor him, offering a wave or weak smile, but it's getting annoying. I think I'd hug him if he managed a threat.

"Anne-Marie's responsible for this, isn't she?" I ask Tobin when he visits.

"She had help. Dante and Silver have been talking you up. Without you being able to confirm or deny anything, the stories are getting better and better."

Stories? Plural?

"Between capturing that Fade, my arm, the cleaning crew at my house, and your stay in the hospital, everyone's jumping to their own conclusions." He takes a seat on the end of my bed, with his legs toward me. "Did you know you killed three Fade with your bare hands?"

"Dante?" I ask, wincing.

"A lower-year named Melisande who's taken to following Annie around. She even acts it out . . . apparently you beat one to death with my door."

"Shut up."

"After saving my life from another two. That's how I hurt my arm, in case you were wondering. The mechanics are a bit sketchy, but I've heard there was definite gnawing."

He mimes chewing on his wounded arm, which is no longer immobilized, but rewrapped into something smaller.

"Remind me to maim Anne-Marie in some public and humiliating way when I get out of here."

"Don't worry," Tobin says. "Dr. Wolff's restricted access to the hospital. No more visitors allowed, only the sick or injured."

"Then how are you here?"

"I have a legitimate reason." He rolls his shoulder forward and makes a comically pained face.

"Pathetic."

"Oh sure," he says. "I come all the way down here, dragging my agony-wracked self to thank the person who sucked the Fade poison out of my shoulder. . . . That one you *can* thank Annie for, by the way."

"One more smirk, and I slap it off."

"Are you annoying my patient, Mr. Lutrell?" Dr. Wolff, emerging from the isolation area, heads toward the half of the hospital I've starting thinking of as "mine." I've been here enough, they should just monogram my name on the sheets.

"I'm innocent, Dr. Wolff, I swear," Tobin says. "I'm only here for you to check my bandage."

Tobin jokes about it, but the stories about his injuries and my medical incarceration have quickly gained the same weight and reverence as the existing rumors of the Fade, and they're no more true.

"How's your arm?" I ask while Dr. Wolff re-dresses Tobin's shoulder.

"Curiously overworked," Dr. Wolff answers for him. "I hope you haven't been overextending yourself with the cleanup. I know we're short on hands, but going slow will benefit you in the long run."

To keep everyone busy, and out of trouble, our elders have decided that anyone over the age of eleven has to help clean up the mess left from the night of the Red-Wall. The adults cleared the rubble from the hall; the kids handling the rest.

"I've been assigned a soap bucket," Tobin says.

"*Assigned* is not synonymous with *used*. I've dealt with teenagers long enough to know misdirection when I hear it." He taps Tobin on the head with his medical file before returning it to its proper place on the shelf.

"As for you, young lady," Dr. Wolff says with a warm smile, "I see no reason you can't follow Mr. Lutrell out of here and help. I know for a fact there are some upturned filing cabinets in desperate need of attention."

"I can leave?" I ask hopefully.

"You may leave. If you're in the room, I think this one will behave himself better."

"I don't need a babysitter," Tobin protests.

"Then consider her your supervisor. I don't want you lifting anything heavier than a scrub brush—understood?"

With assurances that I'll stop Tobin from clearing debris, I'm granted my freedom.

"Are you still working with Anne-Marie in the nursery rooms?" I ask. Areas for the babies were made the first priority after the essential sectors dealing with power and security.

"Unfortunately. Do you know what a diaper bin smells like after it's been sealed in for more than three days?" He slows his pace by degrees until he stops us both.

"You have to go back, no matter how long it takes us to get there," I say, facing him.

"I'm getting very good with my misery face. All I have to do is wince; no one expects me to do anything."

"Sorry, not convincing."

"You were a lot easier to deal with when you were afraid of me."

"I was never afraid of you."

Until now.

I don't know what to think—I *can't* think with him here, and me here, and no one else.

"You were a lot easier to deal with when I could *pretend* you were afraid of me," he amends.

He's so close, I can feel his breath. I try to step in closer, but my legs misunderstand and go the other way, backing up a step as though invisible hands are pushing us apart.

Tobin's face falls, dejected. He thinks I'm rejecting him.

"Maybe we should . . . um . . . Annie doesn't like being by herself for too long." He turns away, and I stumble forward, caught in his momentum.

"How much longer do you think they'll make us do this?" Anne-Marie asks, as a white blob of paint drips down to splatter on her head. She's occupied the far corner of the room for the last two hours, repainting the same spot over and over. It's going to be three inches thicker than the rest of the ceiling when it dries.

"I told you I'd paint if you want to sort files," I say.

Three huge filing cabinets stand broken open and mostly empty against the wall, while I sort scattered stacks of everything from family information to art projects out of the giant mess that formed when they toppled.

"Right, then *you'll* fall off a ladder and break your Fade-proof neck, and everyone else will drown *me* in my paint bucket."

"If it'll stop the whining," Tobin grumbles.

He's not so much cleaning the tables as he is pouring water on them and sailing his sponge across the surface before declaring each one "done."

"I just don't see why *we* have to suffer. We caught one of them, make *it* do the repairs!" Anne-Marie's tirade continues in the form of angry, paint-coated jabs to the ceiling. "It can disappear into walls, tell it to disappear the damage!"

I'm no happier than she is. I already did my four-day rotation in the babies' classes, and have no desire to return. I'd much rather be back outside with my flower bush. Plants don't leave snot on everything.

"We're halfway done," I say.

"And all the way out of paint."

Anne-Marie stomps down the ladder, banging the can

behind her. She holds her arms out, scowling as though she hadn't noticed the paint dripping. Her skin and clothes are covered in splotches.

"I look like I have pasty chicken pox!"

I'm not exactly sure how someone can catch spots from chickens, but the disease is listed in the hospital as something to report should we see the signs. It's a condition from before, like measles and other things with "pox" on the end that now exist only as a distant threat we're forced to memorize.

"I'm going for a refill, and don't you dare leave Marina by herself! If that Fade gets loose and kills her, it'll be your fault!" Anne-Marie's still grumbling when she slams the door.

"So that's what quiet sounds like," Tobin quips. "I'd forgotten."

"Don't let Anne-Marie hear you say that." I tug on one of the few drawers that didn't pop open when the cabinets fell, but it's stuck tight.

"You want to switch? I can handle the paper stuff for a while."

"I'll manage." I've been through the Dark and faced down a Fade. I refuse to concede supremacy to a file cabinet full of finger paintings. "Open up, you stupid hunk of metal."

"If it answers, you're my new excuse to stop working. I'll drag you back to the hospital instead."

I stick my tongue out at him. Talking furniture isn't among my complaints; those are a Fade bent on using my brain as his personal PA system, and Honoria's glare following me around for the foreseeable future.

"You sure you don't want a hand?" he asks.

"Only if that hand is going to lock the door."

"And what could you possibly have in mind that requires a locked door?"

Tobin grins. He's got that spark in his eyes, like the night we went out to watch the star shower, without a hint of the discouragement from the hall.

I can feel myself blushing.

"I want a barricade between me and Anne-Marie before she gets back here and accuses me of 'ruining her system' again." She was the last one to work on these files before the attack, as part of her work-study to become an instructor in the nursery classes.

"I make a great barricade."

"She's on her third coffee of the hour. One more and she'll be moving fast enough to walk through you."

I don't know what's wrong with me; my mood keeps shifting. I'm constantly peeved by things that never really bothered me before, like Anne-Marie's habits. Ten seconds later, I feel horrible for talking about her. Twenty seconds after that, I'm back to wanting to flirt with Tobin.

"I'll take the top ones," he says, sliding past me to start on an open drawer. "You do the bottom."

I drop down, crouching to reach the lowest drawer, when

an odd smell escapes from something that has no place in a file cabinet. With one sharp tug, a half-eaten sandwich with three gooey files attached to it fly out, sending a rain of pages fluttering around us. It's Anne-Marie's handwriting on the folder.

"Do you think it fell in, or did she actually file a sandwich under *G*?" I ask.

"Well, it *is* green." Tobin braves a sniff before dropping the sandwich into an empty file jacket.

"You know what . . . new tactic." I shovel the mess of pages, plus the six-inch stack of paperwork on the teacher's desk, into the open drawer and slam it shut. It takes both of us to latch it. "I say we torch it and claim it all got lost in the chaos."

"Deal."

I face Tobin, and that same jolt goes off like a shock in my chest. I have the sudden desire to look away, but I can't seem to remember how to make my head turn.

Tobin licks his lips. I watch the muscles in his throat as he swallows.

My heels lift off the ground until my weight is on my toes, expectant and strangely hesitant. It's not fear . . . not exactly, but I'm not quite comfortable with my body remembering how to do something my conscious mind's forgotten.

Every breath draws the scent of him in like oxygen, and then . . .

"I . . . I saw my dad. . . ."

Tobin's eyes slam shut. I don't need to hear him say the

words to know he's cursing himself. Whatever traction had us locked in to each other breaks, and I drop back down off my toes.

"When?" I ask.

"The reason I went to the Arc that day . . ."

"You saw your dad in the Grey?"

"Once, about a week after you came in. He just stood there, with the sun setting behind him so there was no light on his face, but it had to be him. He was the right shape, and still wearing his uniform. I waved at him."

"Maybe you only *wanted* it to be him."

"Marina . . . after that day, my dad never came back to the Arc, but I *did* see him again." Tobin gives the room a quick check to make sure the door's still closed. He leans against the teacher's desk, picking at the edge of his sling. "In the White Room, you said that thing tried to talk to me first, but that I couldn't hear it. That's not *exactly* true."

"He spoke to you?"

"Why do you call it that? It's a Fade, not a person!"

"I know, but it's harder to be scared of a real person. What did he . . . *it* . . . show you?"

"All I could make out was my dad's face, and even that wasn't completely clear. He was in pain, and scared."

"Is that what you're afraid of?" I ask, assuming the Fade pulled images from Tobin's mind like he did mine. With me, memories are what I want more than anything; with Tobin, it's his father. Maybe that's the hook. The Fade can latch on to strong emotion.

"It felt real," he says. "It felt like that thing loaned me its eyes and made me see my dad as something weak and small, when he's not."

I want to tell him I understand, but I don't. I know what it's like to have no family, but not to have their memory tarnished or twisted. And I want to ask him how he managed to block the Fade so easily. If all he saw were blurred suggestions, he did a lot better than me. But our moment of solitude has run out.

The door bumps open, struck by Anne-Marie's hip as she lugs two paint buckets back inside. This time she's not alone. Dante, Silver, and two others trail in behind her. The two boys I've never met, but they have patches marking them as three years younger than us.

"I told you we should have locked it."

That free-range feeling of anger starts again, spreading from my feet all the way up to my throat. I'm furious. Not just at Anne-Marie and her timing, but at everything.

"Next time we shove a chair under the handle," Tobin says through a sigh.

"I brought help," Anne-Marie announces.

One of the boys paints a couple of strokes, but doesn't maintain his cover for long. The other pretends to wash down tables, but doesn't bother to soak his sponge first.

"They're staring," I say.

"They think if you're in here, and they're in here, then there's less of a chance that either of them will get eaten if that Fade goes on a rampage."

"Anne-Marie!"

"What?" she asks innocently. "Less work for us, so what's it hurt?"

"Let's just get this over with, and then none of us have to be here anymore, okay?" Tobin says.

He's itching to get back outside; I can see it in the way he watches the door. He wants to be in the open air of the Well, not cooped up in here with too many reminders that there's a Fade on the premises that may or may not have seen his father die in agony and terror. He takes the brush Anne-Marie left behind, reaching for one of the paint buckets with his good arm.

"No way," she says. "Give it back."

"I can help, Annie."

"You're on scrub detail for a reason, Picasso." Anne-Marie dances foot-to-foot in front of the wall to block his access. "Give me back my brush."

"Your name's not on it."

"My teeth marks are," she says. "I chewed the end . . . look."

"Maybe those are *my* teeth marks."

Tobin sticks the end of the brush in his mouth.

"Uh-oh," Dante says. He and Silver back away.

"Prepare to defend yourself against a temper tantrum of epic proportions," Silver adds.

"Toby. Give. Me. Back. My. Paintbrush," Anne-Marie bites out.

Instead, he reaches for an open can of black paint.

"Don't you dare!"

There are five more brushes within easy reach, so I don't get why they're fighting over one.

"Too slow." Tobin gives the now dripping brush a dramatic wave high in the air.

"Toby!" Anne-Marie's voice comes out as a furious shriek. Black spatter peppers the still wet surface she'd spent so much time whitewashing; gravity draws the spots into lines that splinter along the texture as they flow downward.

"Oops?"

"Oops" is not a smart choice of words. In fact, from the look on Anne-Marie's face, "oops" may qualify as the single worst thing that's ever come out of Tobin's mouth.

"Wait a minute, Annie. Calm down."

"Duck and cover?" I ask.

"Quickly," Dante says, right before Anne-Marie picks up the can of black paint and tips it over Tobin's head.

Tobin jabs at her with his paintbrush, leaving a large splotch on her uniform, and she reaches for the closest thing she can get her hands on. She sloshes orange chair paint in Tobin's direction, but misses wide, hitting one of the younger boys instead.

"Hey!" The boy whose face is now half orange flings the blue paint he's still got in his hand.

From there, it's pandemonium. All the stress and nerves from the last few days boil over. Paint flies in all directions at once. Red bounces off white in midair to land in a half-mixed puddle of pink. Black swirls with purple on the floor. Tables and chairs get coated with flecks of every color.

"Cover me," Tobin says, ducking behind the table where I'm hiding.

He runs from table to table, half an inch ahead of bursting color bombs. At the end of the row, he sneaks up behind Silver, who's too busy trading volleys with Anne-Marie to realize he's there. Soon she looks like a giant egg has burst on her head, with yellow running down her ponytail and onto her back.

This is so much better when it's paint instead of bullets.

Everyone's laughing.

I examine the patterns created by the paint on my skin, and what's landed around me. A swirl here, a dot there, smudge the colors together . . . if I relax the muscles in my eyes, my hand blends with the floor and the edges of the chair overturned beside me.

I make myself Fade.

The effect only lasts a second before I recognize that familiar buzz at the corner of my mind for what it is. Even with all the space and floors between us, the Fade's trying to get my attention.

No wonder I've been on edge; the Fade's been messing with

my head. I muddy the colors with my other hand so they're an incoherent mess.

"Go away," I snarl, but I already know there's little chance of him listening to me. I rush out of my hiding place, barely feeling the impact of four different colors against my skin and clothes.

"Not the most effective strategy," Tobin says, joining me in the hot zone. He draws me down to the floor, and I'm grateful for his closeness. It's harder for the Fade to find space to play in my mind while Tobin's with me. "Are you okay?"

I turn to answer, maybe even to confess that the connection I had with the Fade hasn't died outside the White Room, but Tobin's face shocks the words right out of me.

"Your face . . ."

"What?"

He raises to catch his reflection in the metal side of a file cabinet. There's no clear detail, but that only makes it worse. His face is a mess of black lines and dots, and as panic makes his skin paler underneath, the similarity between Tobin and the Fade becomes more pronounced.

"Get it off. Get it off me. Now!" Tobin claws at his face. I try to pull his arm away, but panic makes him unstoppable.

"What's wrong?" Anne-Marie asks. She's in the open now; the others have sensed the change in the room's energy and quit the game completely.

"He looks like a Fade," I say.

She doesn't question how I know, but runs to the bucket of soapy water Tobin had been using to clean the tables and floor. When she comes back, it's with a loaded sponge to clean his face, the same way we'd cleaned the remnants of Tobin's beating off Jove.

The others go back to painting and cleaning, as though they'd never stopped. The airy tone that had left us free to play disintegrates. Even the light looks different. It twists splashes of color into a cruel pantomime of blood and gore as though we'd taken part in some real conflict.

I grab a sponge and eradicate what remains of the lines on the door and trim, but it's going to take a lot longer to rid myself of the memories of my faded self, and Tobin with a face like that thing in the White Room.

The end of our work detail comes as a relief to everyone but me. For them, it's an excuse to escape our mock battleground. For me, it's the loss of anything I can use to keep the Fade out of my head.

He knew.

He knew the exact moment I left the hospital, and the precise instant my eyes no longer opened into the extra bright lights that always shine there. That means he wasn't just in my head when I could feel him; he's been monitoring me somehow, and despite all of the countermeasures of the White Room—this was something even Honoria didn't see coming.

I have to fight to keep my panic off my face, knowing it will raise questions. If it was just Tobin, I think he'd understand—*maybe*—if I remember to call the Fade only "the Fade" or "it." But Anne-Marie would tell her mom at the very least, and the others would tell everyone else. I've tried too hard to convince them I don't hear the voices of the Fade; I'm not giving them reason to doubt me now.

When I get to my room, I close the door and turn the lights on as high as they'll go.

"Stay out of my head," I growl into the empty space, conjuring feelings of repugnance and aversion to create a shield inside my mind.

The Fade breaks through anyway.

Converse, he says. *Speak*.

The Fade's phrasing is awkward and overly precise, as though he's learning the language as he goes.

"No! No conversation!" I grit my teeth and shove back with the memory of using Tobin's door to hit it in the face.

I scan the room to reassure myself that the Fade's not actually there, but nothing shimmers in the light.

Pleas for my attention come in an urgent ramble, broken by reminders that he's seeking his mate. Anger and frustration hijack my own emotions, pumping through my bloodstream like a drug that clouds my judgment and strips me of control.

My mood shifts weren't mine at all—they were *him*.

An abrupt need to move overwhelms my desire to fight,

and I'm struck by the terror of my feet moving against my will.

"Stop!" I cry, but my legs ignore me. They make a hasty turn toward my sink, until I'm forced to face my mirror, but it's not my reflection there. It's a Fade.

Mine. Cherish, the Fade we caught clarifies—*Find. Locate. Release.*

"If she was here, she'd be in the White Room with you," I insist. I try to twist away from the mirror, but my body won't move. I'm paralyzed.

Missing.

"I don't know where to look. Let me go!"

Recollect. Remember.

With those last orders, I'm back to running through the Dark while staring at the female Fade in my mirror.

"I don't remember the Dark!" I sob.

Recall. Locate. Understand.

"I'll try . . . *if* you let me go."

The Fade releases me, but I doubt he'll let me make it to the door, so I focus on the image of his mate and hope I can find an answer that will satisfy him until I can get help.

And I really hope the Fade didn't hear that.

Cherish looks as human as I do . . . mostly, in the same way the Fade in the White Room was surprisingly not a monstrosity. She has that same chalk tone to her skin, and almond-shaped eyes that are metallic in the middle, but vibrant on the edges. The black marks on her face form patterns like on a butterfly's wing, with intricate swirls around her eyes and feathered wisps down her cheek. Three short stripes wrap from under her chin at the jawline, pointed toward her mouth.

She's terrified.

What kind of Fade trick is this?

The rhythm of the thoughts I'm processing changes, like picking up a new voice in a room full of people. It's not the Fade downstairs; this is Cherish.

"She's here," I say out loud, shocked to admit the Fade is right. As soon as I acknowledge her, her presence turns more vibrant, louder, but confused. She doesn't know where she is; it's like she's buried alive. The feeling of suffocation and absolute darkness makes me grab my throat.

I want to go home, she says. Her voice is so strange, and so familiar, bouncing around inside my head like it belongs there. *Find me.*

Understand.

A forceful order from both Fade.

I reach out to touch the mirror, and the image shatters under my fingers, splitting her face into jagged pieces. A rush of pure, hot light spills from between the cracks.

That's when the nightmare breaks, even though I'm wide-awake.

This is real, and I'm left with one unshakable certainty: They're here and they're watching.

CHAPTER 19

How long does it take to open a door?

Outside Tobin's apartment, I pace and pace and get nowhere. I raise my hand to knock a second time, and the door opens so quickly it nearly knocks me off my feet. Someone must have fixed the hinges for him, because the door swings easily, without a sound.

"They're watching." I can't wait for Tobin to ask me what I want; if I stop, they'll find me. I duck under his arm and go inside.

"Who?"

"The Fade—I can feel them. They're watching."

"What do you mean, 'they'?"

"I can't keep him out of my head." I tell myself to stop crying. Tears are not helpful.

"You were fine ten minutes ago."

None of this makes sense to him. There's no way it could.

"He keeps coming back. He's in there with my own thoughts, going through them. And it's not just the one in the White Room. The one he called Cherish, she's there, too."

The door clicks shut behind me as Tobin engages the secondary lock.

"You're going to pass out if you don't calm down. Stop bouncing." He leads me to a chair, then sits on the footstool so he's facing me. He reaches out and takes my hands between his in a gesture of . . . I'm not sure. Maybe comfort, maybe restraint. "Marina, tell me what happened. We'll figure out a way to deal with it."

Every instinct that's survived the endless blank of my past tells me that if I want to live, I need to move. Staying still is to invite death.

"Marina?"

Why does he keep saying my name?

"I heard him again," I say. "It started as soon as I left the hospital, but I didn't know that's what it was. I tried to ignore him. . . . I don't know how you did it, but I can't. The Fade made my legs go where he wanted them to."

"It's trying to make you go outside? Like the people before?"

"No . . . *maybe*. He kept asking me about the other one. I heard her, Tobin. His mate's here." I want to tear the Fade, and the humming buzz that comes with it, from my mind, but there's nothing to latch on to, no way to hurt them.

"Use the emergency call in my dad's room." Tobin hurries off the stool, toward the hall that leads through his apartment. "You have to tell Honoria—"

"I can't!" I chase after him. "I'll have to tell her I can hear them, and if Honoria decides I'm too dangerous to keep around . . . I can't tell her the Fade took control. She'll lock me up. I don't want to go in a cage. Please . . ."

He turns and disappears into the kitchen, and at first I think he's decided to ignore my pleas. I brace myself for the wail of an activated alarm, but Tobin returns almost instantly with the lantern I'd used to burn him before. He lights it, and closes my hands around the base.

"Keep your eyes on it," he says, holding his hands over mine. "If they're seeing your thoughts, then make them see something they don't like."

"Like fire," I say, relieved, and sink into the nearest chair. His furniture's been replaced with ugly, standard metal pieces, but right now I wouldn't trade them for anything.

I put my hand over the flame's peak, where it shines yellow above the white core. Back and forth, I pass my fingers through it, a measured danger to stop a real one.

The light and heat break the connection; even the threat's too much for the Fade.

Another flame appears on the side table. Three more on

the floor. One in Tobin's hand. He lights candles as he finds them in drawers and cupboards. They fill teacups and sit in saucers, until the whole room's lit with mismatched torches. Let the Fade search my mind; all they'll find is fire. I breathe deep and let the soothing scent of soot and wax erase the static buzz from my thoughts.

Finally, Tobin stops scavenging for matches. He sits cross-legged on the floor with two flashlights aimed at the ceiling.

"We should save the batteries in case these burn out," I say, and reach to turn them off.

It's a mistake.

My other hand strays too close to the lantern and its flame bites my fingers. My own yelp shatters my concentration, and I feel the Fade again, waiting just below the surface of my conscious mind. He picks at my defenses, trying to find a way past them.

"Talk to me," I beg Tobin. I need real human words. "Drown him out."

"Come on." Instead of distracting me with conversation, Tobin drags me off the chair. He leaves the candles burning, but grabs the lantern. "Bring the flashlights. If we're farther from the White Room, then maybe it can't get through to you."

At the linen closet, he moves aside so I can flip the latch and push the door into its pocket, clearing our way.

"Remember the ledge," he says, about the same time I

smack into it with my toe. The throbbing ache's a blessing, bludgeoning the Fade's influence by giving me a new focal point. I flex my toe inside my shoe. If being in my head means the Fade feels my pain, then I'll make it worse.

Tobin crowds in behind me, navigating the tunnels quickly while I let the Arclight's natural sounds fill my ears until there's no room for the Fade's voice. The flashlights and lantern chase the shadows out of sight.

"Just pretend this was how we planned it," he says. "This has nothing to do with the Fade; we're going to the Well to watch the stars fall."

I call up images of sitting under the night sky with him, where the Fade doesn't know how to find us. I tell myself I have my eyes closed by choice, only because I want to remember the stars, and that's not the same as being scared at all.

A sudden whooshing makes me stop, even with Tobin chauffeuring me along.

"What's that?"

"Water pipes." He knocks on something overhead. A loud clang echoes down the corridor in both directions. "Someone turned on a faucet or flushed a toilet."

"You're sure?"

It happens again and he nudges my hand against a pipe that vibrates as water rushes through it. "The cold ones are water pipes. The hot ones are for steam. The tiny ones are gas."

It's a perfectly logical answer, but logic doesn't necessarily mix well with irrational fear.

"I've changed my mind," I say. I'd rather tell Honoria the truth. The Fade scares me more than she does. I turn, intending to take the hospital route at the junction.

"We're almost there," Tobin says.

In my head it becomes "we're almost safe."

The farther we stray from the main compound, and the closer we get to the promise of a flame-filled night, the less I feel the Fade's intrusion. I shine the flashlight up to the ceiling and along each wall, following tangles of crisscrossing pipes. Tobin keeps talking, giving me directions, all the way to the Well door, even though I know the way.

Outside, the night's clear, without the clouds that obscured our view before. A brown blanket covers the ground, the same color as the sand in Tobin's water globe. Off to the side stands a cactuslike thing made out of twisted junk painted green. He's even put a hat on it and piled workbooks at the bottom. A rolled-up power cord serves as a rope.

"Surprise," he says, and the Fade vanish from my mind completely. "Do you like it?"

"When did you do all of this? *How* did you do all of this?"

"I don't sleep much lately. Not since . . ." He rotates his arm from habit, and the missing mention of the Fade attack becomes an uncomfortable pause. "I dragged everything down here during the days."

"But your arm . . ."

"Isn't really that bad." He shrugs, wincing as he reaches for a jar beside the cactus. "I even found real sand."

I drop beside him. Tobin waits until I manage to curl my uninjured leg beneath me, then twists the lid off and spills the contents into my cupped hands.

It's cooler than I expected. I thought sand would carry the warmth of the sun, but it reflects the heatless light of the moon in tiny crystal pieces. I catch some in my fist, pouring it from one hand to the other, mesmerized by the texture and sound of such tiny grains falling together.

"I did that for an hour when I first found it," he says as he reaches for another fistful. "Feels strange, doesn't it?" he asks.

"It crunches."

We sit together, mirroring each other's movements until I forget I'm afraid of the night.

"Where'd you get it?"

"In a box when I was looking for the blanket. With this."

It's a picture of a smiling family in the sun. A barefoot little boy in short pants and no shirt pours a bucketful of sand on a man's stomach while a woman covers his feet. Behind them an endless stretch of blue water runs into the sky at the horizon. He flips the photo over so I can read the neat script on the back: *James making a sand daddy. The Cove '23*

"James is my dad's name. He was named for his fifth-greats-grandfather."

I wonder if I was named for someone.

We siphon the sand back into the jar, making sure the lid's on tight so it won't spill.

"Did you know your grandparents?" I ask.

"When I was little."

"I think I knew mine, too."

It feels like there were people in my past who'd been around forever. They existed, and somewhere beyond my sight, they might still.

I hand his photo back and wonder if Tobin can tell that I'm jealous that he knows what his past looks like and I don't. It's not fair; I have the sudden urge to destroy it and put us on even ground.

He folds the photo in half and tucks it back into his pocket, leaving me to feel ashamed for something I never even said or did. The desire was enough.

"How come there weren't many pictures of your mom in your house?"

"She mostly stayed out of camera range." I've made him uncomfortable; his sad smile turns more guarded.

"I'm sorry," I say. "But I don't know what it's like to have a mother."

Forgetting myself is bad enough; forgetting what it's like to be loved is worse.

Tobin reaches into his shirt and pulls out his dog tags, handing them to me. "We get these when we age out of school," he says. "They hold your name and division, that sort of stuff."

"Cassandra Darcy," I read.

"My mom."

"She was a healer?" I ask, running my hand over the snake and staff engraved on the front of the tag.

"She was working with Dr. Wolff on a way to stop the Dark from spreading, but died before it could do any good. I bet she'd have known where you came from."

"How?"

"She was obsessed with life before the Arclight. We used to have a room that was nothing but old books and magazines she'd scavenged out of storerooms and junk piles. Each wall had cut-out pictures from a part of the world she hoped still existed—plants and animals like you couldn't imagine. If there was anyone who knew a place humans could survive out there, it would've been my mom."

He smiles at something I can't see because it only exists in his past.

"I wish I'd known her," I say.

"Dad said she was a crazy kid. Once, when she was like fifteen, the stores ran too low, and they had to authorize supply runs—the ones where Dad got the carpet and chairs. While everyone else was grabbing building materials, she was sneaking kittens into her bag."

"That was a pretty big risk."

"They warned her a dozen times, but they bled red, so

she didn't care; having a cat around made things better for her. She'd have these fits where her whole body would shake and she wouldn't be able to speak. Afterward, it would take days before she could even get out of bed; her cats stuck with her."

"I didn't see any cats in your apartment," I say, and hand the dog tags back.

"They never liked me. After Mom died, they refused to stay inside. I figured they moved into the tunnels where they could catch mice."

I thought pets were supposed to be loyal, not disappear when a kid needs company the most.

"Does any of this look familiar?" he asks. "I was kind of hoping that if you came from the desert, and I made one, you'd remember something."

"Not really," I say, and his entire body sags. "It was a good idea though."

We sit in silence for a while, with me shaking the jar near my ear to listen to the sand tinkle and fall. There's something about the sound that I recognize the same way I know my flower bush, but the details are frustratingly out of my reach.

"You've been here months . . . can't you remember anything?" Tobin looks through me into the space beyond the Well. "If you can remember it, I'll help you find it."

"It wasn't like it is here," I say. "It was easier to breathe. No one was afraid I'd bring death to our door. Maybe that was their mistake."

"You're not a mistake, Marina. You're the success."

I feel like I should be glowing from the heat in my cheeks. Jokes I can handle, mocking doesn't faze me, but I don't know what to do or say when Tobin is serious and the words are still nice. So I shrug and try to shrink out of his sight.

"I remember small things, but the faces are all a blur." Dr. Wolff says it's my mind's way of protecting itself. That's the polite version of saying I probably watched my family die, then decided to think about something else. "There was lots of sound—music and chatter, that kind of thing. Now it's all quiet."

"You don't have to be the only one who survived. The others could be in another place."

If I go by Mr. Pace's dirt drawing, there is no other place. If I go by the sand in the jar, it's possible.

"Do you think it was a good place?" he asks "One you'd want to go back to if you could?"

"Tired of me already?"

It's a joke, sort of, but with some truth thrown in. The fear that he might return to the person I knew before the Red-Wall.

"Never," he says, too quickly to salvage his pride. "I mean . . . forget it."

A brilliant streak blazes across the night, and saves him

from the grin spreading across my face. Behind the first star comes another, smaller, but no less beautiful. The one after that ignites the whole sky.

"You're supposed to make a wish when you see one," Tobin says. The sadness leaves his expression, burned away a layer at a time by each tiny fire.

He settles back on the blanket, with his good hand behind his head as a pillow, then crosses his feet at the ankles. The blipping light from his personal alarm disappears beneath his hair, and I cover mine with my hand just to see what it's like without the constant intrusion. For this moment there's no danger and we don't need the panic button.

"You'll never get a good view like that," he says. "Lie down and look straight up."

I slide closer and lean my head back, but it's no use. Every time I find a star to track, I miss a more spectacular one at the corner of my eye.

"Look there." Tobin points off to one side. "You see those three stars in a line? If you watch those, you won't miss the rest."

Another streak cuts the night in half.

I slip my arm with its alarm under my cheek and turn sideways so my face is just below his.

"I know one thing about the place I came from," I say. "We didn't eat dessert."

"Then you came from a horrible and backward place and

must stay here out of self-preservation."

The last bit of sand still stuck to my skin rolls in my fingers while we lay here, and if I close my eyes, I can convince myself that this is real. We're inside that glass dome with the cactus and falling silver stars where nothing bad can touch us.

"I'm not going anywhere," I say.

We stay still for what could be hours, eternity, or a breath in time. No machines or alarms. No blinking light to remind us that danger could descend at any moment, and in the void, I find a point of focus where his arm wraps tight around my shoulders like a tether to keep me from spiraling into the abyss.

I turn farther so I can hear the beat of his heart and feel it against my own. Shoulder against shoulder. Hip against hip. Ankle against ankle. I refuse to curl up and break the line. It's too perfect.

I can't see his eyes, and that's a good thing. Human eyes don't glow in the dark with a vile metallic sheen. They're soft and brown and crinkle around the edges. They grow dark with anger and intense in concentration. They're a reflection of all Tobin is, and they're the evidence of the soul no Fade possesses.

I feel his breath against my hair. Our clothes rustle against the fabric of the blanket. The faint smell of home—something I still can't put into words—mixes with the scent of Tobin's skin and mine.

The only sense left is taste.

I lick my lips, tilt my head up, and kiss him.

It's not at all like that first kiss in the bunker. Tobin doesn't jerk to a stop when our lips touch or hold his hands stiff away from his body. He doesn't find words to excuse himself from the moment. It's the opposite. He pulls me in close, until he's all I can see.

When we break apart, I'm unsure how to face him, so we settle back into our quiet synchronization, with my head on his chest, watching the sky burn.

He breathes in. My head rises with his chest.

I breathe out. His arm around my waist sinks down.

This is more than close; it's connected.

"There was joy where I came from," I say. Speaking is the only way I know to prove to myself that I'm not dreaming, and that I'm not going to wake from this alone in my cold, plain room. "I think I was loved there."

At some point I had to be.

"I'd be surprised if you weren't."

His voice is dreamy, far away. Tobin is half asleep, and I have to wonder if he'll even remember saying that later. The hand clutching me slackens. His breathing turns even and shallow, blowing into my hair.

"Tobin?" I elbow him in the ribs, but it only spurs him to shift position.

I know he's probably exhausted from dragging everything

out here, and contending with his arm, but would it have killed him to stay awake longer than one little kiss?

I pick up his hand and knit our fingers together, fit my head more firmly under his chin, and watch the stars until they grow dim in the half-step between awake and asleep.

With every one that comes, the wish is the same.

CHAPTER 20

SOMEONE'S watching me.

Tobin's still asleep beside me, his arm around my waist so I'm rolled into his side. The steady thump of his heart beats under my ear. When I try to pull away, he tightens his grip for a second, mumbles something, then lets go so I can sit up.

There's something out there, but I can't see it no matter how hard I strain at the shadows in the curve of the Well.

Another streak flies overhead and I glance up to watch it. When I lower my eyes, he's there. *The Fade.*

No . . .

He *can't* have found me out here, and yet he's standing right in front of me. Bare feet, bare chest, still dressed in the medical scrubs from the White Room. The monitor on my wrist isn't blinking violet or red, so the guards can't know he's gone. I can't make my hand press the button to alert them; something stops me every time I try.

The imaginary bubble of protection Tobin and I found in the Well disintegrates. I push up to my knees so I have at least a chance of facing him on even ground. The Fade closes the space between us, and my throat tightens. He stops like he felt it himself.

Sorry. Regret. Apology.

Is he asking for an apology or making one?

"How did you get here?" I keep my voice low, thankful that Tobin doesn't make another sound.

The Fade replays his journey from the White Room, leaving out the particulars of how he managed to escape the containment cell. There were no guide lines when Tobin and I were down there, but the Fade sees a blaze of pinkish fire along the floor. I watch him enter Tobin's apartment from the tunnels, heading straight for Col. Lutrell's room. At the box of snow globes, the trail reappears, pooling around my favorite one.

Instead of shaking it to watch the glitter swirl, the Fade focuses on the outside, and the shine glows brighter, leading him to the Well, and ending at my feet. Through his eyes, I shimmer. Light rises off my skin like steam; he doesn't see Tobin at all.

"You were following *me*?" I raise myself up a little farther.

He nods.

Assist. Aid. Help.

"I don't know how to get you out of here," I say.

His mental map appears again, with a bold line zipping through the tunnels below the Arclight. He already knows the way out.

"Then what do you want?" I ask, fighting the urge to scream and maybe goad him into an attack. If he can cross the tunnels, he can bring other Fade back through them. There could be hundreds down there already.

Remember Cherish. Locate Cherish. Return Cherish.

"I keep telling you I don't know her. Why won't you believe me?"

Forgotten.

The female appears in my mind, dissolving into a pool of light.

"Yeah, well, I've forgotten a lot thanks to you."

Negative. False.

"I'm not lying!"

Angry?

"No, not angry. Furious. Enraged. I *hate* you for what you've done to me."

Tobin rolls behind me, shifting to his wounded side, and the Fade makes a strange noise. A strangled howl that sticks in his throat as he recalls Tobin in the White Room.

Hate. Anger. Kill. Kill. Kill.

"No!" I jump up too fast and have to grab my leg when it won't hold my weight. "Don't hurt him, please."

I'm stuck trying to balance on one knee while my injured leg splays out to the side—not the biggest barricade, but I'm all Tobin has. A creeping suspicion edges into my thoughts, raising the hair on my arms. Tobin should have woken by now.

"I didn't know about the White Room, I swear."

The Fade's eyes darken. He narrows them, with another tilt of his head, like a curious bird.

"I swear," I say again, though I'm not sure he knows what it means. "I didn't know they'd hurt you. Tobin, tell him."

But Tobin doesn't answer, even when I shake him. That chill moves further up my neck.

"Did you do something to him?"

Sequestered. Put aside.

"Tobin, wake up!"

I slap his arm, but there's no change.

Converse. Speak.

"After you wake him up."

Sadness. Pain. Torment.

A melancholy confusion overtakes the Fade, and the radiant nature of his emotions seeps into my chest, causing his pain to crystalize there as something cold and hard. He walks away, closer to the shadows cast by the building, and farther from Tobin, so I follow, trying to convince myself that if I keep him calm this can still end in our favor.

"How can I feel what you feel?" I ask. "Is that how Fade communicate?"

The Fade responds by pressing the information into my head in a frustrated rush that makes my body lock. Every joint lights up in sequence from my skull to my foot, with pain receptors firing one after the other.

My own knowledge, faces and names and the few facts I'm certain of, skew and mix with the too many things the Fade sends out in waves. The current's so strong, it pushes me back along the dew-slicked grass. I clutch at the ground with one hand, and my inhaler with the other, but the Fade tears it away before I can use it.

"Give it back!"

He pulls harder to bring the ring closer to his face, dragging me with it.

"Let go!" I grab the cord with both hands, using my weight as a countermeasure.

The Fade gives me a split-second warning where the image of the cord breaking against my neck materializes in my mind before he actually does it. And I'm still surprised by the sting when it happens for real.

He shakes the inhaler by his ear, breathes in close to the mouthpiece.

"You could have asked for it," I say.

His attention shifts back to my face; the moment he snapped the cord replays in my mind.

Anticipated. Warned.

"Warning is *not* the same as asking." Getting angry pushes

the fear back. It makes it easier to function.

Apology. Repentance.

"Can I have it back now?" I ask. "That's how questions work, by the way. Your voice goes up on the end so the person you're speaking to knows it's a question. Then they say yes or no."

"No," he says out loud, then adds *Alteration* in his usual non-speech.

"What do you mean, 'alteration'?"

"Changes." He rattles the disk at me and his eyes shift again so the color leaches into the silver center. He's angry. "Alt-er-ation," he sounds out carefully.

"Med-i-cation," I correct. "All it changes is the pain."

The Fade sets the inhaler flat in his palm—offering it, I assume, but as soon as I try to take it, his fingers snap shut.

"Wait," he says. "See."

The thick line swirled across his palm uncurls, spreading out beneath my inhaler. Once it's wide enough, tiny particles—nanites, I suppose—rise off his skin and engulf it completely.

They move in fits and starts, smooth at first, then writhing. Soon the second skin around my inhaler is boiling. The nanites fall apart, dropping onto his palm in clumps.

The Fade snarls, throws the inhaler on the ground, and crushes it under his foot.

"Dead," he says. He shakes his hand like it's gone to sleep, casting off black ash with every shake.

ARCLIGHT

"I need that!"

Inquiry . . .

"Which need?" He tests my "higher pitch" instructions.

"I hurt without it."

The Fade reaches to wrap his hands around my upper arms, and with one swift motion, I'm on my toes looking him straight in the face.

"Will not hurt you," he says.

My consciousness slips into that place that's under his control, where he can pull images out of my mind and make them look however he wants. He goes searching for pain and finds it in the moment where I was shot, only he twists the memory so he's beside me in the Grey. He cuts into his hand until dark blood runs, then holds the cut to my wound. When he pulls it away, we both bleed black.

"I can make you not hurt," he offers, and I'm back in the Well in the present. "You help. I help."

It's not a suggestion. This is his payment for helping him find Cherish.

A rumble starts deep in my stomach, and acid floods into my mouth from the idea that he wants to make me like him. I'm not strong enough to stop him if he tries.

The sky picks this, the worst moment, to throw another fireball across the horizon. An orange streak roars into view, catching the sheen of the Fade's eyes, and making them burn. Everywhere his skin should be white, it reflects the star's tail, blazing with the power contained in that deceptively human-oid form.

Demon . . . Monster . . . Abomination . . .

The rhetoric I've heard since my first moment plays in a loop, and I cup my hand over the panic button on my wrist. Pressing the button would bring help, but it would also cost Tobin his sanctuary.

"Promise you'll leave, and I won't hit the alarm," I say.

The Fade finally lets me back down onto the grass. Calm wraps around me, and my limbs relax before I realize what he's doing.

Safe.

The suggestion imprints over everything else, robbing me of the desire to run. The Fade leans his forehead against mine, close enough now that I can tell the scent of his skin isn't the stench I'd imagined. I want to be afraid of him, but he won't let me.

Trust.

There's an electric tingle everywhere our skin touches. To my horror, it isn't some autonomic response to his proximity, but the very literal rush of foreign matter onto my body.

The myriad of swirls and loops that decorate his skin begin to move as individual particles, smaller than sand, all working together and moving toward a common destination—me.

"Stop!" I choke out.

"Listen," he says instead.

A tiny shock stings my skin for each particle that travels from the Fade to me. Playing the part of conductor, they carry images clearer than those he was able to send on his own, but it's too much. I can't keep up.

My field of vision shrinks until all I can see are those two blue-silver eyes and the ash-white skin around them.

"Too fast," I say.

He's shaking; each tremor sends another wave of nanites onto my skin, compounding the problem. He's almost solid white now, and my hands bear the marks he's surrendered. If fire's the only way to purify exposed skin, they'll have to burn my whole body to destroy them.

"Hear," he grits out.

Desperation. Pleading.

"I need what you know."

My mind pries open, wider and wider, stretching to accommodate new input.

"You see it. I see it." The sound of his voice amplifies in each particle. They shout as one, boring into parts of myself I can't access on my own.

"Take them back!"

Beauty. Hope. Light. Whole.

"They'll kill me!"

He stops. The marks flee my skin, retreating back across our bridge of hands, and I fly backward as sure as if I was thrown by someone ten times my size.

The amount of power contained in his body, those particles . . . nanites . . . whatever . . . is frightening, as much for the magnitude as the revelation that he's been holding it in check when he didn't have to. No way did we bring him down on our own. Not five kids.

"You could have left anytime, couldn't you?"

The Fade turns away, back to hiding in the shadows.

"Look at me," I say.

Am I actually trying to convince a Fade that I want him to stay when he was going to leave me alone?

Alone.

He latches onto the word and sends it back. The world rushes away so there's no sound or sight. Just a starless void with him in the center.

Grief.

The toxic emotion twists my heart, compressing around it. Loss and desperation on a scale I never knew existed.

"You stayed for her."

The Fade didn't come here to kill me, or anyone else. He came for her—*Cherish*. The Red-Wall attack was cover for him to steal inside, a distraction to get him close enough to find her. He never wanted to hurt anyone. This Fade let Honoria Whit lock him up because he was afraid that if he left, he'd never see his Cherish again.

"Start over. I'll listen," I assure him. "But go slower. Okay?"

Hope.

He lays one hand on my cheek, gently, and tilts my head up so we're eye-to-eye. The markings on his face shift into kinetic interlocking lines, but they stay on him.

There's a feeling that a circuit's been broken, but it takes two tries to get up the nerve to lay my hand on his chest. His skin's smooth under my fingers, without any ridging or rise where the patterns should be. They're not *on* his skin, they're *in* it.

That means they were *in* me, too.

It's so strange to feel what I can't see, where his marks blend his body into the night.

The Fade moves my hand until I feel the fluttering beat of his heart, and it strikes me that he's alive. Stories about his kind made them seem like smoke, without body or form, but he's flesh and blood. A heart can't pump without blood.

Cherish.

More than the word drops into my mind. It's a rush of care and concern, set to the beat of a thumping pulse. The images start over as he tries to make me see everything at once, the whole of his mate's life in a single breath.

When I pull back this time, he lets me. His hand's clutched in my hair, rolling the strands between his fingers the way I'd done with the unfamiliar texture of the sand in Tobin's jar.

"Do you have a name?" I ask.

"Cherish is not found," he says.

Confused. Defeated. Rueful.

"Rueful? Can I call you Rue?" I ask.

"Rue," he repeats with a nod. I suppose that's a yes.

The turmoil boiling out of him makes me dizzy with an overbearing sense of failure.

"Try something else. Tell me out loud, in human terms. Maybe it'll trigger something."

I've come too close to give up now. He's so sure I saw what happened to Cherish. Maybe if I find her, I'll find me, too.

"We are infinite," he says. "Words are inadequate."

"They're better than nothing."

"Remember Cherish. Listen to Cherish. Locate Cherish."

"I don't know where to look," I say. "Tobin was born here and even he wouldn't know. The place you were kept was hidden from us."

Mentioning Tobin is a bad idea. Rue's back on the offensive. *Hate. Enemy.*

He paces, looking from me to Tobin on a pause, then returns to his pacing. I'm beginning to think it's a good thing Tobin doesn't know what's going on.

"Leave," he says finally.

"Yes, leave," I agree. "Go look for Cherish."

"You leave. Bring Cherish to home."

"I don't have her," I say, for what feels like the millionth time. "Get out of here before I change my mind and hit the alarm."

But my fingers still refuse to obey my commands.

"We go to home, or home comes to here." Apparently "ultimatum" isn't one of the inadequate words Rue's familiar with. "Home waits. If I remain, home comes to here."

"That's not fair." I whirl on him, causing my hair to flare wide. It catches the moonlight, nearly glowing against the darkness of the Well.

"He will cease," Rue says, and nods to Tobin. "He is finite. With an end."

The sound of that distant heartbeat starts and stops, and the fear that Rue might have somehow killed Tobin even though they're not touching makes me watch until I'm sure he's breathing.

"He will cease," Rue says again, the threat clear.

"If I go with you, you have to promise to leave him alone. All of them—everyone here."

"Mine will stay to home."

"And you'll let Tobin go?"

"He will wake."

A simple matter of numbers becomes the hardest decision of my life. I can stay here and know the nightly onslaught will resume, or I can leave and make a dent in the debt I owe the Arclight for saving me in the first place. It's a near certainty that the Fade will find another breach point. There's a less sure outcome, if I go, but getting Rue out of here will keep Tobin safe.

Actually, it's not a hard decision at all.

CHAPTER 21

I leave my alarm behind, near the door to the Well where I'm sure Tobin will see it. If I leave without a clue, he'll assume I got scared either of the night or of him, and that I've gone back to my room. But no one goes anywhere without their alarm.

Where time moved at a crawl during the Red-Wall, it's flying now. I try not to wonder how long it will take Rue to lose patience with my not being able to answer his questions, or if death will hurt once I'm no longer of use to him.

We're in the tunnels, beyond the safety of the light. We've already passed two collapsed corridors, but Rue picks ways that are clear, finding more pieces of the Arclight that shouldn't exist. He drags me along, clutching my hands with fingers now devoid of the claws that allow him to climb stone walls, and I don't dare separate from him for fear of being lost down here forever in the oldest parts of the Arclight's underground.

It's clearer than ever that the direct assault on our wall was a diversion and nothing else; otherwise, they would have been in and out and never made a sound. Rue navigates the tunnels like he was born to them, sweeping down turns and switch-backs that seem random.

How many times have the Fade entered the Arclight and we never knew? Is Rue truly the only one here with me? I don't hear the click of Fade claws against the walls as we pass, or see any shimmer lines to indicate we have company, but it's possible. All of this whirls through my mind while I try to devise some way to tell Honoria about the hole in the security grid. Once I'm gone, no one will know it's here.

Rue stops so quickly I bounce off his back.

"A little warning would be nice, next time you plan on turning into a wall." I rub my nose, flick the tears from the blow out of my eyes. "You're lost, aren't you?"

The lights here are rusted and mostly broken, with only the emergency beacons glowing. Three out of ten remain, and one of those is intermittent.

"Searching," he corrects, patting the wall here and there.

"For what?"

He sends me the image of my mouth opening to speak, and nothing coming out.

"Don't tell me to shut up," I say, relieved that I can.

An unflinching hand covers my mouth. "Let go of me" never quite makes it into the open air, dying as a muffled squeak in Rue's palm.

"Quiet," he says, then gives me the sense of my voice bouncing from wall to wall down the corridor until it's heard in the Arclight above. "Stay here. Mouth closed."

Rue takes his hand away and directs me to the facing wall.

"You could have just asked," I grouse.

"I did."

"You could have asked *politely*."

"Mouth closed. Politely."

"That's not what I meant."

The muscles across his back tense up, annoyed, and the swirls and loops across them draw tighter into dense coils. The green shine from the emergency lights does strange things to Rue's appearance, making him more out of place in the real world.

"I'm sorry," I say. The last thing I want is an irritated Fade on my hands. "When I can't see, I get nervous."

"Your eyes are damaged?"

"It's too dark. Humans only see what the light touches."

A hand yanks me back across the corridor until I'm directly under the defective light. My body appears and disappears with each short burst of power.

Another minute passes with me sitting on the floor in

my tiny green circle before it shrinks inward. Its filament bursts with a dramatic pop, creating trails of sparks that die out before they hit the ground—a pale imitation of the star shower I was watching only minutes ago.

"Rue?" I call out for the only familiar thing left to me and stretch my foot out, feeling for any boundary I can find. Using a cold pipe for leverage, I pull myself up and along its path. "Tell me where you are . . . ow!"

I catch my hand on a latch in the wall and slam into something hard. Round rungs and sidebars—from the feel of it I've smacked into a ladder that's bolted to the wall by a less-than-sturdy set of brackets. And I could really use my inhaler about now to deal with the pain of discovery.

"Is this what you're looking for?" I ask loudly, over the ringing metal and my ringing ears.

"Yes," Rue answers, closer than he should have been.

"Great. Now what?"

"Climb." He takes hold of the still-wobbling ladder with one hand and tugs at my sleeve with the other.

"I am *not* climbing the rickety ladder of death. It already tried to take my head off. You go first."

Rue swings his weight onto a rung with inhuman grace. He's at the top in no time. From high above, a metal wheel groans, shaking itself loose from rust that falls with clumps of the cement had been used to seal it from the inside. One last, shrill whine and an opening appears at the top of a narrow chute.

There's no alarm on the hatch. I was hoping for an alarm.

"Climb." Rue holds his hand down as though he expects me to jump and catch it. Behind his head, smallish fireballs continue the show I was supposed to share with Tobin.

An enormous meteor drops into the atmosphere. It's bright enough to not only draw Rue's attention, but it illuminates the hallway, giving me an idea of how far I'll have to run before it bends, and I make another instant decision that cancels out my last. I can't leave the Arclight, not with only Rue's word to protect the people here. If he's lying, or if the other Fade decide not to honor the deal we've made, there's nothing to keep them out now that the seal's been broken.

I bolt back the way we came, relying on the snapshot provided by the meteor's burn trail. Twenty steps down, one of the green lights turns on, giving me the next step of my escape. Another meteor trail extends the corridor thirty feet, but also casts a fast-moving Fade-shadow over my own.

My brilliant escape plan lasts mere seconds before Rue catapults in front of me, and I collide full body with him. He drags me up by my jacket.

"Do not run," he scolds. "Cherish was lost when she ran."

He pops me up over his shoulder and stalks back toward the exit ladder. The earthy scent of his skin I'd found such a pleasant surprise before only acts as an irritant now.

"Put me down!" Forget being quiet and not drawing attention; I'm screaming. Kicking, beating him as hard as I can anywhere I can land a punch. Let someone hear.

Rue starts up the ladder and I wrap my arms around the side, holding on to the closest rung with both hands and doing what I can to pull us down. Even a Fade can't balance two bodies on tiny rungs when the ladder is ready to shake loose from its bindings. If we fall, I'll land on Rue, and that means he'll take the brunt of it while I get another chance to run.

I shake the ladder until its ancient bolts wriggle in their slots, clanging to the ground, and the ladder tilts away from the wall.

Rue pries me loose and keeps climbing, even when I jam my hands and feet against the walls. For someone who's supposed to be able to make the Fade cower in their tracks, I'm doing a lousy job of slowing one down.

Near the top, Rue rolls me off his shoulder and we both clear the lip of the opening. My last hope of escape dissolves into the murky disquiet of the Grey and the shallow fog I inhale with every breath. We're deep within its borders, too far from anything else to be of any use.

Rue pauses only long enough to close the cap on the chute behind us and kick some debris back over the edges. The cold color of the metal and the broken cement seal around it blend perfectly with that of the terrain.

He checks the horizon, picks his direction, and marches off into desolation.

"They're going to come looking for me," I say, hurrying to keep up with him.

"They watch where they burn," he says. "They don't watch here."

"So it's safe for you to go in and out."

"Not safe, unwatched."

The black bands on his skin go back into motion, forming a tight web that darkens his complexion. Even the low light here in the space between our worlds causes him distress.

"Does it hurt?" I ask. "When they go in and out of your skin like that?"

"They are me," he says. "I don't hurt me. And I don't hurt you."

He's right. They stung, but didn't hurt; if any seeped into my pores, I didn't notice.

I have no idea how many of those things were on me. They were so small, I couldn't have kept track if I'd been calm enough to try. There's no way to know if any stayed behind.

"I don't have any of those things left in me, do I?"

Rue stops, watching my discomfort as the overwhelming need to scratch nonexistent nerve impulses hits hard. I swat the tingling crawlies in my leg and claw the back of my hands.

"They're not still floating around, are they?" Panic raises my voice an octave when he doesn't answer. Now I'm sure there's a whole colony of the disgusting things multiplying somewhere out of sight. Probably behind my spleen. I'm not sure what a spleen is exactly, but it has a sinister sound to it, and seems like the perfect place for something malevolent to trench in.

"No," he says. His eyes brighten so the silver chases the blue to its farthest edge. I stop fidgeting, angry that he finds this so amusing.

"Would you tell me if there were?" I ask.

"You will doubt if I did," he says, passing me to start our long trek toward the Dark. "You don't trust me."

Of course I don't trust him, he's a Fade. Specifically the Fade who threatened the one person I'd rather not have threatened.

Timed perfectly to thoughts of Tobin, the shrill sound of an alarm cuts the silence behind us, and the lights intensify so that even the Grey brightens. The blue rings in Rue's eyes shrink back to their centers.

"They know you're gone," I say.

"They won't come to home. They're afraid—like you."

"I am *not* afraid of you," I say. If I say it enough, maybe I'll start to believe it.

"You're afraid of not knowing," he says. "You don't know me. You hope I know you."

It's not fair that he's able to pick out information he wants while I'm stuck with whatever flood of upended nonsense he decides to share.

"Move faster." Rue picks up his pace, and I stumble after

him, finding it more difficult to maneuver through the rocks and broken remnants of trees in my shoes than he does barefoot.

"*Do* you know me?" I ask.

"I know what you know."

"Then what good am I to you? I don't have any idea what happened to your mate."

"You have an idea," he says.

"So what? I'm supposed to follow you until my memory comes back?"

"Yes."

I agreed to come with him to give Tobin a chance to survive our trip to the Well. Either I'd escape from Rue, or the Fade would kill me. It wasn't supposed to be an open-ended stay in the Dark.

"What if I refuse to go anywhere, plant myself on the ground, and sit here until the sun rises?"

He reaches for my arm, a warning that I'm about to be manhandled again, or worse, have him take over my body.

"I don't hurt you," he reminds me when I shrink back.

"Good. You cannot hurt me from an arm's length away."

Another blast of the alarm trumpets through the Grey. As it dies, search beams stretch beyond our position, but they never slow down the way they would if someone had spotted us.

¤ ¤ ¤

The wind grows strong in the Grey, where it's free to build without trees or brush to break its reign. Sand and silt and smooth-worn pebbles flow in rivers around our feet, ankle-deep in places, creating a perversion of the paradise Tobin built in the Well.

"Go faster." Rue speeds up again, leaping from one piece of windblown debris to another with no regard for whether they're moving or still. "This is a bad place."

"Rue, I can't keep up. Wait . . . Rue!" But my voice can't compete with the sound of air through the empty places.

At its crest, a pair of dervishes forms, made of dust and untethered things. Dueling jets of air catch my hair and send it flying in all directions.

Rue realizes too late that I'm beyond his reach, and I realize too late that I need his protection whether I want it or not. He makes a vain swipe for my hand that falls short; the next is cut off by a tumbling mass of tangled weeds that strikes him in the chest, knocking him into a roll he can't stop, until colliding with a barely rooted stump does it for him. He wipes a dark trickle from his mouth and forces himself back into the flow of the windstorm toward me.

The stinging pelt of dead leaves and branches steals my breath. My jacket peels up, coming loose from my arms everywhere but the strapped wrists, so the air streams over my skin. One of the buttons catches me in the face, slicing my cheek near my eye.

"Help me," I scream, as my heels leave the ground. In the distance, trees that scrape the sky bend beneath the wind's rage. I don't stand a chance. I lose the ground completely. When I try to scream again, my mouth fills with grit and ash.

I strain for the concentration to locate Rue somewhere in the wilderness beyond my closed eyes.

Help me!

His answer bounces back as a picture of myself with arms outstretched. I do as he says, and fling my arms wide.

Something slaps against my hand, hard enough to make it burn. I try to pull it back against my body, but what I assume to be debris are fingers that draw me closer until Rue can fold his body over mine, bearing the greater share of the storm's wrath. That same strange veil that protected him from the White Room's lamps covers us both. A black rope extends in a braid from the markings on his arm to anchor around a nearby stump so we can't be blown away.

Outside our cocoon, the wind beats against the veil, but the weave proves unbreakable.

We're safe, and a few long minutes later, we're free.

"Thanks," I say quickly, looking down and trying to smooth my uniform back to regulation. This is the second time my enemy's become my hero.

Rue saved me, and injured himself to get it done, but knowing that only heightens the unnaturalness of his being. Already the gashes and scrapes along his skin are knitting back together as though patched by an invisible hand. Where there had been blood, it disappears—called back into his body through the wounds before they vanish, too.

"Go," he says. "The storms will return."

With the light at our backs, and the Dark before us, the descriptions of the Grey as a middle ground fall apart. What most call a buffer zone is no kind of protection to anyone. There's nowhere for a human to hide and no way for a Fade to avoid the light. Everything here is held suspended in a bare limbo. Pools of stagnant water form where rain has filled holes in the ground. Bugs and stinging gnats thrive, unopposed, as the dominant species. Below the water's surface, shining red eyes catch the lights as they rake past, and whatever silent creature they belong to blinks, swimming off. Here, the water's no safer than the air.

Rue no longer tries to speak to me, by voice or otherwise. He crouches against the long exposure to the light, a posture I take up myself. When he turns his head to one side, I do the same, awaiting the discovery of some new and terrible thing that even this Fade shrinks from. I put my feet where he's walked to make sure I don't blunder my way into some other hidden danger.

And then we're there—the edge of the Dark.

It blooms out of the ground as a wall of trees and vines and twisted branches that seem unbreachable to my human eyes. My body locks down, every muscle frozen and refusing to work.

Light is safety; light is life.

I can feel the sun rising in my blood, beckoning me home. But Rue's waiting. The predawn glow catches the outline of his skin as he grasps a curtain of foliage and pulls it aside, revealing an unobstructed passageway.

"Inside," he says. "Where it's safe."

"Maybe for you," I mumble. But even as I argue, I know he's right. There's no way I could cross the Grey here on my own. My only hope is to find the short side, where the Dark bulges so close to the Arclight it's nearly at our gates. And to make it that far, there's nothing else to do but follow.

I gulp to keep the bile from rising, exhale the breath that's started to burn my lungs, and step off the edge into the unknown.

CHAPTER 22

THE amorphous swath of no-man's-land called the Dark is literally the stuff of nightmares. When the Arclight's citizens put heads to pillows at dawn and close their eyes, it's the Dark that lies behind them. Phantoms and ghosts of fears that have compounded on top of each other for generations churn in a new primordial soup that gives birth to the end of the world. It creeps like the misty fog beyond our boundaries, and it's into that void I've now traveled.

Trees with narrow, soaring trunks swallow the sky. There's no up or down or left or right. No depth.

High and interlocking branches steal even the barest light, so I have to bunch closer to Rue in order to follow him. His hand reaches for mine, but I can't tell if the thrumming pulse I feel is a beating heart or the flow of those *things* below the surface. And I refuse to tolerate the touch of hands that may have killed my family. Saving my life doesn't make up for taking it from me in the first place.

I cross my arms around myself and clench my fists into my clothes so he has nothing to hold on to, offering "I'm cold" as an excuse.

It's not even a lie. The crash after my adrenaline spike has turned my blood to ice water.

Here the darkness consumes the light, when the laws of nature say that's impossible. Every breath comes heavy and damp, weighted with layers of dew the sun never bakes away. Even if the Fade don't kill me, I'll sink below the surface and disappear.

Somewhere in the distant parts of my mind, Anne-Marie's voice prattles away about her fears of being locked in with no escape. She becomes my anchor, shielding my mind behind her shrill worries as I wrest memories from my brain by force. I survived the Dark once before; I found my way out. The secret's in there, waiting to be discovered again.

"They're going to come after me," I say. "Tobin will come if no one else does."

Just like his father did.

Disgust.

A pointed jolt stings my skin.

"Ow!" Pinpricks run along my arms, but I can't rub the feeling away no matter how hard or fast I try. "If you disagree, just say so. Words hurt a lot less than the whole mind zapping thing!"

"Sor-ry." He draws out the apology into two long syllables that end our conversation for another thirty meters. I keep rubbing my arms. My hands make heat and keep my skin from feeling clammy beneath my jacket.

"I recognize this place," I say, bracing for the inevitable pain that comes with recollection. This is what Rue showed me outside Tobin's apartment. These are the trees with a fringe of black moss. "But I didn't leave the Dark on this side."

I crossed on the short side, so how could Rue have seen me running this way?

"You remember trees. You can remember Cherish," he says, which isn't helpful in the least.

"Why'd you really bring me out here? I don't believe it's just because of her. If you needed help to kill me—"

No. Negative.

The strength of his response spins my thoughts in twelve directions.

"Nice try, nice lie. I don't believe you."

Belief. Trust. Entreat. Help.

"Just because you're willing to work with the enemy doesn't mean the others are."

"You are not my enemy," he says. "You listen."

We pass some sort of structure, a building ruined and broken, overtaken by the Dark. Vines and growth burst from what had once been windows and doors.

It's a house. Bits of the roof are still in one piece but on the ground, as though something pried them off, and the walls have kept their light rose color without the sun to bleach it away. But where the Dark has touched it, the whole thing runs with black lines like the ones on Rue's skin. If I strain my eyes, I can make out the muted shapes of other houses on either side, arranged around a flat, curved lane.

Something cracks under my foot, and I look down to see a yellow sign shaped like a pentagon, with the silhouette of two children crossing a road. It's metal, like the fallen pole it's still bolted to, and of no interest to the nanites that have consumed the houses. I don't know the symbol, but its meaning is clear: *Humans used to live here.*

"My people would listen if you'd talk like this." I turn away from the one-time homes, now skeletons of forgotten lives the Dark has torn to shreds. "It's confusing your way. They think you can't understand us."

"Talk is difficult." He fits his mouth around each word like it's a solid thing he's not used to having on his tongue. "Imprecise."

That last word makes me shudder; he dug it straight out of my own vocabulary.

"But if you explain . . . Go back with me, and—"

Negative.

"Mouth closed, politely."

Rue strays off the curved path into a rougher area. The place we leave, which seemed so morose, now glows bright compared to what lies ahead.

A black canopy stretches over our heads, the antithesis of the Arclight's safety net, drawing tighter where the Dark has held its grip longest. There are no more leaves, only blankets of foliage with their edges blurred by an unnatural shine. Ebony strands of moss hang from the branches—a perfect match to the impersonation of hair that frames Rue's face, and I'm careful not to let it touch my skin.

I memorize exposed roots and rocks, letting my foot drag here and there, enough to make a shallow trench behind me, but careful not to make it look like anything more than exhaustion of my wounded leg.

"You won't be lost," Rue says out of nowhere, stopping so I crash into him again. I'm starting to think he enjoys it.

"What?" I ask.

"You don't need pathways. I'll show you where to go." He lets me see a line, snaking away ahead of us. "One alone is not safe."

"I thought you said there was no danger here."

"Do not disturb them. They like the quiet," Rue says, and takes up his invisible trail again.

"Who?"

"They."

He keeps walking, but points to the rocks at our feet.

Like everything else, they're covered in a dusting of fine black specks. They move of their own volition in a slow roiling churn, sliding into pools and over the ground. Behind us, my trench is gone, pushed together and filled as though we'd never passed that way at all.

This place can consume me whole and leave no trace behind.

I can't suppress the shudder that comes with spying a glistening shimmer here and there among the trees, even high on the trunks, where near-invisible Fade hang suspended and watching us. They're everywhere.

"What are those things?" I ask, hoping that if I don't act like I've seen the other Fade, they won't react. "Are they nanites, like on your skin?"

"They're voices who don't like to be disturbed. You're too loud."

Our path ends at a large chunk of stone with ruined trees on each side, and deep scars where something cut the rock a long time ago. A straight pair of yellow lines runs down its center.

Nothing's familiar except the repetition of the trees. I'd hoped that something out here would trigger my memories. A sound, a scent . . . anything, but I don't remember this at all. I lean toward the stone, placing my palm against it, but it doesn't feel like rock. It's not exactly soft, but it's not hard enough either.

It's not natural.

I expect Rue to go around, or turn back, but he starts to climb, reaching back for my hand to help me up. Lichen mottled black and green covers the surface so it slides under my hands, tickling my nerves. The lump in my throat becomes harder, threatening to choke me completely before the Fade can do their worst.

When we reach the top, I slap the stains away, scrubbing my hands on every coarse surface I can find that's not coated itself. I pick at the splotches on my uniform, but they won't come off. They spread through the fabric, claiming it as their own, so I tear the jacket off and throw it to them. It disappears where it lands, engulfed.

"They won't hurt you," Rue says, waiting for me to stomp my shoes clean. His posture settles into something catlike for his limbs, with that same avian tilt to his head. It's a weird combination of predator and prey in one body.

"They can," I argue, shaking my fingers through my wind-wrecked hair to make sure none are hiding there. "Honoria says they're parasites. Parasites hurt people. They can kill."

"What is Honoria?"

"The woman from the White Room. Our leader."

I summon every detail I can remember of Honoria's face and clothes, and show him the lines on her face, her sharp eyes, and tight-lipped mouth, then linger over the V-shaped scar at her temple.

"She went silent," he says.

"She doesn't say much, but she's not mute."

I give him an image of Honoria barking orders. I wish I had something to give her a softer edge.

"Her voice fell silent."

Lost.

Rue stands as though he's just heard some cue beyond my range. "Follow me."

The ground turns smooth and flat, forming what I think used to be a road. The same yellow partitions that were painted on the broken stone extend in both directions until they reach the mouth of a wider space. Here, the yellow is replaced by white and blue, bracketing the area into sections. Rusted-out trucks and cars fill spaces that stop at a metal fence with swings on the other side and a tall metal plane that I think was a slide before it went to pieces. There aren't any homes standing here, but it still carries the echo of a human existence.

"What do you mean you lost her voice?" I ask as I scramble after him.

"We heard her voice, now she is silent like you."

"But you hear me fine."

Rue stops; his shoulders heave in a heavy sigh.

"*I* hear you." Rue touches his fingers to my lips, then puts them to his ear. "*We* cannot hear *you*." This time, he rests his fingers in the space where the top of my nose reaches my eyes, then touches the same spot on his own face.

"You mean my thoughts?"

"We pity the silent ones." Rue pauses on *pity*, weighing its meaning to make sure it's the right word. "The silent hide always. The silent live scared."

"The only thing we're scared of is you," I say.

"You said you weren't afraid of me." Rue steps closer and straightens to his full height, so his chin is even with my brow line.

"I used to be," I say, fighting the urge to back up and put more space between us.

He nods again, accepting the answer, then turns around and starts walking.

"Can you hear Cherish?" I ask.

"Her voice was stolen."

Fret. Loss. Desolation. Incomplete. Stripped. Vacant.

Ripping, tearing—it's a feeling so intense my knees buckle under the force, and at the point I know my bones are about to shatter in their sockets, it stops.

I feel like I'm shrinking or drowning, and totally alone.

Please . . . somebody has to be somewhere . . .

But they aren't. No one's anywhere, not even me.

I'm seeing Rue's perspective. His memory. We're back in the Arclight, zooming through the tunnels, and on into the White Room. The lamps glow bright and hot. Fear and pain are all I can feel. There are screams, like the sounds Rue made when the lights burned him, but higher, in a female's voice. Below them, a faint pulse. An entreaty and a promise of rescue, but more . . .

Love.

When the image finally breaks, I'm crying.

He loves Cherish, and somehow she was taken into the Arclight—into the White Room. She screamed for him and he called to her, but they couldn't find each other. And then her voice just stopped. He felt it all, but couldn't help her.

"They destroy us," Rue says finally, and the connection between us shuts off. "Your Honoria destroys us."

"She protects us," I correct, but it's a hard point to make while I'm still shaking. "The ruins we walked through—you did that, not us. This was *our* territory before the Fade killed the people who lived here."

"We are a beginning, not an ending," he argues.

How can I feel pity for Rue losing one person when I'm standing in the devastation that proves the Fade destroyed thousands in this place alone? I lost my family here, why should I care if he gets his back or not?

"Look at this place." I spread my arms out and pivot on my good leg. "This was a playground." I hurry to one of the few swings still standing and test its strength before sitting. "These were children's toys, but the Dark took everything. We have nothing left."

I have nothing left.

He shakes his head, making the crystals around his face clink together, then sits on the other swing.

"We unify. We include."

"But humans like being individuals."

"We know now," Rue said. He pushes off the ground with his foot, starting the swing into a slow sway. "We didn't understand—individuals like being lonely."

"It's not lonely." Hopefully he can't tell I'm lying. I'm the last person who should be trying to convince anyone that it's not lonely living in the Arclight.

"The silent are isolated," he argues with difficulty. "Disconnected."

"What do you know about how humans live? You're a Fade."

"We are not faded—*dimming.*"

There's no way to describe what happens next but to say my eyes open wide. My vantage point expands to take in the whole of the Dark in less than a blink. I'm seeing through a thousand eyes at once. Voices in number and variation I thought impossible stream from everything and everywhere. Whispers and shouts flow side by side and neither overpowers the other.

"What is that?"

"Us," Rue says, then the sounds stop. "And that's human."

Pieces start to align. What Honoria calls a parasite is what Rue calls a part of him. The Fade aren't a contagion—they're a hive, and they don't understand why we're not.

"We are everything. One together." Rue fumbles through descriptions that can't capture a tenth of what he shows me.

Inclusion.

The Fade are exactly what Honoria said—sentient machines responding to their programming, but they aren't parasites; they're symbionts. The human's a host, just like the trees and the birds and the vines, all working together to support the whole. The entire Dark is one massive colony connected at its core. It can't help but expand.

"We listen. They don't hear."

"The people in the Arclight can't hear the voices in the Dark." I nod my agreement, hoping it's my choice to agree and not the delayed result of the Fade burrowing in.

"This isn't dark," Rue says. "You're dark." He pokes me in the chest. "You're silent. You're empty."

Alone.

"You're faded. Not me."

CHAPTER 23

THE Dark stretches on for hours, until I fear it's growing wider even as we cross it, and every step makes me aware of more Fade following us, blended against the darkened terrain. The never-ending movement of the nanite pools along the ground creates a constant sound of tinkling glass.

How can I escape when there are so many watching?

Our journey takes on a tempo set by my leg. It's gone from a dull ache to a throb, and now the first hint of sharper pain shoots down the bone, through the muscle, gathering where the bullet first entered.

I haven't felt so much as a nudge against my thoughts since our argument, and while I'm relatively certain Rue will answer if I initiate the conversation, I don't want him to take it as an invitation to fill my mind as he sees fit. But there's no way I can keep up the pace he's set.

"Here is not a place to rest," he says when I give in to the protest of my muscles and drop on the spot.

We've passed into another group of used-to-be buildings, but like the houses before, it's a ruin. The signs here are red and green, and still standing. One warns people to STOP, while the others form an X, where SEABOUND crosses WINDBOURNE. There's a pedal-bike with a missing wheel tied to the bottom of the post with a lock and chain. It's a graveyard of the world we lost to the Fade, as dead as the people who no longer live here.

"I have to—just for a minute. Tell your Fade friends to come to you. I know they're watching us."

No—*tracking us*. Humans are prey to the Fade. I can't let Rue's temporary civility make me forget that. Fade senses are made for the hunt. Why else would they be so sharp?

I scan the crumbling buildings as far as I can see, but I already know everything's Faded here. Signs that should tell me what this place used to be are bare where the Fade have stripped the wood that used to frame them. One of the doors reads LI YUE PO'S in blue letters against the glass, with a chart of times below, but they mean nothing to me. Inside, the place is empty.

Rue's eyes cut through the Dark, glowing brighter and completely silver. He gestures toward a small, round clearing in the middle of the buildings. More deserted cars sit stopped around its edge.

"Wait here," he says. "I must see beyond."

He drops to his knees in the clearing and lays his hands flat against the ground. His markings rush off the ends of his fingers to mingle with the nanites pooled around him. He goes so still, I'm not even sure he's breathing.

I count seconds in my head, to have some way to mark the passage of time. A minute, then two, with nothing beyond the rise and flow of the nanites along his arms. I fall back on my habit of searching out sounds to fill the emptiness, but rather than the steady comfort of a ticking clock, or whirring power lines that promise safety, there's only the rustle of leaves without wind to cause them, and a whisper.

It's those things, what Rue called voices; it has to be. They're still moving. Maybe over my hands and feet. They're so tiny and light, surely I could miss them scuttling across the toes of my shoes or onto my sleeves. I might not feel them until there's so many they can pull me under like they did my jacket.

"R-Rue?" I call timidly, while rubbing my arms. "Are you almost done?"

I stand and pick up one foot to keep it clear of the ground, then switch when my leg grows tired, but my wounded side's too weak to hold for long. The air grows cold and thick, and I imagine chilly fingers grazing my skin, trying to snatch me away while Rue's unable to help me. I want to scream, but fear a flood of darkness spilling down my throat to overrun me from the inside out if I open my mouth too wide.

"Rue . . . say something. Tell me to be quiet again, I won't get mad this time."

But Rue's still "seeing beyond," whatever that means.

I know the Arclight was behind us when we started, and if I'm right, Rue's taking us near the short side, which would account for his nerves. If I can make it to the Grey, that's safer for me so long as the sun is up.

"Rue? Can you hear me?" I call out, but there's still no answer.

On top of Li Yue Po's, shimmer lines have begun to cluster where Fade are packed in so tight they're interfering with each other's camouflage. Four are completely visible. They're staring at me, but don't seem to know I can see them.

The Fade pools along the ground surge with an influx of nanites.

"Rue . . ."

If I don't take my chance now, I'll lose it. There are so many Fade encroaching on our position, I don't think it'll matter if they agree with Rue about my value to him or not. Surely they can overpower him.

I take a few measured steps away, wondering if I can find the route I took before. If I find that memory, then others could come after it. All I need is something to hold on to that will guide me to my next step. When I feel a wall of those ever-present black vines at my back, I slip my hand inside to pull them back, still walking in reverse away from the buildings.

I glance back at Li Yue Po's to assure myself the Fade haven't moved, but my timing's terrible. I catch the eye of a short, silver-eyed Fade who startles when she realizes I can see her. Another turns toward me, and another, with scores of them dropping the facade of invisibility.

One, two . . . seven, ten . . . fifteen . . . I count them as they appear on other rooftops and my stomach plummets.

No one survives the Fade.

No—*I* survive the Fade.

I now have two certainties about myself. I hate cobbler, and I'm a survivor.

I bolt before I can lose my nerve, head down, into the brush, choosing the path of least resistance, and wagering that the Dark is less dense where the light is closest. The ground becomes easier to navigate, with fewer rocks and jutting roots, and then the dark monochrome breaks, exploding into patches of color—a dramatic contrast of red and blue against the black. Flowers seem so out of place here.

I stop to catch my breath, kneeling off my sore leg, and I'm greeted by an intoxicating scent like nothing in the Arclight's garden. A fine carpet of green covers the forest floor. Not grass, or even moss. It crunches under my touch and brushes off my fingertips like sand. Pink, and in places even an impossible white, show through in the form of tiny shoots and petals, but they're all the same. They look real, but they're not.

They're nanites pretending to be plants, a macabre sort of

photograph of the things they've replaced.

I startle at the cry of a familiar bird the color of a thunder-cloud, and lurch to my feet as realization sets in. It's the bird I rescued—the swirls of black along its tail aren't natural; they're Fade marks. Was I being watched inside the Arclight? Am I still? Is it even a bird, or is it a replication, like the flowers? Can it speak to the hive?

Every step comes with a flinch, as I register the crispness under my feet where there should be soft grass, and feel the glasslike texture of swaying foliage against my skin. Drops trickle down from the canopy in rhythm with the sweat on my face. It's an unplanned synchronization where I'm too in tune with this place for my own comfort. I run harder, pushing my leg against the pain, and slap each familiar thing as I pass it. An act of triumph, ticking it off as a step closer to home, and me being back where I belong. I've gone this way before; I'm certain of it.

I *survive* the Fade.

I'm going home.

I'll tell our elders there's another way to live besides drills and Red-Walls. Rue's reasonable, to a point. If he could speak to Honoria . . . No, Mr. Pace. I still don't trust Honoria. Even Dr. Wolff's questionable, with his hidden rooms and Fade cages.

I'll cross the Grey on the short side, and tell Mr. Pace about the Fade and their easy access to the tunnels under the

Arclight. He'll listen to me, and he'll listen to Rue. He has to.

Eyes appear beside me and before me as I run, shining silver-blue. Fluid faces shift in and out of focus, on even level with my own, then disappear to reform lower, near the ground. I nearly trip on my own feet to stop myself from trampling them.

I dart through a gap in the brush, certain that my leg is ready to quit on me.

For half a second, multiple versions of my own face peer back at me, as the Fade try and recreate my features, and I turn away again. Shimmer lines solidify, creating a ghostly barrier of bodies between me and any possible escape route. I can only go where they'll let me.

Oh God . . . I'm being herded.

I don't know where I am.

The Fade become a chimera, swapping out faces and features of all sizes and shapes with only the dead tone of their skin to connect the flow. My legs stop working and my knees lock down. Panic rises as I recognize the feeling—one of them, maybe all of them, are trying to take control of my body from me.

A confused frenzy muddies my vision as they try and take control of even what I can see. I squeeze my eyes shut until they hurt, causing sparks behind my lids.

This is *my* body. *I* own it. Not them.

"Leave me alone!"

There's no echo to my voice. It strangles in the dank air and falls to the ground.

Vaporous fingers brush against my clothes and skin, taking hold of my hair and lifting it up. They trace my cheeks, below my closed eyes, and slip into my hands, nearly trying to hold them. Something tugs against my pant leg near the aching wound in my calf as though it can sense the burn below the cloth.

And the whole time, whispers swirl around me. Their voices are so strong, I can feel them press in from every side until I'm afraid to breathe because I might swallow them.

"Rue!"

I reach for the inhaler that's no longer there, and curse him for taking it away from me; air would have been safe through my inhaler. The whispers unify into a single question of who and what Rue means. The word ripples out like rings dispersing in a pond.

"Let me go!"

Their control snaps as soon as the words are out of my mouth. I swing around to run again and slam into someone else.

The impact knocks me down.

My first thought is that Rue's managed to get behind me and catch up, but it's not his face; the Fade standing over me is female. Others bunch around her. They're wearing clothes. Human clothes. Dresses and shirts, and pants made of denim.

All that's missing are the shoes. But they're far too still to be real people.

Movement near the female's feet draws my attention there as something small pushes its way through the crowd, and the Fade bends to lift a half-sized creature into her arms.

The Fade have *children*?

I'm sure somewhere in all the things I've learned, I knew the Fade took children along with anyone else, but that's nothing put next to the reality of the tiny, dress-clad creature laying her head against the female's shoulder, popping her thumb into her mouth. Several other young Fade peek out from the pack, but the adults keep them to the center.

"Stay away," I order, horrified by the sight of those innocent faces marked with black lines.

I raise my hand to my throbbing head and it comes away wet with my own red blood—I'm bleeding in the middle of the Dark, surrounded by Fade.

"You're damaged." Rue's voice. He pushes through the group.

"It's not bad." I tear my sleeve off to staunch the bleeding.

The Fade all watch me, but only Rue moves. Are they afraid of my blood?

"One alone doesn't survive. One alone is lost," he scolds. "Cherish—"

"I survive just fine," I rasp, kicking out to create extra space between us. But I make the mistake of using my bad leg.

Something gives with that rubber band feeling of snapping, worse than when it happened in my dream, and I'm every bit as helpless. My calf's on fire.

The Fade stare while I founder, impressions of concern on their stolen faces. Rue's close and getting closer.

I scramble back on heels and elbows until he traps me against a tree trunk, pressing me so hard into the wood that it feels like my spine's going to snap. Sharp crystalline protrusions poke through the back of my shirt, deep enough to draw blood at the shoulder. His nostrils flare at the smell, and he steps away. He reaches his hand out, offering to pull me up. The images he sends my way are meant to remind me I don't like being on the ground with the nanite pools.

"I can't," I say, my eyes blurred with tears. "My leg won't hold. It burns."

Rue crouches beside me, grasps either side of the seam on my pant leg, and tears it open.

Burn?

Before I can answer, he searches for the specifics in my mind, weighing them against what he knows of pain from his memories of the White Room.

"Not that kind of burn," I say, shaking my head. "It's the muscle. Under the skin, from where I was shot."

He runs a finger over the scar tissue, and the echo of injury he dredges out of my subconscious combined with the pressure against the fresh hurt is too much. For a moment, they have me; my mind gets pulled into the hive so my thoughts and those of the Fade form a common well from which we all can draw.

I see it, and not just the fractured mess Rue found among my own recollections. Finally, from his own memory, he pulls the moment I went from dark to light. Through his eyes, I see the uniformed men and women searching for me. I see the water as he hones in on a figure hidden below a wooden pier. He'd heard gunshots, but hadn't known what they were.

"Yes," I say. "That was a rifle. I got in the way."

Pain?

"Yes."

"Heal," he says, cupping his hand over the scar, searching for heat where there is none. He still can't understand burning without light or fire.

"It *was* healing. But something happened . . . it felt like it ripped."

Heal.

Rue slices into the side of my leg with his fingernail, laying the pink scar open as I scream.

"Don't!"

"Defective." He blows out an angry puff of air when the blood runs there, too, and stains my pants.

Another slice comes so quick I'm convinced it only took the space between blinks. He's released my ankle, and his own hand lays open from a slash across his palm. Shining black blood pools there, confined by the bowl of his fingers.

"No! No inclusion. I don't want to be a Fade."

This isn't the same as having nanites on my skin for a few minutes before he takes them back; he's actually going to put his blood in me. Nanite-filled blood, like Dr. Wolff had to cut out of Trey. I can't go back to the Arclight without red, human blood. I'll never see Tobin or Anne-Marie again.

"Please . . . They'll never let me come home."

Calm. Trust.

Rue slaps his palm against my leg, holding his hand still until the blood mingles black and red.

There's nowhere left to crawl, even if I could drag myself any farther. My body won't work. The world loses focus by degrees. Sounds and colors cut in half, and my skin goes numb as my mind begins to spin. Is this inclusion? Screaming on the inside while someone else runs your life? Is there a still-human boy somewhere inside Rue, begging to be freed?

Distant whispers grow loud in my ears, trying to get me to see something that's been invisible until this moment. Layer after layer, they pile on top of each other, agreeing and adding weight to what I've already seen and heard. Everything Rue's tried to show me comes into sharper perspective, clear and close and loud. The Dark isn't silent at all.

Symbiont, hive, inclusion—they're words I understand, but couldn't comprehend before. It's more than shared existence and space. They're one voice, one thought, one will, always in agreement as parts in a single great machine.

One life.

They are many and one, and somehow they've diminished. Those infinite voices mourn the loss of a single note among them. She's Cherish to them all. They implore me to remember and find her as Rue has: *Locate. Return. Know.*

"Never alone," I hear as a chorus and sound of welcome. The warmth of belonging stops me from shaking, but it's a lie. Morphine to dull the pain and slow my mind, a snare meant to trap me so I won't fight or question them. Already I feel my inner self yearning to answer back and reach out for all those invisible arms offering to embrace me as their own.

No! I don't belong to the Fade. I won't be included.

I won't.

I won't.

I won't.

I want . . .

"Marina?"

I hear my human name spoken by a human voice, but there shouldn't be any humans here, especially not ones who sound like Anne-Marie. It's a dream, another trick. It has to be.

"What'd you do to her?" Another familiar voice demands. Tobin shouldn't be here either.

I'm losing my mind already; I thought it would take longer.

Faces in full color push through the gathered Fade—half a dozen people in khaki green, and two wearing the regulation

Arclight blue from last night. Deep brown skin for the face using Anne-Marie's voice, lighter for Tobin. Eyes like Jove's without the hateful squint to them appear near my face, but they belong to a woman.

"You're all right." She sits, takes one of my hands, and covers it with her own.

"Marina?" the one who sounds like Tobin asks, closer now. He kneels beside me, but I can't take my eyes off the woman. This is her . . . the mother I cost Jove . . . the reason he hates me.

"The haze will pass," she says in a clear voice that still sounds so very human. She hasn't lost the natural cadence of her speech like the Fade who uses Rue's mouth to speak, and the lines haven't reached her face. "The nanites are healing your wounds, but they need your nervous system to do it."

"Marina?" Tobin calls again, and this time he refuses to be ignored. He turns my face toward him.

If he's here with Jove's mother, then the Fade have him, too. And Anne-Marie.

I've lost everyone. I'm alone.

Never alone, the whispers argue, but I don't want to hear them.

"Just let me die," I beg them.

"You're not dying, Marina," the thing that looks like Tobin says. "I won't let you."

He calls back over his shoulder, and another of the khaki-green bodies separates from the group, pushing its way forward from the back to say, "She's healing."

I don't want to heal. If I heal, I'll have to stay with the Fade.

"I want to go home," I say weakly.

"Remove!"

The whispers take up the word as a chant until the rhythm falters, interrupted by Rue's rage. He wrenches Tobin's hands from my face, shoving Tobin back at the same time, and inserts himself in the space between us.

"Get away from her!"

Tobin's on his feet, pushing back. He grabs Rue around the waist, the same way he took Jove down in the bunker. Rue could break him in half, but Tobin has more experience in a hand-to-hand struggle; neither of them can find a way to best the other.

"Do something!" Anne-Marie screams.

The khaki-clad man who responded before wraps an arm across Tobin's chest, using a hold common to the Arclight's security teams, and walks him backward. The Fade-woman I'd seen with the little girl lays her hand on Rue so lightly that I'm surprised he feels it, and a forced calm spreads through the open link I've been drawn into with the Fade. Even I'm not worried anymore.

Rue glances back at me, catches my eye; his face is grim.

He will cease. You will find my Cherish, and he will cease.

Rue lumbers away and vanishes into the Dark, not stopping when the other Fade reach out to him. The khaki-covered arms restraining Tobin let him go, and he returns to my side, while his captor takes up position at my feet beside Jove's mother.

"Are you okay?" Gentle fingers prod my leg where Rue cut me. There's nothing there but numb. *Everything's* numb. I can't feel the nanites anywhere but in my leg. They're not branching out or drawing lines across my skin. There's no sensation of my humanity draining away.

"I'm . . . I . . . I'm . . ."

There's no longer a clear path between my mouth and the words I want to speak.

"Stop fighting them, sweetheart," Jove's mother says. "Close your eyes and it'll be over by the time you wake up."

I won't let it be over. I fight the suggestion to let the Fade absorb me into their shared self and turn to Tobin.

"You're supposed to be safe," is what I want to say, but the words are slurred and mangled.

"I crossed over the boundary on the short side," Tobin says, taking my other hand. I hadn't realized I was so cold, but I feel the warmth from his skin more than anything else. "I came to find you . . . and I was right, Marina. My dad's alive."

He's beaming.

My eyelids stop moving, half-open, half-closed, and the last thing I see before the rest of me goes as numb as my mind is the face of the man in khaki smiling beside Jove's mother.

It's James Lutrell.

His eyes are silver.

CHAPTER 24

GREY light.

My eyes open into the endless dawn of the space between light and dark.

A crumbling pier that's fallen half into some kind of lake, the remains of boats in various stages of decomposition. One of them looks like it might still float if someone was desperate enough to try it. I'm in the water, up to my neck.

The air smells dull and laced with mildew. I hear a sound from the shore, and at first it looks like a clump of bushes moving, but bushes don't walk or carry the sound of heavy boots.

When I try to get a better look, my hand slips off the piece of wood I've used to brace myself and makes a splash.

Step by step they creep closer to the rotted mess that serves as my hiding place. Lt. Sykes, Mr. Pace, and someone else. . . . I know him. It's the man in khaki—Tobin's father. His eyes are still human brown.

Oh . . . this is a dream. Maybe I'll see my mom and dad.

"Ripples," Col. Lutrell whispers with a finger to his lips, pointing toward the water under the pier.

I shrink into the shadows; Col. Lutrell steps to the fore and extends his hand from the shore.

"Come on, sweetheart," he says.

I cling to the post, not daring to trust him.

"James! Look out!" Mr. Pace slams his hand into Col. Lutrell's back, shoving him face-first into the silt, only barely avoiding the path of flying debris that would have taken his head off.

So Rue's here, too.

The scene explodes into shouts, terror, and gunfire. My mind is assaulted by images and echoes of feeling from the Fade as they fill in my gaps, mashing our realities together. This is my memory, but from their perspective, too.

Rage. Anger. Fear. Outrage. Guard.

It comes from all directions at once. I shut my eyes for a moment to block the Fade like I did before, but it doesn't work. These aren't my real eyes.

"They're behind us!" someone shouts; I can't tell who.

The scenery moves. Trees, ground, and grass, all break into the shimmering outlines of crouched forms that match the terrain. They pop out of nowhere, stepping into existence from open air. Ghostly mentions of Rue's mate reverberate through the chorus. The humans took a Fade-girl, so the Fade are determined not to let them have me.

"They're everywhere," Mr. Pace shouts.

Both sides rush the middle and get hit hard.

"Get her out of here!" Tobin's father yells above the rest. "Elias, get her inside!"

Lt. Sykes stays at his back; Mr. Pace wades in to get me, but I pull against him. I want to vanish, so the monsters can't see me. I want to be safe.

"Come on, kid," he says. "We'll take you home."

He drags me out of the water, shivering and confused, dripping so my clothes and hair lie plastered and dark against skin that's too pale from being out of the light so long. I break his hold at the bank and dash away in the wrong direction— toward the line of Fade.

"She's running," he shouts. The rifle at his side swings up.

Having the Fade in my head is twisting things. They're trying to alter my memory . . . make me see my rescue as something else.

"Stop," I scream at myself in the dream, but this has already happened. I can't change it.

My movements are wild and unsteady, driven by terror rather than logic. I head for the ridge above the water; high ground is always safest. Rue breaks away from the other Fade, running to intercept me.

"Colonel?" Lt. Sykes shouts.

"Do it," Col. Lutrell answers.

Lt. Sykes fires toward the ridge; the explosion from his rifle rattles through every whispered voice in my head, confusing the Fade who weren't used to a sound so loud outside of thunder.

I fall at the base of the slope. Blood from my leg mingles with the mud under my body, and the Fade scream in outrage and pain as the connection they've forged in my mind forces them to endure the agony I felt, too.

"Marina? Marina, can you hear me?" Col. Lutrell's voice morphs into something more feminine and familiar, jarring me back into the conscious world.

For once, I wake without pain. I can feel the softness of a mattress under my body, and drop my hand from where it's draped across my stomach to the sheets. If there are sheets, this is a bed. But why is it so dim? I can barely see anything.

Someone please tell me that inclusion doesn't mean I lose my senses, too. To be locked away inside myself without hearing or seeing. If this is what is what the Fade do to their hosts, then I'm ashamed to ever have pitied Rue in the White Room.

"Marina? Are you awake?"

"Anne-Marie?"

No. No. No. NO! She was a hallucination; she had to be. Unless . . .

"Where's Doctor Wolff?" I ask. If he's here, then I'm back

where I'm supposed to be. These are hospital sheets.

"Did you go blank again?"

"What?" I blink, hoping maybe I can pick up a few more details of the room.

"You're not in the hospital, Marina. We're still—"

"—in the Dark," I finish. We're still in the Dark. *We*. Both of us. That means Tobin's here, too. I didn't dream them at all. I didn't dream Tobin's father or his inhuman silver eyes.

I've failed. I let Rue convince me there was a chance the Fade were something other than what I've been told, and my misplaced trust has cost me the very ones I came here to save.

"You're one of them." I scramble backward in the bed, until I'm scrunched against the panel at the top.

"No, I'm not," the thing wearing Anne-Marie's face says.

"Anne-Marie's not this quiet."

Her face draws up in a scowl as her fingers begin to drum against her crossed arms. That's definitely one of Anne-Marie's habits, but if the Fade included her, they'd know that . . . wouldn't they?

"Fine. Don't believe me. Serves me right for volunteering to babysit." She flops dramatically onto the end of the bed.

As my eyes adjust, more bleak details emerge from the shadows. Furniture, and even a door that wobbles on ancient hinges, makes it clear that this place is formerly a human dwelling. A house, most likely, similar to the ones in the neighborhood Rue and I passed through. There's a mirror hung on one wall, and a window facing the outside, though it's overgrown with vegetation bearing the Dark's markings. There are curtains hung, slightly askew, but still there. Leaves litter the floor, with vines growing in through a holey roof.

Rue? I call out silently, but he doesn't answer. It's just me and Anne-Marie. Phantom bits of soft, indirect light filter through, landing on her skin; there aren't any marks on her.

"If you're really who you look like, then where's Tobin?"

"Outside with his dad."

"His dad's dead."

"He's not. . . . I swear, Marina." The frustration leaves her face. "It's not like what they told us at all."

"Why would you leave the Arclight?"

"We went Red-Wall. Toby ran in, totally freaked because he couldn't find you. He had your alarm, so I knew something bad had happened."

Her voice slips into the familiar rush I'm used to, with one word running over the next.

"He was hoping you'd had another headache and were waiting in the hospital."

"You were in the hospital?"

"Well, I wasn't going to leave Jove and my brother alone when the walls were blinking red," she snaps. Her temper's definitely still intact. "I tried to convince Toby to go into the shelter with us. . . . *Sorry* . . . but I really did think you'd go there. *Sorry*."

"Anne-Marie, focus," I say. "I'm not angry with you for getting yourself to safety . . . assuming you're actually you." This is giving me a headache of a different kind. "How did you end up here?"

"Toby took off. He thought our Fade had taken you." She hunches in on herself. "I didn't think they'd do that. It didn't make sense for them to want you . . . er . . . *alive.* . . . Sorry."

"Stop apologizing."

"Sorry." She winces.

"So, what—the two of you decided it was a good idea to go outside in the middle of a Red-Wall?"

"No! We went to find help. Honoria came barreling down the hall at a dead sprint and flattened me. And she wasn't happy to see your alarm and the crushed inhaler. She turned sheet-white and ordered us into the bunker. But Toby headed out here and I couldn't let him go alone, so . . . well, we both came."

I fight the sound of Honoria's voice warning that the Fade are smart, devious, liars, *killers.*

I *want* this to be my friend, and I *want* there to be a chance that Tobin is still the boy I know. How can I return to the Arclight and tell the people there that two more of their own were lost because of me?

The barely functional hinges on the door creak and pop, and I brace myself for an influx of Fade, but only one, Tobin's father, enters.

"She's awake?" Silvered eyes watch me from near the door.

I glance frantically around the room for something to use as a weapon, but the only thing within reach is a moldy pillow.

"Swear to me you're who you say you are." I turn to Anne-Marie and look her straight in the eye—something I couldn't convince myself to do until now. They're deep and dark, without a hint of shine in them.

"It's me, Marina," she says.

"TOBIN!" I scream as loud as I can, then pull in air until my lungs burn, and do it again. "TOBIN!"

Another creak comes from the door's hinges.

"Marina?" Tobin's voice asks before I can see his face. I leap off the bed and rush toward the sound. There's no hitch in my calf when I launch myself at him, wrapping my arms and legs tight.

"Is it you?" I ask, glancing up, and cringing at the possibility that his eyes will shine, but they're as clear as Anne-Marie's.

"Of course it's me," he says. "We came after you. Didn't get far, though. A group of four jumped us less than a klick inside their territory."

I take his face in both my hands, testing the temperature of his skin, the way it feels under my fingertips to see if there's any movement besides his pulse—anything to prove this is Tobin, and not some Fade-riddled imposter.

"They knew me," he says.

"What? How?"

"Because of me," his not-father says. "A side effect of saving my life."

"It's not *your* life." I climb down so I'm a barricade between Tobin and the lie he believes. I wrap my arms backward, linking my hands behind Tobin's back; his wrap forward around me, turning us into a human infinity symbol. "It was James Lutrell's life. You stole it."

With Rue, it's easier to think of being Fade as his normal, but it's different when you know who the human was before the Fade.

"Marina, it's really him," Tobin says. "Listen to him."

I am so sick of people telling me to listen! No one listens to me, why should I listen to them?

Tobin shrugs out of our embrace, despite my attempts to hold him back.

"I know you want this to be your father, Tobin, but it can't be. You know better. You've got to go home and tell Honoria to seal up the tunnels."

"Have the voices stopped?" the Colonel asks when I stop shouting.

"I don't hear voices," I say automatically.

"When the Fade used his blood to heal your leg, it would have opened the connection."

My stomach does another flip.

My head, my arm, my leg . . . everything I know should hurt or ache . . . they're all perfect. I race for the dirty and cracked mirror on the wall, checking my own eyes this time. I yank my sleeves up and pull at my collar to examine the skin below my neck, to make sure there aren't any lines there. The only indication that I was ever wounded is the scar on my leg that's returned to the way it looked before Rue cut it open.

"You're clear," the Colonel says. "Once you healed, the Fade reclaimed his nanites. Just like with the rest of us once they'd patched us up."

"If that's true, then why do your eyes still shine?"

"They can't fix what happened to me in the skirmish, so they don't accept I don't need them anymore. A small colony of them refuse to leave. I'm not the only one—Elaine Crowder has nanites replacing three major arteries and a heart valve, near as I can tell."

"He bleeds red, Marina," Tobin says. "They all do. All the people we thought we lost . . . they're here."

"Then why haven't you gone home?"

"Honoria's locked us out," he says. "We've checked."

"That's what the alerts were," Tobin says. "After you came in, when we had blue lights every night, it was our people checking the tunnel hatches to see if they could get back in, but they couldn't breach the seals from outside."

The tension in the room holds us all suspended. I keep to my place by the mirror, while Anne-Marie stays on the bed. Tobin and his maybe-father take the position in between.

"Didn't you have your radio?" I ask.

"Standard procedure," the Colonel says. "The Arclight assumes anyone taken will be turned Fade."

"Then go in through the front doors. Send someone whose eyes don't shine to tell everyone what happened."

"It wouldn't matter. SOS orders would have been in effect from the second sunset."

"Isn't that a distress call?"

"Shoot on Sight, if it comes from Honoria. They'll drop anyone who approaches the Arc at this point, except maybe one of you kids. You're still inside the window. Those like Elaine and I were down for four solid days in something I can only describe as hibernation. The others were afraid to leave us behind. Even those who'd had minor injuries could hear the included and weren't completely convinced they weren't turning. It was another week before we knew enough to be certain the Fade had no designs on us beyond patching us up."

"If I ask you to bleed, will you show me?"

The Colonel reaches into the pocket of his uniform and pulls out a field knife.

"Do you want to do it, or should I?" he asks, holding the closed knife out on his flattened palm.

"You can do it," I say. "But I don't want your blood anywhere near Tobin."

Tobin joins me near the wall while his father reaches for a strapped compartment on the leg of his pants, this time pulling away a metal flashlight. He tosses it to Tobin and doesn't even flinch when Tobin turns it on.

"Watch," Tobin says.

The Colonel slides the knife into his hand, slicing downward, then angles his palm into the flashlight beam so we can see the bright red, *human*, trickle. Red blood and silver eyes—an impossible combination. While I'm trying to reconcile the two, Anne-Marie glances down.

A diminutive Fade-child with gogglelike markings around her eyes has hold of her hand; it's the one I saw when Rue healed me. Anne-Marie stands, lifting the girl to her hip like she's still a real child.

"She's been following me since they brought us here," Anne-Marie says when she catches me watching.

"Does it . . . er . . . she have a name?"

"Not one I can repeat," Anne-Marie says, grinning. "She's tried to tell me, but all I get is a white wall. I call her Blanca." She points to me, then turns to the Fade-child and says, "That's Marina, the friend I was looking for."

The girl tilts her head and glances back and forth between me and Anne-Marie before Anne-Marie shakes her head.

"You have to say it out loud," she says. "Otherwise, all I get is a buzzing sound. *Bzzt*." Anne-Marie pokes Blanca in the stomach with the sound, and she giggles. "Say it here." She puts the girl's hand against her own throat so she can feel the vibration when Anne-Marie says *friend* again, as though she were teaching one of Arclight's babies a new word in class.

"Fw-en-duh?" the Fade-child struggles out. Even her speech reminds me of Rue's first attempts.

Where *is* Rue? I thought he'd have been the first Fade I'd see here.

"Marina is my friend," Anne-Marie repeats with a nod, and carries the child closer to me.

"M'winna," the Blanca says, training her metallic eyes on mine. Her stature and movements, even the way her Fade-coated hair curls into heavy ringlets, are very much like the sniffly little thing who attached herself to Anne-Marie during the Red-Wall.

Simple pictures, the equivalent of nursery school finger paintings with bright colors and shaky lines, flip through my mind until she settles on something that shows a misshapen person with white hair standing in the midst of a ring of mal-formed Fade.

"M'winna hear?" she asks in her tiny, tinny voice.

"It's easier if you talk out loud," I say.

The solemn concentration on her face dissolves into pure child's delight. Giggles tumble into a fit of laughter as she leans forward in Anne-Marie's arms toward me.

"What's she doing?" I ask as her little fingers pat my skin.

"The Fade are fascinated with those of us unconnected to the whole," Tobin's father says. "The young ones especially."

"You should see it, Marina," Anne-Marie says excitedly. "They're all over the place. Little ones like this, and a ton of them our age."

"That's horrible." Worse than horrible, it's unthinkable that they'd infest a child and steal her life before she even had one of her own.

The way Blanca's wriggled past Anne-Marie's defenses, getting close enough to be held and cuddled, laying her head against Anne-Marie's shoulder, like a still-human toddler in need of a nap—Blanca's a weapon of innocence, with camouflage beyond her markings.

I stare at the girl's features and wonder if her real human name isn't buried somewhere in my forgotten past. Maybe I wasn't alone when I ran through the Dark. Maybe I didn't lose an older sibling who was trying to protect me, maybe I was eldest and responsible for this baby-Fade in her scruffy dress with red flowers dotted on the front.

"It's not what you're thinking," Tobin's father says. "She was born this way."

"Born? As in . . . *born?* As in birth?"

"We were surprised, too."

I watch Anne-Marie sway to the rhythm of imaginary music to comfort the girl snuggled against her. As she drifts, Blanca takes on Anne-Marie's features and coloring, disappearing into the curve of her neck and shoulders until only those goggle-eyes are visible when she pops them open to fight sleep. Even her dress shifts to mimic Anne-Marie's uniform.

She can't have been born like that.

"It's complicated," Tobin says.

"Complicated? You've been here less than a day, and already you're willing to let them rewrite the history you've known your whole life."

I have to put some distance between myself and Blanca, with her half-altered appearance, but I don't really want to stand near Tobin's father, either. I wish this room were bigger.

"The history hasn't changed," Tobin argues. "We just didn't know all of it."

"Look where we're standing!" I've settled near a cabinet full of drawers with old photographs encased in cracked glass stacked on top. I grab one and shake it at him, turning the smiling couple in the image into an accusation. "This was a human house before things like that"—I jab a finger at Blanca—"destroyed it!"

Blanca blinks awake, startled by my flaring temper. More of those finger-paint pictures bore into my brain. Outstretched arms and smiles.

Her innocent attempt to cheer me up triggers some sort of spasm. Tiny fissures open in the wall separating me from everything I've forgotten, like a crack in an eggshell. What spills out burns until I think I'll catch fire right here.

"Make her stop," I beg, desperate to break past the roar in my ears.

"Marina?" Tobin asks. I feel his hands on me, but they grate like sandpaper over raw blisters.

I open my eyes, and through the haze of agony and light find Anne-Marie angled away now, as though I'm a threat to the tiny monster in her arms. I can see the lines on Blanca's skin even with the flare behind my eyes, so I focus all my torment and confusion toward the source of my pain, hoping she'll understand she's causing it and stop.

Blanca shrieks. Glistening tracks appear on her cheeks, and remorse stronger than anything I felt from Rue slams into me as she shimmies out of Anne-Marie's grasp. The lights in my mind dim.

"What did you do?" Anne-Marie demands. "She's a baby!"

"She was hurting me."

Blanca backs away toward the door, still repeating her silent apology. A hesitant, embarrassed offer of something that looks like a messy pink and white flower from my hidden bush pops into my mind, followed by the scent of roses. A peace offering, but again, it's too strong. If I ever get back to the Arclight, I'm ripping that bush up by the roots; I'll never be able to smell another flower without getting sick.

Blanca's desperation and desire to hide tear through the room, making me shake with her fear.

"You're too . . . *loud*." I fumble for the last word, not sure what I can use to get the point across. I try Rue's way of saying be quiet and show the girl her own face without a mouth, but I'm no better at communication than she is.

Blanca squeaks and shuffles backward.

"Wait," I try again. "Let me—"

She's gone.

Not invisible—gone. Her blue dress with the red flowers lies in an empty heap on the floor where she sank into it and vanished. The constant buzz that filled my head from the moment she entered cuts to silence.

"You didn't have to scare her off!"

Anne-Marie hurries out the door as Tobin helps me off the floor.

"Give us a minute," Tobin's father says to him.

"Will you be okay?" Tobin asks me.

"I'm fine now that she's gone."

Slowly, Tobin makes his way to the door. The man I hope is his father takes a seat on a broken table near what once was a window. He crosses his legs and adjusts his weight every few seconds. His eyes don't stay fixed or stare at me. He picks at his fingernails. They're all human habits.

"Tobin said he saw you, beyond the Arc," I say, because I can't stand having to weigh every silent nervous tic against the possibility of it being an act. "But you never came back."

"Letting him see me was a mistake." He stands and starts to pace the filthy floor, moving around the vines and debris like he's memorized their placement.

"And your solution was to send the Fade in as a raiding party?"

"Not my idea. When your friend, Rue—"

"He's *not* my friend!"

"When Rue," he corrects himself, "found my knowledge of the Arc and the layout of the compound in my memory, he came up with the plan on his own."

"Do you know what happened to his mate?"

Col. Lutrell doesn't answer right away, and that is its own, terrifying admission. Maybe Cherish isn't in any shape to be found after her time in the White Room. If she's permanently beyond Rue's reach, I don't know what he'll do.

"What I know of Cherish, they've already gleaned," Tobin's father says.

"Why should I believe you?" I ask. "You bleed red, so what? Until a few days ago, we were rock-solid sure that Fade couldn't pass through the Arc, but they found a way."

"If I were standing where you are, I'd want to know the same thing. I wouldn't want to be alone with me either. But you *can* trust me."

Nowhere does he give me an actual reason, but there's too much of Tobin in him for me to truly fear him.

"What happened to the little girl?" I ask. "How'd she slip through the floor like that?"

"The ones who are born as Fade—" He scrubs his face with his hands, swipes across the back of his neck. "I have to figure out how to say it so it makes sense to a human mind."

A cold chill pimples the skin on my arms and neck.

"Your mind isn't human?" I ask.

"It is, but when they were doing their repair work, it was . . . indescribable."

"That's what it was like when Blanca was trying to talk," I say. "Rue I can manage, but with her it's like we were incompatible systems."

"Most of the included have no concept of human speech or how their way of all speaking and thinking everything at once sounds to us. Their bodies aren't static; their natural state is in flux, so they're used to it."

"You mean Blanca slipped between the floorboards like turning over a glass of water?"

"A human can't pass through solid matter because our body exists as a whole; a born-Fade can break apart into its component pieces and return to the whole at will." He traces through the air along the dark lines that decorate the ceiling and walls. "Her body isn't made of cells and tissues the way we think of them."

"Are you saying her whole body is nanites? No host?"

"The nanites evolved. Human DNA is the basis of their life, but each of her cells is a single entity that can exist apart or in the colony that is her body. She left here, followed the trail, and most likely went back to the place she shares with her family."

"She did not," a voice says from the shadows where Blanca had fled.

"Rue!"

He steps out of the darkness, holding the goggle-eyed Fade-girl, who's now wearing the uniform jacket I abandoned on the trek here. I check to see if Anne-Marie gave hers up, but "Marina" is stitched on the name bar.

"M'winna me," she says, brushing the jacket's collar under her nose.

"She came to me," Rue says. He's ditched the scrubs he'd worn inside the Arclight, exchanging them for clothes like the ones from Tobin's magazines. Blue denim pants and a shirt made from blocks of color, but these have that same sheen to them as the flowers in the Dark. They aren't cloth, like what he wore to cross the Arc—they're nanites. "She thought she had injured you."

"I'm okay," I say, holding my hand out toward Blanca.

"M'winna fw-en-duh?" she asks sheepishly.

Friend? Not really, but if this Fade-child was truly born this way, and not taken, then there's no reason we should be enemies.

"Speak with words," I tell her. "The other way hurts." I pinch my hand and make a face to get the point across.

She pops her thumb out of her mouth and reaches for my hand, curling her tiny fingers around mine and leaning in an unmistakable request to be held.

"She can cause you no more pain," Rue says. "Her voice won't reach you."

"Emp-ty," she says as she picks at my fingers, then shows me her own hand with its circular loops.

"Human," I correct.

"M'winna silent?" She turns to Rue, face scrunched up in consternation, and a moment of communication passes between them.

"What'd she say?" I ask. I've begun swaying, like Anne-Marie does to comfort the babies when they're upset. Blanca lays her head over on my shoulder without letting go of my hand.

"She wants to know why she can't hear you," Rue explains. "I told her your voice has been lost, so she's keeping your hand until it comes back."

I don't bother to point out that I don't want it to come back. The only voice I want in my head is my own.

"She hopes it will return with your finding Cherish."

"How am I supposed to find her if I'm here and she's not?" I ask.

He glances at Blanca again, then back to me.

"She saw Cherish. You spoke of her here." Rue lays two fingers against my head.

"No, I didn't."

"She saw." He tilts his head toward Blanca. "She saw; you saw."

"She's a kid, they make mistakes."

"She did not mistake Cherish. Cherish is her other."

"Her other what?"

His expression disappears in a swirl of loops and lines as they rearrange on his skin.

"Her next to," he tries again.

"I still don't—"

Rue turns sharply to Tobin's father. "Correct the word," he demands in a clipped voice.

Tobin's father shivers as Rue says things to him I can't hear.

"Ah . . . sibling . . . sister," Tobin's father says.

"She is my Cherish's sister. There was no mistake."

"Then she understood more than I did," I say. "Colonel, is there somewhere other than the White Room where Honoria might hide something or someone?"

Thinking of the White Room brings back flashes of the light that seared the backs of my eyes a few moments ago, and the echoed pain of all that heat bubbles up, racing along my nerves to spread through my body. Blanca pats my cheek, clinging tighter when the dull throb turns sharp, so that my hand goes automatically to my eyes, trying to force it back.

"Do you have your inhaler?" Tobin's father asks.

"Rue thought it was dangerous. He broke it."

"Poison," Rue says behind him.

"It was medicine!" I insist. "Medicine I could really use."

Blanca wriggles at my side, trying to get away. She takes

the less-than-pleasant ideas of what I'd like to do to Rue for breaking my inhaler in the literal, and scurries off to hide behind his legs.

"You haven't had it since yesterday?" Tobin's father asks.

I shake my head furiously, but it does nothing to throw off the stinging zaps.

"Pain?" Rue asks, stepping closer. "Heal?"

"No! I mean . . . no . . . it's not broken, not like my leg. There's nothing to mend." I've never had an episode last like this. As a dull ache, sure, but not this endless feeling of a white-hot poker trying to split my skull.

"What do you remember?" Tobin's father kneels in front of me. "If the suppressant's been out of your system for hours, then—"

"Suppressant?"

The look on Tobin's father's face is one I don't think I've ever seen before. He's nervous and apologetic and even a bit fearful.

"Let's try something else. Tell me about my son; replace the pain with what you know of him."

"Tobin took me into the tunnels. He was trying to put space between me and"—I glance up at Rue—"what I was afraid of."

Rue snatches Blanca off the floor and turns away.

"He'd made me a desert." It's actually helping. Talking through the memories is pushing out the pain. "I still don't know how he managed with his arm. . . . Wait, why didn't they fix his arm?"

I look back at Rue, who refuses to face me.

"Rue?"

He scoffs at me, but offers no other answer.

"Tobin refused," his father says. "I wasn't able to refuse when they entered my system the first time. Tobin was, and he did."

"But I told Rue not to put his blood in me."

"It's complicated," he says.

That seems to be the qualifier for everything concerning the Fade.

"How's your head?"

"Better. Thanks."

"My wife, Cass, had seizures. There was a lot of pain involved, and sometimes all she could do was talk through it until it passed. She'd focus on something and tell Tobin a story—usually about one of her snow globes."

"What does it mean?" Rue asks, appearing so suddenly at my side that I have to wonder if he actually walked across the room or did that floor-slide thing.

"A snow globe's a ball of water with a little sculpture inside," I say, and offer him the image of the dancing couple in Paris; I don't think he'd appreciate the desert the way I did.

"This marking," he says, and points to the name bar on the jacket draped around Blanca's shoulders. "She asked what it means. I'm not certain why you wear it."

"It's my name," I say. "Me. That's my uniform jacket. That way people know who it belongs to. Those are letters, if you want something more specific." Specific always seems the way to go with Fade. "Different letters make up different words. Look at Colonel Lutrell's. *J* is his first initial, for James, and Lutrell is the family he comes from. Mine just says 'Marina,' because I can't remember my last name."

"I have seen this," Rue says. "This isn't you."

"You've seen my name written somewhere?"

"You are still difficult."

Rue trains his eyes on Tobin's father, and for a while, it appears that they're just staring at each other, but then I realize Col. Lutrell's eyes aren't still. They move side to side, in an overloaded spasm.

"What?" I ask, but they don't answer.

Tobin's father shakes his head and says, "No. You could make it worse." His body begins to tremble. "If you go too fast, it'll increase the chance of trauma."

Rue looks furious, more so than I've seen him since the Well when he threatened Tobin. A trickle of red blood drips from Col. Lutrell's nose.

"Rue, stop! You're hurting him!"

Blanca puts her hands on either side of Rue's face and pats his cheeks, finally drawing his attention away. He puts his back to me and Tobin's father, who's stumbling toward the floor.

"What was that?" I ask him.

"We had a disagreement," he says. When he opens his eyes, they're not silver but a milky, muted green.

"You're blind?"

"Only for a few minutes. They've gone to repair the capillaries that burst in my nose."

"The nanites from your eyes?"

He nods.

"I kept them off my hand for your sake, but now they're becoming impatient with my injuries." The slash he made in his palm closes over with new skin, so the only marks left are the burns I'd seen in Tobin's photo.

"What did Rue say to you?" I ask.

Tobin's father slumps forward on his palms, catching his breath. I storm across the room to where Rue's stewing. Blanca reaches for me.

"What did you say to him?" I demand, picking her up. "You were talking about me—what did you say?"

"He promised to help find Cherish. He hasn't helped," Rue mutters.

"You've got to stop doing this. I understand you want her back, but Cherish wouldn't want you to hurt people for her. I know—"

"You do *not* know," he snaps. The bands around his irises

widen and constrict wildly so his eyes seem to pulse. "You do *not* understand. If you understood, you would find Cherish. You can't even find this." He jabs a finger toward Blanca's chest, and my name bar. "You've gone silent," he snarls. My arms tighten protectively around Blanca.

"You're right," I say carefully. "I *don't* understand what my name has to do with anything."

"You are not . . ." He pauses, assembling the words he needs into something I can comprehend. "This is dead water," he says finally, and shows me his view of a vast body of water meeting a greyed horizon. "This tried to end you."

"Are you talking about the uniform?" I ask, still confused. "The Arclight?" How could my name mean "water" in the Grey?

"You are not dead water."

Rue's impression of the Grey and its still, stagnant water, comes again, but changed. It churns with the bits of memory I've reclaimed from my rescue. Tobin's father, Mr. Pace . . . they said *sweetheart*, they said *kid*, but they never asked me my name.

I set Blanca on her feet and stare at my jacket hanging to her knees, reading that one slim line of stitching over and over and over: *Marina . . . Marina . . . Marina . . .* I have to be Marina. I don't know how to be anyone else.

"Marina, please let me try to explain," Col. Lutrell says behind me.

I stumble away from him, but that takes me closer to Rue. I back toward the door, overcome with the sudden, undeniable need to run away from this place and these people—human and Fade. My own mind, the self buried beneath that wall of white, is screaming for me to finally hear her.

"M'winna see?" Blanca touches my hand. She's followed me, and the light pressure of her fingers is enough to spur me into motion. I charge out through the barely there door.

There's no hesitation, I just let my legs take over and run.

CHAPTER 25

WHEN Rue put his blood in me, it did more than heal my skin and reknit the muscle. I'm faster, more sure-footed, stronger; I no longer feel like I might pitch off my feet at any moment. It hardly registers that the house I'm fleeing is part of a community, which is now full of Fade mimicking the human lives that flourished here before they came.

The Arclight's survivors sit among them, as though in conversation. If Honoria saw this, there'd be no way to convince her that Jove's mother and the others hadn't turned. They're too comfortable here.

Sharing your body and brain with another being can knock down your personal barriers pretty quick. That's the only reason I don't yelp when Rue steps out of the shadows in front of me.

Tobin runs over, with Anne-Marie right beside him. Behind me, I hear Col. Lutrell; Blanca snaps into view, like a fast-growing flower, reaching for Anne-Marie's hand as soon as she's fully formed. She is still wearing my jacket, but the hem of her dress now rests below the mangled edge of my uniform.

"Move," I say to Rue.

"Did he hurt you?" Tobin demands. He jerks Rue around by his shoulder, but size isn't necessarily an advantage against the Fade.

"No one's hurt, Tobin. Move," I say again, hoping to distract them from each other, but neither gives quarter. "Fine. You two stay put; I'll move."

I slip around them and take off again, ignoring the familiar feeling of being watched that trails down my back. They're following. Whether Rue or Tobin broke first doesn't matter—neither stayed behind.

A bright line glows before my feet as sure as if someone painted it with phosphorescent dye. It cuts a path I couldn't have found on my own, skirting knots of roots and rocks and taking me through the trees where the branches hang low enough to skim the top of my head. I don't care if it's real or Rue's creation. For once, I'm running *to* something instead of away from it.

The Dark passes in a blur. The promise of answers shines up ahead.

"Marina!" Tobin's feet pound behind me, but I can barely hear them over the sound of my own. "Slow down."

"No!"

Not until I know for sure.

I know I should be afraid . . . I *am* afraid. These are the sorts of nerves that come from standing on the edge of something, with nothing underneath to catch me when I fall.

"Marina! Dad says it's not safe out here."

Even with my newfound speed and grace, Tobin catches me, but it doesn't matter. We're in the Grey. We're here.

"We have to go back."

That's what I'm trying to do—go back. Hopefully it'll be far enough to do me some good.

"What are we doing out here?" he asks, glancing nervously at the water as though one of those red-eyed creatures might be lurking nearby.

"Looking for answers," I say.

"It's him, isn't it? That Fade." Tobin spins me around to face him, though he's looking over the top of my head. I don't need to see him to know Rue's there. "He lied, didn't he? He left some of those . . . *things* . . . in you, and he's back in your head."

I'm not sure what to say. It's not Rue calling me out here, but I think it's the Fade.

Rue was right to destroy my inhaler. Now that I've lived with the pain for a while, I remember the fog that manifested with every breath through that little silver disk. I remember how close I'd come to latching on to something from my past only to watch it wither and drown beneath a fresh coat of whitewash. I'd lose the pain, but I'd also lose my train of thought, and by the time I found it again, another headache would require another hit to start the process over.

And over.

And over . . .

Alteration.

Or maybe it's Tobin who was right; maybe Rue missed a few nanites and, like drones, they're trying to line up my thoughts with the hive. How would I know? All the things I thought I knew are suddenly as insubstantial as a daydream.

"Answer me," Tobin says, frantic.

"No."

"You can fight this, Marina."

"I wasn't arguing. 'No' was my answer. It's not Rue."

Tobin's expression clouds over. He throws another fierce look over my shoulder and leans down. I assume he's going to whisper something in my ear, but he smashes his mouth on top of mine so fast all I see is the disheveled black mess of his hair where it's fallen in his face.

I think my heart may have actually stopped. I certainly can't breathe . . . there's no room for air between us.

"Stop it!" I gasp, using him as leverage to push myself back.

"What'd I do?" he asks. His voice is choked with hurt; his

face marred by betrayal. "It helped before. You said if you didn't think about him . . . I thought . . ."

A storm builds in the space behind me, making the air crackle with current, but there's no mistaking this for an act of nature.

"Rue, don't," I say sharply, pivoting into the path of a tenebrous haze.

Pure toxic intent rushes past as a wave, smooth and fluid. It's so thick in the air, and so heavy with loathing, I can actually see it spearing toward Tobin. He has the smallest inkling of what's happened, shuddering when it touches him, but there's no way he interprets the hatred that makes up the cloud's mass.

Tobin's father, Anne-Marie, and the Fade who followed us struggle to keep Rue's rage in check, physically restraining him, and an unfathomable reality of my life before the Arclight begins to dawn on me.

I know what happened to Cherish.

"This is where it happened," I say. "It's where they found me."

What Rue called dead water stretches toward a misty horizon. The water's perfectly still, with a frosted mirror surface. Boats lie smashed along the shore and bare trees jut from water. No way are there any fish in there.

"I was under that deck when I saw your father." I glance up at Col. Lutrell, and he gives me a slight nod.

The memory begins to solidify.

"I didn't think he saw me, but he sent Mr. Pace in after me. He told me I was safe, but I was terrified."

"Of course you were," Tobin says.

"Of him, Tobin. I was afraid of your dad. Mr. Pace and Lieutenant Sykes, and all the others . . . they just kept coming. And they made so much noise."

Memories roar back into the vacuum of my empty mind, all topsy-turvy and backward.

"You didn't know what you were doing," Tobin says. "You'd been out here alone all that time—of course you ran when you heard people. You probably thought they were Fade."

"I don't think so." His version makes sense, but it's not what happened. "I was trying to get somewhere, but then they came . . . I had to hide from—"

The worst pain of my life takes me to my knees beside the water.

"You need your inhaler," Tobin says.

"No! That's why Rue smashed it, he knew—" Another stab, and my fingers curl into the squish of saturated sand, but there's nothing I can anchor myself to.

It's not the first time this has happened to me.

Another kind of sickness hits my stomach as one memory filters through the jumble completely clear.

"He knew . . ."

I can still hear Dr. Wolff tell that first, worst lie: *"You're safe here, Marina."*

This time, when the pain comes, I use it for fuel. Another shard of myself breaks free, hacking its way out of the void, propelling me forward, back onto my feet.

"I didn't know my name," I say desperately. "I didn't recognize it when Doctor Wolff said it."

Another jolt nearly knocks me over. It feels like all I can do anymore is scream.

"Where is it?" I call to Rue. "Where'd you see it?"

"Near the water."

I run, stumbling, using my hands for balance when I need them, toward a pile of debris that's been heaped against the pier by the water's natural ebb and flow.

I focus on Tobin's father as I fling junk out of my way. Pieces of wood fly out of my hands as fast as I can fill them, and all the while the sun sinks farther so that the sky changes color.

"Marina, what are you doing?" Tobin reaches for me, but I take a step farther down the pile.

"Let her be, son. I tried to warn this one that forcing her memories out could do her more damage, but he wouldn't listen." He jerks his head toward Rue, and Rue blows an angry puff of air out of his nose.

"It's here." Everything comes back to the water. "It's . . . there!"

Tobin reaches for the faded piece of wood that holds the key to everything. He hands it to me, curiosity and confusion on his face.

"Where are we?" I ask, facing him with the board hugged to my chest.

"Marina, you're scaring me," Tobin says. "I don't care if you're getting your memories back, it's not worth this."

The only one not scared or confused or even angry anymore is Rue. He's smiling. Relief breaks across his skin like dawn itself until he nearly glows. A gentle humming sound comes from his direction, almost like laughter or purring, and the hive takes it up, making the air vibrate with their joy.

Blanca drops Anne-Marie's hand and scampers over the uneven terrain. She stops beside me, throws one slim arm around my leg, and leans in.

"M'winna hears," she says resolutely; one of my hands drops to rest on top of her head.

"What is this place?" I ask Tobin again. "The water, what is it?"

"I don't know. Some kind of lake or reservoir. It's too small to be the ocean."

I turn the piece of wood in my hands so he can read the washed-out and cracked paint: CYPRESS HILL MARINA. "I'm not Marina—this place is."

With that one, simple admission, the inhaler-fueled

barricades in my mind shatter, blowing apart from the inside. As each one goes, it pulls another with it, and another, and another until there's nothing left to hide behind.

Smell's the strongest impression, and what comes through first is the scent of antiseptic, mixed with mildew from soaked clothes, and fear. I can actually smell their fear.

"Where was she caught?" Honoria's voice asks.

Funny that my brain changed *caught* to *found* so long as I believed the lies she told me.

"Klick and a half into the Grey, almost to the Dark. She was hiding in the water."

Yes, I was hiding. Hiding from them.

The memory rewinds, starting over at the point I started listening to them.

"They got lucky. Seems like our girl was a free spirit even in the hive. They found her out alone and stunned her with a first dose of suppressant, but it wasn't enough. She panicked."

"How is she?" Honoria asks.

"Confused," Dr. Wolff says. *"Which is to be expected. Her viable parasite load is below measurable levels, which means it's either non-existent or hovering. Her blood's gone red. All we can do is wait and see how she does."*

"Keep her away from the others until you're certain."

"And here I was planning a party."

"This isn't a joking matter, Wolff. We're handing them a real, honest-to-God survivor after all this time. Even with the casualties,

morale's barely taken a hit. I'm not going to be the one to tell them it's a farce."

They either don't know I'm awake, or don't think I can understand them because they speak openly, and I hear every word from where I'm tethered to the hospital bed.

"I know exactly what it means," Dr. Wolff says. "Don't forget who burned the bodies of ones who came before her. I have no intention of letting anyone see this child until I'm sure she's not another one of your mistakes."

"What came before was progress. All that matters now is what comes after."

Honoria heads for the door.

"With the nanites suppressed, her conscious memories no longer exist. If she was taken young enough, she may not have any memories independent of the hive. She may not have a name," Dr. Wolff says.

"Where was she caught?"

"Klick and a half into the Grey, almost to the Dark. She was hiding in the water."

"Marina, it is," Honoria says.

Hot tears fall on my hands; a soft weight leans against my hip as Blanca props her head there. Either regaining my memories makes it possible, or Rue lets up on the reins, because another one of those flower impressions pops into my head, and despite myself, I laugh.

"Thanks," I say softly, hugging her.

"M'winna hear?"

"Yeah . . . I can hear you."

An excited squeal bursts from her mouth and suddenly she's not leaning on me, but hanging off my neck like a strangling vine.

"I'm sorry," Tobin's father says. "We thought you were a kid like one of ours. We thought . . . I'm so sorry."

I can't answer him, so I nod against Blanca's crystalline hair, holding her as tight as I can.

"Colonel Lutrell?" Anne-Marie finally speaks. She's bouncing around like she's ready to pop. "Is Marina all right?"

"I don't know, Annie," he says. "I truly don't."

"Marina, look at me," Tobin begs. He's beside me, trying to pull my face away from the tiny Fade-girl in my arms, but I won't let her go. Not again. "Look at me!"

I can't. Instead, I raise my eyes and look past him, to the line of pale bodies standing near the brush line to avoid the last bit of the day's light. Their markings have migrated toward the setting sun, leaving them with meridian lines down their faces. In a few moments, the Arclight will be turning on the lamps, knitting together that web of solid light I used to think protected me.

Rue stands alone. That odd glow I thought I'd seen before is nothing compared to what I see now. It's a full-color aura, radiating off his skin and pulsing in time to his heart.

I hear that distant *thump, thump, thump* he'd tried to make me understand before. The Fade are all there, blended and blurred into a constant drone, but his . . . notes, I guess—they stand out. Louder and richer. My own heart answers right back, but with a duller sound that's more melancholy.

I've found Cherish.

And she's never felt so alone.

CHAPTER 26

"**I'M** a Fade."

I test the words, but the part of me who still clings to what I learned inside the Arclight rejects them. That part of me bristles, disgusted by the suggestion, while Cherish, who has been chained inside Marina's static form for too long, thrills at the chance to breathe again.

This isn't what getting my memories back was supposed to be like. I don't feel whole at all; I feel like someone's drawn a line down the center of my mind. The human me occupies one side and the Fade takes the other.

I am a Fade.

I am *a Fade.*

I *am* a Fade.

No matter how I say it, nothing changes the meaning into

something better. It doesn't make me who or what I thought I was. Mr. Pace was right—there *is* something worse than not knowing.

"What?" Tobin shakes me, as though he could jar me hard enough that I'll forget myself again.

"I'm a Fade."

He steps back. Forward. Back again. He looks to his father, but Col. Lutrell won't meet his eyes or mine. Tobin even risks a glance at Rue, but Rue's attention is on me. *Cherish*.

Cherish who is a Fade.

Cherish who is his mate.

Cherish who is not Marina.

Marina never existed, because she is Cherish.

I can't think of Cherish as me. The barrier's still there, like pressing against that glass wall in the White Room, being able to see and hear, but not touch.

"I was a Fade, but they changed me."

"Doctor Wolff would have known," Tobin says desperately.

"He did."

It's such an easy answer. If I remove everything I was told by Dr. Wolff and Honoria, then all the assumptions of my being and the stitched-together explanations of my survival fall away. They knew I was a Fade this whole time, and they changed me into . . . *this*. I'm not a cure sent into the Dark to save what was left of humanity. I'm not the hope for a better future. I'm someone's science experiment.

"He said you were a survivor," Tobin argues. "Why would he lie?"

"Because we thought she was a human turned Fade," his father says, his voice thick. "We thought they all were. Honoria and the Doc have been enhancing your mom's suppressant for years, trying to make it into something viable to cure those beyond the Arc so we could regain some footing in the world. But all we did was drag her back over a line she never crossed in the first place."

Another apology hangs on the end of his words, but he pulls it back.

"You saved her." Tobin turns stubborn, refusing to humor his father's confession. "You went into the Grey because she was human. You said—"

"I lied, Tobin—every time we went out. We knew if the suppressant worked, we'd need a way to explain how a new face appeared in the compound, and we thought the lie would be easier on everyone."

"But why?" Anne-Marie asks the question I don't have the nerve to ask myself. All I can do is sit here on my knees, watch Rue while he watches me, and not let go of my . . .

Blanca's my little sister.

My family. My own blood. It's a painful truth, but there's been too much pain too fast for me to feel anymore. It simply insinuates itself among the rest; I'll feel it later.

Blanca picks up my thoughts as though I'd called to her out loud, and holds tighter.

The inaccuracy of the name Anne-Marie's given her becomes clear. Her name isn't Blanca, or anything that can be spoken. This baby-Fade clinging to my neck and wrapping her legs around my torso is the scent of air and the way it sounds when it blows through the trees, the color of flowers at our feet. My flowers, hidden and protected in the Arclight's garden. Flowers that flourish in my mind, drawn by a child's imprecise hand, over and over.

A wail comes out of my mouth so full of agony, and so far from human, that I don't recognize it as my own voice until Blanca squeaks and runs to hide behind Anne-Marie.

"What's going on?" Anne-Marie asks. Blanca shifts her colors, becoming a matched extension of Anne-Marie's uniform.

"She was trying to tell me her name," I sob, with my arms around my middle to contain the ache. "She wanted me to remember her."

"The little one's her sister, Annie. That's why she kept following you into Marina's room. She was worried." Col. Lutrell sits heavy on the ground, as though my grief is contagious.

"Does this mean Marina can't go back with us?" Anne-Marie asks.

"No," Tobin answers at the same time Rue chimes in with "Yes."

"Cherish remains to home," Rue says.

"This isn't her home," Tobin insists.

"I brought Cherish to home," Rue argues; the marks on his skin stretch into thinner lines with sharper edges. "Cherish remains."

"Honoria fixed her. *Marina* belongs with us."

As if I needed further proof that I can't bridge the gap between my Fade life and my human one, even my name becomes an argument.

"M'winna me," Blanca says from behind Anne-Marie. I can hear the tears in her voice as she disputes Tobin's claim. "M'winna me! M'winna me!"

Rue joins me and lifts me up off the ground. Through Cherish's eyes, his name changes from an expression of sorrow to a bird song, and cool rain through the canopy leaves—that unnamable something in the Dark that drew me into synch with every step I took deeper into its heart. My bird and my flower bush, the things I protected inside the Arclight for fear they'd be taken from me or destroyed . . . now I know why. I'd already lost them once.

Cherish catches me off guard. Free to act, she throws my arms around Rue's neck and holds tight.

No . . . *I* hold tight. Cherish is me, not some foreign spirit inside my body.

I feel like I'm wearing a costume. These aren't my arms, and this isn't my skin. My hands, my hair, none of it's mine. And when Rue returns the embrace, radiating that same fierce concern, followed by relief that turns my muscles into jelly, the divide that shouldn't exist becomes clear. I'm Cherish, but she's not me anymore.

"Marina . . ."

I meet Tobin's eyes over Rue's shoulder. Anger I would have expected, but not vacant, bereft shock. He's the shattered shell from the photos taken after his mother died.

"Put me down, Rue," I say, wriggling out of his arms.

He sets me on my feet, but doesn't let go; his hands settle on my face. That brilliant aura turns dingy, and the joyous vibration I'd felt when I first found myself stutters, losing momentum.

"Cherish is still silent," he says, confused.

"Why didn't you tell me?" I ask. "You recognized me in the hall when we caught you."

I hadn't understood at all. What I assumed was a plea for me not to hurt him that day was his first promise not to hurt me. Rue was trying to tell me I was safe with him.

"I gave you my Cherish's image."

"But you didn't tell me what it meant."

It's a twisted proving of my own assumptions. I *was* the cause of all the turmoil, but not for the reasons I thought. As I clung to the people who stole me away, I was hiding from the one trying to rescue me.

"You didn't say 'Marina, you are Cherish.'"

"You're not dead water. I can't say 'You are Marina, you

are Cherish.' We should return to home," he says, taking my hand and tugging me back toward the trail I'd taken from the Fade houses.

"As should we," Col. Lutrell adds. He nods into the distance where the Arc has begun to shine through the night sky and into the Grey. "If there's any chance at all for us, we have to go before the kids are locked out, too."

Agreement passes through the Fade, followed by hope that Col. Lutrell and the other survivors are able to return to where they want to be. It's laced with a mild sting, anticipating the loss of their presence among the hive. Separation is the Fade's greatest fear.

"A couple of us are going to have to hang back until we can explain what happened," Col. Lutrell says nervously.

"They are welcome to remain," Rue says.

"Thank you," Col. Lutrell says. He glances at me, then away to Tobin and Anne-Marie, and I know what he wants to ask, but Anne-Marie beats him to it.

"You're coming with us, aren't you?"

Blanca tugs my shirttail, and grateful for an excuse to turn away from Rue's over-acute focus, I cling to the sister I barely remember. She settles into my side, leaning against my shoulder as though this is something she's used to.

One more awkward reflection of a life I can't believe is mine.

"M'winna me," she says again, twisting strands of my hair in her fingers.

"I . . . I don't know, Blanca," I say. There's no way to verbalize her actual name, but the one Anne-Marie's come up with doesn't seem to bother her. "I don't think I can stay."

How can I exist in the Fade's world without the nanites required to experience it? Whatever Honoria's suppressant did, my body's static now, unlike Blanca's or Rue's. His nanites healed me, like they were designed to do, but they didn't bond to my cells. They couldn't fight what the injections and inhalers did to me. They can't turn me back into the creature made of a billion parts working as one.

I'm immune to my own nature.

"Cherish belongs to home," Rue says.

"We're not going back without *Marina*." Tobin tilts forward onto his toes. It's a subtle shift in his posture I've come to recognize as the tipping point of his temper.

"Stop it, both of you," Anne-Marie orders, making the questionable choice to step between them with a hand on each one's chest to hold them apart.

"You can't want to leave her behind," Tobin says.

"Of course not," she says. "But we can't go dividing Marina up like the last cupcake at snack time."

"Annie's right," Col. Lutrell says. "Marina, it's up to you. What do you want to do?"

It seems like someone should have asked that sooner.

"What happens if I stay?" I ask.

"You remain Cherish," Rue says, but I don't think that's

possible. Even if I could accept Rue's offer and take the nanites back into my system, I'm not completely sold on the idea of ceding part of myself to the hive. I've spent too long trying to figure out who I am to be redefined again.

"If I don't go back with you, what will Honoria do?" I ask Col. Lutrell.

"Assuming Tobin and Annie can talk some sense into Elias, I'm hoping he'll force Honoria to bring us in. We'll have to spend some time in quarantine, which is why I want to go first. Someone like Elaine would die under the lamps."

"But the nanites correcting your vision will be fried," I say. "Honoria won't let you out of the White Room until the shine's gone."

"These people are my responsibility, Marina. If there's a risk to be taken, then I'm the one who takes it."

"The people, but not the Fade, you mean?" I charge. "They saved your life. It's not your risk, it's theirs."

"And if they'd agree to leave my body, I'd let them, and head home blind, but they won't. They're actually quite stubborn." He glances at Rue, then back to me. "So is Honoria."

"She's going to keep doing this, isn't she?"

Dr. Wolff called me the success that came after her failures. I'm the lucky one, and that's a terrible thing to consider.

"As long as she has what she believes to be a viable cure"— he winces at the word—"she'll use it."

"And if she takes someone younger next time, or they die

like the ones who came before me?" We're past the point of evasions and excuses. "What if she takes Blanca?"

"She won't," Anne-Marie says. "We won't let her . . . right?"

Col. Lutrell's answer is a look that's anything but encouraging. Honoria will call me proof of success, and use that to justify another scouting party—and another, and another, until the forgotten fight between humans and Fade turns back into a war.

I left the Arclight believing it would make the people I cared about safer, but now I know the only way to save anyone is to go back.

"Are you sure they'll let us in?" I ask.

"They'll be cautious, but containment procedures allow you to reenter."

"No," Rue growls. "Cherish won't go back to burn."

He's right; Cherish isn't going back at all. All this time I thought I'd lost myself in the Dark, and it was the Light I'll never recover from.

"I'm going, Rue. We have to find a way to let the Arclight know the truth."

"No," he says again, stalking closer.

"They think the Fade are sick humans," I say. "As long as they believe that, and so long as they think that what you call voices are some kind of malignant parasite, they're going to keep taking us. If they know the truth, then there's a chance they'll keep Honoria from stealing anyone else's voice the way she did Cherish's . . . mine"

"M'winna me," Blanca says, and shows me another drawing of the two of us tied together. I'm sure it's her idea of a threat—*you're staying here if I have to tie you down.*

But I don't waver. Not on this.

"Think about it, Rue. The place they put you was built to hold your kind."

"*Your* kind," he says automatically.

"It used to be," I say, and feel the dizzying rush of confusion and hurt my words send his way.

"Burned," he says, opening his own memory to give me a taste of what it was like for him when Cherish was in the White Room where he couldn't reach her.

"I know you're scared. . . . *I'm* scared. But, we're stopping this here," I say.

"You need to go back to the White Room," Col. Lutrell says.

"No!" both Rue and Tobin shout, for once in total agreement.

"If there's proof Marina didn't start out as human, then it'll be there," Col. Lutrell says. "Find it. I'll be there to back you up."

"How are we supposed to get you around the SOS?" Tobin asks.

"Your friend here popped the lock on one of the ladder chutes. We can get in that way, but it's dangerous. We need a diversion . . . if you're still willing to help us," he says to Rue.

The nod Rue gives in return is automatic, as though he'd already decided to follow us whether we needed him or not.

"Good." Col. Lutrell turns from the Fade to Anne-Marie. "Annie—do you trust me?"

"Of course," she says, but some of her enthusiasm dies down when Col. Lutrell reaches for her hand and Rue's, and joins them together beneath his own, just before the lines on Rue's skin drain away, transferring to hers.

CHAPTER 27

AN oppressive sort of dread descends once the Arc's close enough to see clearly, burning through the gloom around me and Tobin and Anne-Marie without making a dent in the chill. She's fallen into step beside him, as I walk behind. Every time he cuts his eyes over his shoulder to see if I'm still here, I want to turn and find someone else, farther back.

"This isn't going to work," Anne-Marie whispers to him. The problem with ears that can hear everything is that you hear the things you'd rather miss. "Not if you two act like you're allergic to each other." She stops and grabs his sleeve to make him face her.

"That's my bad arm!"

"Your arm would be good as new if you hadn't refused to let them help you. And I don't feel like explaining to Jove that we lost our only chance to bring his mom home because you want to pout more than you want to do what needs to be done."

"I am *not* pouting!"

"I spend twenty hours a week with four-year-olds—I know pouting when I see it. You won't even look at her."

Tobin does it just to prove her wrong, but the instant our eyes meet, he looks away. The whole thing takes less than a breath, but the sting lingers.

"She's one of *them*, Annie. One of them pretending to be one of us."

I've become an other, a changeling who stole away the person he'd come to accept as part of his world and replaced her with someone else. I don't know how to make this better for either of us. How am I supposed to make up for something someone else did?

"She didn't know."

"You really believe that?"

"Your dad does." Anne-Marie speeds up when he tries to get away from her. "She's our friend, Tobin. And she's every bit as upset as you are—*look* at her!"

He keeps his head down, letting the light on the ground guide him home.

"At least Marina has a reason to go sullen and surly on me," Anne-Marie hisses. "You're just being an ass. What happened to wanting to bring her home?"

"She's not coming with us because she wants to; she's coming to protect the rest of *them*."

"Yeah, the same way she went with Rue to protect *you*. Don't you get it? She doesn't know where she belongs, and having you turn on her ten minutes after nearly knocking Rue's head off to stake your territory isn't helping."

"Every time I think about what she's supposed to look like. . . ."

An image flashes over my own thoughts: me and Tobin, in the Well . . . that spontaneous kiss that surprised us both . . . only now, I look like Cherish.

"She lied to us," Tobin says quietly.

"When?" Anne-Marie asks.

"When she said she was a human named Marina who escaped the Fade."

"I never said that." They turn to me. "I never said anything about who I was or where I came from that I wasn't told by someone who supposedly rescued me. I'm the one who kept telling people I *wasn't* Fade-proof or a Fade-killer or any of the other stupid things they came up with as reasons to loathe or love me. I'm not the one who lied—they are."

Hours ago, had Tobin's father mentioned a chance to save someone like Blanca by turning her human, I would have agreed with him. Reclaiming a human life seemed more important than anything, but my life was never supposed to be human. And now that I know that, and the twisted, melted parts of my existence are coming back . . . what am I supposed to do?

The reason Honoria Whit doesn't trust me isn't a mystery anymore. I'm a Fade; altering my face doesn't change that. No wonder she was waiting for me to break and run back to the Dark. The closer we get to the Arclight, the louder Cherish cries for the Dark and those she left behind. She fights my control and tries to make me turn around. It's that "itch" that kept cropping up near the boundary line.

Tobin still walks ahead, holding himself too stiff for me to believe he's not as confused as I am.

We're about half a klick from the Arc when Anne-Marie stops him.

"We're getting close," she says.

I nod mechanically, and wonder if it's still a human gesture now that I know I'm not human. I wonder if my posture or mannerisms have changed so that someone would know there's something off about me just by looking.

"If we're going to pull this off, then they can't catch us walking apart," she says.

It would be difficult to sell the idea that she and Tobin had to carry me back if they did. Tobin stiffens further when I move close enough to touch him; at least this time he tries to hide it.

"What are you doing?" he asks as I bend down to pick through the broken stones that litter the ground.

"You know they won't buy it unless they see it for themselves."

There's one detail we've chosen not to discuss. No one inside the Arclight is going to take our word that the Fade didn't turn us; the only way to make them believe it is to give them as many visual cues as possible before they have the chance to doubt us. Without proof, they'll treat us the same way they did Tobin's father. They have to see red blood where they expect black.

I select a stone that's flat and thin, and close enough to sharp, but I hesitate before making the cut. My hand hovers over the ragged rip that used to be my pant leg before Rue tore it in two.

"Do you want me to do it?" Tobin's shadow appears at my side. I can tell he's uneasy with the idea of spilling my blood, no matter how hard he tries to keep the sound out of his voice.

"No," I answer. "I've got it."

For as much as it represents, the narrow and not-quite-straight line I dig into my shin is unimpressive; the scarlet tint deceptively normal. It doesn't even hurt.

I toss the stone away when I'm done. I could have just dropped it, I guess, but flinging it and watching it fall feels cathartic. It's freeing to hurl something into the void and know there's no reason to fear it.

Anne-Marie mangles her hair, adding dirt and sticks before smudging her face. She uses another broken rock to make a cut above Tobin's eye, then takes the flatter side and scrapes her cheek. She does the same to her hands. A few strategic rips in both their clothes, and we're good to go.

Tobin leans down so I can slide my arm around his neck, then shoulders my weight; Anne-Marie takes my other arm.

"You're going to have to actually lean," he says. "It won't look right if you don't."

"I'll bleed on you," I point out. Tobin's attention drops to that winding trickle that's begun to pool beside my foot, and for a moment he loosens his grip.

"I didn't mean—" He starts to apologize, but I cut him off. There've been too many things that people didn't mean to do or say for me to tolerate another.

"Let's just get this over with, and get everyone back where they're supposed to be, okay?"

And maybe make Honoria answer for what she did to me, and tried to do to Rue.

"Where is that for you?" he asks hesitantly as we hobble off together.

"You should ask one of the Fade to fix your arm," I say, instead of answering. "Keeping the injury is stupid."

I honestly don't know what I'm going to do. Anne-Marie and Tobin hardly speak for the entire population of the Arclight, and even if they're willing to accept what I really am, there's no guarantee the others will be so accommodating once they discover their supposed hope for destroying the

Fade is actually one of the enemy. If the nanites can't bond to my body, then I can't go back to the Dark. I don't think like a Fade; I'm not sure I ever will again.

"Marina, I—"

"Quiet," I say, holding a finger to my lips, then my ear. "Listen."

"It's not one of those sand things, is it?" Anne-Marie whispers.

"Patrol," I say. The rhythmic thump of boots is unmistakable. "Go ahead and do it."

Tobin's grip tightens, as does Anne-Marie's, and then they begin to shout.

"Somebody help us!"

"Is anybody there? Help!"

"They're coming," I say. The patrol's cadence breaks, speeding to a run, and changing direction so they're headed straight for us.

"Go limp," Tobin says.

I drop my weight on their shoulders. They straighten up so my feet drag, and shuffle forward, calling out for help as we go. A rifle spotlight cuts through the Grey's fog, forming red dots on our clothes. This is a search party, not a patrol. There are five members instead of the usual two.

"Lieutenant Sykes!" Tobin plays his part to perfection, filling his voice with relief and hope.

We must be quite the picture: the bleeding leg that I have

to remember to favor, Tobin's still-bandaged arm, and Anne-Marie's melodramatic limp.

"Stay back," Lt. Sykes warns, commanding those with him to halt.

"She needs help," Tobin says, twitching the shoulder I'm leaning on.

Lt. Sykes takes the radio off his belt. "We've got them. No, three . . . they've got the girl with them." He looks us up and down, focusing on one after the other, starting with Anne-Marie, then me, then Tobin, then back to me. "They're banged up; the girl's in a bad way . . . yeah," he says, focusing on my leg. "It's red. All three are still red. You'd better get over here."

I pick up the sound of more boots running, and Mr. Pace emerges from the fog. We've been here long enough that it's settling uncomfortably on my skin, turning it clammy.

"Help us," Anne-Marie says.

"Please," Tobin adds.

Instead, Mr. Pace stands with the others, rifle in hand, but pointed down.

"They're scared, Tobin. We've been gone too long," I say.

"Her blood's still red." To my surprise, Tobin slips down so that Anne-Marie has the bulk of my weight and reaches for my leg. He wipes his fingers across the cut I made and holds them out to our teacher.

Our teacher who may want to kill me.

"Look at me," Mr. Pace orders.

"Please," Anne-Marie whines. "She's heavier than you think."

"Stay still."

He shines the spotlight from the end of his rifle into each of our faces in turn. Tobin and I hold steady, but Anne-Marie's hand digs into my shoulder, fighting the urge to flinch away and close her eyes. She blinks and looks down as soon as Mr. Pace draws back.

"Tell me what happened," he says as he puts the light away. "We lost your alarm signals toward the edge of the Grey."

"We found her," Tobin says. "That thing took her and we found her."

"Did you go into the Dark?"

"It abandoned her on the rim." Anne-Marie lies beautifully. "She was hurt. . . . I mean she *is* hurt. Marina needs a doctor."

"It wounded you?" Lt. Sykes asks, backing up a step.

"I tried to run," I say. Tobin stands again, letting me lean on him so Anne-Marie doesn't have to hold me up. "But my leg couldn't take it. The Fade left me out there to die."

I have to ignore Rue's plaintive chant of *negative* and *false* in my head.

"I tried to get back, but couldn't drag myself that far."

"How'd you cut yourselves?" Mr. Pace asks. "The blood's fresh."

"My fault," Tobin and Anne-Marie say together.

"It was me," Anne-Marie insists, grating the words through

her teeth. "We'd been carrying her for hours, and it was getting dark. I tripped a few meters back and took them both down with me."

"My head's killing me," I say. "That thing destroyed my inhaler before we left. I need Doctor Wolff."

If Tobin's father was telling the truth, losing my inhaler will get a rise out of them.

"You haven't had it at all?" Mr. Pace asks, fear creeping into his tone.

I shake my head.

"No, and I really need it. Please . . ."

"Elias—" Lt. Sykes starts. He pulls Mr. Pace off to the side. "Don't be stupid."

I think we've failed. That they'll turn away and abandon us out here—or worse, put us all down like rabid animals where we stand. It's what Lt. Sykes wants, I'm sure, but there's an obvious struggle going on with Mr. Pace.

"Is my mom okay?" Anne-Marie asks, before he can tell us no. This doesn't sound like one of her random blurts, but a calculated bit of leverage, and I find myself rethinking the times I've compared our teacher to her brother. Maybe there's a very good reason the two are so similar. "She has to be going nuts. Is she okay? Is Trey? My running off didn't make him worse, did it?"

"It didn't make him better, Annie."

"Will you tell them I came back?" she asks. "I don't want

them to think I'm wandering lost out here. Even if you have to lock us up, Mom can focus on Trey if she knows I'm okay."

His decision's set in that instant. I had no idea Anne-Marie was this brilliant.

"You can tell her yourself." Mr. Pace slings his rifle over his shoulder, so it hangs by the strap down his back.

"You can't!" Lt. Sykes pushes him back when Mr. Pace starts for us.

"They're within the window, Sykes. I'm taking them inside."

He ducks down so he can replace Anne-Marie at my side. Mr. Pace slides one arm around my waist and one under my knees to lift me off the ground.

"Thank you," I say.

"Come on, kids. We'll take you home," he says, just like he did the last time he didn't really rescue me.

CHAPTER 28

MR. Pace leaves me and Tobin in the White Room, just like Tobin's dad expected. He locks the door, posting guards outside while he takes Anne-Marie upstairs. One well-placed temper tantrum coupled with a few tears and a perfect pout are enough to make him decide that since all she's got are scrapes, she's not much of a threat. Tobin and I have been exposed to the Fade by blood, but he has no reason to doubt her.

"Sorry," I say when we're alone. "I didn't think they'd lock you up, too."

"It won't be for long," he says. "They'll figure out I'm clean and—"

"I'm not?" I ask.

"That's not what I was going to say. I'm . . . I don't know how to process this."

"Try it from my side of the argument."

"We're not arguing."

"Shut up and help me with the computer."

Since Rue destroyed the containment area when he escaped, there's no way to separate us from the main console that controls the room itself. All the records have to be there, including the proof of my origins. If we can show everyone that the Fade only wanted to rescue one of their own, and that they had no designs on the humans living here, it should be easier for the Arclight to accept that their lost citizens weren't turned. And if we have any hope of backing up the survivors when they come home, we'll have to find whatever we can before Honoria gets involved.

"Where do we start?" I ask.

"Push buttons, tap screens, and hope we don't need a retinal scan," Tobin says.

We get lights in different colors and intensities. We get sounds like music, but garbled and far too loud. Tobin slides his finger across a screen, and the broken wall of the containment area tries to retract, but it's too damaged to move properly.

Desperate, I go still and beg Cherish for help, but all she knows is the agony of being inside the cell. She retreats from any mention of the White Room.

"This isn't working," I say. "There are too many choices."

"If you've got a better idea, I'm listening." Tobin has been trying to work a plastic dome with a control panel beneath

339

it loose, and as it finally snaps in his fingers, I wonder if he would have been strong enough to break the dome before Rue cut him.

I'm thankful Tobin isn't looking my way when it sinks in that I killed my own kind. I murdered who knows how many Fade when I burned them out of him. Rue and the others had to have known what I did. . . .

I turn my head to hide the tears stinging my eyes. Rue tries to help from a distance, but the feeling of forgiveness makes me hate myself—and Honoria—more. Those I killed were a part of him. How can he not hate me?

A screen rises from some hidden compartment made to look like a floor tile. The lights and controls still confuse me, but it's a safe bet that the one blinking is the one I want.

I lay my hand flat against the blinking panel, and the screen snaps on, filling the room with soft light. White letters scroll on the smaller screen in front of me: SELECT FILE, followed by a chain of numbers in columns. The first twenty or so carry the tag "Regression Test," and I try not to believe they're all that remains of Honoria's failures. The next five say "Fatal Failure" in red, with "Darcy," and a qualifier that would only make sense to the person who created the file.

"That's my mom." Tobin gasps. He tears the dog tags out of his shirt. "Dad called her Cass, but to everyone else she was Darcy . . . Do you think my mom is responsible for what happened to you?"

"Just because they used her research doesn't mean it's what she had in mind."

"Get it off the screen," he says softly, tucking the tags away. His certainties have been shaken as much as mine the last few hours. While I discovered that I wasn't who or what I thought I was, Tobin's problem is the opposite. He's stayed the same, but everyone around him has changed into someone barely recognizable.

I slide my finger down the list until I hit an arrow that zips through the names all the way to the bottom, where a new category appears in blue: "Fade Regression: Success. MARINA."

"Punch it," Tobin says.

A security feed of the White Room appears on the screen. Honoria and Dr. Wolff stand at the console while the Fade-girl, Cherish . . . *I mean, I* . . . prowls inside the cage where they kept Rue.

Cherish looks exactly how I saw her in my mirror. Ashen skin with feathered markings on her . . . *my* . . . face. Fury and terror struggle for control as the me on the screen realizes she can't escape the light. The sentient tattoos that decorate her skin leap to her defense, creating the familiar veil, but Honoria turns the light higher until Cherish falls to the floor in a writhing heap. Her protective bubble shatters, sifting down as ash. I watch Cherish's body go into convulsions I'm glad I can't remember.

"No way Dad knew this was going to happen." Tobin

makes a sound like he's about to throw up right there on the keyboard.

I stop the playback, searching the list for anything else with my name attached to it. Three more files appear in the queue.

In the first, Cherish is still in the cell, awake but too weak to move. The lights overhead shine so bright I can barely see her until her fingers appear splayed out against the glass. I feel an imprint of her despair from not knowing why she was apart from the hive or why no one came to rescue her . . . *me*.

On screen, black lines melt off Cherish's arms, to end up as puddles on the floor; that was when we lost the hive completely. The skin I see isn't bleached out anymore, but red and blistered—the last wounds the nanites are able to heal, and the ones that finally push them past their limits. The blood trickling from her mouth and nose tints scarlet behind the black. She curls into a ball, trembling and scratching at the glass with one fingernail.

A very real sickness overtakes my body in the here and now while I stand watching the people I trusted torture me.

"I . . . I didn't," Tobin stammers. "I didn't know, Marina. I swear."

I give him a sharp nod because I don't trust my voice.

The next film shows the men in hooded plastic suits who burned Tobin's carpet. They drag my limp body out of the cell by my arms. It's easier to think of the me on the screen in terms of myself now; nothing's left of Cherish's appearance to make me think otherwise. The bare tops of my feet slide across the tile; long strands of white hair cover my face. They throw me into a reclined chair, fix straps to my arms and legs, then return to the cell to scrub it down with acid and liquid fire.

The buzz, signaling Rue's presence in my mind, peaks into a frenzy. I was so focused on the screen that I hadn't considered how what I saw would affect him or the others in the hive. He hadn't known the specifics of Cherish's imprisonment either. Now that he does, I hope he can keep control of himself long enough for the rest of Col. Lutrell's plan to be put in place; otherwise all of this is for nothing.

"It was the eyes that gave us the most trouble." Another voice in the room shocks me; the videos have all been silent.

Honoria stands in the doorway with a small remote in her hand, as though this is some filmstrip she's presenting. Tobin turns, too, taking a half-step in front of me, holding his arm out as a barrier between us. But this time, I'm not the one who needs protection.

This is the woman who stole me from my family, the one who caged me and left me crying in agony until she'd destroyed my life. This is the woman who's always treated me as though her fears are my fault. I want to tear her apart with my bare hands.

"We weren't sure they'd ever turn," she says, ignoring our

reactions. "Blue was a surprise. Given your features, I thought they'd settle on brown."

One step into the room and she stops to lean against the wall, feigning boredom. She looks like she did the last time I saw her—hair that curls where it's fallen out of the tie she keeps it in; the same scowl sits on her face. But I know so much more now. How can she be the same when the world's a different place?

She taps her remote and the last video plays. A very human me, with cut hair and perfect skin, lies restrained in a hospital bed. A massive spasm bows my back nearly to breaking before I pitch over the side and vomit black fluid.

"The poison inside went last," she says as I watch Dr. Wolff console the me on the screen before giving her a shot that knocks her out.

Honoria pauses the image on a close-up of my face.

"It took almost a week for the melanin in your skin to activate," she says. "We got lucky. An albino would have been difficult to sell, and we were already pushing it by trying to explain away your senses. Fortunately, people tend to see what they want to see."

She moves off the wall and joins us behind the console, slinking across the floor in a way that's almost predatory. The hand holding the remote disappears into her pocket and reemerges with a small glass tube, which she sets on the panel. Her face is impassive, unblinking, with a practiced calm that disguises how alert she actually is. Her eyes, grey rather than silver—a distinction I never thought important before—are sharp as ever.

"What's that?" Tobin asks.

"Open it," she says to me.

I'm not sure what she's up to, but I stay behind Tobin. I'm done following her orders.

"I was surprised when Elias said you'd come back. Without the suppressant, you could have reverted by now. The fact that you haven't says we're getting closer. You can thank Tobin's mother for that."

"My mother didn't know about this."

"She knew more than you can imagine." Honoria grabs my hand, pulling it out straight as though Tobin and his temper are no deterrent at all. "Thanks to her, we have our first real shot at reclaiming our rightful position on the planet. The only trick is to keep the host alive long enough to survive separation."

She picks up the vial, pulls the stopper out with her teeth, and spills the contents into my open palm. A small pile of black crystals sits there.

An acrid odor hits my nose. I know what this is . . . *Fade ash*. In the background Honoria's still trying to talk to me, but all I can focus on is the putrid scent. I can't get away from it.

Rue rescues me again, sending me the impression of clean, cool air. I feel strength pour into my arms and legs, steadying them as sure as if he'd braced me up himself.

"Thanks to Darcy, the death toll was one-sided with this one." Honoria leans toward my hand and blows the dust away. They're someone's remains, and she's treating them like table salt.

"Who was it?" I ask when I stop shaking. For all I know, it was what's left of my parents.

"You," Honoria says without so much as a twitch to suggest regret. "Or rather, the parasites that used to reside in your body."

"They're not parasites," Tobin growls.

She laughs. A mirthless sound devoid of any real emotion, like a filler.

"They weren't designed to be, that's true," she says. "But it's what they became. They become whatever it takes to get you to believe them. Whatever you saw out there, Tobin, it's not real."

"Rue's real." I refuse to let Honoria cow me. "He came here for me. He risked his life just so he'd have a chance to find out what you'd done to me."

And he's still here.

"He was a scout, nothing more."

"He loves me." The words come out quiet.

"Maybe the host does," she says. "But the parasites that control his actions won't indulge his fascination for long. You, your Rue, the people we lost, they're just shells programmed to advance so long as there exists a place they don't control."

"No, they're not," Tobin says, again defying the woman who's controlled almost every aspect of his life since he was a child. He can't intimidate her the way he can most people, but she can't intimidate him anymore, either. "They didn't understand free will at first, but they do now . . . we saw it."

"I knew Elias was dreaming when he said you didn't go into the Dark." Honoria smirks at me. "Your precious Fade took you straight back to their nesting ground, didn't he?" She turns on Tobin. "And you—as stubborn and reckless as your father—wouldn't get that close without diving in to find out what happened to James firsthand. Am I right?"

Tobin clenches his fists as his sides, and his muscles lock the way they do when he's ready to punch something or someone.

"He did, and the Fade didn't hurt him," I say. "They aren't dangerous. They found another way to fulfill their purpose. They can have children of their own—like me."

"And you think that makes them *less* of a threat?" Honoria asks.

She's not surprised. She doesn't flinch the way Col. Lutrell did when he realized the Fade had changed—she knew.

I go cold. An accident or a mistake I could accept, but not this. This is vile . . . calculated . . . *evil.*

"How many were there before me and Rue? How many did you put in here?" I ask. Renewed courage comes, not only from having Tobin in reach and Rue in spirit, but from the hive—demanding answers for those of their own who were hurt, and ultimately lost. They give me a sense of new purpose.

"You were the first success; that's all that matters. The others took their hosts down with them."

"They were trying to save them!"

"*We* were trying to save *you*. I'd say we succeeded."

"Save me from what? Existing? You knew I was born Fade! What gave you the right to turn me from what I was into . . . *this*?"

Suddenly my own skin disgusts me because I can't stop thinking about how wrong it is.

"You shouldn't have *been* born," Honoria scoffs. She starts to pace, nervous and angry and a dozen other emotions I can more than see. Cherish reaches out with senses I didn't know I had, realigning the world. "The idea of your kind procreating, like they had a right to breed with the bodies they stole—you're nothing but a lie."

"If I'm a lie, it's one you told. *You* sent those people to rip me out of the Dark, knowing what would happen to them."

Anger gives me a bolder voice.

"I didn't—"

"You knew the Fade would fight to protect their own! And you sent your people to kidnap one knowing that."

"They knew the risks. They chose to go because what we could gain was worth more than what they'd lose."

The more she says, the more certain I am that returning

to the Arclight was the right choice. Not only is she unapologetic for what happened to me, or her own people, I'd bet she's already planning another run into the Grey to try again.

"Why me?" I ask.

"Providence. Fate. Statistics." She shrugs. "You strayed away from the others, and made yourself an easy grab. That was my first clue that something was different, and then I saw you and I knew. When someone turns, their skin retains the scars of their human lives. Yours was perfect, aside from the gunshot. No scars, no vaccination marks, no healed breaks in your bones, no incisions from surgery or piercings. No one gets to your age without a few scrapes unless they're not human to begin with."

"You really don't regret any of it, do you?"

"Only that the process was flawed. You've remembered too much, but there are ways around that now that we know your generation can be healed."

"You don't even have a conscience left," I say.

"What does a Fade know of conscience?"

"I thought you said she was human," Tobin says coolly.

Honoria's face twitches, her arrogance cracking at last. She's disgusted by her own success. In her eyes, I'm still less, but I'm also the closest thing she's got to what she wants. She can't destroy me without losing that.

Knowing that makes me stronger than her.

"How do you face the people here, and still pretend to

care about them after all you've done?" I ask.

My words don't seem to anger her at all.

"You say you remember, Marina—"

"That's not my name!"

"Fine, then what do they call you?"

"Something beyond your comprehension and ability to voice. Sound and texture and feeling, even taste. You couldn't begin to understand."

I know now why Rue said that he wasn't "Fade" but "Everything." He doesn't experience the world; he *is* every part of it, and every part of it *is* him. Whatever I was before Honoria named me Marina, I'm so much . . . *less* . . . now.

"You diminished me beyond words, and fractured me to less than nothing—a single voice pulled from the roar of the wind."

"Very moving," Honoria says. "But your story lacks perspective."

All I have is perspective. The only way to truly know the Fade is to be the Fade. The only way to truly know the human is to be human. I'm both and neither in a single breath.

"That roar? It's the voices of the ones they took. Those who ran in terror for days and weeks and months and years until they were chased down and devoured. If anything remains of who they were, it's chained without the ability to speak or move or even think for itself. The creatures who spawned you—they're a farce of the lives they ended." Her voice turns nearly gentle, and I wonder if this is how she sounds telling stories to the children. "You weren't there. You don't know what it was like to run in the middle of the day or burn your house as you went because you hoped it would keep them back. To count your living friends and family down like a timer set for Armageddon until you only needed the fingers on one hand. But I do."

"That was generations ago," Tobin says, tossing a look at me. It's not possible for her to have memories that old, unless the Arclight holds bigger secrets than even he knows.

Honoria begins to pace again. Each time she passes us, I'm reminded of the pistol tucked into the back of her waistband; she's never harmless. Even Tobin looks like he's scared of her now.

"It started here, did you know that?" she asks. "With my father, in this room." She sweeps a hand through the air, letting her eyes rove over the White Room's expanse as though there are vistas drawn with lines Tobin and I can't see. "His dreams lived and died here. He said they'd unlocked the secrets of life. There'd be no more disease, and people would live forever—but one tiny miscalculation and he was the first one to fade."

For the first time, I see true emotion on her face, but it's buried so deep she doesn't know how to express it.

"The Fade took my family. I watched friends walk out as their minds were overcome, and they surrendered their bodies to a deathless oblivion. Trees, grass, animals, even the bacteria in the ground gave birth to the Dark. One night, my brother swore he heard his best friend calling to him, and when he took the walk, I went after him."

She pauses long enough to push her hair back from her brow line so we can see clearly how far the V-shaped scar extends. Below it, her eyes shine, giving the grey a silver cast.

"That's where I got this—when the thing that stole my father's face took my brother from me. I heard them calling for me, but I fought. I held a piece of heated metal to my skin until it melted and they couldn't speak to me anymore . . . I was sixteen."

So that's what Rue meant. Honoria removed herself from the hive; she went silent.

"It happened over and over as the ones I couldn't reach replicated and spread. So I'd burn them again until they went quiet." She turns her head, baring the back of her neck, pulls her sleeves up at the wrists. Her skin is nothing but scars on top of scars.

"How old are you?" Tobin chokes out. If Honoria was here to see humanity fall to the Fade, then she's at least as old as his sixth-greats-grandfather.

"Old enough to know the Fade never truly leave a body once they've taken it." She brushes her hair back over the V on her head. "There were billions of humans on this planet when I was a girl. In the course of three years, that number dropped by more than ninety percent. Over the next thirty, it did it again. We went from dominant species to endangered species in a single generation, and as we fell, they rose, using our own hands and feet to stand against us. So forgive me if I don't tear up when you say the Fade felt the loss of *one* I dragged into the light."

No.

She doesn't get to turn this around so I pity her.

"You want to know why I survived when the others didn't, Honoria? You want to know the big magic secret? *Rue*. That's it. He kept me sane. He was more afraid of the void than the pain, and he refused to let the others shield him from it. We aren't like the Fade you knew; we're born connected. Because of you, I can never get that back."

I expect Tobin to be furious, hearing me talk about Rue and what he meant to the me-I-used-to-be, but instead, he steps closer. He doesn't say anything, but his arm draws me in and I settle against his side.

"We can cure your friend as easily as we did you. We intended to, as soon as we had the data we needed, but he ran off before we had the chance. All you have to do is bring him back and you'll never have to miss him again."

"It's not a cure!" Tobin says exactly what I'm thinking. "Don't you realize you did to Marina the exact thing you accuse the Fade of doing to your family?"

"And I'm going to make sure that everyone here knows it,"

I say. "The only danger they have to fear is the one you've put them in."

"Go ahead." Honoria stands aside. "Walk out that door and tell your friends the truth. Tell them exactly who you are and where you came from. See how fast they turn on you."

"I don't have to," I tell her. "The people you tried to sacrifice will say everything for me."

"What are you talking about?"

I count the surprise she can't cover as a small victory, hopefully the first of many to come before sunrise.

"They're coming home. Like they've been trying to do since *you* locked them out."

"To *protect* the compound. They've been exposed too long."

"I saw them," Tobin says. "Marina saw them. Annie saw them. They bleed red."

"How many?"

"All of them. The Fade healed them and let them go."

"Impossible," Honoria says, but her assertion is countered as, one by one, the different security zones light up on-screen, screaming breach.

She brushes us aside and enters a swift sequence of commands into the console. The chain of file headings disappears, replaced by a grid of camera feeds from the Arc. Near each one stands a familiar face: Silver, Dante, Trey, Becca, nearly all the members of our year plus Trey's. They're jumping back and forth across the barrier to overload the sensors, throwing things at the lamps, and taking out the bulbs and lenses by shattering them.

Honoria selects the camera nearest Anne-Marie. It zooms in as Anne-Marie kneels down and places her palms flat to the ground so the nanites hidden beneath her sleeves rush off now that the Arc's gone darker on the boundary. She steps back and watches them fan out into lines while the first signs of doubt appear in those close enough to see it happen.

Up to now, it would have been easy for them to believe Anne-Marie was still herself. But seeing those marks on her skin, and seeing them move, the others must be questioning whether or not they've just sealed their own fates.

"What is she doing?"

"Opening the door."

Rue rises from the ground. He grows large on the screen as he nears the camera, and sets a path straight for the Arclight.

"I don't have to call Rue back," I say. "He never intended to leave me behind."

CHAPTER 29

THE Arclight's in chaos, the walls screaming red, when we leave the White Room. Honoria tears out so fast, she doesn't bother to check the door. Why should she? The Fade have just been ushered across the Arc; we're the least of her worries.

Posts go unmanned while those responsible for them try to locate their kids. As one parent after another checks their wrist alarms to track their families, their faces turn an apprehensive grey. They huddle up in the hall, comparing their findings to those of the others around them. If the plan's on schedule, then the trackers should be going off-line.

"We need to find Annie before Honoria does something stupid," Tobin says.

In her present state of mind, she could very easily write Anne-Marie off as an acceptable loss. No one will question that Anne-Marie's turned; not once they know she's the one who let the Fade in. No one will balk at the suggestion that she's not really Anne-Marie, but an imposter who fooled the other teens into helping her.

After all, everyone knows that's what the Fade do. It doesn't matter if it's true or not.

"Get to your bunker," a guard in the hall says absently, while pressing the command buttons on his personal alarm. He doesn't wait for a response.

We sprint through patrols and groups of younger children being herded toward the safety zones as they wail for their siblings. We try to keep our heads down so no one notices us, but eventually our luck runs out.

"Tobin?" Mr. Pace skids to a halt on his way around a corner at the end of the hall, between us and the door we need to reach.

"This way." Tobin snags my arm to lead me down a different corridor.

We take off, leaving no question that all pretense of my injuries in the Grey was just that. Mr. Pace is right behind us, and much faster than I've ever realized.

"Get back here!"

"Go help Annie," Tobin says. "I know how to handle him better than you do."

I doubt anyone's going to be able to "handle" Mr. Pace right now.

"He's less likely to chase you," I argue. "Find your dad."

I stop on the spot, not giving him a choice. Tobin scowls at me, but keeps going. If he slows down, we'll both be caught, and he's of more use to the others than me. There's a chance that the guards might listen to him; with me, they'd likely shoot first and worry about asking me questions if I survive.

"Tobin, stop," Mr. Pace calls, pulling up short when I block his path. He glances at my leg, with its now missing limp. "You weren't hurt."

"Sure I was," I say, crossing my arms to make a stand right here in the hall. I'm not much of a deterrent size-wise, but my rising temper makes up for it. "But the Fade make better medics than Doctor Wolff." I guess now I know why he was so insistent that I'd be a natural healer.

One of those split-second emotional shifts lets me see fear on Mr. Pace's face before it's covered again.

"Trying to figure out how they healed me if I still bleed red?"

"How'd you get out of the White Room?"

"Honoria ran when the alarms sounded. Tobin and I decided not to stay behind and maybe get locked in for good."

"Where were you going?"

"It's an exterior door. Where do you think? We both know I don't belong here."

This time it takes more effort to cover his surprise.

"They're not what you think, Mr. Pace." If I can make him

believe the Fade let me go voluntarily, then it'll be easier when Col. Lutrell arrives. "I came back to help Tobin and his dad."

"James is dead, and you just sent his son outside in the middle of a Red-Wall."

"Anne-Marie's out there," I start to say, but I'm drowned by a screeched "Annie!"

Anne-Marie's mother rushes from person to person in the hall, gripping their hands frantically in turn.

"Elias!" she calls as they point her down the hall.

Mr. Pace's attention snaps to the sound of her voice.

"Dominique?" he calls.

"She's gone, Elias," she blubbers, nearly wiping out on the tile. She grabs Mr. Pace's hands in her own, shaking them while she trembles. "Annie wasn't in the apartment when I got back. . . . I went to get her something to eat. I was only gone five minutes."

"You were supposed to keep her in sight," he charges. "I told you she was at risk."

"She said she wanted a shower. I didn't think it would hurt, but she's not there. Look!" She raises her arm, jiggling her wrist alarm at him. "It's dead, Elias. The kids' alarms are dead. Someone turned them off. Who could do that?"

Tobin's father, for one.

"Did you check the hospital?" Mr. Pace asks. "Trey—"

"Jove's alone. He gave me this." Anne-Marie's mother opens her other hand and unfolds a paper napkin that's been clenched in her fist. The word *outside* is scrawled across the wrinkles.

"Outside, Elias. *Outside*. Why are my babies outside?"

"Trey thought he was going after his sister," Mr. Pace says, resigned to the dark end he sees ahead. Tobin, Anne-Marie, Trey—in his mind, they're already gone.

"Trey's not in danger," I say. " Anne-Marie needed his help, and Silver's, and—"

The Red-Wall cuts off without warning, but instead of producing the usual blinding light, or going back to its inert state with a blinking blue indicator, the hall's bathed in an eerie yellow-green.

"Where are the lamps?" Anne-Marie's mother asks, clinging tighter to Mr. Pace.

"This is emergency power," he says. "From the old generators. We're on fumes."

He turns from Anne-Marie's mother back to me. There's not much left of the unflappably calm man I know as my teacher and protector. I'm on the other side now—the thing he's protecting someone from, and the determination I'd found comforting as his student gives me chills.

"Where's Annie?" He doesn't have to raise his voice. That restrained whisper is the most sinister thing I've ever heard. "Where did she take them? What did she do?"

"The only way for Colonel Lutrell and the others to come home was to knock out the lights," I say. "Mr. Pace, please.

Tobin's father said you were his friend, that you'd listen. . . ."

Anne-Marie's mother comes unglued.

"What did you do to my daughter? She's out there because of you, and now you're inside while my Annie's out there with those . . . *things!* They should have never brought you back here." Her hand comes down across my cheek in a stinging slap.

"I know that!" I'm also tired of shouldering the blame for what others have done to me. "I know I shouldn't be here, but he"—I point to Mr. Pace—"and his friends brought me here so Honoria could play mad scientist. If you want to hit someone, hit him!"

"What's Honoria got to do with anything?"

"Only everything."

Shock from hearing Col. Lutrell's voice stops Anne-Marie's mother from landing another strike on my cheek, but Mr. Pace isn't so easy to surprise. He's got his rifle off his shoulder, with Anne-Marie's mother swept behind him, before anyone can say anything else.

"I'd rather you didn't point that in my son's direction, Elias," Tobin's father says.

"J-James?" Anne-Marie's mom asks, trying in vain to scoot back around to face the man she thought was dead.

"Didn't you tell him?" Tobin asks me.

"It's not easy to talk when someone's trying to slap your mouth off." The top edge of my cheekbone's still vibrating from the impact.

"That's not James," Mr. Pace says. He locks the rifle sight on Tobin's father. "It's one of them, Dominique. Annie let them in."

"My Annie wouldn't do that."

"How many did she take?" Mr. Pace demands, straight at me. "Trey, Silver, and who else?"

"No, no, no, no, no. No!"

Anne-Marie's mother flies out from behind him so fast that she knocks Tobin's father to the ground, shaking him by the front of his uniform.

"Give her back," she screams.

"Dominique, get clear," Mr. Pace orders.

"She's just a baby! Please, give her back."

"'Nique, stop it!" Tobin's father pleads as he attempts to guard his head from her hands. "Annie's fine. I swear!"

"He's telling the truth, Ms. Johnston," Tobin says. He wraps his arms around her from behind, pinning hers against her sides until she stops squirming.

"We were out too long, 'Nique. We had to find a way around the SOS."

"Elias?" Anne-Marie's mom looks over her shoulder hopefully. "Is it possible? It's possible, isn't it?"

Mr. Pace shakes his head.

"His eyes, Dominique."

Behind the hands he's using as a shield, Col. Lutrell's silvered eyes shine up at her and she howls again—pure rage and pain. She digs her fingernails into his skin, gouging his face.

"Dominique, no!" Mr. Pace shouts. He pulls the slide back on the rifle.

"Don't!" Tobin darts in front of our teacher, putting his hand on the end of the rifle to keep it pointed at his own chest. It's a calculated risk at best. "He's not a Fade."

I rush Anne-Marie's mother to pull her off of Tobin's father.

"Look at your hands, Ms. Johnston," I say. "Look at his face where you scratched him."

"Blood," she says in a hollow voice.

"'Nique, get clear," Mr. Pace orders again. "I am not losing anyone else to these things."

"Elias, wait!" Anne-Marie's mother staggers to her feet with her hand raised. "It's red, Elias. His blood's red."

"No . . . not possible," Mr. Pace stammers. "I saw you fall. The Fade took you."

"They saved us," Col. Lutrell says. "And now they're trying to help us get back where we belong."

"How many came back?"

"Four of us to start. There were complications with Elaine and some of the others."

"Where are my children?" Anne-Marie's mother asks. "James, please tell me what's happened to Annie and Trey."

"They should be back with Jove by now," I say. "Anne-Marie wanted to stay in the hospital with him, and she was afraid Trey would be too scared to let them heal his arm after the way he was injured."

"They're already inside?" Mr. Pace reaches for the radio on his belt.

"Leah wanted to see her son and to make sure his injuries were dealt with first thing," Col. Lutrell says.

"They're not here to hurt anyone," I say. "But if you don't stop Honoria . . . I know what you did, Mr. Pace, and I know why, but you weren't saving a human girl the Fade had taken."

"You're human, Marina," Mr. Pace says, but he still doesn't drop the rifle. "You were taken too young to remember, but you're human."

"I'm not supposed to be."

"And Honoria knew it," Tobin says. "You don't know what she did. If you saw what happened in the White Room, you'd be helping us."

"Maybe we should hear them out," Anne-Marie's mother says. She lays her hands gently on Mr. Pace's arm, pressing down against the rifle.

"Give me a chance," Col. Lutrell says. "If you don't believe me when I'm done, then shoot me."

It's a stalemate. Mr. Pace stands guarding Anne-Marie's mother. Col. Lutrell stands guarding his son, and Tobin gradually works his way closer to me.

"There've been too many secrets for too long, Elias," Col. Lutrell says. "They've almost destroyed us." Very nearly the same words Mr. Pace used to accuse Honoria what feels like a lifetime ago.

"You're sure Annie and the Fade she let inside are in the hospital?" Mr. Pace lets his rifle droop so it dangles from his trigger hand, toward the ground. He unlatches his radio, picking at it with his fingers.

"Yes."

The Arclight's people who came in with Rue are in the tunnels by now, getting all of the kids who helped Anne-Marie out of sight until things cool down, so no one makes a mistake they can't take back later. That was Col. Lutrell's idea; having Rue go with them was mine, to placate Cherish. I know he'll keep them safe, but it's more than that. I don't think I could deal with him and Tobin and possibly Honoria all at the same time, and if things get bad, he'll be able to get out. They'll never find him in the shadows if he has to hide.

Knowing he's down there, somewhere, makes me feel better.

"Annie was trying to help," Tobin says. "She wants Jove to have his mom back."

Mr. Pace raises the radio, pressing the button on the side as it reaches his mouth.

"Be advised," he says. "We have a breach. Multiple hostiles."

"Always stubborn at the worst times." Tobin's father gives a heavy sigh.

"Elias, no!" Anne-Marie's mother makes a grab for the

radio. "Tell them that room's full of Fade and they'll kill anything that moves—including my kids."

"Proceed to hospital. Converge, but do not engage," Mr. Pace amends. "I repeat: do not engage. Containment only."

"Did I hear that right?" Lt. Sykes whines through the radio. "You *don't* want us to kill these things?"

"We have no confirmation of exposure. Lock down the ward."

"But Honoria—"

"Anything Honoria has to say, she can tell me to my face when I get there," Mr. Pace snaps. "Create a perimeter and hold the line. I'm en route."

He slips the radio back on his belt, raises his rifle again, and uses it to point us back down the hall.

"Let's go," he says.

Anne-Marie's mother runs ahead of us. Tobin laces his fingers though mine, draping his arm around my waist so that I'm in front and he's between me and Mr. Pace as we follow.

CHAPTER 30

My senses are swinging back toward Fade levels. It's no longer just my hearing or even my sense of smell telling me that Lt. Sykes is already outside the hospital ward when we arrive. Emotion ceases to be an abstract; it's tangible, with a taste and smell all its own.

Tension has an acidic bite. Fear's the feeling of being crushed between ceiling and floor by the air itself, but its scent turns surprisingly sweet. After a few more steps, Cherish informs me I'm picking up an amalgam of worry: from Anne-Marie's mother for her children, from Col. Lutrell for his son. Even Tobin and Mr. Pace contribute, their anxiety pinging off my skin. The sweet smell is their concern.

"Status?" Mr. Pace says.

"We've got two of them inside, plus your kids and Leah's

boy . . . she came back," Lt. Sykes says. "How'd they get through? The Arc was solid, then it was just gone. They'd have to be inside to trip the grid."

"Annie gave us a hand."

Lt. Sykes jumps, only now realizing who's accompanied Mr. Pace. "Colonel?"

He shifts his rifle nervously in his hands, unsure if he should point it at us or at the hospital door. The suffocating crush becomes more intense as the others with him—M. Olivet and two I've seen patrolling the halls—do the same. The faintest hint of a line becomes visible, shining from the infrared scopes on their rifles as my eyes continue to readjust.

"Stand down," Mr. Pace says.

"I stood down in the Grey and let you bring those kids inside. Look where that's gotten us." Lt. Sykes looks away, carefully checking each of our faces, separating friend from enemy. "We've got the hospital on lockdown. No one can figure out how they doused the lights. Honoria's got half our people out trying to round up however many of our kids we've got left, but they've disappeared into thin air; the other half's on Fade watch. One SOS has come back for her son, and here you are with another telling me to stand down. So no, I won't. Not until you convince me there's a single reason not to think you're as far gone as Leah and James."

"I would think *not* shooting you would have been your first clue," Mr. Pace says, but it doesn't do any good. When the enemy can look like anyone, trust is a luxury you can't afford.

Anne-Marie's mother, impatient with their bickering, tries to rush the ward, but she's barred by the guards with Lt. Sykes.

"Get out of my way!"

"You can't get through, 'Nique," Lt. Sykes says. "Quarantine seals are one of the few things the old generators were set to preserve in case of power failure. It's a small advantage, but I'm not going to waste it."

"It's creepy having those things walk around in clothes, like real people," M. Olivet says. Her hands tighten on her rifle.

Through the window, I see Anne-Marie sitting on Jove's bed, holding his hand, while his mother takes the chair beside them. A female Fade stands in their midst. She's small, fine boned, with eyes that sit like mine above high cheekbones. I recognize her as the one I saw with Blanca and wonder what her name is. If she's close to Blanca, then she's close to me, maybe even family. Her face brings memories of the scent of pine trees and the prickly snag of green needles, so in my mind, the Fade-woman becomes Evergreen.

While Evergreen sees to Jove, lending him her nanites to heal his body, a tall, severe-looking Fade in black denim, whose presence conjures images of storm clouds and lightning as it splits a rotted tree, approaches Trey. To anyone who didn't know better, they'd look like a couple of teenage boys shaking hands, until Trey unwraps his wounded arm, displaying his burn.

M. Olivet raises her rifle.

"Get the door," she says. "It's an easy shot."

"No!" I shout. "He's trying to fix Trey's arm, Mr. Pace. They need to see."

"Get the door, Sykes," M. Olivet says. "I can't shoot through the glass."

But Mr. Pace catches Lt. Sykes' hand.

"It's too late," he says.

Bolt, which is the name I decide on, holds Trey's wrecked arm steady while the angled pattern of slashes and stripes transfers from him to Trey. It's not easy to see them once they leave Bolt's ashen skin for Trey's and sink into the deeper sepia tone there.

Trey's movements turn sluggish with the healing stupor, and he falls backward toward the bed. Bolt keeps him from slipping off, straightening Trey's legs and folding his arms over his chest. He takes a seat on the floor, cross-legged, waiting for the process to finish.

"Is Trey breathing? I can't see him breathing!" Trey's mother cries, trying to force her way through, but the guards won't budge. I wonder if there was a time my Fade-mother became as frantic over me when I went missing.

"You can't help him, 'Nique," Lt. Sykes says. "He's gone."

"He's in stasis," Tobin's father corrects. "Once the damage is repaired, he'll be good as new."

"Will his eyes shine?" Anne-Marie's mother asks.

"Not if Trey's injuries aren't permanent; the nanites will leave once he's healed."

She nods, faster than someone would to simply say they agree. Another note underscores the mix of fear and worry—one that's pure, clean, and cool.

Emotion's supposed to be private, but I'm mind-snooping again. With Anne-Marie's mother, I know exactly how much of her worry's hidden, how hard she's struggling not to break down in the floor, and how uncomfortable Lt. Sykes makes her. With Mr. Pace, he wears a thin shroud over an aching concern for Anne-Marie's whole family, but I can feel his nerves settling.

I focus on Tobin, afraid that the friendly facade he's worn since the White Room covers his revulsion for my true self. But instead of touching something toxic from him, it's beautiful. My whole body turns warm, and I'm grateful that the odd color of the emergency lights masks how pink I must be. Tobin doesn't want me to be Cherish—that hasn't changed—but not because Cherish is Fade . . . because she's Rue's. He doesn't hate me. It's the idea of loss that disgusts him.

That's what this whole thing boils down to. Human or Fade, it doesn't matter—no one wants to lose the ones they love.

Cherish tries to turn my attention back to Rue, and the idea that she should leave with him, but I can't. Whatever part of Cherish I return to the Fade would be forever trapped behind a piece of Marina-shaped glass, just out of their reach. To live like that would kill me; I'm not sure that denying Rue would do any less to him.

Tobin thinks I belong here, with him, in the human world, but Cherish will always be in the background to remind me how out of place I am here, to tell me Fade names that I have to distill into words like Evergreen and Bolt because Marina's mind is linear and lacks the dimension necessary to say more.

I wish I could split myself in two and take both roads.

Anne-Marie's mother knocks against the hospital's glass quarantine doors. Anne-Marie raises her head, scowling at our group in the hall. She stands and starts our way.

"Mom?" Anne-Marie says. I read the word on her mouth, but the sound doesn't pass through. She tries the door, but it won't open.

Lt. Sykes and the guards prepare for the worst, expecting her to try and break it, or for the Fade in the room with her to turn violent now that they know they've been spotted, but Bolt stays on the floor beside Trey's bed. Evergreen stands beside Jove's, comforting his mother.

"The door's locked." Anne-Marie presses the microphone button on the quarantine controls and tries it again.

"I know, baby," her mother says. "They can't let you out yet."

"I'm sorry I ran off, and I know I'm in a lot of trouble, but—"

"I'm not mad at you," her mother says. Her eyes redden

with new tears as she lays her hand against the glass. "Is your brother all right?"

Anne-Marie glances toward Trey's bed.

"It's weird the first time you see it, but he's good." She's smiling wide when she faces the door again. "He'll still have a scar from where Honoria burned him, but they'll fix the muscle. Trey'll get to use his arm again."

"Honoria burned him?" Anne-Marie's mother whirls on Mr. Pace. "You said he was hurt during cleanup."

"He was," Mr. Pace says.

"Trey breached containment. Honoria did what she thought was best," Lt. Sykes says.

"Containment like locking my kids in that room?" Anne-Marie's mother takes on the same lethal tone I'd heard from Mr. Pace earlier.

"It was a necessary precaution."

There's a subtle shift in the air as another body is incorporated into the hall. It's sharp as a razor, and poised to cut. The mark of someone who's efficient, with absolute conviction, and it fits Honoria perfectly.

Inside the tunnels, Rue's picked up on the change in my thoughts; he's losing patience. Inside the hospital, Bolt and Evergreen have turned their attention from their patients on to us, trying to gather information from their angle, most likely to pass it along to him.

We really don't need a jumpy Fade on our hands right now.

"Hello, James," Honoria says derisively. Her scraggled orange hair tints the glass of the ward door as she approaches. She carries a rifle, on its strap, at her side, but not yet in her hands. My new eyes see a darkish blue halo around her skin that seems a foul copy of the aura that surrounds the Fade, showing their harmony in a way only other Fade can see. Another, similar but brighter, hovers around Tobin's father, strongest at his eyes where it's very nearly the same shade as that of the two Fade in the hospital.

It's a fascinating effect as it manifests. Anne-Marie is barely blue at all, with a dusting on her hands and face, but with Trey, they're speeding through his tissues as they repair the wound in his arm. Jove looks like a patchwork quilt. It's hypnotic; I could watch it forever if things weren't so serious.

"Honoria," Col. Lutrell says. "I hope you aren't planning on shooting me before I say my piece."

"You can say anything you like once you're in quarantine. It'll be a nice change. We haven't had much luck getting your people to speak so far."

"Only because they were too busy screaming in agony to make real words," Tobin says. He draws closer, one carefully placed step at a time, until we're shoulder to shoulder.

"Hyperbole doesn't suit you, Tobin," she says. "As Marina can attest, the one affected carries no memory of the episode. Had she not seen it, she wouldn't have known it happened and neither would you, so there's little reason to argue the point.

However, I do have my concerns to address, the first being the fact that I can't seem to get the lights on. Your doing, James?"

She turns from Tobin to his father.

"The system's taking a break until it's safe for the Fade to leave."

"I'm not unreasonable," Honoria says. I've never heard her sound this way before; she's so artificially pleasant it makes my skin crawl. "You can leave the ward as it is, but I'd appreciate if you restored power to the rest of the compound. We've got a lot of scared people out there—your friends, if you're truly James Lutrell. And they'd appreciate knowing what you've done with their children."

"The kids are safe, but they're staying out of sight for the time being."

"In the tunnels?"

"No fair asking questions you can answer yourself, Honoria."

"And you seem to have an answer for everything," she says. "The advantage of so many opinions at your disposal through the hive, I suppose."

The way they speak is too formal, with a layer of civility covering something far darker and more dangerous. They're both checking for weak points in the other, figuring out where to go next.

"If you're determined that we wait for Trey and Jove to recover, then perhaps we should move everyone inside the ward," Honoria says. "It'll be difficult for you to prove your point if we're all out here."

"Are you serious?" Lt. Sykes asks.

"They'll behave themselves," she says. "If they don't, James loses any hope of convincing us otherwise. And he *wants* to convince us more than anything, because he knows all I have to do is wait for dawn and open the shutters manually—nature will handle things for us. Open the door, Sykes."

Anne-Marie's mother sprints into the room as soon as the quarantine door slides back. She runs straight for Trey's bed, oblivious to Bolt, who has stationed himself beside her son.

"He's okay, Mom," Anne-Marie says as her mother lays her fingers against Trey's throat to check for a pulse. "I promise."

"He continues," Bolt assures Anne-Marie's mother, startling her when he touches the hand at her side. "The damage is healing."

"You can talk?"

"Yours are our base. We do as you do."

"They sound kind of funny until they get used to talking, but they've picked up a ton of human habits," Anne-Marie tells her mother.

"Like biting your fingernails?" Honoria asks as we're shuffled into the room along with her.

Anne-Marie drops her hand from her mouth. "I'm not a Fade," she says.

"Of course not. My mistake. Sykes, seal the door. You can

leave if you want, but I'm staying here until sunup."

"So am I," Mr. Pace says.

"We'll try and get the personal trackers on the kids working again." M. Olivet doesn't wait long enough to see if the invitation to leave is open to all; she takes the out.

"You should go, 'Nique," Mr. Pace says.

"I'm not leaving my kids."

The outer door slides shut, locked from the outside, with the familiar hiss of the closed ventilation system. Honoria's unusually calm, considering she believes that only she, Mr. Pace, and Anne-Marie's mother are completely human. I watch her scan the room, pausing on Bolt, then Evergreen, and finally Tobin's father.

"How long does it take?" she asks.

"The nanites are efficient. They can heal minor wounds in a matter of minutes. Severe injuries can take days."

"And their marks will be gone until the process is complete?" Honoria's trying to calculate the chance of sunrise hitting the Fade while they're unprotected. A half-formed fuzzy image of her making an attempt to "cure" Bolt and Evergreen nudges its way into my mind, but dissolves as though Honoria pulled it back when she realized I could see it.

I feel a presence at my shoulder, one Cherish finds familiar. *Evergreen.* She doesn't do anything other than stand in that particular way the Fade have of going still, but I no longer find it odd or unnerving. The air grows warmer like a soft blanket, and I realize she's trying to reassure me; she's here if I need her.

"Will daybreak kill off anything in their system?" Anne-Marie's mother asks.

"If the parasitic load is light enough," Honoria says. "But if they get a foothold, the nanites will spread and multiply. Once they reach critical mass, there's no way to purge them without losing the host."

"But Marina was with them for years."

"Ah, yes, our little loophole," Honoria says. Her haughty, self-righteous smile is back. "The rules aren't quite the same for your generation, are they?"

"Wait," Mr. Pace asks. "You mean she's right? Marina was never human to begin with?"

Honoria shrugs. "She's human *now*. It doesn't matter how she got here."

"Don't listen to her, Mr. Pace," I say. "You made a mistake when you took me from the Fade. I understand why you did it, but if you don't stop her, they'll go to war to protect the hive, the same way you would to protect your own children. If that happens, the blood will be on your hands, too."

Confusion explodes into a writhing cloud around him, with all the options vying for his attention. There are definite groups here—Anne-Marie's family, me and Tobin and his dad, Honoria and Lt. Sykes, the Fade—but there are no clear sides. The lines are blurred where they cross from one group to the next.

"We can beat them back," Honoria says, desperate now that's she's in danger of losing her advantage. "We made some mistakes, sure, but trying to cure the ones who've turned isn't working. If we can't save the ones we've lost, then we can at least take the Fades' future the way they took ours."

She suddenly sounds much younger, and much less sure of herself and her position, as though she's Mr. Pace's subordinate rather that his superior.

"This is our last chance," she pleads. "Darcy came as close as anyone had in decades, and we lost her in six hours when she was exposed, even with her suppressant. Her death doesn't have to be a failure."

"You're wrong," Col. Lutrell says. "About everything. Marina, the Fade, Cass—"

"If Marina had reacted like Darcy, she'd be dead by now," Honoria snaps.

The mentions of his mother make Tobin tense. He's taken her dog tags out of his shirt and slides them along the knotted chain, using the click of metal on metal to ward against whatever new horrors are lurking nearby to taint her memory further.

"Cass didn't die because she failed. She died because she succeeded."

"I think the Fade have finally hit your grey matter, James. You're babbling."

"Look around you, Honoria. Their first priority is to heal."

"And?"

"And Cass had seizures. Her brain wasn't wired right, so they tried to fix it. When we dosed her, they died. We killed the only thing keeping her alive." Whatever the Fade have done to his eyes hasn't stopped them from being able to create tears.

"You killed my mother?" Tobin asks, shattered.

"We didn't know. Cass shut down almost immediately . . . we thought they were killing her."

Sorrow's a horrible experience. Damp and heavy, it clings to my skin.

"They've certainly made you a better orator, James," Honoria says coldly. "Though I'm not sure Darcy would share your sympathies."

"My mother wouldn't have wanted any part of this," Tobin says.

"How would you know? You barely remember her."

Her words are too cruel to be accidental. She's baiting Tobin and his father, trying to negate the sympathy Col. Lutrell's story has created in Mr. Pace and Anne-Marie's mother. Right now, there's every chance they'll turn on her.

Instead of reacting the way I expect, Tobin lets out a breath and relaxes. The dangerous haze around his body lifts, subdued by a rush of clear air.

"Maybe you should ask the Fade to fix whatever's wrong with you," he says. "Because right now your people skills aren't doing you any favors." He gives her a fairly good imitation of her own mocking smile, then closes his eyes and takes another deep breath. "Thanks for the cool down," Tobin says. "I almost lost it."

"Who are you talking to?" Honoria demands.

"Him." Tobin glances at the Fade I've named Bolt.

"I miss your voice."

Bolt has taken Honoria's fixation on Tobin as an opportunity to get closer. His sudden appearance in her personal space chips the shine off her phony calm. She steps back, raising her rifle between them. He examines the red dot on his chest, curious. He puts his hand in the beam, seemingly satisfied when the dot appears there instead.

"You went silent," he says. "I miss your voice."

"Back away," she orders; he does the opposite.

Bolt matches her step for step until they're toe-to-toe, then reaches up for her hair where it covers her scar and moves it aside.

"We were confused . . . now we are regretful. Will your voice return?"

Honoria's face can't pick a color. It goes white, then red, finally settling into a sickly greyed-purple.

"Get away from me," she snarls.

"I came here for you," Bolt says. His words are smooth, like maybe this isn't the first time he's spoken this way.

"Were you human?" I decide too late that's probably bad timing for the question.

"I was as my other." He points to Honoria. "I came here for my other. My other came *from* here for me."

"What's he mean by 'other'?" Anne-Marie whispers behind me.

"She's his sister," Col. Lutrell answers before I can explain.

"He's the one you followed out of the Arclight when you were a kid," I say.

I find myself questioning Dr. Wolff's assumptions of my age. Honoria's decades older than her appearance, but Bolt could pass for Trey's age. Is it possible Rue was serious when he said the Fade are infinite?

"My brother's dead," Honoria snarls. "This *thing* isn't even his ghost—and he's certainly nothing of mine."

But she hasn't taken her eyes off of him.

"What do we do?" Anne-Marie asks.

"I don't know," I say.

I'm not sure Bolt understands the danger he's put himself into. If he keeps pushing her, Honoria's going to react, and he doesn't have his nanites to do anything about the damage she'll inflict.

"Marina." Tobin nudges me with his shoulder, drawing my attention. A panel nestled between two mounted cabinets sinks back into the wall and slides open along a track, like the one in Tobin's linen closet.

"Is that—"

"It's Rue," I say. A barely there disturbance in the air marks

Rue's edges, and the familiar *click-clack* sounds as he drags himself up the wall and onto the ceiling. "How'd he get here?"

"Left tunnel, Hospital," Tobin whispers, reminding me of the junction in the tunnel.

We follow him with our eyes until Rue reaches the point where he's suspended completely from the ceiling.

He strays too close to one of the emergency lights, and pieces of one side of his body come into view: an arm, half of his furious face, and snatches of his clothes where gravity pulls them toward the floor. I give him what I mean to be a discreet signal to move out of range, and even tell him to do so without audible words, but it's too late. Mr. Pace is already tracking Rue across the ceiling; he starts to raise his rifle.

"Don't," Tobin says. "He's only here for Marina. That's the only reason he was ever here; he won't do anything that could get her hurt."

Miraculously, Mr. Pace listens; his arm relaxes, but he keeps watching.

"We're sorry," Bolt says again. "*I'm* sorry. Will you return your voice?"

He reaches for the memory of a sister who no longer exists as he knew her, and it's one step too close for Honoria. She doesn't have to pretend to tolerate Bolt the way she does me; he's a Fade and nothing more.

The sound of a gunshot in such a confined space is worse than the memory of it from the Grey. Somehow it's even worse than that first Red-Wall when I lost count of how many times someone fired into the night.

Her bullet cuts the air in slow motion, creating a bent channel that collapses as it passes. It strikes Bolt's shoulder, spearing straight through. He doesn't cry out or wince the way a human would, but the shock of being hit, and the momentum of the bullet, topple him.

A pair of chalk-white arms wraps around me from behind, pulling tight, as a body shields me from danger. I'm wrenched sideways, and when we stop, I realize the hands locked across my shoulders and chest are too delicate to belong to Tobin or Rue. It's Evergreen.

I glance back, looking her in the face from a breath away while Cherish reaches out across the threadbare link between us, seeking comfort and protection. A rush of warmth responds with another wave of pine.

"M-Mom?" I stammer, desperate to have a confirmation from Cherish or Evergreen or both. "Are you my mother?"

Mine. A soft voice says. *Yours.*

She was standing two meters away and I didn't recognize my own mother's face.

Rue lets go of the ceiling. He drops down, turning in the air as he becomes visible to all, and lands on Honoria hard enough to knock the air out of her. Her rifle clatters to the floor, and Rue stands up with the gun in his hands, then snaps it in half.

"No more burning," he says to Honoria as he tosses the pieces away.

That's the gesture that finally breaks the others. Everything they've ever been told about the Fade says that what's happening isn't possible. It's an accepted fact that if the Fade breach the Arc, they come to kill, and yet, the only ones who've threatened harm since their arrival tonight have been humans.

Mr. Pace falls back on his training and tries to help Bolt. He forgets his rifle altogether.

"He's bleeding out," Mr. Pace says. There's no hesitation when he presses his hands down over the wound in Bolt's shoulder. Black blood bubbles up through his fingers. "What's wrong with him? I thought the Fade could heal themselves."

"He gave his nanites to Trey, for his arm," I say.

Bolt's confused more than in pain, but I know from experience the shock won't last long. When it's gone, the pain will come.

"Tobin, get the radio off my belt, tell Doc to get back here ASAP. We're on frequency four. 'Nique, I need something to stop the bleeding on this kid."

Anne-Marie's mother grabs a sheet off the nearest bed while Jove's mother and Col. Lutrell ransack the cabinets. And in the middle of all our unfocused, human panic, Rue simply walks over and brushes Mr. Pace's hands aside. He lays his palm flat against Bolt's shoulder.

Rue's marks spill across Bolt's skin, toward the wound,

packing and sealing until the bleeding stops. Slowly the blackened blood pulls back; the edges of the gunshot shrink in. It takes less than a minute to go from critical to cat scratch. When it's over, Rue's marks return to their rightful place and Bolt retakes his seat beside Trey's bed, his posture beaten down and defeated. Anne-Marie's mother slides down to sit beside him.

"Thank you," she says, timidly stretching her arm across his shoulders. "For my son." She holds Bolt's head when he lays it against her shoulder mournfully.

"What are you doing?" Honoria rages as she regains her feet. "Have you all lost your minds?"

"I think we may have just found them," Mr. Pace says.

"Do you *want* to go back to the way it was in the first days? The hysteria? The grief?"

"We're jumping at the shadows we've created ourselves, Honoria. Maybe the balance didn't settle the way we hoped, but there's no reason to keep fighting when we don't have an enemy anymore. We can move on."

"Our enemy is in this room!"

I see the idea before the action, as sure as if I pulled it out of her head. Honoria's hand snaps to her back, retrieving the silver pistol she's never without. She points it at me, dead center on my chest. Evergreen slips in front of me, and even though I want to cling to her, and bask in the knowledge that I have a family who loves me enough to defend me, the gesture's not needed. Honoria hates me, but I'm not her target. Even if my blood was black below my skin, all it would prove was that I'd gone back to what I was before. She needs to give Mr. Pace evidence that the Fade have taken one of the humans he thinks is safe. It can't be Col. Lutrell, because his eyes haven't convinced anyone of anything, so she picks a better target, determined to draw blood she's sure isn't red anymore.

Her arm swings wide and she fires.

CHAPTER 31

FOR a moment, we're lucky; it's a miss. Then I notice Tobin's face. His nerves and muscles can't agree on an expression and he ends up with a tic that makes one side twitch.

"Tobin?"

The whole front of his uniform turns red, fanning out from a spot on his chest.

"It's red. . . ." The pistol drops from Honoria's hands.

"Of course it's red," Col. Lutrell shouts.

A tiny, out-of-place smile quirks the corner of Tobin's mouth as he falls. He tries to break his descent, but there's nothing to grab onto besides me. He's too heavy to hold, and I end up crashing onto the floor next to him.

"Last time we ended up like this, you kissed me."

"You could have just asked for another one."

When he laughs, red spray comes with the sound.

The air's buzzing with the energy off his father's emotions; the scent's so thick, I'm breathing sand. His larger hands press down on Tobin's chest, trying to control the bleeding, while Anne-Marie's mother and Mr. Pace make use of the supplies they hadn't needed for Bolt.

I see Honoria on the fringes of my vision, but she doesn't make a grab for her pistol again. She reaches for the radio on her hip, moving like she's in shock.

"Wolff, where are you?" she demands. "Get down here! We've got a man down."

"Who?" crackles through the handset.

"Just get here!" Her temper flares as she pitches the radio across the room. It bounces off the shatterproof glass.

A blood-choked gurgle covers the *ga-gunk* of Tobin's heart and drowns the rasp of air in and out of his lungs. His eyes open sluggishly, with the appearance of murky amber glass. If he sees through them or not, I don't know.

But I know what needs to be done.

"Rue!"

The risk of becoming Fade is worse to Tobin than death, but there's no other way.

"I will not stand here and watch you die," I tell him. "You have no right to expect me to. Tell me it's all right."

A smile ghosts across his lips again.

"Do it." Col. Lutrell nods, whether Tobin wants this or not.

"Forgive me," I whisper. "If not, at least you'll be around to hate me again."

I fold over and kiss him. It's just a quick touch of my lips against his, and he's in no shape to return it, but it more than makes up for the one in the Grey.

"Rue!"

Rue stands in the open, as far removed from us as he can manage, the only Fade in the room who still has enough nanites to do any good. In the quick burst of information he sends my way, he says he's never seen a person die before.

Interesting.

"No, it's not," I say out loud, startling those around us who don't have any idea who I'm answering. "It's terrifying."

Conflicted images of Tobin present and absent shift in and out of focus as Rue tries to understand how death works. For all his talk of things that are finite, he doesn't understand humanity any more than I understood the Fade.

Reclaimed is what he settles on. His head tilts to the side, expecting to see Tobin blend away into the floor the way the Fade return to the hive.

"That's not it at all!"

Silence. Removed. Zero. I try and convey the full weight of something I hardly understand myself, but it's a mourning-choked jumble.

"You have to help him."

Negative. Against.

Honoria should have shot me instead; if it were me on the ground, Rue would have already saved me.

"If he dies, it's like what happens when Fade touch fire. But you can save him."

I feel his heart break, and for once the bond between us doesn't catch me off guard for its intensity. It's just a reflection of what I felt the moment Tobin fell.

Transient.

"Exactly. Humans don't stay forever. I can't stand to lose anything else, Rue. Please."

Infinite. He points to himself.

Finite. Tobin.

A smug tone colors his declarations. Rue takes it as a fact that at some point Tobin is going to die, and that without Tobin, things will go back to the way they were.

I'm on my feet before I even know I'm moving, flying straight at him.

"So am I!" The force behind the words shocks him as I jab his chest with my finger.

Cherish. Infinite.

"No, I'm human." My rage stalls out. "I have an end, just like Tobin, and I don't want *his* end to be now."

Behind me, Dr. Wolff's in triage mode; he and Col. Lutrell are arguing over Tobin's body. Dr. Wolff wants to move Tobin to a bed, but Col. Lutrell doesn't want to risk lifting him. Honoria's drifted to the far side of the room.

"Marina!" Tobin's father yells. "If he's going to do something, it's got to be quick." He trains his eyes on Rue. "Please save my son."

Anger. Hurt.

Rue starts to argue, then goes blank. The connection between us cuts off as if he's pulled a plug, leaving me empty and cold. He's tuning us out.

I reach out and grab Rue's hand, using those razor nails of his to cut into my skin. Lines of red run down my arm to drip off the end of my fingers and onto the floor.

"Red blood, not black." I streak my hand across his chest where I left a smear of Tobin's blood when I poked him. The color's identical. "Do I need to spill more to make you understand? I'd give every drop if I thought it would help him."

Rue catches my hand as it's poised over my arm, ready to shred as much skin as human fingernails can manage.

There's only one other argument I can think of. Somewhere deep within my memory lies the moment he showed me before: Rue and Cherish, side-by-side. I take that memory and twist it, forcing Tobin's face over Rue's, and changing Cherish from Fade to human.

"I'm not your Cherish anymore. If it takes suppressing my memory of you again to get that point across, then I'll do it. Save him, or I swear I will."

Rue dreads the void. That emptiness is what he's fought against since I was taken. Fury and fear cause his marks to expand, swirling parts of him away into the background.

"Marina!" Col. Lutrell screams again. "Doc! His heart's stopped!"

"Move!" Dr. Wolff's on the floor in an instant, pushing against Tobin's chest to get his heart beating again.

"Please do this for me!"

"For you," Rue says. The tight coils of the lines on his skin relax as he lets go of his anger. He leaves my side and, bending next to Col. Lutrell, Rue positions his hand over Tobin's chest.

"Wait," Dr. Wolff says. "What are you—"

"Let him be, Doc." Mr. Pace pulls him back.

"But Elias, he's—"

"Going to save Tobin's life."

Rue holds his hands there for what feels like forever, and we all hold our breath, watching what a week ago would have been our collective nightmare. Finally, Tobin gasps, and Rue steps away, leaving him to his father and the healing stupor that will finish the job.

"For you," Rue tells me again as he steps close. He takes my hand and examines the mess I made of it. "For me," he says, then joins our hands, threading his fingers through mine. I feel the tickle that comes with the transfer of nanites from his body to mine, and the odd twinge where my skin's reknitting.

"You held some back," I say. "You shouldn't have. It's not bad."

"All wounds are bad for my Cherish."

Behind his voice come the whispers, that harmonic melody of so many voices, joyous at the prospect of hearing me among them again, if only for the moment. Through them, I know exactly how much it took for Rue to take those few steps and save the person he sees as his rival.

Not enemy, *rival*. I see the distinction just before the fatigue of the Fade's presence overwhelms my conscious mind.

"Thank you."

I don't think the words make it to my mouth, but I'm sure he hears them.

I feel my center of gravity start to shift and I tip, fully expecting to hit the ground, but it never happens. Rue's there before I land so I'm in his arms.

All pain is bad for my Cherish.

He lays his forehead against mine, as much a kiss as if he'd touched my lips.

Never alone.

CHAPTER 32

"MARINA?"

The last voice I heard before I surrendered my consciousness isn't the one I hear when I wake into light. This one makes my heart flip—Tobin's alive.

I turn toward the sound, blinking. When I open my eyes again, it's to a stretch of burning sand littered with tiny silver stars.

"Tobin?"

I can't see him. The light's too bright, and my eyes blur from the intensity. I blink faster, trying to clear my vision, but the desert and its cool, static stars never fade. It can't be real . . .

"Where is this?"

I reach out to touch what I hardly dare believe. If the

desert's a dream, then what does that make Tobin?

"You're in the hospital," Tobin says. "We both are."

For the first time, I realize I'm lying down.

I hear a click near my head and the lights dim by half. Tobin smiles down at me, where he stands holding the chain from my lamp. He lets it drop and takes a seat on the edge of my bed. The desert's still there, sitting on my side table, safe inside the snow globe from Tobin's apartment. He hands it to me without so much as a wince. There's no sling or bandages.

"Rue did it . . ." My arm drifts up, incredibly light for as heavy as I feel everywhere else, and I reach for what had been the point of impact on his chest. Even though it's buried beneath crisp white hospital pajamas, I know the wound is gone.

"Yeah, he did," Tobin says.

"You said he, not it."

"It's hard to think of someone as an 'it' once they've saved your life. Even if the only reason he did it was to make you happy."

"He did it because it was the right thing to do."

"If you say so."

It takes a couple of tries to get my momentum going, but I manage to prop myself up so Tobin and I can truly face each other.

"What are you staring at?" he asks.

"No eye shine."

I'd worried that Tobin's injuries were too severe or complex. The nanites Rue lent him could have left him marked in a way he'd think worse than the bullet.

"There was at first," he says. "I wasn't a fun guy to be around when I woke up with them in my head. They're too cheerful—like Annie on too much sugar, and twice as loud."

"The voices?"

"Everything started to dissolve after Fade-boy took his crawlies back. They've backed off to static now, and Dad says they'll stop altogether after a while. Look." Tobin leans closer and pulls the collar of his shirt aside; the nanite lines that had appeared while he was healing have vanished, leaving a neat circle of shiny pink tissue. "They even fixed my shoulder while they were in there."

"Rue's gone, isn't he?"

It's not a surprise. Even if he never physically suffers at the hands of our elders again, he'd be trapped away from the hive and forced to endure the constant reminder that I didn't—couldn't—choose him. For Rue the Arclight means only torture.

"He left after I woke up," Tobin says.

I tell myself it's okay, Rue is where he belongs, and I'm as close to that place as I can get for now—sitting in a hospital bed, shaking fake stars from a water-logged sky. A yearning echo comes from the backmost recesses of my mind, where

Cherish's memories—her essence, maybe —have settled. She's
still there, separate, but hopefully that will change.

"How are you awake before me?" I ask. "I had like three
cuts on my hand. Honoria shot you point-blank in the chest."

"Doctor Wolff sedated all of us . . . just to make sure, you
know? Mr. Pace says we were down for a week, but you've been
out days longer. I think he double-dosed you. Supposedly
tomorrow's the day they turn us loose."

I've been so focused on me, Tobin, and the immediate
space around us, that I completely overlooked how packed the
hospital ward is.

Col. Lutrell and the others who had been left to die in the
Dark occupy most of the beds, some sitting up, some lying
down. A group of three are playing cards on a table pulled
between them. They've lost the chalky pallor from being in
the Dark, but Tobin's father, Elaine Crowder, and one other
still have the distinct eye shine that came from having the
Fade in their systems.

There will never be another night without Fade inside the
Arclight.

Anne-Marie sits cross-legged on the foot of Jove's bed
while he's in the same position at the head. He must have
said something to annoy her, because she throws a handful of whatever she's eating at him and he responds in kind.
From there, it's all-out war with bits of snack food flying in
barely aimed lobs. They're both laughing by the time their

mothers try to break it up, but Anne-Marie and Jove join forces, turning it into a two-on-two fight no one wants to stop. The presence of relief in the room makes me feel like I'll float to the ceiling at any moment.

"I guess we missed the fallout," I say, curious about what happened when our year-mates came out of hiding.

"Silver and Dante said things were pretty crazy for a couple of days when people started coming back. Dante's parents wouldn't let him in the house or around his little sister. Honestly, I'm kind of glad I slept through it. I've had enough crises for a while."

"Yeah." I reach for the inhaler no longer around my neck, out of habit rather than need. Heartache has replaced headaches. I can still feel the hive out there, as close as my own breath.

Honoria was right about the connection being for life, no matter what. Thanks to Rue, it's a life that's mine to define for the first time. There's no way to reciprocate for that.

Wait . . .

"What happened with Honoria? Did they do anything to her?"

"There's not much they *can* do. The White Room's trashed, and there's no other holding area besides the hospital. Mr. Pace and Doctor Wolff have pretty much stepped up to replace her, but unless they turn her out, they've done all they can."

Tobin looks suddenly uncomfortable. He takes the snow

globe from my hands and pitches it back and forth between his own.

"She wants to know when you're awake," he says.

"Why?"

If there's another apology coming my way, it's too soon. She might regret hurting Tobin because he's human, but I refuse to believe she regrets shooting him. I've heard it out of her own mouth—making a mistake doesn't deter her from trying again. The others may think she's not dangerous, but I know better.

"I don't know," Tobin says. "She doesn't say much to anyone. She just comes to the door and watches. Usually, she's got that old white ball of hers. I think she's living in that office underground, Marina." He rolls his shoulder as though it gave him a twinge, even without the injury. "She really thought I was a Fade."

"I know."

"No one knows what to do about her. No one remembers the Arclight without her . . . they all knew. My dad, Mr. Pace, all the adults knew she'd been around that long, but they weren't supposed to tell us until we aged out."

She's my inverse. I had too few memories; Honoria has too many. Centuries' worth of fear and hiding so strong she still can't cross the Arc herself. It's no wonder she's nearly lost her mind. Who wouldn't?

"Those scars she showed us were nothing," Tobin says.

"She's been trying to kill off the Fade in her own body since she was a kid in the first days. She experimented on herself with light and heat and chemicals, but nothing worked for long. She's been aging at a crawl. Dad says they're not sure if she can even die."

She's been torturing herself as much as anyone else.

"Her brother, the one with the wicked-looking marks on his face, keeps coming back. I think he wants to help her understand, make peace . . . something. I'm not sure he can; I'm not even sure we should try after everything she's done."

"Of course we should," I say. "If we don't we're no better."

The bandages, the IVs , they're all useless, so I unwrap them, wincing as I pull the needle out. Rue's nanites have repaired the damage I did to myself; it's like it never happened. Only my memories tell me different.

Thanks to Rue, I'm getting those back, too.

I miss him . . . not just Cherish, but me, and in the space between heartbeats, I hear him say the same: *I miss your voice.*

"So what do we do when we get out of here?" I ask, wondering if the blush I feel on my skin is actually visible.

"Probably go back to class." Tobin sighs, but "back" isn't possible. Nothing's the way it was before. "Mr. Pace and some of the other teachers tried to get permission to have lessons in here, since we've been out so long, but Dr. Wolff refused. They say everything outside's normal again . . . well, almost."

He raises his wrist alarm from his lap and holds it in front of my face. It's dead. I twist so I can see the light above the door, but it's not blinking either. It's glowing green.

"Half the Arc's been down since Annie and the others broke the lamps. After the first few nights, when the Fade didn't attack or even appear, people started to wonder if there's a need to keep hiding. The ones that work are still on, so it's not pitch-black, but they say you can see the stars now. I think I want to see for myself."

"Me, too," I say. Maybe next year, when the stars fall like they did in the Well, the Arclight will look like that picture on the front of Tobin's magazine, with everyone outside sharing the experience. The stars won't be our secret anymore, but we can still keep the Well.

Tobin goes back to absently tumbling the snow globe.

"How'd that get here?" I ask.

"Mr. Pace brought it to me. I thought you might like see it when you woke up."

He tosses it over, and I give it a shake, watching the little stars swirl while the hospital lights shine through the glass. We used to live like that—stuck inside, where nothing was quite real.

Nature's righting itself. Light and dark can exist in their own spaces, side-by-side, and so my world still consists of three.

Cherish, the me-I-was, who knew only darkness, and refused to succumb to the void, even after she'd been buried.

Marina, the me-I-became, who knew only light, and found that it hid viler things than even shadows dared. And the me-I've-yet-to-be, bought with the blood and sorrow of strangers, and friends, and those can't be called either because neither is sufficient to explain them.

I've become the Grey, suspended at the point between two worlds, touching both and being neither.

Through Rue, the me-I-was still exists somewhere undiluted by a vessel too small to contain it. Surely in that great and vast expanse, there's room for him to find someone else. My world is so much smaller, and I did. Tobin may not know the name I can no longer speak for its complexity, but the meaning of it is there in the way he looks at me. The concern mixed with joy; hope spread over worry, all swirling around like stars in water.

Or maybe I'm looking at it wrong. The world's no longer stuck in a jar, or contained to places deemed safe. It's as vast as a night sky, and as big as I need to be.

There are no boundaries anymore, only the promise of something new over the horizon.